FIRST EDITION
www.hfcunningham.com

Content Warning: Violence, gore and strong language

Cover Design by Vivian Reis www.vivianreis.com
Map Design by Jessica Slater www.jslaterdesign.com
Developmental Editing Report by Anna Bowles annabowles.co.uk
Copy Editing by EB Editorial Services

REMNANTS OF BLOOD

H.F. CUNNINGHAM

THE FIVE KINGDOMS
STONESTEAD
CASCAIRN
TARK
WOODREN
RILL
ARMODAN
SHEY RIVER
TAYFORT
THE BROCHLANDS
GORMBRAE
RAVENSMORE
N
W
E
S

Thank you.

Firstly to my sister, Kay, who was my first reader and first fan.
Secondly to Erin, who read many early versions and always had infallible advice.
Thirdly to Athina, who is my rock.

And lastly, to myself for writing the damn thing in the first place.

Chapter One

The Funeral

The sun was warm on the back of Tannin's neck as she watched the cheap pine box being lowered into the grave. The straps holding the coffin creaked with the weight of it, and she could hear the puffing of the gravesmith's assistants as they struggled to keep it level. Other than that, the silence was oppressive. Only two other people were there to observe the funeral rites and cast long shadows over the disturbed earth. The old woman who lived next door to the deceased and couldn't resist fresh gossip and Tannin's best friend Flint, who'd tagged along for moral support.

Not that it could be called much of a funeral anyway. No one had bothered with any amulets or tokens for the deceased. There had been no speeches. No tears. Just a quiet confirmation that her grandfather was indeed dead and gone. It still didn't feel real, and the dizzying humidity of the early summer day wasn't helping with her odd sense of detachment. She'd had the nightmare again last night, and the lack of sleep weighed heavily behind her eyes.

With a thunk, the coffin settled into its final resting place. The old woman edged closer to the gravesmith, and Tannin could hear snatches of her whispered croaking.

"... a drunkard so he was... I always tried tae be neighbourly you see... such a waste..."

Tannin gritted her teeth as she took a step closer to the grave, feeling the old woman's stare boring into the back of her skull. She gazed down into the hole and sighed.

"Rest in peace, you miserable old bastard," she murmured with a wry smile and tossed a handful of dried heather onto the coffin lid.

She'd barely seen the old man since she had moved out three years previously, just turned fourteen and sick of his drinking and his yelling. And his debts. She'd only become aware of his money problems when debt collectors from the Lenders' Guild had barged in in the wee hours only to be paid off with her grandfather's once prized timepiece – a gold lined piece with glittering cogs. He had promised it would be Tannin's when she came of age.

In the years they'd lived in this town, he'd discovered the lure of 'shine, a poor man's whisky, and his once proud stance had become stooped, his muscles had wasted away and his hair and beard had turned wild. He had become bitter and resentful – especially to Tannin. Did she even know what he'd done for her? Where would she be without him? Still, she had some fond memories of him and now, looking down at his coffin, it was strange to think he was actually gone.

He'd taught her how to fish and which mushrooms were safe to eat. She'd loved his stories of "good ol' days" and of a childhood she didn't remember. She didn't remember anything before they'd come here to Armodan six years ago.

Tannin turned away from the grave, dry-eyed. She had already missed him so much over the last few years that his death didn't feel like much of a bereavement at all.

Flint raised a hand to shade his eyes and then gestured at something behind her. "Hey, Tan, look. What's he doing here, you think?"

Tannin turned and took in the bulk of the man standing by the edge of the graveyard. She groaned.

"What a bloody nerve. Couldn't even let the old man get in the dirt before he muscles in."

Morey Clach leaned on the edge of the low crumbling wall that bordered the graveyard. Despite the heat, he was, as always, wearing his distinctive purple cloak pinned with a gaudy brooch to remind the good people of Armodan of his title. He'd sent several messages requesting her presence over her late grandfather's business dealings in the past few days, but she'd ignored them all. Business dealings. She could guess what that meant. Clach, as well as being the unofficial Laird of the area, was a prolific moneylender and all-around arsehole in Tannin's opinion.

"I can't be arsed dealin' with him right now. C'mon."

Even though he hadn't had anything to do with her grandfather's death – a drunken fall down the stone steps of one of Armodan's many public squares – Tannin couldn't help bitterly thinking Clach may as well have given him the push.

He certainly didn't have a problem pushing the old man towards another bottle of 'shine with his constant harassment and bullying.

She didn't know the details of whatever business they'd had together, and she didn't want to know.

Tannin and Flint headed to the gate furthest from Clach with a backward glance to confirm that he wasn't following. As graveyards went, it wasn't the most depressing place. The ground was dried up and yellowish this time of year but, come spring, wildflowers would brighten the graves with purples and pinks, and the gnarly old tree that stood in one corner would shade mourners under soft new leaves. From the graveyard, if it was particularly quiet, you could even hear the bubbling and churning of the nearby stream as it wound its way down through the Brochlands to splash into the broad Shey river that bisected the kingdom.

They walked in silence back towards the town. Well, towns. Sort of... Armodan was a sprawl of old towns and villages that had long ago merged together around the ancient walled citadel. Technically, only the inner citadel was called Armodan. The ramshackle civilisation outside of it was the Skirts. Or to Flint and Tannin, home.

Tannin scuffed her feet on the path as they walked and watched the dust puff up around her shoes.

"Not exactly the most fun time ever but still, thanks for comin' today Flint." She looked over at her best friend and he gave her a shrug.

"It's what I'm here for." He draped an arm around her shoulders and gave a squeeze.

Tall and lanky, Flint would've stood out in a crowd even without his unique style. Today, he had dressed a little more mutedly seeing as it was a funeral after all, but a feather still stood proudly in the jauntily angled hat perched on his dark blond hair that matched her own. The two of them were often mistaken for siblings or cousins at least even if he was almost a foot taller than her. Tannin, however, did not share his fashion sense. The only concession she'd made to today's events was to wear slightly less scruffy tunic and breeches than usual. Like she had anything else to choose from.

Recently, the pair had increasingly less time for each other but, on rare occasions like today, neither of them had work and they could spend the rest of the day how they liked.

Tannin had joked that the underworld must've frozen over when Flint told her he had an actual honest-to-the-gods job. It all made much more sense, of course, when he admitted that while technically he was only supposed to be inspecting the imports that arrived at the citadel gates, some of the rejects didn't always find their way back out again. There was always a buyer somewhere, he'd reasoned at the time, and nowadays he made good money with his network of back-alley salesmen and con artists.

"What're you gonna do about Clach?"

"Screw him."

"Ew, really? And I thought you had standards - oof!"

Flint clutched his side dramatically where Tannin had elbowed him.

"Prick." She let out a deep breath. "I'll deal with him somehow."

Flint gave her a sly look. "And that dealing with it is a tomorrow problem?"

"In theory... Why?"

"Well, as the amazing and caring friend that I am, I thought you might need a little distraction today." He grinned. "What did you do?" Tannin narrowed her eyes.

"I may have... liberated some whisky from one of the wagons." He patted the bag slung over his shoulder with a knowing wink.

"Flint!"

"Awk, I was careful. Don't stress!"

"You are honestly-"

"You saying you don't wanna come drink it with me?" He pouted and blinked his big brown eyes.

Oh, not the puppy dog face...

"You gonna make me drink alone? Alooooooone."

"Oh, shut up." Flint was reckless, but even as she shook her head Tannin couldn't help returning his mischievous grin.

"Yeah?"

"Aye, okay then." She elbowed him again. "Can't say no to that face."

Flint whooped and linked his arm through hers. "Ruins?" "Ruins." Tannin grinned.

The ruins were a crumbling old shamble of stones that stood a little way outside the town, not far from the graveyard. It had apparently once been one of the thousands of Brochs that covered the kingdom and gave it its name but was now just a mess of toppled masonry.

Skirter children from the town told ghost stories about druids and monsters to scare themselves silly when they snuck out at night and lit little campfires in the hollows around the huge stone blocks.

Tannin hadn't been there in ages, and it felt almost traitorous to the childish memories of scrambling over the boulders playing stupid games to be sitting on them now swigging stolen spirits out the bottle.

She peeled off the wax top of the bottle that Flint handed to her with her knife and popped the cork out. She sniffed at it suspiciously as the sweet smokiness rose from within and then brought the bottle to her lips.

She grimaced at the taste.

"That is vile." She coughed.

"Yup." Flint flashed her a gratified grin. "That's how you know it's the good stuff. That's not your standard 'shine, I'll have you know."

"Oh, well in that case." Tannin raised the bottle and gave a mock salute with it. "Sláinte."

Hours later, Tannin stumbled down the stairs to the kitchen entrance of Fletcher's Bakery. The building itself was much like the others in the more residential districts in the western Skirts, with rough stone walls for the ground floor and weather-stained wood for the upper floors where the Fletchers themselves lived. Age, harsh weather and hasty construction meant that most of the buildings in the Skirts bent and creaked and leaned in on each other haphazardly, and the bakery was no exception.

Sometimes, the houses leaned so far out over the narrow streets they gave the feeling of walking through a forest path where the canopy of trees stretched to block out the sky.

Tannin wiggled her key into the lock as quietly as she could, managing on the second try to get it in. The kitchen was dark, and she moved from memory to where she knew the sink was with the idea of a mug of cold water before passing out under the big wooden table that stood in the middle of the room. She knew better than to return to her rented room in the lodging house at this hour and definitely not when she was drunk. Even though she did have a soft spot for her most of the time, her landlady, Mrs O'Baird, would definitely murder her, and the old lady could do without the stress. Plus, the streets after dark weren't somewhere she wanted to be, especially when she was this much in her cups.

Tannin felt along the counter with one hand, guiding herself in the dark in search of the drawer that had the matches in it. She was so preoccupied trying to keep a steady hand to light the clunky, old, glass panelled lantern she didn't notice the door open or the soft footsteps behind her.

"Good evening."

Tannin yelped and leapt backwards, knocking over a tower of trays and bowls that clattered to the floor.

"What the –"

A quiet schikk of a match ignited another lamp, and the soft yellow light fell across the leering, repulsive face of Morey Clach.

"Clach? What the hell?" Tannin asked weakly, clutching her chest where her heart was hammering into her ribs.

"I think we need to have a little chat."

Tannin rubbed her eyes. "It's the middle of the night." "I'm aware. I've been waiting for you."

"You can't just walk in. 'srude."

Tannin turned back towards the door, meaning to throw it open and tell him again to get out, but her path was blocked by a wall of muscle in the shape of a man. One of Clach's many lackeys.

"Aw, you brought a wee pet? Well, you can both fuck off and come back at normal people time." She grabbed a pan off the counter and held it aloft in what she hoped was a menacing way.

She went to take another step when a massive hand reached out, ripping the pan from her grasp. Tannin lost her footing and fell forward, catching herself on the table before she could hit the ground. She would've let herself sink down onto the cool stone floor and give her spinning head a moment to catch up if Clach's man hadn't shot out a hand to grab her arm and haul her back up.

"Hey – arrrgk!"

He spun her around and threw her into one of the straightbacked wooden chairs at the table.

"I don't think you quite realise the situation. Threatening me is not a wise decision."

Tannin swallowed hard and tried to breathe evenly. The sudden movement had sent her stomach lurching, but otherwise she found herself quickly sobering up.

"What d'you want, Clach?"

"Your grandfather and I had a lot of business together, as you know, and his untimely demise has left me with somewhat of a shortfall." He spoke slowly and deliberately as he paced the length of the kitchen and back. "To put it simply, he owed me a lot of money and that debt is still outstanding. A debt which you have now inherited." He smiled at her in a way that a cat might smile at a mouse. "Five thousand crowns."

Tannin gaped. That was a colossal amount of money.

"Horseshit."

"Oh, I'm afraid it's not. This," Clach said as he took a sheet of parchment and laid it on the table, "is a signed contract from the Lenders' Guild naming you as next of kin." He jabbed at her name with a thick finger. "Signed and all in order."

"That bastard! I don't have any money," Tannin said in disbelief.

She squinted at it. It was unmistakably her grandfather's scrawled signature. She reached for it, wanting a closer look. The stamp looked official.

"You can keep that," he said. "I have my own copy, and another is with the Lenders' Guild. I would have sent this by courier, but I imagine you would have ignored it like all the other communications I've sent." His small eyes glittered in the light of the lantern. "Besides, I think it's good to start a business relationship with a personal touch, don't you? And as it is a rather large sum of money, I think you and I are going to be working together for quite a while. I am, of course, a reasonable man, and I won't demand it all at once, no, no. One hundred crowns by the first I think should be enough to start us off."

He smiled his horrible catlike smile again and added quietly. "And don't you be thinking of running off now. You wouldn't like how that turns out."

He gave a curt nod to the big man who stood by the door, and they both turned to leave.

“Until the first then, my dear.” He tipped his hat as if to a lady and sauntered out into the night.

The first of May. That’s Beltane.

Tannin sat for a few moments trying to organise her thoughts in her muddled head. Five thousand crowns. She rested her elbows on the table and ran her hands through her hair.

Fuck.

Chapter Two

The Morning After

Tannin must've fallen asleep where she sat because she woke with a start what seemed like only minutes later, neck sore and mouth dry, to the sound of her boss, Eve, bustling in through the door. She quickly unstuck her cheek from the table.

"Oi!" Eve thumped a load of linen down in front of her.

Tannin groaned.

"Hey!" Eve clapped her hands loudly. "Wake up!" "I'm up, I'm up..."

"Yer a disgrace is what ye are. Drunk and droolin' all o'er my table." Eve chucked a fresh apron in her face. "Ye should've had the first batch in already."

"I'm not droolin'," Tannin muttered, dragging herself to her feet and wiping her chin with her sleeve. Even now that she was standing, Eve towered over her, hands on her hips and a face full of disapproval.

"Get a move on!"

"Gimme a break." Tannin donned the apron and massaged her temples.

"Oh no, ye've got work to do. Work that ye should've started ages ago. Make yersel' useful and get the ovens lit, and if yer gonnae be sick do it ootside 'cause if ye throw up on my floors –"

"I'm not, I'm good," Tannin mumbled through a wide yawn.

"Better be."

Tannin stretched and headed for the matches and kindling when Eve caught her arm.

"Hey, you awright?" Her voice was soft. Tannin could see concern in her eyes. As a boss, Eve was a bit of a tyrant, but as a friend she had a caring side.

"Aye, I'm fine." "Ye sure?"

Tannin shrugged. "He was old. It happens right?"

She wasn't up for explaining the Clach situation right now. She'd barely gotten her head around it herself, and she didn't fancy a lecture.

"Still..." Eve trailed off and then straightened up and gave her head a small shake. "Right, we've got tae get movin'. By the gods, we're so behind today."

The kitchen was simple with walls of bare stone and dark wooden cabinets lining everywhere that wasn't taken up by the colossal wood-burning ovens. Shining copper and steel pots and pans hung from rails across the ceiling over the big square table in the middle, which was consistently covered in a thick dusting of flour during the day. The kitchen was also stiflingly hot.

Sweat dripped down the side of Tannin's face as she pumped the bellows to keep the fires in the giant clay ovens roaring and hefted the heavy trays to and from the shelves within. She usually loved the smell of the fresh baking bread, but this morning it made her stomach churn and her head ache. Eve darted around the kitchen like a madwoman kneading, cutting, mixing, shaping, flour flying everywhere. She'd been a baker at Fletcher's for years and could have made a perfect loaf in her sleep, but even the high demands of the morning crowd sometimes took their toll. Even though she was maybe only ten or so years older than Tannin's seventeen, her furrowed brow and the flour settling in her black curls, streaking her hair with white, made her look much older. A streak of dough stuck to her brown cheek where she'd absentmindedly scratched it.

"Oi! You just gonnae stand aboot and look bonnie, huh?" Tannin snapped out of her daze. "What?"

Eve rolled her eyes and groaned. "Here." She steered Tannin round to the table where a basin of freshly made dough sat. "Knead that and keep oot of my way."

They'd been working full steam for hours, battling the constant demands from the shop for fresh loaves, when the scraggly figure of Mr Fletcher stormed into the kitchen and demanded what was taking so long. His raspy voice grated in Tannin's already aching head as he glowered at them expectantly.

"Sorry, Mr Fletcher. We had a slow start this mornin'." Eve might've been the boss in the kitchen, the rest of the bakery was the domain of the Fletchers. They'd owned this bakery for generations. It was their lifeblood, their pride and joy. Every morning, a queue would form long before the doors opened.

"It's my fault," Tannin interjected before Mr Fletcher could have a go at Eve. "I had a funeral and –"

He cut her off by holding up a liver-spotted hand. "I dinnae want tae hear it. We've a reputation here, and I've had a line of angry customers out there all morn." He turned back to Eve, waggling a finger. "I've told ye before, if yer assistant isnae up to scratch..."

"She is. It willnae happen again." Eve gave Tannin a pointed look.

"Aye, sorry. Won't happen again." Tannin promised.

"It better not. Consider this a warnin'." He stomped out of the kitchen. Tannin rolled her eyes as Eve let out a long sigh, wiping her brow with the back of her hand.

"Oi, dinnae roll those eyes. He's serious, Tannin. You've got tae take this serious like or yer out on yer ear."

"I do take it serious. He's just such an arse." Tannin glared at the closed door as she slid another tray into the oven. She grabbed the lower tray of browning bread with a pair of thick gloves and swore as it slipped from her grasp. As she tried to grab the tray, her forearm grazed the inside of the scorching oven door. She let out a cry and reflexively jerked back, spilling the tray of hot, fresh bread across the floor.

"Argh! Fuck! Shite." She clutched her burned arm and looked forlornly at the loaves scattered over the floor. "Eve, I'm sorry. I –"

Damn, that hurt!

"Right, come here." Eve grabbed her and steered her to the sink, took the thick gloves from her and splashed cold water down her arm. "Let the water run o'er that for a bit. As for the bread, we'll just not tell them, eh?" she said, giving Tannin a conspiratorial wink while deftly scooping up the fallen loaves and putting them back on the tray.

"I'm sorry –" Tannin started but Eve interrupted her.

"Take the rest of the day. The mornin' rush is over. I can handle it from here."

"You sure?"

Eve gave her a soft smile and lifted her arm out of the stream of water to have a look. "Aye, I think yer more hazard than help today. Ah, that's gonnae sting a bit, but ye'll be fine."

Tannin sniffed. It really did sting. "Thanks."

"Go find that boyfriend of yours to take care of ye. I'm sure I have him tae thank for yer state this morning." Eve grinned slyly.

Tannin rolled her eyes again. "He's not my boyfriend, I've told you a hundred times."

Flint was more like a brother to her than anything else, but gossip never stopped.

"Mhm, ye can do better."

"Like a certain delivery lad, you mean?" Tannin said mischievously.

Eve shot her a look. "Now how'd ye know aboot that?"

"Oh, like you two are subtle."

Eve flapped a dishcloth at her in response.

"Graeme's too innocent for you. You're gonna corrupt the poor man." Tannin teased.

"Out! Go on, get oot of here 'fore I change my mind about lettin' ye have the day off." Eve shooed her out of the door, but she was smiling.

Tannin toyed with the idea of going home for some sleep. Gods knew she needed it. Her eyes prickled with tiredness and her limbs felt heavy, but she knew that now she was sober and away from the chaos of the kitchen that worry wouldn't let her sleep so easily.

Five thousand crowns.

Flint wasn't home, but she found him lounging in the shade beside the stables, watching the horses. Flint never spoke about his family, but Tannin got the impression he had come from money once upon a time. He'd told her once he'd had his own horse when he was young and when he was finally a rich man it was the first thing he'd buy.

"Don't you have a job?" She plopped down beside him on the dry grass.

"Don't start 'til three." He looked her up and down and chuckled. "You look like shite. How's that hangover treating you?"

"I feel like shite," she groaned. "I need to talk to you." "Not my fault if you can't handle your drink, mate." "Clach was in the bakery when I got in last night."

Flint's eyes widened a fraction and he raised himself up on one elbow. "You okay?"

"Peachy." Tannin lay back on the grass and moved her arm over her eyes to block out the light. "My old man owed him a shit ton of money, Flint... I'm fucked."

"How much is a shit ton?"

"Five thousand."

Flint let out a low whistle. "Aye, you're fucked. What're you gonna do?"

Pray probably.

Tannin didn't really believe in gods, but Armodan had a hell of a lot to choose from if you did. There was a god for everything. God of merchants and travellers, of health, of war, the skies, nature... There was someone up there responsible for everything if you thought about it enough. There was probably even a god of lost causes somewhere up there that could be her own personal patron.

"Who knows." She sat up, unable to stay still, and tore a handful of grass from the ground. "I've got a month to get a hundred together or I'm probably gonna lose my damn kneecaps."

"You're not gonna lose your kneecaps."

"I probably am. May as well say my farewells to them now." She poked at them mournfully.

"Tan."

"What? I've literally got –" She rummaged in her pockets "Three... and a half crowns to my name, and I'll only make fifty total this month and I've got rent... Goodbye knees."

"He's got to know you can't pay that."

"Oh, he does. I'm just waitin' on some other sleazy offer from him."

The conversation trailed off, both of them lost in thought. As well as back-alley loans, it was rumoured that Clach lined the pockets of gang members all throughout the various territories in the Skirts as well as owning half the brothels.

Brothel or debtor's prison. Oh joy.

Tannin rubbed her eyes. She, thankfully, still had some avenues to explore before it came to that. It would not come to that.

"My grandad still has some crap at his house I'm gonna look through. See if there's anythin' I can sell. If the old bastard hasn't sold it all already."

"You want a hand?" "Nah, I got it."

"All right, lemme know if you do. I'll be about. And I've always had my eye on that pipe of his..."

Chapter Three

Rags and No Riches

To call it a home was generous. It was more of a collection of things in a space. Tannin could see nothing of the grandfather she knew in the mess of belongings strewn around the rooms. But then again, in the last year or so he'd become a man she didn't know at all. She pushed open the door to what would have been the study and stepped over the empty bottles that littered the floor.

Charming.

She remembered when they'd first arrived in the Skirts and she'd lived here with him. He would sit at the desk in this room with the light from the window streaming in behind him, turning him into a silhouette, and write in his journals for hours. The study also used to have a decently stocked bookcase too.

His desk now stood in the same place but with half the drawers pulled out and piled on the floor. The bookcase was still there, but the shelves were empty. Tannin's hand came away with a film of dust when she touched it. The books were long gone. She cast a glance

around the room. Of course, there was nothing here. He'd have sold everything long before he'd have gone to Clach. She massaged her temples and tried to think.

Stupid, fucking, selfish old man.

He'd been bitter and distant, but she'd never thought he'd do this. Leave her completely alone with a crushing debt. Tears pricked her eyes. She wiped them away with an angry grunt as resentment washed over her. She was not going to cry for him. She stalked back through the hallway, peeking in at other rooms which were equally in disarray.

The bedroom was a mess of dirty clothes and bedding on the floor. The curtains bellowed a cloud of dust as Tannin pulled them open, making her cough and splutter. The light that came in through the window was weak and marred by the layers of dirt and grime streaking the glass, but it illuminated the room a little better.

The truth of it was she hadn't wanted Flint to come because she knew it would be like this. He'd already seen her grandfather as the pitiful wreck he'd become, and she didn't want to confirm that any further. She didn't want to pollute his image any more than he'd already done himself. Half the town knew him by the sight of him slumped in doorways after a heavy night or by his incoherent ravings as he screamed in the street at anyone who dared let their eyes linger on him for more than a split second. Tannin had been in a public shouting match with him more than once.

"He's working for them! They want to kill me!" Her grandfather would scream. He'd never elaborated on who he thought "they" were, but there always seemed to be a "them" out to get him. The healers had said the paranoia would only get worse with age. And it had.

Countless times, he had been covered in cuts and bruises whenever she visited and refused to tell her what had happened. Once, here in the bedroom she stood in now, she'd even caught him re-bandaging a worryingly deep cut in his side that looked like he'd haphazardly sewn it up himself. Appalled, she'd tried to make him tell her what happened. Had he been attacked? Had he had an accident? When had this happened? He had just looked at her with wild eyes and said, "Some secrets we take to the grave, my dear". He'd then laughed such a manic laugh that it scared her. He'd refused to be taken to a healer and feigned memory loss any time she'd asked about his injury. Or maybe he wasn't faking. Maybe it was the 'shine taking its toll.

Tannin combed through the room, looking half for things to sell and half for memories to keep. She found his old oilskin cloak crumpled up at the bottom of an empty wardrobe. It was filthy and the fabric was cracked in the creases, but she couldn't help the sad smile that pulled at the corners of her mouth. He'd been wearing this cloak when they'd made the long journey to Armodan from somewhere she couldn't remember. She'd been sickly from the cold and the wet, and he'd told her stories to take her mind off her misery. Of times gone by and ancient magicks.

He had spoken with practiced ease like he'd been telling the same stories for years, and she'd listened intently as he told her of an ancient race of human-like beings but who had special and unusual abilities gifted by their magical blood. The Fair Folk. He had told her how the power of these beings had merged and mixed with humans, and how every so often there were people with traces of this magic and incredible abilities called Remnants who still existed to this day. He'd performed a silly magic trick with a disappearing coin at that point, and even now Tannin chuckled and shook her head at the memory.

Of course, she'd soon learned that the legends of Remnants were a common myth and had been surprised – and a little disappointed if she was truly honest – that her grandfather hadn't made up the story just for her.

For so long, it had felt like it was just the two of them in the world. She knew she'd had parents at some point, obviously, but her grandfather hadn't spoken about them much except to tell her they'd died a long time ago. Tannin paused in the kitchen. It had been here that he first told her she looked like her mother when she wore her long hair down about her shoulders. Apparently, Tannin had her soft brown eyes too, but wherever her freckles had come from remained a mystery.

She half-heartedly pulled open every cupboard in the place. They were either empty or full of junk except one small cupboard under the sink where something poking out from the top caught her eye.

She tugged at it, and a sheet of loose parchment came out. She recognised her grandfather's handwriting immediately and some of his favourite rants. "Do they know? Can't let them have it." Triangular, twisting symbols were inked all over the page with such force the paper had torn a little.

Tannin felt around the top of the cupboard until she found the latch. Opening it, the false board came away and half a dozen dog-eared books fell out. Journals. She crouched, peering up at the hollow space. It was a much bigger space than she'd anticipated. The edges were still rough, and her hand came away with sawdust on her fingertips. It was clear he'd installed it himself and recently.

Picking up one of the books at random, Tannin flipped it open and was met with more of her grandfather's heavy- handed scribblings. On half of the page she held, water from the sink had evidently dripped down onto the books. Ink leeched from one word into the next, smearing the sentences into an unreadable blotch. Not that the undamaged part was any more readable. Tannin held the page up to the light. She tipped it left to right. Turned it upside down. Those were not words she knew, and yet they were familiar.

She flipped through a few of the pages until she found one that was legible.

"I think I have identified a Possible. Her name is Laurel Strongholde of the Black Dog Blacksmithery. I've been watching her for some time."

"Ew, grandad," Tannin muttered, but she read on.

"Her strength and power have to be seen to be believed. I've known giants of men who would struggle to lift what this extraordinary woman throws around like little more than an ear of corn."

"I spoke with her today. Such a gentle woman for one her size. We spoke for some time. She is cultured and intelligent and is a Smith of pure artistry. She is a fascinating woman and the more I see the more I am convinced."

"I see Laurel most days now. I can't help but find excuses to stop by."

"The council is raising taxes this month and Laurel is furious. The Black Dog barely turns a profit as is, and they can't keep up. I've warned her about bringing attention to herself, but she's dead set on speaking up at the next meeting. She spoke of uniting the artisans to make a point. I can't help but feel this is dangerous. There is talk of rioting against the tax rises."

"Laurel is dead. The walls of the Dog collapsed around her as she slept. I truly cannot believe she is gone."

"I looked again at the wreckage of the Dog. Those walls were solid. I'm now more than ever convinced this was foul play. Surely, the council wouldn't take her out over a measly tax complaint or even inciting a little violence. She was far from the instigator. No, this was the Triquetra. I'm sure of it."

"My sweet Laurel."

Tannin re-read the excerpts in stunned silence. The first of the dates scrawled in the margins were when she still lived in this house with him, yet he'd never mentioned a Laurel. The dates progressed past when Tannin had moved out. She'd already been living in her lodging house when this Laurel apparently died and remembered the brutal rioting around that time vividly. He'd mourned her alone. Tannin sighed heavily.

Well, that sort of explains the drinking. But why had he never said anything?

Dust tickled her nose and she sneezed.

Time to go.

She'd take the bits and pieces she'd found and the journals with her and read them at home. This place had given up all it was going to. There was nothing else worthwhile here, only the sad remnants of a sad old man that would disappear entirely when the new tenants moved in in a few days' time.

She was about to leave when she noticed a pipe kicked into a pile of debris in the corner. She dusted it off with her sleeve and held it up. A slight crack ran down the bowl, but it would still work just fine so she tucked it in her pocket for Flint. She knew it by sight as one of her grandfather's spares. It wasn't the one Flint had admired – that one was a sleek and shiny polished wood and brass that looked almost marbled as the dark and lighter woods mingled together.

That had been her grandfather's favourite and she'd made sure he'd been buried with it tucked inside his chest pocket.

Chapter Four

The Slippery Slope

One month. One hundred crowns.

Tannin sat on her narrow bed and shook the last of the coins she'd scrambled together out of her coin pouch. She'd sold the few assorted bits and pieces from her grandfather's place that weren't completely unsalvageable and earned a few more coins from doing extra odd jobs for Mrs O'Baird around the house.

"Mony a mickle, maks a muckle," she muttered to herself. It was one of Mrs O'Baird's favourite sayings. Many smalls make a big.

Not bloody big enough.

Tannin knew it wasn't enough, but she counted it out anyway. After rent, she had sixty-seven crowns, four silvers and a handful of copper pennies. Twenty of those crowns Flint had pressed into her protesting hands. Her pride had begged her to refuse it, but she really couldn't afford to.

Even with Flint's charity, she was still short. She clenched her fists and squeezed her eyes tightly shut, fighting the urge to hurl the meagre collection across the room. Losing a coin down a crack in the floor would be just what she needed now.

She let out a shaky breath and blinked tears away angrily.

Options. I need options. There has to be options.

She swept the coins back in the pouch. If she didn't turn up with the money the following evening, someone would be by to collect. She wondered what Clach would do to her if he had to send someone to chase up the coin. Nothing good. Maybe break a few fingers for a first offence?

She fidgeted, pulling at a loose piece of skin at her thumbnail. She'd already had to pull so many splinters out of her hands after fixing the ancient upstairs shutters, and her ankle still itched like crazy where she'd brushed up against unruly nettles in the courtyard while pulling weeds. And after all that, she was still short.

Borrowing money elsewhere would only double her problems, and the last time she had asked for an advance on her wages, Mr Fletcher had laughed in her face. She could ask Eve maybe. Tannin scoffed. Like Eve would have that kind of money just lying around.

An unwelcome thought that had been circling her mind for days surfaced again. Money lying around...

What choice do I have?

The bakery coin chest... They'd know it was her immediately. She'd get caught. Unless she ran? The inevitable decision had been a dull weight in the back of her mind. She had to get out of the Skirts. Run away from Armodan completely. Change her name. Get away from this.

Well, if I'm running anyway, I may as well burn some bridges.

A pang of guilt struck her as she thought of Eve, but she pushed the thought out – she wasn't stealing from her, it was the Fletchers', and they could spare it. She decided not to tell Flint she was going until the last minute in case he tried to talk her out of it. She'd made up her mind and even had most of her possessions packed up already and her canvas bag sat next to the door ready to go.

She'd have to leave a lot behind. Her eyes trailed over the assortment of odds and ends that littered the top of her chest of drawers. A collection of little unusually shaped pebbles filled a fancy goblet that she'd lifted from a tavern one night. A broken cat skull sat beside it. Flint had called her a morbid wee creep when she'd picked it up, but she'd liked the sharp little fangs and she'd wanted to make a candle holder with it like she'd seen one of the strange little shops in the citadel. Of course, it broke immediately when she'd tried to make a hole in it, but she still had the pieces. Her quilt... that was going to physically hurt her to leave it, but at the end of the day it had come with the room and wasn't even really hers. It was fraying, faded and got washed far less often than it should, but it was oh so comfortable. Tannin hugged it to her chest and breathed in its familiar scent to calm herself.

She'd miss so much if she ran. Maybe Flint would come with her though. She really hoped he would. Even for just a little while. That would make it easier. She could make use of his contacts. And she wouldn't be alone.

Tannin glanced out her window. It was nearly midnight and dark outside. She'd go tomorrow and not let herself dwell on it. If she thought about it too much, she'd never go through with it.

Get the money, deliver it, run.

She blew out her candle and stared up at the ceiling in the dark. She knew sleep wasn't going to come easy, but when it did come it came with the same night terrors that had haunted her since she could remember.

It always started with the drums.

Tannin could hardly see through the gloom. Her feet slammed into the wet ground with every step, coldness seeping in through her shoes. She could hear both her and her grandfather's laboured breathing. And the drums. She could hear the drums. Trees flew out of the foggy darkness.

She didn't know where they were going – just that if they stopped, they died. Horribly.

Every nerve in her body was on fire. Her head was pounding. Dizziness. Only the big hand gripping her small one and dragging her onwards kept her from slowing.

Their pursuers were gaining.

Thorns and twigs pulled at her clothes and tangled in her hair. Roots caught at her ankles with every step. Bright spots appeared in her vision, clouding out the dark shadows of the trees, but she couldn't blink them away.

A whistling sound blew past her ear and an arrow buried itself in a tree in front of her, splitting the wood.

She cried out. The sound reverberated in her chest and echoed through the air. She couldn't hear anything else. Adrenaline was surging through her veins and the bright spots in her vision were blinding her. She couldn't tell if she was still running. She felt like she was falling.

She was *falling. They'd reached a sharp drop in the earth where the ground had slipped and the floor dropped jaggedly downwards. The tree roots at the top were like gnarled tripwire, hurling them straight over the edge and tumbling out of control.*

Her grandfather was talking. Shouting. Shaking her by the shoulder. She wasn't listening. She had hardly felt the impact with the ground. The intense pain in her head had spread to her chest, and the heat was incredible. Her burning lungs couldn't take any air. She kept her eyes squeezed tightly shut and her face pressed to the earthy forest floor. Her hands clenched and unclenched of their own accord.

The snapping and crunching of bone sickened her to her stomach but not as much as the writhing of her own muscles as they fought to grow, overlapping each other and tearing through skin as if alive and frantically clawing their way out from within. Her back arched and her limbs jerked, slick with blood. Her vision was clouded with the red mist of pain as her fingertips ripped open, baring the bone underneath.

She would have screamed if she could. The last thing she saw as her jaw cracked and contorted was the cascade of small, white teeth tumbling into the dirt.

Chapter Five

A Life of Crime

Her heart felt as heavy in her chest as the purse of stolen coins in her pocket as Tannin dragged her feet up the stairs to Clach's offices. She didn't know whether he lived here or just did his business from here, but it was in one of the nicer parts of the Skirts. The streets were a little wider and cleaner than where Tannin lived, but there was no escaping that shabby outer city feel even if the houses were bigger.

She glowered at the wagons that passed by with merry clip- clopping sounds of hooves on cobbles. Thoughts of Eve's pained expression if she ever found out filled her head. It had almost been too easy. A small wedge propping open the shop door from the kitchen. A rusty old nail to pry the coin chest open. The real money would be locked up somewhere else, but she only needed another thirty or so crowns. She hadn't even emptied the chest and, as bad as she felt about it, there really was no going back now.

She rapped a closed fist on the elegant carvings on the wooden door, ignoring the gold knocker in the shape of a griffin's head, and waited. No answer. She waited a bit and pounded on the door again. Still nothing.

Tannin thumped the door.

When there was still no response, she jiggled the handle and the heavy door opened stiffly.

"Hello?"

Muffled sounds emerged from somewhere further in. The hallway was lavishly furnished with polished wooden side tables and antique looking paintings adorning the walls. As she stepped inside, her feet met soft blue carpet that ran through the hallway and slunk up a gold banistered staircase.

Ugh. I guess money doesn't equal taste.

She swallowed her bitterness. Clach made good money for a reason and it was why she was there – he always collected.

She'd only taken a couple of steps inside before a door to her right burst open and a scruffy older man with whisps of white hair rushed through. He had a roll of bandages in his hand and stopped dead when he saw her.

"Who the hell are you?"

"Uh –"

"What are you doing here?"

"I –"

"Get out!"

"Clach's expectin' me!" Tannin blurted as the man made to shoo her out.

"Clach?" The man's eyebrows knitted together, and he pursed his lips as if he was weighing up his options.

"Come on then." He grasped her elbow. "Next time, use the backdoor."

He propelled her at an uncomfortable speed through a corridor and down a narrow flight of stairs. The muffled noises she'd heard earlier were getting louder.

The older man nudged her into a side room. "Wait here."

He slammed the door on the way out. Tannin straightened her tunic and puffed out a long breath.

Waiting it is then.

The room resembled a waiting room of sorts but without any of the luxury she'd seen upstairs. The few chairs were rickety and old, and the floor and walls were plain stone. The window looked out almost straight into a brick wall. Tannin peered out at a set of stone steps leading upwards outside to the street level.

Guess this was the backdoor I was supposed to have somehow magically known about.

As time dragged on, Tannin found herself pacing. She wished she had a timepiece. Without one, she had no way of telling how long it had been, but it felt like an eternity. The noises from elsewhere in the building came and went, and once she thought she'd even heard a stifled scream.

Her stomach churned, and she couldn't have said if it was more from impatience or nervousness. Her pouch of gold felt heavy in her jacket and kept pressing into her ribs. She would be almost glad to be rid of it.

She slumped into one of the chairs. It was an uncomfortable as it looked. She just wanted to be out of here and on the road already. She would go east, she'd decided. To the marshes of Woodren that her grandfather told her she'd grown up in. She didn't remember any marshes but maybe being there would spark some memories.

A nearby crash startled her out of her daydream. Running footsteps clamoured in the corridor outside followed by the sounds of muffled shouting. Tannin poked her head out. Voices thundered through a half-closed door just up the corridor.

Should I be getting out of here?

Anxious and unable to sit still any longer, Tannin crept along to where the noise was coming from and peeked gingerly around the doorframe. The curtains were drawn, and the only light came from a cluster of candles on the table. Two men and a woman, all in some state of distress, cast long shadows across the room. Further in stood a battered-looking sofa, and Tannin could see the outline of someone lying on it.

"We cannae change the plan now!"

The light flickered on one of the men's faces as he leant forward, revealing deepset wrinkles and a chin of greying stubble. He was hunched over the table and jabbed a finger at parchments on it as he spoke.

"I know that! What do ye want me tae dae?" the woman's husky voice replied in a growl.

A weak "Sorry..." came from the figure on the sofa, but the woman hushed it gently. Tannin could see she wasn't a tall woman – maybe only a little taller than Tannin herself but much stockier. Her black hair was drawn back into tight braids that ridged across her scalp and cast a spiky shadow across the wall. The woman picked up a cloth and bowl and moved around the sofa, out of sight. Tannin instinctively leaned a little further trying to see.

"What d'ye think yer doin'?"

Tannin almost leapt out of her skin with a yelp at the voice that tickled the back of her neck with hot breath. Before she could turn around, she was shoved roughly into the room and into the light of the candles.

"I didn't see anythin', I swear!" She garbled and then started. "Holy shit."

As she stumbled into the circle of candlelight and stern faces, the reason for all the commotion became horribly clear. Lying on the couch was a boy who couldn't have been more than fourteen. His pale, panting face made even paler by his shock of bright red hair peeking out from under his cap. He was dressed in the tatty, multi-layered garb of a beggar. His pasty face was covered in a sheen of sweat. The boy's leg bent out at an alarmingly unnatural angle, and blood had seeped through his breeches, staining the cushions. A glint of whitish bone peeked out through the ripped, bloody fabric. Tannin steadied herself against a wave of nausea.

"What's this?" the older man demanded.

"She was listenin' from the hall." The man who'd caught her was a thin, reedy man. His sharp features made him look more rat than man.

"Ye said this place was secure, Clach," he sneered.

Tannin couldn't have seen him from the door, but as she turned in dread there was Morey Clach in all his jowly glory.

In a few short steps, he closed the distance between them and seized her by her collar, shoving his flabby, rapidly reddening face close to hers and forcibly tearing her gaze away from the boy's mangled leg.

"What the hell are you doing here?" he spat.

"You told me to come here." Tannin tore herself out of his grip and wiped spittle from her cheek. She rifled in her pockets to produce the crumpled debt notice and her coin pouch and thrust it at him. "Ring a bloody bell?"

Clach glared but snatched the note anyway, giving it a cursory once-over. "Then you wait until I say otherwise. Get out!" He threw the note back at her but kept the pouch, weighing it in his hand with his eyes narrowed in suspicion.

Tannin scrambled to snatch up the scrap of parchment and turned to leave, breathing a sigh of relief. Who knows what these crooks were up to? The sight of that mangled leg was enough to make her want to run as fast as she could and not look back.

"Wait."

Shite.

Tannin turned to see the woman looking her up and down before her lips tugged into an appraising smile. She was older than Tannin had first assumed. Crow's feet crinkled at the sides of her black-rimmed eyes.

"What?" Tannin asked warily, itching to bolt for the door. The woman circled her, stroking her chin in thought.

"She'll do."

She looked at the older man, eyebrows raised as if looking for agreement or approval.

"Aye, that she will." The man replied with a smile that didn't quite reach his eyes but showed a glint of gold in his teeth.

"Will what?" Tannin said. Tension knotted in her shoulders and her skin prickled anxiously. There was little doubt in her mind that these people were from one of the bloodthirsty gangs that stalked the Skirts. They had that mean look about them.

No, no, no.

"I am not paying you for improvisation, Hamish!" Clach growled, rounding on the man.

"Yer payin' us tae get a job done, Morey," Hamish replied evenly.

The men exchanged a tense stare. Clach broke eye contact first with a grunt. Seemingly taking that as an agreement the man, Hamish, turned to Tannin.

"So, yer gonnae dae a wee job for us tomorrow night and earn yerself a wee bit coin, right?"

"I'm just here to drop off money. That's it...." Tannin backed away towards the door, but her the woman blocked her path.

This wasn't the plan.

"You. It's your lucky night," Clach said, growling through his teeth and pointing a ringed finger at Tannin. "Do what he says and your debt's paid up for this month. I'll keep this for next month's payment." He jiggled the pouch so that the golden coins within rattled.

She opened her mouth to argue.

"One more word out of you, and I'll go to the judge first thing in the morning to demand what I'm owed," Clach sneered. Tannin had already noticed that the due date on the agreement was long past. She'd been hoping it was a mistake. "I own you until the debt is paid, unless you want a trip to debtor's prison. I say you have a job to do and you're going to do it, understand?"

Tannin shut her mouth with a snap. She didn't trust her voice not to crack so she simply nodded.

"Tomorrow night. Midnight. Here. Dinnae be late," the woman commanded before turning back to the papers on the table.

A moment of silence passed where Tannin wasn't sure what she should be doing until Clach snapped at her to get out and she gladly scurried for the door. Once outside, she ran her hands through her hair and exhaled with frustration.

This wasn't the fucking plan.

If she didn't show up the following night, she may as well sign her own death warrant, but getting involved with organised crime was way beyond anything she was comfortable with. These were serious people, and one job with people like them never ended at one job.

She needed to think, and she needed advice. A quick glance up at the darkening sky told her that it wasn't too late to seek out a second opinion.

Chapter Six

Thinking Juice

It was a gamble which tavern she'd find him in, but The Broken Sword Inn was a firm favourite for them both. Only the most gullible of travellers actually took a room at the Sword intending to sleep there. It was more of a stay by the hour kind of place, but the ground floor and basement made for a surprisingly nice pub for a casual drink. A smoky fire crackled in the hearth, bathing the long wooden tables and booths in a soft glow. Dice and game counters littered some of the tables where patrons could spend an evening frittering away their last few crowns.

More often than not, someone took up a fiddle and filled the room with jaunty tunes. The heavy maroon curtains that blocked the windows and the candles littering the tables gave the low-ceilinged rooms a feeling of perpetual late evening, and Tannin and Flint had often lost track of time there. It wasn't just the atmosphere or reasonably cheap drink that kept them coming. Tannin suspected Flint's recent favouritism had a lot to do with the new barmaid and her low-cut dresses.

Sure enough, Flint was lilting along with a bard's bawdy singing from the bar when Tannin entered.

He was with a group of men she vaguely knew by sight, but it seemed her expression was enough for him to give her his full attention because as soon as he saw her, his grin became serious, and he claimed a booth in the back for some privacy.

"Spill," he said immediately, all trace of tipsiness gone. "Clach made me an offer instead of takin' the money,"

Tannin said and then snorted. "Offer. Like I could refuse."

Flint grimaced. "Like..." he paused and then said in a hushed tone, "a sex thing?"

"Ew! Gods, no." Tannin mimed throwing up. "I swear, I'd take debtor's prison before I did that."

Maybe...

Tannin was no stranger to hard work, but potential years of hard labour as a debtor was a harrowing prospect. Especially since she hadn't even borrowed the damn money in the first place. Running away was a much more likely option but, even then, she didn't know how far she could realistically get if Clach sent someone after her.

Flint shrugged. "Don't be so high and mighty. It's an honest job, you know."

"Oh, shut up," Tannin said, leaning her elbows on the table and putting her head in her hands. "It's not that. It's a crime thing."

"Ahhh." Flint nodded knowingly. "And you don't know if that's too far down the unreturnable road into sin? I get it."

"It's not so much a moral issue." She paused. "Well, it is a wee bit. I just don't want to get into somethin' I can't get out of."

"But you're a dead woman walking if you don't." Flint finished for her cheerfully. "You know what you need? Thinking juice."

He didn't even wait for her to respond before he was off bouncing back to the bar. Tannin scratched at the peeling varnish of the table. Someone had carved a heart around "G+D" at the place directly in front of her. A little further along was a charming illustration of the male anatomy.

Tannin smiled wryly. Some things you could always count on. The sun would always rise in the morning to set again in the evening and people would always draw dicks on things.

Flint returned with two full goblets and set one in front of her.

"My treat. Since you're beyond broke and your life is basically trash right now."

"So kind." Tannin rolled her eyes and then inspected her drink. "This isn't juice. It's mead."

"It's got fruit in it, doesn't it? Therefore, it's juice."

"Flint, this is made with honey, dafty. There's no fruit in it."

"Huh." He peered into his goblet at the amber wine within. "Then it shall be renamed Thinking Beverage, Your Great Highness of all Knowledge."

Tannin raised her glass. "To Thinking Beverages then."

They clinked goblets and took a gulp.

"So, what's the job?"

"I have no idea. All I know is that it's tomorrow night. I'm goin' in blind as a bloody bat."

"You're gonna do it?"

"I can't get out of it, can I?"

Flint agreed. "Nope, he'd hunt you down for sport, my dear. Well, not personally, he'd hire a sellsword or a bounty hunter or something. God. I'd love to see that man try to run though."

"You are not being helpful."

"'fraid I can't help ya with this one. No gettin' round Clach when he wants something." He patted her hand consolingly. "If you find out more about the job before then, gimme a heads-up though and I'll see what I can swing for ya."

"Thanks," Tannin said miserably.

"Oh, it's not so bad." He waggled his eyebrows. "Crime can be fun you know."

She rolled her eyes.

"So... to the unreturnable road of sin, did you say?" She raised her goblet again unenthusiastically.

"You know I love a good sin." He winked.

Tannin declined another drink after draining her goblet. She confirmed yet again that there weren't any loopholes or Plan Bs she could use. Flint patted her shoulder in consolation.

"You've just got to do it and hope it's a one-time thing. Be careful though," he said, suddenly serious again. "You're expendable to them, remember. If it starts getting sketchy, like too sketchy I mean, then get out of there. Just run as fast as those little legs will take you."

"It's already too sketchy." Tannin stood up to leave. "If I need to suddenly flee the city for completely unrelated reasons, you'd be down for a trip, right?"

Flint laughed. "Only if you pack enough Thinking Beverages for the road."

Night had fallen as she aimlessly meandered through the narrow streets. She didn't want to return to her lodgings just yet. Going home meant that today was over and it was closer to tomorrow, and Tannin was dreading tomorrow. So she dawdled. She ran through a bunch of possibilities in her head of what the job could be. Something illegal definitely but how illegal? Extortion? Bribery? Robbery? ... Murder?

Tannin frowned. No, she'd be replacing that scrawny boy with the broken leg, and he didn't look like the murdering sort. But then again, looks were deceiving.

She took the widest and best lit route home, still dragging her feet as she walked under the oil lamps that illuminated the street. The watchmen, who lit them every night with long, wick tipped staffs, must have been and gone while she was in the Sword with Flint because little pools of light lengthened her shadow against the cobbles.

Houses and shops meshed together in the shadowy darkness outside of the lamp's reach.

If she hadn't walked this route a million times, it might have made her nervous. The towering buildings jutted out and loomed overhead where parts had been added and beams and bridges between the houses mingled with the laundry strung up between them, creating strange shapes in the gloom. Each one was its own kind of unique with different parts in wood or stone depending on what had been within arm's reach when the buildings had been thrown together. Steeply slanted roofs pointed up into the clouds haphazardly and although she couldn't see them right now, Tannin knew a lot of these old houses had lost tiles last winter and many were still loose. There was not much chance of them getting replaced. People in the Skirts had other things to spend the little money they had on, so the old buildings just hung on until they collapsed in on themselves and then they were simply rebuilt from the rubble. New life from old corpses. That was the Skirter way. Tannin kept well away from the decrepit buildings to avoid falling debris while stepping carefully over the odd pile of horseshit that littered the road.

Would Clach accept a tile to the skull as a valid excuse for not showing up? Probably not.

She kicked at the new weeds already clawing their way up through the cracks in the courtyard paving when she arrived home. For a lodging house in the Skirts, it was actually holding together pretty well. With the repaired window shutters, the old brick house even looked semi-respectable despite its lopsided chimney and weather-stained façade.

Technically, she could have afforded a larger room somewhere else with the wage she made, but her little room was comfortable enough. Mrs O'Baird was a more than fair landlord and what was more, she didn't just accept any old tenant, and so Tannin hadn't had any drunken late-night visitors trying to break her door down like she'd heard of happening in other places. Besides, she was settled here.

She certainly felt more at home here than she ever had at her grandfather's place. There, she'd always felt like she was intruding or doing something wrong, but here she was free to do as she liked as long as she paid her rent and didn't actually set the place on fire. She definitely liked the freedom.

Tannin scowled. And now she was indebted, trapped and completely screwed. Once more, she cursed her grandfather for being so stupid. So heartless. So dead.

Still refusing to admit the day was over, Tannin strolled around the back to a ramshackle stable. She'd heard the newest tenant actually had a horse of his own, and sure enough a pretty white-and-brown thing was chewing lazily and snorting. She'd never ridden a horse and although she saw them constantly on the street, she never went near them. People got weirdly defensive about their horses.

"Hello, there," Tannin said gently, holding her hand out for the horse to sniff at. She wasn't sure why, but that was what you did with dogs so why not horses?

She had barely extended her hand when the horse whinnied and bucked away from her.

"Woah! Woah there." Tannin took a measured step backwards.

The horse snorted and pawed at the hay covered ground in agitation.

"Aye, okay I get it," Tannin muttered annoyed. All she wanted was to give his mane a stroke and forget her worries for a minute or two.

Snort.

"Well, I don't like you either then, Horsey."

SNORT.

"All right, I'm goin'! Calm it!"

Chapter Seven

The Job

After an agonising day at work, waiting anxiously to see if her theft would be discovered, Tannin was a bundle of nerves as she tried to steel herself for what was still coming. She liked a bit of adventure and didn't have a problem bending the rules a little in times of need, but the prospect of being dragged into the actual underbelly of the Skirts was more than daunting. The guilt of taking a few coins was already eating her alive. She wasn't cut out to be a criminal, and she was already thinking of ways she could slip some money back into the till when she eventually had some. Her stomach clenched every time she thought of going back to Clach's offices, but Flint was right. He'd track her down if she didn't.

She passed the evening sewing up a hole in a pair of her breeches, and the result was messy to say the least. Her hands were shaking too much for the stiches to be neat, so she gave up, throwing the whole thing into the corner with a grunt of annoyance after she'd pricked herself with the needle for the fourth time. She sucked the little bead of blood from her fingertip. If she survived the night, she'd ask Mrs O'Baird nicely to sew them up for her.

When it was time to leave, Tannin had to take a swig of whisky from a flask Flint had given her "for courage" to even make it out the door and force herself to walk to the imposing building that held Clach's offices. She had learned her lesson from before. Instead of knocking on the front door, Tannin skulked around the back and slipped in the basement entrance, slightly surprised that it was unlocked.

Waiting room? No, confidence is key. That was what Flint had told her. She swallowed hard, puffed up her chest and strode straight to the room they had all gathered in before, but her courage failed her at the last second and she knocked timidly instead of charging right in.

The door opened a crack. A black-lined eye glared at her before it was fully opened and she was ushered in.

"Right oan time," the woman said dryly, shoving a dark green bundle into Tannin's arms.

The others were already present and before she could even ask, the older man from before was giving her a staggeringly quick explanation of the situation.

"Right. I'm in charge here – name's Hamish. And that's Fergus, Beck and Nyesha. That's all ye need tae know." He pointed at each of them in turn.

Tannin thought she recognised Fergus as the ape-like man that Clach had brought to the bakery. He stood with his thick arms crossed and gave no sign that he recognised her.

Beck was the skinny man who'd snuck up on her before. She would have called him tall if he wasn't standing next to Fergus the apeman. His eyes were unsettlingly pale as he watched her intently with his head cocked to the side. She shivered. The woman, Nyesha, was dressed in livery, the same dark green colour as the bundle she'd given Tannin, with her braided hair partially hidden by a flat cap.

"Right, rundown of the plan. Newbie, listen up." Hamish set out a rough hand-drawn sketch of a building on the table. "This is the hoose. I'll be goin' in as a guest here." He circled a scribble on the map with a thick, gnarled finger. "Newbie, yer gonnae come in here and keep watch here –" Another jab at the parchment. "Signal is three quick knocks. Go on, knock on the table. Three times. That's it. Good lass. If anyone comes near this side of the hoose while I'm daein' my thing, then we get oot sharpish. Got it? Good. Nyesha is gonnae be on lookout here and once we're in, she's gonnae wait ten minutes and then head here to prep the horses. Beck and Fergus take the perimeter. Newbie, what's yer name? Put that uniform on, otherwise ye'll stand oot like a sore thumb."

"Tannin," she mumbled, putting the oversized coat on over her clothes and pulling the cap down over her hair. She was drowning in fabric, but hopefully it would do its job and keep attention off her.

A robbery then?

It sounded simple enough from that vague explanation. She could keep lookout. That was much better than the grim scenarios she'd come up with in her head as she tossed and turned the night before. She could still do this job and get out of the city with a head start. She could leave as early as tomorrow morning.

"What is the job?" she asked.

"Ye dinnae need tae know aboot the job, ye just need tae stand watch. Clear?" "Aye, but –"

She eyed Beck and Fergus anxiously even though she couldn't hear the words they were muttering between themselves. They were looking at her. Clearly, no one was happy with the change of plans and their discontentment was palpable in the air.

"Right, we've got tae move now. Let's go." Hamish clapped his hands.

Tannin barely had time to think before she was rushed out the backdoor and boosted up into the front seat of one of two waiting carriages beside Nyesha, who took the reins and gave a sharp "H'YAH".

She didn't register where the others had gone and focused on finding something to hang onto as the carriage jolted off. She could hardly believe what was happening as she clutched at the side rail and they picked up speed.

Tannin swore as the carriage thundered over some uneven cobbles. "Fuck! Will you slow down!"

"Watch yer mouth and sit up straight. Try and at least look professional." Nyesha gave her a withering look out of the corner of her eye.

"I will when I'm not about to die in a damn carriage crash," Tannin blurted as she was jostled and bounced around on the hard seat however tightly she clung to the side rail. Nyesha ignored her and urged the horses onwards at breakneck speed.

Before long, they passed neatly arranged trees and gardens and the road changed from cobbles to packed earth. The clogged city fell away behind them to be replaced by suburbs of spacious estates and meticulously maintained manors. These were the estates of the rich folk who didn't deign to live amongst regular people, even in the luxury of the inner citadel. There were only a few ways to get rich enough to afford property out here in the clean clear air while still being close enough to Armodan to do business regularly and none of them were honest.

Only once they were well and truly away from the Skirts and all trace of oil lamp light was no longer visible did Nyesh a slow their pace. She turned to Tannin, stony faced.

"Listen tae me, ye dinnae say a word. Follow my lead and not a peep. Get it?"

"Got it."

"When we get there, I'll tell ye where tae go. Ye dinnae move 'til I tell ye."

"Where are we going?"

"Just do what yer told."

They turned at an imposing gate with tall, sharp spikes topping it and were waved through by a set of green liveried servants to follow a road that passed a finely manicured lawn and huge leafy topiaries.

They drove up the winding drive, pausing only for a brief second to let Fergus and Beck jump out from the back of the carriage into the shadows. The house they approached was bigger than any one house ought to be in Tannin's opinion. The manor could have swallowed her whole lodging house and then some, with three or four floors of stone with rose bushes lining the lower windows and carved statues flanking the arched front door. Each chunk of the house rose to a different height in steeply pointed peaks, as if the architect couldn't quite decide where the roof should be.

Nyesha directed their carriage off to the side where a stately stable stood already full with proud beasts and massive, gilded carriages. Instead of stabling their horses, she urged them a little further to park behind the stable, hidden from view. The few people they'd passed on the way up hadn't given them a second glance.

Nyesha hopped out and tied off the reins, beckoning Tannin to follow her away from the stables and the house and into the gardens.

"Don't creep about like that. Ye look suspicious. Just walk normal like."

"Right, okay." Tannin blushed. She had been almost half in a crouch, glancing about furtively with every step.

They walked around to the side of the house in the dark, giving the building a wide berth. Beck and Fergus were waiting for them there, their eyes fixed on a dark window that stood ajar high above them. Really high above them. They looked at Tannin expectantly.

"Absolutely no fucking way," she hissed, coming to a stop.

"Get over there." Nyesha growled.

"You want me to go through there? Not happenin'."

"Hamish is inside waitin'."

"I'll fall! It's too high!"

"Yer not gonnae fall. Get up there."

"Ha. Not a chance. I didn't agree to this." Tannin made to back away when Nyesha blocked her path.

"Move."

"Seriously?"

"Time's tickin'. We dinnae have time for any horseshit, and yer the only one wee enough tae get in there. So get."

"This is all horseshit," Tannin muttered but she really did not like the glint in Beck's eyes.

Nyesha raised her eyebrows and gestured again to where theothers were waiting. "After you, newbie."

They stared at each other for a moment. The threat didn'tneed to be said out loud.

"Fine." Tannin walked back to the others. "Let's do this. And my name's not 'newbie', it's Tannin."

As she went to step up onto Fergus's interlocked hands, Beck caught the back of her coat and leaned in so that his lips were almost touching her ear.

"Just remember," Beck whispered sweetly, "Ye get in any bother? And ye rat oan us? I'll cut yer tongue out myself."

Getting in the window was no easy task. Even standing fully upright on Fergus's shoulders, Tannin could barely reach it. Her fingertips only just managed to brush the ledge.

"I told you, it's too high!" she whispered and then suppressed a yelp as Fergus grasped her ankles and thrust upwards, launching her another foot in the air.

She scrambled for the ledge and managed to throw her elbow over the sill, her legs scraping off the brick as she fought to pull herself through. She dragged herself inside and landed in a panting heap on the carpet.

The room she'd landed in was probably, at one time, a very elegant bedroom but now it was clearly just used as storage. White sheets covered chairs and cabinets and other shapes Tannin couldn't even hazard a guess at. Gold framed portraits were piled leaning against the wall, the foremost of which showed an imperious-looking man. The painted figure looked upon the fine layer of dust that covered everything in distaste.

"Here." Hamish stepped out of the shadows where he had been waiting and offered her a hand. As she accepted it, he was already hurriedly whispering.

"Right. Target is in the office on the floor above us. I'll go in and get it. You stand watch. Still just lookout, right? Ye good, aye? Come on, quietlike now."

Tannin nodded. Her throat tightened, and her heart was still thumping from her scramble through the window but that wasn't all. This was suddenly uncomfortably real. She was breaking and entering, and she didn't even know what for.

With no other option, she followed Hamish out of the room.

What the hell have I gotten myself into?

Chapter Eight

A Change Of Plans

In the light of the hallway, Tannin saw Hamish clearly for the first time. He wore the clothes of a nobleman with white ruffles at his throat and a sleek black velvet vest above a black kilt. His greying hair was pulled back and held by a black bow at the nape of his neck. If she hadn't known better, she'd never have taken him for anything other than some Laird or other. Only when he spoke did he give himself away.

They climbed up the stairs. She tried to make her footfalls as silent as possible on the soft carpet, hardly breathing, constantly looking back to check they were still alone and undiscovered. Whereas Hamish moved with practiced ease, soundless and stealthy. When they reached the office, she stood wringing her hands, but Hamish took only a second to pick the lock and they slipped inside.

The room was dark. Even when Hamish lit the small oil lamp on the desk, it did little to illuminate the bookshelves that lined every wall with huge, imposing tomes. Tannin wondered vaguely if they were ever actually read or if they were just there for show. That seemed like a rich person thing.

Everything had to say "oh look how important and smart I am". The desk, too, seemed designed for show. A statement of power and class. All shining wood and green leather inlay with glittering silver nibbed quills and crystal ink pots. The room was watched over by a huge oil portrait that hung behind the desk. She guessed that must be the man of the house or a relative or something. He was ugly.

Hamish wasted no time in admiring the office and instead snapped at her to keep watch by the door.

Fair enough. That's what I'm here for after all.

She stood with her eye pressed to the tiniest crack in the door, looking out into the corridor. Even so, she couldn't help having a peek at what Hamish was doing. He had swung out the huge portrait. Behind it was a safe. It looked like it must have weighed a ton. Even the handle to open it was larger than any door handle she'd ever seen. She quickly turned back to the corridor as Hamish glanced her way. It was blessedly empty outside, but that didn't do anything to quiet her nerves.

If we get caught...

She didn't even want to think about it. She didn't feel particularly guilty stealing from people who owned houses like this and would sooner spit at her than offer her a kind word, but that didn't stop her from being actually guilty in the eyes of the law. Thievery would get her hand chopped off and mounted on one of the cruel spikes on the huge walls that surrounded the city Gaol. It would wave at her mockingly until carrion birds carried it off piece by piece.

Maybe I could talk my way into just a trespassing charge...

She strained to hear anything at all besides her own heartbeat. It was hammering impossibly loudly in her ears, but she could still hear the gentle clinking of whatever tools Hamish was using on the safe. He seemed to be chanting some sort of mantra under his breath. She didn't understand the words, but it made the hair on the back of her neck prickle. It was slow going and every sound made her jump and imagine that there was a whole squadron of guards about to charge down the corridor any second.

Eventually though, the tumblers inside the mechanism seemed to move and fall into place. Hamish muttered a low stream of curses.

"What is it?" Tannin whispered, panicked.

"Sh! Someone's got here 'fore us." He swore again and then came the sounds of him resealing the safe and hurriedly packing up his tools.

"They're probably still here somewhere." He growled, reaching around her to open the door fully. "They're gonnae regret takin' my prize."

She could do nothing but trail after him as he stalked out of the office and back down the stairs towards the increasing noise of music and celebration. The corridor led them to a delicately banistered balcony that overlooked a grand hall where a lavish party was in full swing.

Traditional May flowers for the Beltane celebrations hung in ribboned garlands and overflowed from huge golden vases all through the room. Tiny flame-filled braziers lined the long tables down the sides of the hall like dainty bonfires. Tannin

couldn't help but gape at the finery of it all. Couples swayed and spun on a glittering marble dancefloor as musicians played a slow but joyful tune. She could have watched the fluttering dresses, flapping kilts and intricate steps all night. They were like the exotic birds she'd seen once in one of the peculiar store fronts in the artisan district.

This was an entirely different world to her early morning bakery shifts and scraping by day by day. If she lived a life like this, a hundred crowns a month to pay off Clach would be pocket change. Hell, if she could afford one of those gowns, then the full five thousand probably wouldn't make her sweat. She wouldn't have to do Clach's damn dirty work ever again.

Tannin sighed. The only way she'd break into this upper circle of finery would be if by some miracle she managed to marry into it. Not that she wanted to marry at all. Although marrying someone rich and getting Clach out of her face once and for all... That was an attractive thought.

"Him." Hamish turned her by the shoulder, jolting her out of her daze, and pointed out a man weaving through the groups watching the dancers.

The man in question was broad shouldered and finely dressed in dark blue. Tannin couldn't see many details from this distance, but she was willing to bet it was as richly embroidered as the other guests'. Judging by the grey streaks in his hair, she guessed he was probably around the same age as Hamish.

"How d'you know?"

"Let's just say oor paths have crossed," he said grimly. He slid his hand into his vest and nodded almost to himself.

Tannin didn't doubt that there was at least one deadly blade hidden in there. A sgian dubh. *Black dagger.* She swallowed hard and prayed that he wouldn't need to use it.

"Can't I just go?" she asked desperately. "If the plans changed, then you don't need me here anymore."

"I might. Ye never know. Now look. Remember what he looks like." He gauged Tannin up and down critically. "Try and stay out of sight. We dinnae want tae spook him."

Tannin looked down at herself. Sure, she was wearing the right colour of one of the servants of the house, but she was also wearing a coat indoors, which would look strange to anyone paying attention not to mention she was far too small to fit in with the burly servants she'd seen on the drive up. Maybe they were the security though and her small stature wouldn't seem out of place inside with the indoor servants.

Hamish nudged her again and pointed. She hadn't been paying attention to the target at all but now, following Hamish's pointed finger, she saw him slip through a side door. She caught a little more of his bearded face this time but only for a fraction of a second.

"Cellar," Hamish muttered, taking off down the stairs.

Tannin hurried after him, keeping as far away as possible from the mingling nobles and ducking behind pillars. She knew her disguise was a feeble one, and it would only take a second glance for her to be busted. Her heart was in her mouth until they managed to slip through the little door and disappear.

At the bottom narrow stairs, she could finally breathe a little easier as the music faded away almost entirely and the dull grey walls sheltered them from the revelry. The cellar seemed to be a mass of interlinking rooms, each section storing different wares. One was half filled with rolled up rugs and carpets and another with crates upon crates of fabrics or maybe clothing – she didn't get a chance to snoop properly before Hamish moved on. The man they were pursuing seemed to have vanished into thin air until they ended up in a room storing wine and spirits. The unmistakable sound of whispering reached their ears.

Tannin followed Hamish as they edged around stacks of crates and peeked through gaps. Their target stood by an open trapdoor in the floor, but he wasn't alone. A smaller, dark clothed figure stood beside him, and they were speaking in hushed voices.

Hamish whispered as they watched, "We can still follow.We just need tae - Argh!"

He had misjudged the shelf he'd been leaning on, and a cascade of glass bottles fell and shattered, spraying the room in frothing wine and giving him away immediately.

"You!" Recognition sparked in the man's eyes followed by nothing short of pure fury. He thrust the package at the other figure. "Take it and go. I'll take care of this."

Hamish spewed a stream of curses and took off in a long- legged sprint in the opposite direction, leaping over the spillage and broken glass.

"Wait!" The black-clad figure cried but couldn't do anything to stop the man charging after Hamish. He was so focused he sprinted right past where Tannin was crouched, frozen, and she thanked whatever god was watching over her.

The figure muttered angrily as she stood over the trapdoor. Tannin could see her more clearly now through a gap in the crates. It was a girl. She didn't look much bigger than Tannin, and didn't seem to be armed

Maybe I can jump her and get the package? No, that's a stupid idea. What do I care about the package?

All she had to do was get out of this stupid house, and that tunnel was her best chance at a way out. She'd wait until the coast was clear and then sneak out.

Crashing noises from above startled both her and the girl at the trapdoor. Whether it was the two men or the entire household's security flooding the cellar with swords drawn, both girls made the same split-second decision and made for the trapdoor. Tannin was as quick as a hare, too quick for the girl to see her in time. She couldn't stop in time and crashed into her, knocking them both through the hole in the floor.

Luckily, they didn't fall far. Even more luckily, Tannin thought, she'd landed softly on top of the other girl who coughed and wheezed as Tannin rolled off her.

"What –" She gasped.

Hm. May as well.

"Look, it's not personal," Tannin blabbered, ripping the package out of the girl's loose grip. "But I need this sorry – Oof!"

She was less winded than Tannin had expected, and a foot caught her hard in the back of the leg, sending her sprawling onto the ground. Tannin returned a kick in the girl's general direction and heard a satisfying grunt as her foot made contact. She gave a last glance over her shoulder as she scooped up the package from where she'd dropped it and darted off into the tunnel.

Her leg throbbed as she moved through the darkness with only the vague outlines of sconces on the walls that should have held flickering lamps to guide her. She clutched the package close to her chest.

I have the prize! Not bad for a first job.

Tannin beamed with pride and then paused to give herself a mental shake. She wasn't supposed to be enjoying any part of this, although the thrill of it was undeniable. Her fingers traced the wrapped bundle she carried. It was surprisingly heavy for its size. As soon as she was out of this darkness, she was definitely going to check out what was worth all this bother.

She tried to keep her speed up, but now that the adrenaline was wearing off, weariness set in fast. There hadn't been any other tunnels branching off this one. The other girl could be on her at any time – Tannin had no doubt she was giving chase – so she kept up a slight jog when she could. The upside of one tunnel was that she had to be going the right way.

Tannin couldn't tell what direction she was heading, but from the strain in her muscles, the tunnel was definitely inclining slowly upwards. Her mouth and throat were as dry as ash, and she wished she had some water. The dust and dirt in the tunnel weren't helping, and neither was the layer of grime clinging to her damp skin.

I am never doing this again.

The brief excitement was not worth this filthy tunnel and the risk of losing a hand to the city guards. Fuck Hamish, fuck Nyesha and fuck Clach. She was getting out of this city as soon as possible.

It didn't take long before a strong orange glow was visible ahead.

Yes!

She barely managed to keep going, but if she could just get out into the city streets, she could lose her pursuer and find somewhere to catch her breath. The glow seemed to be coming from a part where the tunnel widened out into a chamber. There must have been a lantern or a torch there, because Tannin could see a room beyond the opening. Her legs felt leaden as she stumbled out of the tunnel and onto flagstones where she skidded to an unsteady stop. Her relief vanished instantly at the sound of weapons leaving their sheaths.

"Oh shite." At least six shadowy figures converged on her from where they had been lounging on crates and barrels or against the walls. Sharp steel glinted in each hand.

Tannin had just started to reflexively raise her hands – in surrender or defence she wasn't sure – when the other girl came charging through the entrance behind her, pink cheeked, her long dark hair in disarray and breathing hard but with a smug smile plastered across her face.

"I'll be taking that back now." She held out her hand for the package. For a thief, she had a surprisingly cultured accent and, as Tannin's eyes raked over her sizing her up, she had to admit she was also very attractive.

The audacity.

She gripped her prize tighter for a second, but feeling the circle of bandits creep closing, she tossed it over to her.

"So not worth it," she muttered.

The girl turned the package over in her hand, tracing the contours of whatever was inside. A crinkle of worry formed on her forehead as she laid the parcel on the flat top of a barrel and, flicking open a knife, carefully cut through the covering.

As attention shifted to the package, Tannin spotted the exit across the room. She steadied herself, deciding to make a run for it. She must've made it obvious somehow because the next second a blade was levelled at her throat. She froze.

"Don't you even think about it," the thug at the other end of the short sword growled.

Dammit.

"NO!"

Everyone's attention snapped back to the girl and the package. The fabric had been sliced open and folded back. Nestled in the middle was some sort of brass device. Several attachments hung forlornly from its sides with a large slightly opaque but very cracked lens sat in the middle. It made a sad ticking sound in the quiet of the cavern.

The girl gingerly lifted the device out of the packaging, open-mouthed in dismay. One of the lens shards slipped free and thudded back onto the top of the barrel.

She fixed Tannin with a murderous look.

"I didn't –" Tannin didn't even get to finish saying she hadn't meant to break it, that she didn't even know what it was, when a fist connected with her face.

She didn't register the pain right away, just the fact she'd hit the ground and she could taste blood. Her cap had flown off and her hair fell about her face as she pushed herself up a little and spat out a mouthful of red onto the ground. She swore as she ran her tongue over where her tooth had sunk into the inside of her lip, gouging a chunk out and spurting blood into her mouth. It hurt like hell, and her fancy coat was now spotted with red stains.

"Enough! I said no violence!" The girl barked at the man who'd punched Tannin. "Just search her."

"Get off me!" Tannin struggled as she was lifted off the ground and held tightly by both arms as the man who'd hit her rifled through her pockets.

How is this girl the one giving the orders?

"If that thing's broke, we're still gettin' paid, right?" the man demanded, narrowly avoiding Tannin's attempts to kick him. He was an ugly brute, who looked like he'd taken a fair few punches to the face in his life too.

"An agreement is an agreement," the girl replied curtly.

One of the bandits holding her flicked the lapel of Tannin's dark green coat. "That's the real deal. She's not alone for sure. Unarmed except for this knife though."

Tannin growled as he pocketed it.

"Attilo went after the man she was with back at the house. He seemed to know him. How many are with you?" The girl turned her interest back to Tannin.

"I dunno," she spat, squirming like mad. As grim as her current situation was, she hadn't forgotten Beck's promise to cut out her tongue as she fought ineffectively against the strong hands. "Get off me!"

The girl raised an eyebrow. "You don't know how many people you came here with?"

Tannin didn't answer and looked away. The ugly thug massaged his knuckles.

Hope that's broken, arsehole.

The dark-haired girl called to one of the figures who was hanging back. "Have you seen this girl before? Do you know whose crew she's with?"

A grubby-looking man with tattered clothes stepped intoTannin's line of sight. He looked like a pile of dirty laundry come to life and his matted beard looked like it could house several small rodents.

"Don't look like none I've saw hangin' about before." He stepped up closer to Tannin. The smell of stale beer and body odour pouring off him was enough to make her gag. She tried to turn away, but he grabbed her chin and tilted her face to the light of the lanterns, his filthy nails scratching her skin. "Nah, not seen 'er."

He let her go and stepped back. Tannin took a much- needed breath.

The girl sighed. "We don't have time for this. Let's just go." "What about her?"

"Leave her here for one of her friends to find. They'll come down here eventually."

"No, wait!" Tannin protested as she was hauled backwards further into the cavern. She was then unceremoniously dumped on the floor next to a supporting beam that propped up the ceiling and pushed against it. A dagger was brandished threateningly in her direction with a growled bark to not move as her arms were again seized and pulled behind her.

"Argh! Don't!"

"Oi," a gruff voice from behind her snapped as she shifted uncomfortably. "Stop movin'."

"Oh, I'm sorry. Is this *inconvenient* for you?" Tannin snapped back.

"Aye. It is actually. I'd have sooner slit yer worthless throat and be done with it."

Tannin bit back a retort and sat still, letting whoever was behind her finish binding her arms behind the wooden post. She flexed her fingers and wiggled her hands, grimacing.

Fuck, I'm not getting out of this any time soon.

The girl was the last to leave.

"You're really gonna just leave me here like this?" Tannin called desperately.

The girl rounded on Tannin with such a venomous look that she flinched.

"Do you even know what you've done?" She spat. "Do you even know what this is?" She held up the piece of lens.

"Wee bit of broken glass?" Tannin hazarded.

"Very funny."

"We've got to go, Ava," someone called from down the passage.

"Look, Ava is it? I'm sorry about your fancy... clock or whatever. But you can't just leave me here!" Tannin tugged at her bonds in emphasis.

Ava scoffed. "You're lucky you're not –" She froze, a strange look appearing on her face. She looked at the twisted hunk of metal and glass in her hand. She looked at Tannin, then back to the device, then lifted it to her ear and her eyes widened.

"Lucky I'm not what? Dead? How considerate of you," Tannin muttered.

"Ava!" The big man from upstairs who had gone after Hamish had finally made it through the tunnel. He was red- faced and puffing as he took Ava by the arm, barely giving Tannin a second glance. "We're leavin'. Now."

Ava gave Tannin a bewildered backward glance as she was steered out of the cavern, leaving a lone lantern standing on a crate.

Tannin listened to their footsteps echoing down the tunnel. Her heart sank with each step as she was left well and truly alone. I really hope Hamish isn't dead. She brought her knees up tight to her chest and was trying to feel around for knots when the lantern started to sputter.

"No no no no! Come on!" Tannin moaned as the lantern finally spat its last spark, leaving her alone in the pitch black.

Chapter Nine

A Late Night

Tannin hadn't managed to loosen the rope at all despite her struggling, and she'd been wondering what historians would think when they found her body in a hundred years still slumped against this damn post when she heard footsteps.

"Hello?!" Her voice cracked as she called out. Gods, her throat was so dry.

A dim orange light came into view from the tunnel followed closely by the creeping figure of Hamish holding a covered lantern. He looked nervous but otherwise none the worse for wear.

"Hamish!" she called, almost laughing with relief.

"By the bloody gods." Hamish rushed the last few steps across the room to kneel down beside her.

He lifted the lantern to shine light on her bruised face andswore. "What the hell did ye get yerself intae?"

"Those two weren't alone. Get me out of here."

A couple of slices of his knife took care of the bindings around her wrists before Hamish helped her to her feet.

"Ye good?"

"Aye, I'm fine." She rubbed her wrists and touched her swollen cheek. "Ouch."

"What happened?"

"I had the package and I made it to here and there were like ten thugs waitin'. The lens thing's broken by the way – it wasn't my fault! – and..."

"Awright, awright. We'll no worry aboot that now." He gave her a tilted head smile, exhaled a long breath and then clapped her on the shoulder. "Ye did alright for yer first job. I'd say ye've earned yerself supper."

The tunnel exit led them up through a grate back into the Skirts. Tannin was heartily thankful to be back on home ground. She followed Hamish into a shabby-looking tavern that she wouldn't have looked twice at except for the fact it still seemed to be bustling with people despite the late hour. She must have walked past it a hundred times but never thought anything of it. The windows were encrusted with years' worth of grime, and the post jutting above the door just had slightly swaying chains where a sign should have been hanging. She had just wanted to go home and sleep, but since he had mentioned supper, a dull ache had developed in her empty belly.

A hot meal is a hot meal.

As Hamish made his way inside the dark smoky tavern, people seemed to know to move out of his way and didn't meet his eye as he headed straight towards a booth at the back.

Tannin was vaguely surprised to see the rest of the crew lounging in the booth, nursing mugs of ale. They must have planned to meet here after the job was done. At the looks she got from them, through the pipe smoke that Beck puffed in billowing greasy clouds, Tannin got the distinct impression that she was an unwelcome intrusion on their gathering. She studied a new hole in the knee of her breeches to avoid their eyes. Mrs O'Baird was going to be thoroughly annoyed with having to sew another pair.

"Well?"

"We ain't celebratin' tonight, boys," Hamish said with a sigh. "Another crew got there before us. We didnae get the prize, but Tannin here proved herself." He clapped her on the shoulder good-naturedly.

With a single hand gesture to the barkeep, two more mugs of ale and steaming bowls of some kind of stew appeared on the table for them.

Hamish recounted the tale of the evening and revealed that he and the other man had played what sounded like a very tense game of cat and mouse amongst the partygoers until the other man had given up. By the time he had gotten to the part about finding her in the cavern, Tannin had almost cleaned her bowl. She hadn't realised how hungry she was, but the meaty smell of the stew had made her so ravenous she'd attacked it with enthusiasm. She dragged a hunk of bread around the edges to get the last of the thick gravy.

"And where were you durin' aw that?" Nyesha asked pointedly.

"Gettin' punched in the face," Tannin said drily with her mouth full, returning the older woman's glare.

"And this other crew," Beck said eyeing Tannin suspiciously, "they just happened to know we'd be there?"

Fergus answered before she could.

"No, Beck, they knew the package was there. They didnae know we was gonnae be there. That's what he said."

Beck responded with a grunt but didn't argue the point. Nyesha retained her stern expression but also kept her thoughts to herself. Trust was clearly hard-earned with these people.

"Tannin did good," Hamish said, thumping her on her back again and causing her to spill ale into her lap. "In fact, I'd be up for keepin' her on. What d'ye say?"

Tannin looked around the table. Was this the kind of offer that she could even refuse or was this more of him just informing her of the situation?

"Uh... thanks," she said slowly. "I'm not sure this is really for me though."

Nyesha gave a bark of laughter. "Can't handle the heat? Aw, poor baby."

"Aye. Actually." Tannin shot back. "And I didn't see you down there helpin' me fight off an entire crew. Doubt you could've done much better than I did."

Nyesha scowled and sat back with her arms crossed as the rest of them gave a round of low hooting and chuckling.

"That's you told, Ny," Fergus said, elbowing her.

"Whatever," she muttered.

Hamish rooted in his pocket for a moment before handing something to Tannin.

"What's this?" she said, accepting it.

"Yer cut," he said with a grin. "Still thinkin' this ain't the life for ye?"

Tannin looked at the coins in her hand. She'd never even held a fifty-crown piece before let alone three.

"But we didn't get anythin'."

"Ye did your part." He shrugged. "We pay our crew well regardless of the outcomes."

"I'll... think about it," Tannin said carefully. She was pretty sure that she never wanted to do anything like that ever again. Her face hurt and she could honestly have died tonight, but the glint of gold from her curled fist was intoxicating. She wouldn't have to worry about Clach again, that was for sure. In one night, she'd made more money than she could've dreamt, and way more than she'd earn at the bakery.

The bakery. Oh gods.

She bit her lip. She had to put the money back before anyone realised what she'd done.

"I have to go," she said abruptly. "I've got something I need to take care of."

"All right." Hamish's gold tooth shone as he smiled. "We'll be in touch."

Tannin felt a fresh pang of guilt as the bakery came into view, but she didn't expect to see the fluttering of light through the window. She risked a peek through the glass. If someone else was in there robbing the place, then she was in the clear. Her heart fell when she saw the familiar figure of Eve standing at the counter, holding her head in her hands. Tannin tried to back away slowly. She could talk with Eve in the morning but right now her body ached for sleep.

Unfortunately, her movement must've caught Eve's attention because her head snapped up and Tannin knew she'd been seen. She froze as Eve opened the door and bathed her in soft yellow light from the bakery.

"Tannin? What are ye dain oot here in the middle of the night?"

"I –" Tannin didn't even know what to say. What could she say?

"What happened to yer face?" Eve asked in alarm. "Are ye in trouble?"

Something clicked in her head and her eyes narrowed.

"Ye wouldnae happen to know anythin' some missin' coin, would ye?"

The truth must've been written all across her face, and Tannin was too tired to even try and think of a lie.

"I'm sorry." It slipped from her lips before she could stop it.

The disappointment on Eve's face was worse than she could have imagined. She'd been disappointed with her countless times before, but this was a new depth of heartbreak as she wordlessly turned to go back inside, leaving Tannin on the doorstep.

"I came to give it back!" Tannin tried to follow her in to explain, but Eve held up a hand.

"I dinnae want tae hear it," she said quietly. "I dinnae want tae hear anything from you. Go home, Tannin."

The door closed with a very final thud.

Stupid. Stupid. Stupid.

How had it all gone so wrong? And so quickly? Tannin kicked a stone in her path. It clattered into the wall of one of the shuttered shops lining the street. She'd left one of the heavy gold coins in the mailbox outside the door after Eve had slammed it shut. It was all she could really do now.

Stupid. She had just set up to kick another stone when she heard a low whistle in the alley to her right and saw movement in the shadows.

Shite.

She hadn't been paying attention and now the dark, empty streets were suddenly far less peaceful and much more foreboding. She picked up her pace. She was about halfway between the bakery and her lodging house. She could make it home.

Another shadowy movement ahead caused her to instinctively dart around the next corner. She glanced over her shoulder as she did so. The streets seemed deserted. Tannin was halfway through a sigh of relief when a couple more steps showed her her mistake. The alleyway ahead was blocked off by a solid wall. Dead end.

Oh no.

"What have we here, boys?" The voice came from the mouth of the alleyway behind her. Three men sauntered towards her. She cursed herself in her head. If she'd been thinking straight, she never would have come this way. She should've kept to the main streets.

So stupid.

"You're out late." They kept ambling closer and closer.

"Ye got coin on you? Seems a shame to keep it all tae yerself"

She backed away until she hit solid brick.

"I've not got anythin', I swear."

That's a lie. You've got a hundred crowns in your pocket, eejit.

Tannin reached into her pocket, intending to throw the coins and run when they were distracted.

"That's all right," one of them said, reaching out a hand to stroke her shoulder and tease a lock of her hair that had come loose from its knot at the back of her head. "There's plenty ways to share."

Her heart stuttered at the implication and she froze.

The hand on her shoulder moved to stroke her swollen cheek. The man gave a mock look of sympathy from under his hood. "Looks like someone's been awful mean to you. We'll be nice. Ain't that right, boys?"

Her heart was thundering.

They laughed jeeringly and jostled each other in anticipation. They were everywhere. Closing in from all sides. More of that jeering laugher.

Tannin's hands clenched into fists, her fear turning to anger. How dare they laugh.

Grinning, leering faces swam in front of her eyes.

They were laughing. Fucking laughing. A rage of an intensity she'd never felt before blacked out any other thoughts.

Another hand reached for her and the knot in her stomach twisted violently.

Heat.

She couldn't breathe.

Fire.

She couldn't see.

Red.
Blood rushing in her ears. Roaring. Ringing. Deafening.
Red.
Everything was on fire. Her body was being pulled apart by the flames.
Red.

Chapter Ten

An Awakening

Tannin woke groggily and struggled to open her eyes. They were gummed together. She rubbed at them, groaning. Dry hay jagged into her from all sides. She blearily looked around.

Hay?

She went to rub her eyes again and balked at the sight of her hands. They were crusted in half-dried blood. She sat bolt upright. What the hell?!

Weak sunlight dripped through the wooden slats of the stable walls and mottled her bare legs with pale blotches of light. Bare legs. A quick downwards glance confirmed her suspicions. She was stark naked. And lying in a horse stable. Covered in blood.

Tannin blinked.

What the hell happened?

She staggered to her feet and took a few wobbly steps on achy legs, clutching her head. She felt like she'd run a hundred miles with a hangover. She brushed as much hay off as she could, but it stuck to the congealed blood covering her.

Using the wall of the stall to steady herself, she spied a water trough. The notion disgusted her, and on any other day she wouldn't have dreamt of drinking from a horse's water. The salty metallic taste coating her tongue, however, was making her gag. She sank to her knees in front of the trough, scooped a handful into her mouth and spat pink water back out onto the straw on the ground. The taste lingered. She splashed water on her face and up her arms and tried to scrub the blood off as best she could. The water was lovely and cool on her skin. She rinsed her mouth again.

I have to get out of here.

There had to be a blanket or coat she could grab. She crept along to the next stall, occasionally swatting at buzzing, thick-bodied flies that flew at her face. She peeked around the corner and recoiled, clamping a hand over her mouth to stifle a shriek.

Lying still in a pile of straw was a horse that Flint would have called magnificent. Its beautiful black coat was once sleek and shiny and its mane carefully combed and braided. No longer. The soft, glossy coat was matted with blood and gore. Wide strips of flesh had been carved away, showing glints of white bone beneath. The stomach was sliced open spilling a slimy mess of innards onto the stained floor. Huge black eyes stared glassily from a face frozen in a silent scream.

A horse's scream cut short. Teeth clamping down on a throat and bones crunching. Feeling the pulse slow and warm blood ooze. Ripping. Pulling. Tearing... The savage joy of it.

Tannin's knees gave out as she retched. She vomited until there was nothing left and she could only heave and choke. She wiped her mouth with the back of her hand and crawled shakily until the body was out of sight.

What the hell did I do?

She had to get out of here. She had to get out of here *now*.

She pushed down the rising panic in her chest and took a deep breath. Okay. One step at a time. Find some clothes. She took off more quickly this time past the other stalls, and silent relief flooded her when she passed the last one with no sign of further carnage.

So, I ate a horse. Could be worse. Could have eaten two. A giggle escaped her throat before she could stop it. What the hell was wrong with her? She ducked into one of the empty stalls and leaned on the wall as she doubled over, both hands over her mouth to try and contain the manic laughter bubbling out. Tears rolled down her cheeks as she tried to muffle it. It took a few minutes before she could get a hold of herself again. She closed her eyes and ran her hands through her tangled hair. Another chuckle threatened to burst forth. She quenched it with another deep breath. Deep breaths. Deep breaths.

Okay focus, eejit.

Hanging on a peg near the entrance was an old coat that probably belonged to one of the stable hands. Tannin dragged it on half grateful for the covering of her nakedness but half resentful at the added warmth. She was already sweating, and she wasn't sure if it was from stress or actual warmth, but she felt clammy all the same. The coat went halfway to her knees and the sleeves drooped past the tips of her fingers. She clumsily folded them up so that her hands could at least peek out the ends and fastened up the front.

"Okay, problem one solved. Now where the hell am I?" Tannin muttered to herself.

She smoothed her hair back from her face and tried the heavy door. It slid back with a thunk. She peered out into the pale light. From the lack of people to the lack of darkness, she guessed the sun had only just risen. Probably what had woken her.

Or maybe it was indigestion.

She snorted in laughter again. She was definitely feeling a little un*stable* right now.

Hahaha. Cut it out you need to focus!

Tannin gave her head a shake and blinked hard. People would be up and about very soon. She looked around and thankfully recognised the surrounding buildings. She wasn't far from home.

The mad dash back to her rooms was a bit of a blur, one she managed without incident, dodging between buildings and ducking behind walls to avoid the first early risers of the day. She finally got to her lodging house and dashed to the front door. The locked front door. Dammit. Her keys were in her pocket. Wherever her pockets had gotten to.

Fuck.

She had one spark of hope. Mrs O'Baird sometimes forgot to close the kitchen window at the back of the house. As Tannin snuck around the weed-filled alley to the back courtyard, she clasped her hands together and sent a silent thank you to the gods for giving her aged landlady such a shitty memory.

She waded through the straggly bushes under the window, wincing as her bare feet stepped on sharp stones, and clambered up onto the window ledge with the help of an upturned plant pot before sliding her way through onto the kitchen counters.

I'm really making a habit of breaking and entering these days.

Tannin dragged herself up stair after stair to her room on the third floor, the tired achiness making itself known in her legs again. By the time she finally got there, she could barely take another step. She said another silent thanks this time to her own stupid self for forgetting to lock her door as she slipped inside, snapped the bolt back and pressed her forehead against the hard wood. The cool surface reminded her of how much she was overheating still wrapped in the heavy coat. She ripped it off and kicked it under her bed. She'd deal with it later.

She pushed her hair back from her forehead, raking her nails along her scalp. This couldn't be real. She looked down at her hands, imagining them as the cruel claws that had shredded through a horse's skin like a knife through parchment.

Dried blood still filled the creases in her knuckles and clung to her fingernails. The sting of vomit rose in her throat again. She needed the blood off her. Right now.

She practically leapt to the other side of her room where she had a wash basin and a creaky old faucet, which she cranked on full. There was a shared bathroom across the hall where she could take proper baths, but she couldn't risk leaving blood all over the place. She grabbed a hard bar of yellowish soap from the shelf next to the basin and attacked her hands and arms in a fury of lather and splashing water. As the water turned a foamy pink and the sight of her arms returned to one of freckled normality, Tannin breathed a little easier.

"Oh shit." She cursed as she caught a glimpse of herself in the mirror. She'd managed to clean a bit of her face at the water trough, but red still streaked her flushed cheeks. Her neck and chest were a mess of smeared blood and pale lines where water had trickled down. Her blonde hair was thick with half dried blood and hay.

Memories of dark tunnels, broken lenses and tight ropes came streaming back as she inspected the purplish bruise mottling under her eye. How long ago was that? Hours? Days? She didn't know. It was foggy. Her brown eyes were bloodshot and stared widely back at her from a pasty, sick- looking face in the mirror. She pulled the plug in the basin

and refilled it with more cool water, holding the sides of the wide basin for support before plunging her whole head into the water and scrubbing vigorously.

She'd barely pulled on her night shirt when a light knocking came at her door. Pulling it open revealed the shrivelled form of Mrs O'Baird.

"What're ye doing making all this racket?"

"I'm sorry I just – Woah." A sudden wave of dizziness washed over her. Tannin grabbed the door frame for support.

"Miss Hill?"

"No, yeah. I'm fine." She gave her head a little shake. "Sorry about the noise."

She went to take a step back to close the door again when another wave of light-headedness set her off kilter and she stumbled. Black splotches clouded her vision mixed with stabs of bright light.

"Oh."

She was vaguely aware of movement and sound and the solid firmness of the wooden floor before the darkness took over completely.

Chapter Eleven

Last Chances

Fever scorched her veins as time passed in a haze of heat and delirium. Tannin lost all sense of time and place until it finally broke and she found herself back in her familiar, narrow bed, piled high with blankets, vaguely aware of someone sponging her forehead with a damp cloth.

"Mrs O'Baird?" Tannin croaked, her mouth dry.

"Oh, there she is. Thought we were gonnae lose ye." The old lady helped her sit up, propping her up with an extra pillow. She offered her a glass and Tannin gratefully gulped at the cold water.

"What happened?"

"The fever, dear," Mrs O'Baird replied, setting the glass on the table. "It's been a bad year for it, very bad indeed. Yer through the worst of it now though, so dinnae fash. Drink all that water and get yer rest. I'm a busy woman, ye know! I'm no healer."

Tannin didn't say anything as the old woman rearranged her blanket and bustled out of the room with more mutterings and grumblings. As grouchy as her landlady was at that moment, Tannin had a sudden urge to ask her to stay and sit with her a while. Her grandfather had always sat with her when she was sick.

He would make her sweetened tea and stroke her hair. She pushed the memories away before they became painful and pulled her blanket up to her chin.

Tannin was able to rise properly the next day, fortified by Mrs O'Baird's sworn-by broth, and she gratefully soaped off the cloying sickly feeling in a hot bath. Startled at the news she'd been out of it for three days, she rebuffed Mrs O'Baird's insistence that she stay in bed and made her way across town to the bakery. Eve would have thought she'd run away or something after being caught out with the money. The mostly faded bruise under her eye was a reminder that her adventure into the world of crime wasn't just another fever dream. She shuddered as she remembered that dream she'd had with the horse. Fever did strange things to your mind.

She wasn't sure what kind of reception she'd receive given how she'd left things with Eve, but she definitely didn't expect her to throw her arms around her and squeeze her half to death while gushing that she was so glad she was okay.

"What's goin' on?" Tannin asked, bewildered. "I wasn't that sick."

"Oh, ye willnae have heard! Oh, Tannin I was so worried when ye didnae come in that mornin'."

"What happened?"

"There was an attack just doon the road. Like real gruesome stuff. They think it was some kind of wild animal from the forest came right intae town in the night. There's been a curfew and everythin' 'til they find it." Eve was breathless as she rattled off the details. Three men had been torn apart. "They still havnae found all the pieces. And then ye didnae show up... I should never have let ye walk home alone at that time of night. I went round of course, and Mrs O'Baird said..."

Eve continued talking but Tannin had tuned out. She gripped the back of a wooden chair for support. Blood drenched memories flooded in.

Heat. Flesh. Screams. It wasn't a fever dream.

"Ye dinnae look well. Ye shouldnae even be up and aboot," Eve said gently.

Tannin nodded vaguely.

"Oh, and I havnae forgot oor conversation from that night either," Eve said, her warmth shifting to something much sterner "I am willin' tae forget... certain things... as they've been put right. Ye understand me?"

"Eve, I –"

"We'll speak no more aboot it," she said curtly.

Clearly, whatever trust Eve had in her was either gone completely or incredibly low, but at least she wasn't fired just yet.

"Whatever trouble yer in, Tannin, get it sorted and keep it the hell away from here." Eve jabbed a finger at her to emphasise the point. "I know this is hard with yer grandad gone, but ye've got to get yer shit together."

"I promise. I'm done with it. It'll never happen again," Tannin said earnestly.

"It better not. If it does then I'm throwin' ye to the wolves. I mean it. Last chance, okay?"

Before she could reply, Mr Fletcher came in through the shop door and flung an envelope at Tannin, who promptly dropped it.

"This isnae yer own personal post office," he barked.

Tannin scooped up the letter, bewildered. Who was sending her letters? She'd never had a proper letter in her life.

Dear Ms Tannin Hill,

We know what you are and we want to talk. Merchant Square fountain. Midnight on the day of the new moon.

A Friend

"Who delivered this?" Tannin demanded.

Mr Fletcher was already halfway through the door to the shop and didn't answer her. She shouldered past him, earning herself a few choice words and sprinted into the street, her footfalls slapping loudly on the cobbles, scanning around wildly for whoever had left the note but there was no one around.

"Dammit," she swore.

She crept a little way down the empty street, keeping a wary eye out in case they'd disappeared into one of the many closed doors, but it was hopeless. They could be anywhere. She was just about to turn back when an ear-splitting wail ripped through the still air. She clapped her hands over her ears with a gasp, almost doubling over half in shock and half in pain, her teeth clenched tightly. And then, as quickly as it had started, it stopped, leaving Tannin staggering. What the hell was that? She scanned the street and all its dark windows again, but it was still as empty and silent as when she'd got there. She rubbed her ears with a grimace. They were still ringing as she took off in a jog back to the bakery.

"What was aw that aboot?" Eve asked when she returned. Tannin shook her head. "Doesn't matter."

Eve gave her a stern look. "Yer on yer last chance, remember? Keep that shite away from here."

"I will, I promise." Tannin fought a yawn.

"Go home, Tannin." Eve patted her on the back. "I'll send Flint round to check up on ye later. He's been asking after ye."

By the time Tannin stumbled back into Mrs O'Baird's house, she was yawning with almost every step.

"Ms Hill? Is that you? Letter came by for ye."

Tannin rubbed her eyes and picked up the thick parchment envelope from the cabinet. It was the same handwriting as the letter that came to the bakery. Looping, neat letters in black ink.

She closed her eyes and massaged her temples, taking a moment before she tore it open. The same message as before looked back at her. Whatever this was, it needed brain energy and Tannin didn't have any at the moment. She crumpled it into her pocket, yawning again. Her bed was calling for her and who was she to resist?

Flint found her a few hours later snoring and buried in a nest of blankets and pillows.

"Hey." He poked at the soft pile of quilts. "Wakey, wakey."

Tannin merely groaned and retreated further into her cocoon. Usually guests weren't permitted, especially in the bedrooms, but Flint's charms had obviously worked on Mrs O'Baird as he wafted the scent of fresh bread towards the quilted lump.

"I've got food," he crooned.

Tannin poked her tousled head out. "Tell me more."

"Eve gave me a seed loaf. She said you like that one, and I got some of that soft cheese from the market."

"I do like that." Tannin admitted, sitting up and wrapping her quilt tightly around herself. "Thanks."

"Heard you've been pretty sick. Gotta get that strength back up." He gave her a playful punch on her arm. "You missed some big excitement though."

Tannin tore a chunk from the loaf. Clearly, Flint had been snacky on the way over because the bread was half hollowed out of the soft inside. "Aye, I heard."

"There's a monster on the loose," Flint whispered in an exaggeratedly spooky voice. "Ooooohhhh!"

Tannin rolled her eyes, her mouth too full to reply properly.

"There's been a curfew and everything these last few days, but they haven't found it yet. People are freaking out," Flint said, checking a gold timepiece that Tannin strongly suspected he had not paid for. "There's another announcement happening soon. The last one was actually pretty funny."

"How can an announcement be funny?"

"Cause the new head of the city guard is an arse. Fancies himself some kind of knight in shining armour gonna save all us poor defenceless citizens from the fearsome monster."

Tannin chuckled. "Sounds like a hero to me."

"They've put together another company for 'round these parts specifically for getting this beast. Like those blokes weren't just killed, they were destroyed. Torn to pieces and no one heard a thing. I didn't see the bodies, but apparently it was well gruesome. Anyway, apparently this one guard's been wanting to lead a company for years."

"They put that together quick."

More guards in the area would be a real nightmare for most people. Smuggling and gambling, thievery and begging were all commonplace throughout the Skirts with gangs controlling almost every street.

You could always spot the guards a mile off dressed in the distinctive uniform of red tunics usually overlaid with some sort of light armour with a belt laden with sword and baton. They patrolled mostly within the citadel walls but sometimes they ventured out into the wider city when there was trouble to deal with or trouble to make if they were bored.

"He was all 'My dear people!'." Flint leapt up from the bed and puffed his chest out theatrically. "As you all know, the beast that we hunt is still at large." He paused dramatically. "But rest assured that I will personally not rest until the creature is dead by my own beautiful hands."

Tannin snorted as Flint continued.

"We shall shoot the beast with our darts!" He waggled his eyebrows and mimed aiming some sort of crossbow. "And when it is down, we shall take its head!"

"Darts?"

"These," Flint gestured widely, still in character, "are a new technology that I, because I am so very smart, have commissioned for this hunt. With just one of these babies, you could knock out a horse! And then we cut its head off and I am the greatest person who ever lived!"

"He fancies himself a bit, does he?"

"Oh aye. Big time." Flint flopped back down onto the bed and motioned for Tannin to scoot over so they could lay side by side. "So, you want to tell me about the other night?"

She groaned. "It was... fine."

"Oh Tan, you know I'm going to need details." He chided gently.

She told him a brief version of events ending with Hamish's implications of further work.

Flint looked at her reproachfully. She thought he was going to tell her to stay away from the gangs, but he just shook his head sadly and said, "We really need to work on your storytelling abilities. Where was the drama? The intrigue? The romance?" he complained. "Only you can make breaking and entering, a midnight chase with a mystery girl and being captured by murderous bandits sound like a trip to the market."

"Oh, I do apologise," she said sarcastically.

Wait till you hear the one about my trip to the stable. There's your drama.

"It's fine." He sighed. "I will be embellishing it for retellings in the pub."

"No." Tannin warned seriously. "No tellin' anyone. This is secret."

He huffed about it for a few minutes but eventually swore himself to secrecy for the time being.

"Oh, I almost forgot. I got this today." Flint handed Tannin a crumpled envelope from his pocket. "It's for you. Dunno why it came to me".

Tannin's stomach dropped slightly. Another letter with neat, looping, black letters. This was more than just persistence. They were letting her know they knew where she lived, worked and who her friends were. This was a threat.

Chapter Twelve

The Strong Stuff

Dear Ms Tannin Hill,

We know what you are and we want to talk.

Merchant Square fountain. Midnight on the day of the new moon.

A Friend

"Well," Flint said, reading over Tannin's shoulder. "That is not good."

"Oi! Privacy?"

"You need to fix that, rapid."

"Oh, you don't say?" Tannin ran her hand through her hair and pushed it back from her face. "What do I do?" She groaned.

"I have an idea."

Half an hour later, Tannin begrudgingly followed him into the Swords tavern.

He had bullied her out of bed and insisted on coming here. She already had an idea of what his brilliant idea was.

More thinking juice. This time, they sat at a table way in the back instead of in a booth.

Sure enough, when he returned from the bar, he had two drams of whisky. When she reached for one, he slapped her hand away.

"Ah, ah. These are both mine. No strong stuff for you 'til you're all better."

One of the barmaids swooped in behind him and placed a steaming mug in front of Tannin.

"Tea? Flint, I could have had tea at home. In bed." She groaned.

"Yes, but I didn't want tea." He winked taking a sip from the glass and then clearing his throat loudly. "Ah, that's the stuff."

"You dragged me here so you can get pissed?"

"No, we're here for brain fuel," he said and tapped his glass, "and to make a plan. Show me that letter again."

Tannin handed him the crumpled parchment and warmed her hands on her mug as he scrutinized it.

"We know what you are." He read aloud in hushed tones. "Now that is dramatic. I assume this is about your wee adventure the other night, and you don't have anything else to tell me?"

Tannin made a noncommittal noise into her mug. Should I tell him? What would I even tell him? Shit, he really likes horses.

"Hmmm. New moon," Flint said, his brow furrowing. "I won't be back by then."

"Why, where are you off to?" Tannin asked with a frown. "Acquisitions," Flint said mysteriously. "In Tayfort."

Tayfort was a large city on the coast, a bustling hive of exoticness and trouble. It was through its harbours that the Kingdom of Rill on the Western coast earned most of its riches. Tannin had never been, but traders came to Armodan via Tayfort all the time, bringing all kinds of treasures with them. The people Flint worked with basically controlled the route between the two cities and had their noses in everyone's business. Flint usually stayed in Armodan, and although he had gone on trips to Tayfort before, it was unusual for him to travel.

"Uh, no. You get to know all my secrets, so tell me what you're actually doin'."

His eyes glinted with mischief "All I will tell you is that there is an item that a buyer of mine is interested in and a certain gentleman doesn't want to sell."

"So, it's a con." Tannin sighed. "How long will you be gone?"

The journey to Tayfort itself took at least a few days on a fast horse.

"Two weeks at least." He winced.

"I should come too and just go into hidin'," she said, half-considering it. "Armodan has become way too messy for my likin'."

"Ha, no." Flint downed the rest of his whisky. "No?"

"Your new friend has my address." He smacked his lips loudly. "And I like it here."

Tannin groaned. "They sent one to the bakery too." "You're screwed."

"Yes, thank you, Flint. I know that."

"I'll see what I can do about getting out of the Tayfort job and come be your back-up muscle."

"You have no muscles."

"You wound me, woman," he said mildly.

Tannin swirled her tea, watching the leaf fragments tumble and sink to the bottom. *We know what you are.*

Could that mean a thief or a criminal and not whatever happened to her later that night? Tannin wondered. What had happened? She still hadn't had time to process it. A monster, Flint had said. Was that really me?

She tried in vain to suggest to herself that maybe she'd just been in the wrong place at the wrong time and just been a bystander to the monster's attack, but that didn't explain how she'd woken up with a mouth full of blood and memories of both men and horse's dying screams wheezing out of throats clamped between her teeth and of warm innards spilling out. She shuddered.

"You okay?" Flint peered at her. "You're all peekit."

"Yeah...um." Tannin pushed her empty mug away. "I think I'm gonna go home and sleep it off."

"Good idea. I'll, ah, stay here." Flint's eyes slid from Tannin's pale face to the smiling, buxom barmaid. He leaned over to give her a flirtatious little wave.

"Think with your brain and not your dick this time please, Flint," Tannin said as an exhausted sigh escaped her. "This is a nice place, and you're gonna get sleaze all over it."

"How dare you," he said but he was already smirking. "I am a gentleman."

Out in the fresh air and away from the stillness of the tavern, Tannin leant on a fence and took several deep breaths. She couldn't tell him. She couldn't tell anyone.

They're either going to think I'm insane or a monster.

She didn't feel particularly monstrous. Holding out her hands, she inspected the light freckles that dotted the backs of them. No, she felt quite human. Vulnerably human. She shivered again despite the warmth of the day.

What to do, what to do?

If someone knew what she'd done, then why not set the new guard company on her? Or take her out themselves? What did they want?

It couldn't be money. She already had less than nothing to her name. Information? She might've gotten herself involved with the shady side of the Skirts, but that didn't mean she knew anything at all. All that was left was that whoever it was had wanted her to do something in exchange for keeping her secret. A favour of some sort.

Tannin swore under her breath. She really was screwed. And the one person who might have been able to shed a light on what was happening to her had had the audacity to die, the bastard.

Back in her room, Tannin flipped through her grandfather's journals without enthusiasm – not reading but scanning for the word monster. She'd have even settled for creature or beast or a god damn demon reference. Anything. Anything at all. But there was nothing that looked remotely helpful. Hurling them back under her bed, she then flopped onto her blankets with a frustrated grunt. Hopeless.

Maybe I'm just losing my mind.

Chapter Thirteen

A Friend

The day of the new moon arrived far quicker than she would've liked. Tannin still hadn't made up her mind if she was going to go to the mysterious meeting or not. Flint hadn't been able to get out of the Tayfort job and had left already. She'd be going alone. If she ignored the letters, she didn't know what would happen. But what would happen if she went?

In the end, it was the sound of Eve's voice in her head telling her to keep this kind of thing away from the bakery that made her decision for her. If she didn't go now, whoever it was would come back with more than just letters. And so, she found herself on the other side of the town as the sun disappeared and night cloaked the streets in a dim grey. The new moon rose high as an impossibly thin sliver behind the clouds. She half hoped no one showed.

The letter had specified the fountain in the square of the merchant's quarter. Although they still called it that, it wasn't so much a merchant's area now that any business that had a shred of success had moved away from the dilapidated square and inside the city walls or over to the other side of town. The only wares sold in the shops and stalls set up in these streets were dregs and scraps from other shops bought cheap or stolen and resold.

If ever you were looking for something shady, the merchant's square is where you'd find it.

Tannin kept close to the boarded-up shop fronts, a wary eye on any alleyways, as she weaved through the tightknit and winding streets until she reached the square. Almost every district had a public square from the times when they had all been separate towns, even if their names were long forgotten. Most were just empty, paved squares where people hocked their wares or listened to the travelling bards who lounged there during the day. The merchant's square was centred around an old fountain which, in more prosperous times, would have had water bubbling merrily from the mouths of the proud sculptures, but now stood barren and cracked.

She wasn't about to become a sitting duck, waiting for the unknown at the stone basin, so she skirted around the outside of a vacant building that overlooked the square. That way she could see who was coming and be better prepared. She'd even shown up a full hour early to see if anyone was scouting the place out. She was privately quite proud of being so organised. She even had an old spyglass she'd found tucked away in Mrs O'Baird's attic when she was up there cleaning. It was an old, heavy, metal thing that bumped around awkwardly in her satchel.

Before leaving her lodgings, she'd reread the journal entries about Laurel before she left. It had been a terrible idea. Tannin was extra jittery and constantly looking over her shoulder for invisible enemies as she skulked towards her chosen spot.

The vacant building was a hulk of age-twisted wood over five stories tall. Slipping inside was almost effortless – the ground floor windows had been smashed a long time ago. Broken bottles littered the ground and the strong smell of urine assaulted her nose. The next floor up was cleaner, if barely. The soles of her shoes stuck to the wooden floorboards as she tried to find the least offensive place to put her feet.

Maybe this wasn't such a good idea.

Movement in a corner made her jump. A rat skittered along the floor. She breathed a sigh of relief, glad it was just a rat and not a drug-addled squatter foaming at the mouth and ready to bash her brains in.

This was definitely a bad idea. She made to leave but movement out the window had her pause. Tannin took the spyglass from her bag and peeked through the age-speckled lens. A dark figure was indeed lurking at the mouth of an alley.

Well, well what do we have here?

"Come on," Tannin muttered. "Come on so I can see you."

She took the glass away from her eye, meaning to give the lens a rub with her sleeve when a shadow fell over the window ledge.

"Don't move."

Fuck.

She jerked to the side and swung the heavy spyglass, cracking it into the face of the figure who had crept up noiselessly behind her. He yelped and went down like a sack of bricks, clutching at his face and dropping the crossbow he'd been holding. Tannin leapt over him to the stairs just as another figure rounded the top of them. She hefted her spyglass in both hands.

"Don't take another step!" she yelled. "I mean it."

"Wait!" A female voice came from further down the stairs.

Tannin frowned. She knew that voice.

A dark-haired girl pushed past the man at the top of the stairs and approached slowly with her hands outstretched in the kind of stance one might do to calm a frightened dog. It was the girl from the tunnels.

"Wait, we're not here to hurt you."

"Ugh, it's you." Tannin didn't lower her spyglass. "Should've bloody guessed."

"I just want to talk."

Tannin shook her head. "I should never have come here."

Ava rounded on the man, who had now risen clutching his bleeding forehead. "What did I tell you explicitly *not* to do?"

The man with the crossbow had recovered enough to get to his feet and hefted it up to rest on his shoulder. "Didnae shoot her, did I? Yer welcome." He gave a mocking bow. "Oh, and I'm fine by the way."

Now that she could see him more clearly, Tannin recognised him from the tunnels aswell. Was he the one who'd punched her? She glared at him.

"Get out," Ava said disgustedly.

The man spat on the floor and gave Tannin a filthy look but stalked down the stairs at Ava's order. The other man – the man who'd gone after Hamish that night – still stood at the top of the stairs, arms crossed, blocking Tannin's way out.

She stepped back towards the window. The man had the build and the stance of a guard or a soldier. Maybe both. His stare made her nervous.

"I apologise for this. I wanted this meeting to be civil." Ava's tone was authoritative, but she looked young. Younger than Tannin maybe.

Tannin snorted. "Aye, very civilised. Just tell me what you want and quit harassin' me."

"Come to think of it," the girl said lightly, stroking her chin as if deep in thought, "maybe an armed approach was a good idea considering I know what you are."

Tannin raised an eyebrow.

"And that is?" She tried to make it a sneer but even she heard the uncertainty in her voice.

Damn it all.

"You know exactly what I'm talking about. But let's start smaller. Your name is Tannin Hill, correct? May I call you Tannin? I'm Ava."

"I know your bloody name. What do you want?"

Ava took the piece of broken lens from her pocket. "Do you know what this is?"

"I feel like we've had this conversation before. You know, right before you left me tied up under a cellar?"

Ava ignored her. "This," she said and held it up to her eye, "is a sightlens."

As Ava looked at her through the cloudy glass, Tannin shifted with unease and readjusted her grip on the spyglass.

"Is that supposed to mean somethin' to me?"

"It shows a person's true nature. What's hidden in their blood. Or it did before you smashed it to pieces."

"And what does it show now?"

"Enough to know you are a Remnant."

"As in the myth?" Tannin gave a bark of laughter. "All right, you're clearly insane so I'll be goin' now."

Yeah, sure. I'm descended from Fair Folk and I have magic powers. Pull the other one.

Ava tilted her head and kept watching Tannin through the glass. "What I don't know," she continued over Tannin's protests, "is what kind. However, certain... events shall we say? ... have given a few clues. I'd say there's a definite Remnant power to whatever tore apart those men on Pine Street."

Tannin could feel the blush creeping across her face and knew her cheeks were turning pink. She hoped the light was dim enough that it wasn't visible.

"What do you see in that thing?" she asked.

"What are you worried I'll see?"

"You're lyin'."

"Then how would I know?" "Know what?"

"What you are."

The silence hung between them until Tannin broke it.

"So, what is this? Blackmail?"

"By the gods, no. I want you to work for me."

"Excuse me?" Tannin said bewildered.

"Some people will be looking for something other than a wild animal for what happened on Pine Street. A lot of people know Remnants are more than a myth, even if they pretend not to, and sooner or later they will know about you. Some of these people are bad people. I, however, see the usefulness in monsters, and I'd rather have them on my side than hunt them."

The word "monster" rang in Tannin's ears.

Is that what I am?

Ava clearly realised her mistake because she quickly added, "I believe Remnants have useful skills. Skills that could benefit everyone. Imagine the battles that would be won. How much better our kingdom could be. I think everyone can agree the current situation is... lacking."

"I don't want any part in that. I'm no soldier. I just want to be left alone," Tannin snapped, her resolve hardening.

"It's only a matter of time before they find who killed those men."

"I don't know anythin' about that," Tannin said quickly.

"You're really bad at lying, and you need to do a whole lot better than that if the wrong people come asking around." Her voice softened. "You need to get control of yourself. I know things that can help you. I can help you understand. We can help each other."

Her condescending tone grated on Tannin's already fried nerves, and Ava's voice betrayed her. She was no commoner and sure as hell no Skirter. Even the fact that she had sent Tannin a letter gave it away. Most people in the Skirts didn't read, and if they did it was only a few words here and there. There was a curious pride element to it.

You got what you wanted by going and talking to people face to face. What did they want with fancy bits of parchment? Tannin had no idea when or where she had learned herself, but she must have as a child. It was a big assumption to make, one that a noble wouldn't have thought twice about. Ava was some noble's daughter probably. A Laird or something. Maybe she was even a Lady herself.

"Oh aye? You want to help me understand? You know nothin' at all. You want help from a monster so you can go play all your wee rich-girl power games with all your noble friends? Yeah, I noticed you're one of them. Sorry to disappoint, m'lady." She gave a sarcastic curtsey. "But I think you need a new hobby and to leave me the fuck alone."

Ava blinked. She struggled to regain her composure while her face glowed in embarrassment. Her lips parted as if to deny it, but no sound came out.

Tannin scoffed. "You want more shiny jewels on your tiara? Then you do it yourself. But you think you know my secrets? I definitely know yours. Someone like you sneakin' around in tunnels with thieves and lowlifes, tsk tsk."

Ava was speechless. Her mouth opened and closed like a fish blowing bubbles.

"Oh, and if you come near me again or send some of your wee friends after me, there might be some more monster stories for your collection."

"Enough."

The man at the stairwell that Tannin took to be a guard stepped forward. She'd been expecting this since he'd blocked the stairs. They weren't going to let her just walk out. She had already subtly taken a couple of steps while they were talking until the backs of her legs pressed against the windowsill.

"No, wait!" Ava cried as she noticed Tannin glance down.

Tannin swung her legs over the sill and took a deep breath as the two of them scrambled to reach her. She was only one floor up.

What's that, twelve feet? Ten? Fuck it.

She jumped.

She'd heard somewhere that you were supposed to roll when you jumped from something high. She tried it as the cobbles came rushing up to meet her and half managed a tumble but gasped as pain lanced up through her ankle.

That could've gone better.

Looking back up, she saw Ava's shocked face and the guard's grim one. She flashed them a wide grin and a very rude hand gesture before darting off into the shadows.

Chapter Fourteen

The Changing of the Seasons

By the time the sun rose, the ovens in Fletcher's bakery were crackling and filling the kitchen with a heavy warmth as Tannin hobbled around preparing the first batches of the day. Eve arrived with the rising of the sun as usual and gave a cheery greeting that turned into a gasp when she saw Tannin's limp.

"What on earth have ye gotten up to now?" Eve exclaimed.

"I...fell?" she replied sheepishly.

Eve immediately sat her down and went to work treating her swollen ankle, berating her for not getting help sooner.

"I put a cold cloth on it," Tannin said defensively, raising her leg up on a chair so that Eve could get a better look. For the next few minutes, Eve poked and prodded and bent her joint, nodding knowingly when Tannin winced.

"Well, I dinnae think it's broken, so yer lucky there." She gave Tannin a long look and she just knew she wanted to ask again how it had happened, but thankfully Eve said nothing as she bandaged up Tannin's ankle tightly with strips of cloth.

She insisted Tannin stay seated for the majority of her shift, meaning Tannin was on mixing and shaping duty while Eve worked the bellows and fetched and carried.

"I like this way of workin' much better." Tannin grinned, stretching luxuriously in her seat as Eve hefted tray after tray from the ovens.

"Hmmph. Dinnae get used to it. As soon as that ankle's better, yer my dogsbody again."

The pain and swelling took a few days to subside, even under Eve's watchful care. As her ankle got better, Tannin was able to put more and more of the strange meeting out of her mind. Remnants and secrets and strange girls with lenses. She shook her head. She was in a much better mood now that the source of the threatening letters had been revealed as just some rich girl trying to play at being smart.

Tannin had little interest in the affairs of the nobility. As far as she was concerned, so long as she had a roof over her head and enough coin to get by, she couldn't care less which noble was kissing royal arse most effectively or what they did with all their mountains of gold. Most Skirters held similar sentiments, although no one could resist if the gossip was juicy enough.

Between trying to win back Eve's trust and paying off Clach, Tannin had enough to deal with. She'd sworn colourfully and smashed a teacup when she realised the coins she'd gotten from Hamish were long gone along with the rest of her clothing from that night.

She also still had no idea what was going on with her. She couldn't deny what had happened and not understanding it was torture. She was too lost to attempt her plan of fleeing the city right away. In her spare time, she had been reading through the legible parts of her grandfather's journals to figure out what the hell she was, but she hadn't found anything useful. Just the bitter ramblings of a man who thought the world owed him and more of those triangular symbols.

As summer faded, the trees started changing colours, and the leaves were a golden hue when the autumn sun shone through them. Rain lashed the cobbles every few days, and the fields south of the city were a-buzz with workers from the rural areas who travelled from farm to farm, bringing in the year's harvest in exchange for a full belly and a few coins.

The coming of the harvest season, and the Lughnasadh festival, also spelled big news for the city of Armodan. The Five Kingdoms used this time of year to show off their prosperity with their neighbours. It also served as an excuse for making new alliances. Almost all matchmaking took place when the regal families visited each other for feasting and celebrations of plentifulness. This year was no different. The only difference being that the princess of the Brochlands, Princess Avalyn of Armodan, was now of a marrying age and the visiting royals were seen as potential suitors.

The city's nobles and commoners alike buzzed with gossip about likely matches and which kingdom they wanted a closer tie with. The streets buzzed with talk of fur trades with the kingdom of Gormbrae to the south with its wide grassy glens and thick forest or iron and weaponry from the craggy mountains of Cascairn of the north.

The speculations were never-ending, and Tannin was thoroughly bored of it. On the rare occasions she tended the shop instead of slaving away in the kitchen, it was the only topic on people's lips. That and the rain.

The invitation, when it came, was a complete surprise. Tannin and Eve were prepping for the day when both Mr and Mrs Fletcher came flouncing into the kitchen. That Mr Fletcher was flouncing alone would have been a dead giveaway that something big had happened, but his babbling and laughing like a child was downright unnerving.

"We've a royal commission!" He thumped a thick piece of parchment down on the table. With its curling letters and gilded border, it certainly looked very official. The calligraphy alone must have taken some poor scribe ages.

Tannin craned her neck to see what was written.

Esteemed Owners of Fletcher's Bakery,

You are hereby given the honour of commission to cater to His Majesty King Florian's guests on the third day of the Lughnasadh Festival.

The requirements are thus:

What followed was a list of desired quantities of various baked goods – more than they would produce in a month for that one day of the festival.

While Eve and the Fletchers cheered and danced at the prospect of "moving up in the world", Tannin could only stare in disbelief at the invitation. Royal events were catered by only the most luxurious providers. Never in a million years would she have thought they'd consider a regular bread-maker for one of their fancy parties.

What little Tannin knew about the royal family, she'd learned fully unwillingly from her times minding the shop when she ended up being a captive audience for the babblings of gossiping mobs of elderly women. Men too sometimes, she reflected. No one could completely avoid the inane gossip from the court though, and Tannin was no exception. Princess Avalyn's reputation was that of a pious and sheltered young girl spending most of her days in the chapel in silent contemplation. The king himself, King Florian, wasn't particularly beloved by the people but neither was he disliked. He was tolerated. As for Queen Giordana, she hadn't made a public appearance since their first born's, Prince Florian's, accidental death a few years previously. Prince Justus, now the eldest and heir to the throne, was a bold warrior keener to play with swords than to actually rule, and it was probably lucky that King Florian was in good health for the time being.

Last year, when the new baby, Prince Sontar, was born, it was all people could talk about. Of course, the national holiday proclaimed for the birth greatly helped in that respect. When word of the new arrival reached the neighbouring allied kingdoms, dignitaries had sent lavish gifts and processions to welcome the little royal bundle of joy, or more likely Tannin thought, to ingratiate themselves with the king. After all, although they were supposedly equal allies, the Brochlands was by far the largest and wealthiest of the kingdoms. Woodren to the East didn't involve themselves in politics much, and the other kingdoms were happy to pretend the swampy wastelands didn't exist. It would be exactly the same show of wealth and friendship in the bid for the princess's hand.

The days before the festival passed in a flurry of flour and chaos as the small bakery clamoured to prepare the enormous list of requirements. Most they could pre-bake and transport up, but they were also taking basins and basins of dough to cook more at the castle itself. A polished, uniformed servant from the castle had appeared the same day as the official invitation with an absurd list of rules and schedules. Tannin had scowled at the dress code.

By some miracle, they managed to be on track with the schedule and Tannin found herself dressed up in a brand- new, grey dress that Mrs Fletcher had insisted upon "to look professional".

She strongly suspected the cost of it was going to come out of her own wages, but she'd argue the point later. It had been a while since she'd worn a dress. She'd taken to wearing breeches or overalls when she was working after having scorched the hems of her skirts when they brushed too near the open flames of the ovens.

She walked beside the painted wooden caravan they'd rented to carry the small mountain of bread to the palace while the Fletchers drove slowly through the packed streets. Eve walked on the other side, fidgeting nervously. Mrs Fletcher had given them a stern warning before they'd left to stay alert for "ruffians and beggars" who'd ransack their wagon in a heartbeat if they sensed weakness.

Fortunately for them, they were not the only common traders to be invited to the palace, and once they entered the walled citadel itself through the main gate, they formed a procession flanked by guards in a winding snake that led from the old walls all the way through the narrow streets to the castle high on the hill in the centre.

Entering through the main gate meant crossing the old wooden drawbridge where the horses' hooves echoed in loud thuds over the deep ravine that once was a moat.

There hadn't been water in the moat for a long time, and Tannin could see it was now full of long grass, broken parts of carts and mud as she peered over the edge of the bridge. Eve walked determinedly not looking down as they crossed the chasm and begged Tannin to come back from the edge with a groan.

Other bridges made up of junk piles and wooden slats reached over the moat all around the old city walls, but since the procession was by royal request, they used the official entrance to the citadel and the main thoroughfare up to the castle.

Tannin and Flint used to come into the citadel quite often to wander around the colourful markets and strange tiny shops of the lower quarters where the artisans hocked their wares. Where the Fletchers' caravan trundled now, however, making their way higher and higher to the heart of the city, was definitely a much richer environment than any of them were used to as they left the seedy comfort of the Skirts and the colours and textures of the artisans and finally reached the cultured refinery of the upper quarters. Ladies and gentlemen, lavishly attired in reds and golds for the harvest festivities, gazed in wonder at the parade of common wagons traipsing through their streets.

Tannin had never actually been all the way up to the castle. The walk was further than she had realised. Nearing the castle itself, she was overwhelmed by the sheer size of it.

From a distance, it looked big and imposing but up close it looked like an impossible architectural feat. It could have easily covered the entire street the bakery was on. More even. The walls were pale glittering stone, and as they passed underneath the perilously sharp iron spikes of the gates, Tannin quickened her pace. Guards lined the inner courtyard and directed merchants and entertainers to various wings and kitchens and gardens, checking invitations carefully.

The kitchens in the castle were like nothing Tannin could have ever imagined. The towering ovens were lit from beneath and burned some kind of gas that was piped through a maze of copper pipes that ran up the walls and over the high ceiling. The oven also appeared to get ferociously hot much quicker than the old wood burning ovens at Fletcher's. Tannin's first batch was charred and smoking before one of the regular kitchen staff took pity on her and showed her how to work the damn thing properly. The kitchen was a stewing broth of the chefs and servants grabbing glittering silver platters teeming with delicacies, the contents of which Tannin couldn't even begin to guess and her mouth watered jealously at the tantalising scents.

Chapter Fifteen

A Royal Appointment

The Fletchers' team was slightly removed from the main chaos as their "lower quality" bread was going to the coach houses and guard barracks for the hundreds of additional staff the guests had brought along. Throughout the day, they would need waves of fresh loaves at key times, and since they had brought a wagonload of pre-baked breads, they had a few hours to get acquainted with the kitchen. The rest of the kitchen seemed comfortable with the process, and after a period of madness, the room itself seemed to sigh in relief and half the staff went out into the fresh air to smoke pipes and watch some of the entertainers practicing.

It was during this lull that a guard, a tall wiry kind of man who looked like he'd never smiled in his life, barked at them all to vacate the room. Mutterings of irritation and confusion erupted, but a guard's order could hardly be ignored. The kitchen clatterings soon subsided as the staff left by the side indicated by the stern pointing of the guard's bony finger. Tannin made to follow but he stopped her.

"Not you," he said curtly.

She looked between him and Eve in confusion and shrugged at her when she gave her a questioning look.

The guard waited until the last of the kitchen workers had left before following them through the door and closing it with a snap, leaving Tannin alone in the suddenly quiet room.

What the hell did I do?

A few heartbeats passed before the main door opened and a figure entered and glanced around the room furtively. Tannin's confusion increased for a second and then a broad grin spread across her face.

She would have never recognised her, she had to admit. In a fine dress of royal blue that billowed out from the waist in ruffles and with ivory lace frothing from the sleeves and top of the bodice, Princess Avalyn was almost reminiscent of a turbulent sea. She would stand out starkly against the autumnal colours most people wore for Lughnasadh. The guests of honour were from Rill. Maybe the blue was a nod to them and their coastal kingdom.

Even her face was different. Some expensive powders or expert shading had given her the appearance of high cheekbones and ruby red lips. The simple knot she sported when they'd last spoken was replaced by partially braided soft waves that cascaded past her shoulders. Her piercing eyes, however, were unmistakable.

"Ohohoho! It's Princess Avalyn, isn't it?" Tannin clapped her hands. "Ava. Avalyn. Very clever," she said dryly.

"Keep your voice down! I know you're going to have questions, but I need you to just trust me and come with me right now," the princess said with an urgency Tannin failed to see the cause of.

"Trust you? Suuuuure." Tannin looked the princess up and down, taking it all in in amazement. "This is an interestin' look for you. I would've expected somethin' a wee bit more subtle since I'm guessin' your less than appropriate activities sent you skulkin' in here."

"Quiet!" she snapped, still scanning the room.

Her abruptness took Tannin aback. She held her hands up in mock surrender. "All right then. You obviously schemed to get me here - despite me tellin' you to leave me alone I might add - so say your piece."

Tannin was quietly impressed at the scheme. She hadn't suspected for one moment, and there was no way the Fletchers could have refused a royal commission, plus they'd need all hands on deck so she was guaranteed to show.

"I did. I admit that but it was a mistake, and you need to leave now." Her voice bore an edge of worry and her speech was hurried.

"Uh, I'm workin'. I can't just leave. We have orders to fill."

Tannin gestured to the general mess of the kitchen.

"You don't understand. You need to leave." Avalyn reached for her arm. Tannin danced back out of reach.

"Why, what's goin' on? What did you do?" Tannin narrowed her eyes.

Avalyn bit her painted lip. "There was an alert. I don't know, there might be a Seer here, and if they See you then you're in danger."

"And a Seer is?"

"Someone who can See someone like you," she said with deliberate emphasis on the word See.

"Like your lens but without a lens?"

"Exactly. Keep your voice down."

"And you led me right in here?" Tannin asked accusingly. "What is this, some kind of trap?"

"If it were, would I be here right now trying to get you out?" Avalyn was fidgeting, twisting a silver ring on her finger.

"I can't just leave I've got things to do. Eve –"

"Miss Hill! You do understand that they could kill you, don't you?" She gave Tannin a pressing look. "There have been others. And there have been accidents."

"Wait, no one said anythin' about killing. What others?" Tannin's thoughts snapped to Laurel in her collapsed smithery. Was there actually merit to those scribblings?

"We do not have time for this. You need to go before anyone comes in here."

Tannin paused and mulled it over. If she stayed, she might get Seen – if that was even a real thing. If she left, she'd definitely get fired.

"No," she said firmly. "I'm not goin'. I'd lose my job and I can't afford that. Nothing you'd know anythin' about I'm guessin'."

"Ugh!" Avalyn groaned. "You don't understand –"

"No, princess. You don't understand."

"Look, either you come with me now willingly or I'm calling one of my guard and have you dragged along," Avalyn said crossing her arms.

Tannin narrowed her eyes. "You wouldn't."

"Oh yes, I would. I can't have you ruining –" A rumble of footsteps and voices sounded from the corridor outside.

Avalyn grabbed Tannin's wrist with surprising strength and pulled her to a small door in the shadow of one of the colossal ovens. She shoved her through unceremoniously and followed quickly, pulling the door almost shut behind them. Tannin had been too surprised to resist but now turned to Avalyn with a glare.

"What the h– mmph!"

The princess clamped a hand over Tannin's mouth and pushed her back against the wall as deep, hushed voices came from the kitchen.

"Shh!"

Tannin glared at her indignantly. They were so close that Avalyn's skirts fluttered against her legs and she could see all the individual gems stitched into her distractingly well- filled bodice. One strand of her glossy hair had gone rogue and dangled from her forehead between them as they stood almost pressed against one another. Avalyn's bright blue eyes stared down at her intensely as low voices sounded from behind the door.

Inappropriate thoughts raced around in Tannin's head about possible other circumstances where a pretty girl could have her pinned against the wall. She swallowed hard and abruptly forced them away.

Not the time. Not the time. Not the time.

They stayed like that not moving and barely breathing until the voices subsided.

"Let's go," Avalyn whispered, finally taking her hand away from Tannin's mouth.

"Get off me," Tannin hissed, pushing the other girl away and praying inwardly she hadn't noticed how flustered she was. "What the hell was that?"

"Those were no cooks," Avalyn said grimly. "They were plain-clothed guards." "The Seer?"

"I don't know, but they were looking for something. Or someone," she said pointedly.

"I swear if you're fuckin' with me..."

"I'm trying to help you, you fool."

"Tryin' to help yourself more like. I know you still want somethin' from me or I wouldn't even be here in the first place!"

Avalyn ignored her and went to peer around the corner of the short corridor they found themselves in.

"Are you coming or not?"

"Do I have a choice?"

"Not really. Follow me closely and quietly."

Tannin followed the princess through another set of doors which led them into the servant's corridors.

Avalyn explained in hushed tones that since almost every servant was attending to festival preparations, or tending to their new guests' needs, she was reasonably confident they wouldn't meet anyone on their way through.

At the first set of stairs, Tannin stopped. "Wait, if you're kickin' me out why are we going up? Out is down."

"There are passages. Just trust me."

"Why should I?"

"We have already established that you don't have a choice," the princess replied primly.

They made it up several flights of stairs and through multiple corridors, occasionally ducking into side corridors to avoid wandering servants, until Tannin was utterly certain she'd never find her way back even if she wanted to. She still didn't fully believe the princess's Seer story. Or any of it for that matter, but her anxiousness was infectious, and Tannin found herself glancing over her shoulder.

They finally reached a set of dark wooden double doors which had elaborate carvings etched into the grain. Tannin momentarily forgot where she was and stood trying to decipher the depiction. There were horses and swords and lots of little soldiers.

Avalyn cleared her throat.

"Oh, right. Aye." Tannin hurried after her into smallish, domed antechamber then further inside.

"These are my rooms. No one will come in here. You're safe for now."

Being the Princess of the Brochlands afforded a life of utmost luxury. The room they had entered had the makings of a fine sitting room with richly embroidered sofas and vases of fresh exotic flowers that Tannin had never seen before. The suite continued further, and delicately decorated, gold handled doors led to multiple other connecting rooms. She caught a glimpse of what must be a bathing room covered in decorated tile and marble.

"This way," Avalyn said, leading the way into a room to the left which she unlocked with a key she produced from somewhere within the rustling folds of her gown.

The floors were covered in carpets that had been hand stitched to depict the royal coat of arms. Tannin's feet sank into their lushness as she walked. Heavy curtains surrounding the carved four poster bed were adorned in the royal colours of deep purple and gold. The stained glass in the windows splashed the room with every shade imaginable.

"You brought me to your bedroom?" Tannin said, raising her eyebrows suggestively.

Avalyn gave her a withering look. "Will you be quiet and come over here?" She seemed to be fighting with a large wall tapestry depicting the five kingdoms.

"Just sayin', points for effort but not the smoothest, princess."

"Are you always this irritating when someone is trying to save your life?" she demanded, finally managing to detach the tapestry from its fixings and hold it aside, revealing a seemingly smooth section of wood panelling.

"Well, I don't know. The whole life endangerment thing only started when you showed up." Tannin crossed her arms and stared at the section of wall. "Am I supposed to be seeing somethin' here or...?"

Avalyn reached out and pressed one of the panels, depressing it slightly beneath her immaculately manicured fingers. The subtle clicking of a mechanism sounded, and a square section of the wall swung inwards.

Tannin peered inside at the dank passage. "Ohh."

So, this is how you sneak about.

"Follow the path for around twenty minutes. You'll come out in the old necropolis."

"You're not comin'?" Even Tannin heard the apprehension in her voice and she inwardly cringed.

"Does it look like I'm dressed for creeping around in the dark?" Avalyn gestured at her outfit and then it was her turn to give Tannin a smirk. "Not scared, are you?"

"No!" Tannin said with a huff.

"Off you go then. When you reach the end, there are stairs to your right that will lead you out. Other than that, do not touch anything. I mean it. I hope you understand what a risk I'm taking even showing you this tunnel. Or getting involved with you at all."

"I didn't ask you to get *involved* with me. In fact, if I remember rightly, I specifically said to leave me alone."

"Well, you're involved now whether you like it or not. They were looking for you in that kitchen."

"And whose fault is that?"

Avalyn merely stepped back gesturing for her to enter the passageway. The door was small and even Tannin had to duck her head to go through. "You're welcome for the escape plan."

"Which I wouldn't need if it wasn't for you." Tannin wasn't even sure why she was arguing at this point. She felt she needed to, though.

"Just get out," Avalyn snapped.

"Fine. And this time when I say leave me alone from now on, I mean it!"

Avalyn simply scoffed and closed the door.

There was a series of mechanical clicks again and then silence. The hidden door fit so snugly in its frame that it didn't even let the slightest trickle of brightness through. The tunnel was pitch black and Tannin realised all too late that she didn't have a light.

"Aw shite."

Chapter Sixteen

The Crypt

"Twenty minutes, my arse." Tannin grumbled as she finally stumbled into the weak light of what looked like an old sanctuary. Her eyes had adjusted to the pitch darkness of the dusty corridors better than she'd expected them to, and now even the wispy light jutting into the hall was enough to make her squint. The light trickled in from cracks in the ceilings and parts of the walls where the mortar holding the bricks together had crumbled away over the years.

The floor was made up of wide square stones, worn down with age and interrupted every few metres by pillars that rose like thick tree trunks. They stretched, widened and joined each other to make the tall, ribbed arches in the ceiling. It reminded Tannin of the monastery cloisters where once a year in the late autumn the monks sold their self-brewed beer in giant flagons.

In recent years, it had drawn such a crowd, with even the richer folk from the inner citadel abandoning their comforts to slum it in the Skirts for a few days, that it was becoming a festival in its own right.

She and Flint would stagger through arched walkways that surrounded the inner garden, laughing and singing along with whatever crude song the crowds were belting out and sloshing beer all over themselves. It was a harsh contrast to the cold and empty chamber she found herself in now.

Tannin's footsteps echoed unpleasantly as she wandered through the cavernous room. Plaques lined the walls with words in a language she didn't know. She assumed they were names. She'd heard about places like this. Instead of being buried in a graveyard with a headstone, some people gave their body to the fire to have it reduced to ash, believing their soul would be carried away by the smoke.

Whatever was left when the fire burnt out was collected in a clay pot and sealed up in a place like this. Tannin shivered at the thought of all those remains bricked up in the walls. She didn't want that when she died. To be stuck in a little pot for eternity.

Is a pine box really any better?

She hadn't ever given death much thought but standing here surrounded by the dead, she couldn't help it.

Ava had said whoever was looking for her wanted her dead. Would they bury her after? She wondered idly. If they did find and kill her, that is. Would they bury her casketless body in some unmarked grave?

She paused, looking at a particularly decorative plaque with a floral wreath circling the name.

Better that than here, she decided. She'd rather have the possibility of real flowers growing on her grave than some sad carving. She shuddered at her morbid thoughts.

The air was still and held the underlying tang of death. Even the sanctuary itself seemed to be in a state of decay. The stone walls were holding themselves together purely out of tradition and a stubborn reluctance to give way to the moss that was already poking through some of the gaps to creep towards the plaques.

At the far side, opposite of where she'd surfaced, was a set of sturdy wooden doors. From the light squeezing in the tiny gap between them and the shadow that interrupted it, Tannin could already see a thick beam blocking the door from the outside. She gave it a push regardless. It whined at her as it rocked back and forth a little before settling but remaining solidly shut.

There has to be another way out.

There was no way she was climbing all the way back up that damp, musty tunnel.

Especially in this stupid dress.

Tannin quickly spied the top of a wrought iron banister in the shadow of a pillar that she'd missed before. Hadn't the princess said something about stairs? The stone spiral staircase attached to the banister went down deeper into the belly of the mausoleum and Tannin paused. She really didn't want to go downwards, but she didn't see any other direction to go.

The banister was cold to the touch and the metal wound in and around itself in an intricate pattern interspersed with some long-forgotten coat of arms. The stairs themselves dipped in the middle from being worn down smooth.

The gloomy light from above followed her downwards but grew weaker as she reached the bottom. Tannin breathed a sigh of relief at the sight of spiked torch sconces that held torches and gladly lit them with a tinder box that was helpfully tucked into its own nook set into the wall beside them.

In the room she now stood, a large space had been cleared of debris and a circle was marked in chalk. Outside the circle, leaning against the wall, were a host of training weapons and equipment that must've been liberated from the guard barracks. Wooden and dulled steel swords, spears and axes. At the other side of the room, atop a marble sarcophagus, a map was pinned down with thick books at each corner with notes and diagrams scribbled across every inch. Dark wooden bookshelves and cabinets lined the back wall, overflowing with strange books and artifacts.

"What is this place?" Tannin wondered out loud.

Although she had no desire to go near that stone coffin, curiosity needled at her. She edged a little closer to check out the parchments on top. This was clearly the princess's base of operations.

Tannin smirked at the thought of that girl planning a rebellion of any kind in her fluffy blue dress, but the smirk quickly left her face at the sheer level of detail neatly penned on outlines that she recognised as the house Hamish's crew had tried to rob. The memory of Ava giving orders to a bunch of cutthroat bandits swam through her head.

Maybe I shouldn't write this girl off so quickly.

Judging by the documents, she had been far more prepared for that heist than they had been. It was sheer luck Tannin had managed to get her hands on that package in the first place, and she would've never been able to leave with it. It seems the princess had paid off some of the Guards, some of the servants and had her thugs waiting in the tunnels.

She'd covered every way out.

Damn.

The stacks of books caught Tannin's attention. She stopped to read the titles, keeping a wary eye on the sarcophagus. The thing gave her the creeps. The top three books seemed to be part of a collection. She squinted at the peeling spines.

An Account of Remnants in the Age of The Sun

She had no idea what the Age of the Sun was meant to be, but she'd heard pretty much all the stories about Remnants. Everyone had.

She'd heard them from her grandfather and overheard snatches here and there in the pub or a mother reciting a tale to a fascinated child in the park. They were firm favourites to tell throughout the city. The result of mythical Fair Folk mixing with humans and giving them extraordinary abilities.

Yeah, right.

Men who could shoot an arrow into an apple at a thousand feet away. Women who charmed woodland animals with a song. Thieves who infiltrated an impenetrable fortress without a whisper. Sailors with command of the waves.

Those were Remnants. Not monsters who tore horses apart. Tannin pushed memories of unseeing glassy black eyes from her mind and flipped open the first book. It wasn't like she had anywhere she needed to be right now.

Her eyes widened as she read the chapter headings.

Kelpies, Balors, Selkies, Druids...

Okay, so maybe they are monsters...

She'd heard stories about each of them. Kelpies were vicious water demons that took pleasure in drowning children in rivers. Balors, in turn, were giants who ate full- grown men for breakfast. Selkies bewitched the minds of fishermen and drove them to their deaths. Druids... druids did just about anything they could manage with their herbs and potions.

Still a bunch of bloody children's stories.

She was about to slam the book shut when she read the next heading. Triquetra.

Oh, well that's something.

Tannin traced the symbol on the page with her fingertip. One twisting line that overlapped, coiled and came back together forming a triangular knot-like symbol. She'd seen that before. Messier versions of this were doodled all throughout her grandfather's journals.

She definitely wanted to read this book but not in a creepy crypt underground when she had a perfectly good room to go to with blankets and tea. She cast a furtive look around. Maybe she would just borrow it for a little bit. She could see if the symbol really was the same or she was imagining it.

With no bag or pockets big enough to fit the book, she tucked it under her arm and then gave her dress pocket a pat to feel the comforting weight of her keys still in place. A sharp pang of guilt hit her when she thought of Eve left alone to cope with the massive orders today. How on earth was she going to explain why she'd disappeared?

Never mind Seers and monsters, Eve is going to bloody murder me herself.

Tannin quickly found the exit – a trapdoor that was angled inward awkwardly but had cracks of light coming in from the sides. She popped her head through and could see that parts of the upper floor must have long ago come crashing in. The collapsed pillars blocked the entrance to the lower level from view from the outside. As she hauled herself out of the crypt, she was met with the grim view of a thousand cracked and looming gravestones.

How lovely. More death.

The one place in this damn city that the inhabitants hadn't swarmed over in their masses was the ancient necropolis that rose just outside the walls. The hill of the dead. The small hillock was crusted with decaying tombstones and caved-in mausoleums over which a hundred varieties of moss and fungus creeped. The legends of the Sluagh, the unforgiven dead who roamed places of death, were still whispered in hushed tones by the old women in the city to their terrified grandchildren when it got dark. In the stories, the Sluagh could either try and earn their forgiveness or they could be bitter and vengeful against the living. There was no way to tell until they came for you. Tannin shivered just thinking about it. Unlike the old ruins, the threat of the Sluagh actually kept people away from this place.

Smart princess.

Back at her lodgings, Tannin brewed a pot of tea on the stove downstairs and took the whole pot up to her room. There, she sat cross-legged on her bed, holding her mug in both hands and with the book open on the blanket. Her grandfather's journal lay beside it. The symbol was unmistakably the same. Tannin took a slow sip of her tea and began properly from the beginning.

Chapter Seventeen

Sorry Isn't Enough

Her tea had long gone cold, and her candle was almost burnt down to the wick. There was so much to take in. The old stories always described them as monsters, but this book told a completely different tale.

Kelpies were Fair Folk who ruled the rivers and waterways, selkies claimed the sea, balors took the mountains and the druids took the forests. That was how the kingdoms were originally split. The humans were supposed to take the moors and grasslands. Apparently, that had all gone to hell quite quickly. The kingdoms of Woodren, Rill, Cascairn, Gormbrae, the Brochlands. It made sense... sort-of. Tannin squinted at hastily drawn maps.

So many different authors, from each corner of the five kingdoms, had written their lives into the pages of the Accounts, and Tannin was overwhelmed by it all.

Kelpie-bloods could hold their breath underwater and swim like otters apparently. The stories were mostly how they smuggled goods up the rivers by swimming. Like boatless pirates.

Selkie-bloods seemed to have a powerful sway over people – there were no entries from selkies themselves but only those who had been seduced, enthralled or conned by them. They seemed to like to steal people's boats.

Balor-bloods... giants with inhuman strength. The mention of strength sent Tannin reaching for her grandfather's journals. Hadn't he said Laurel was strong? Had he actually said the word balor?

She rubbed her stiff neck and stretched before diving straight back into the old pages. She alternated between the Accounts and her grandfather's journals. She reread the passages about Laurel. Her grandfather mentioned her several more times. It seemed her death had hit him hard.

He also spoke about Tannin more than once.

"It's better that Tannin doesn't remember. It's better that she doesn't know. She's a headstrong girl. If she knew, she'd want to be involved. It's safer this way."

"Doesn't remember what though?" Tannin muttered running her hands through her hair in frustration.

The later sections of *An Account of Remnants in the Age of the Sun,* after the Remnant entries, was a depressing read of attempts at fighting against a mysterious group that called themselves the "Triquetra" and, from what she had read so far, failing every time. It seemed they really had it out for Remnants.

The last section she'd read had been the partial memoirs of a man called Ignelious Strongholde, who was surprisingly not a Remnant at all.

"Strongholde.... Strongholde..."

She flicked through the pages of her grandfather's journals as, again, the name flickered in her memory and there it was. This man, Ignelious, must have been an ancestor of Laurel. Her grandfather. Or great grandfather? She had no idea how old these writings were.

He had been a Triquetra recruit from an early age and maddeningly spoke very little about it. Instead, most of his tale had been a tragic love story.

"I am in turmoil. I am in the most inescapable grips of love, and I know this love to be true, but my love has revealed her secret to me. She is of the balor-blood, of those dark and wicked creatures I have sworn to destroy. And yet her heart is so pure. Never have I known a being so gentle and kind. How could such tainted blood run through such a heart?"

"The unnatural strength she possesses can only come from this evil source, and yet I cannot think her to be evil. Could it be I have been deceived? Blinded by her beauty and charm? I think not for I love the very soul of her and she, mine. Is the source of the deception, then, from my tutors, my masters? Could it be that evil resides not in the blood of the Fair but in the heart of man?

I am in turmoil."

Tannin was not big on reading usually, preferring to hear stories from books Eve had read over clouds of flour as she animatedly recounted tales of knights and strange creatures and faraway lands, but this one gripped her attention so fiercely she couldn't stop. Ignelious continued his writings as fervently as she read them. They'd married in secret. He joined with the group of Armodian Remnants to betray the Triquetra from the inside. His entries became less about love and more informative. Times and dates of meetings and detailed sketches of the inside of some official looking buildings. No names though. The Triquetra members never exchanged real names and instead referred to themselves with codenames. Ignelious's codename was Black Dog.

Again, Tannin flipped back through her grandfather's journal. Laurel's smithery was called the Black Dog. There was no way that was coincidence. She felt a buzz as the connections lined up. Her excitement mounted until she read Ignelious's last entry.

"My name is Ignelious Strongholde and I think I am going to die. Tonight, they have called a gathering of great importance and I believe it to be my execution.

I am afraid, but I know I did the right thing. I think the Triquetra elders finally know that it is I who is working toward their downfall and not the unfortunate Ackaster whom they previously suspected. I believe Ackaster may indeed have been working against their interests but for profit and not for the Remnant peoples. The man's chief loyalty was always to his own purses.

My wife and my son are safe and that is all that matters to me. The Remnant clans of the western side have fled the city and are free of the ever-tightening net that the Triquetra spins around this once great city. They will know by now that they have all fled. I stay in the hopes that, perhaps, I am undiscovered and can continue this noble cause. If I am discovered, then I can only hope I can divert their attentions from my family in my last breaths."

It was Ignelious's last entry.

Tannin exhaled and sat back against her pillows. He must've been killed but his family survived – Laurel was proof of that – and had come back to Armodan sometime after fleeing. Why did they come back? Did the Triquetra connect her to the traitorous Black Dog that they'd killed so many years before? Did the Triquetra still exist? Was that who had been looking for her?

Too many questions remained unanswered, and this one book wasn't giving her any answers. She'd have to go back to the necropolis and look at the rest of them. Maybe there was something there that would give her answers about what happened to poor Ignelious. Or even better, something that would answer her burning questions about what the hell she was. About all the things her grandfather had decided she was too young and headstrong to know about. Maybe the princess had allies like these Remnant clans? Was this what she meant by work with her? Fight against these Triquetra people?

That would be utter madness.

She snapped the book shut. None of these stories had happy endings, and she was not keen to add her own. But equally, she couldn't just leave it alone.

Something big was going on right under her nose. She stared at her ceiling where a tiny spider was weaving a silvery net. Whatever this was, she was up to her neck in it whether she liked it or not. Maybe if she managed to get some answers her grandfather's work wouldn't be in vain.

Even after a night of tossing and turning and dreams of black dogs being caught in spider webs, Tannin rose as usual before the sun. She still had no idea what she was going to say to Eve. Sorry was hardly going to cut it, and she couldn't tell her what really happened.

Oh sorry, Eve. The princess kicked me out via a secret tunnel because I'm secretly magic. By the gods, this was going to be bad.

Tannin was surprised to find the door already unlocked and the fires started when she got to the bakery. That was always her task. Before she even stepped through the doorway, Eve blocked her path.

"Oh, look who shows up." Her expression was as hard and cold as iron.

"Look, Eve, I'm really –"

"Don't you dare say yer sorry. I dinnae care what excuse ye have." Eve's eyes glistened with tears, but her voice was

pure anger. "Do ye even know what kind of a day I had yesterday? Do ye?"

Tannin stayed quiet. She deserved this.

"A royal commission. How could ye do this to me? Answer me!"

"I... Something came up... I..." Tannin stumbled over her words under Eve's furious gaze.

"Something came up? Something came up? No, not good enough. You, at the very least, the least, Tannin, had to have my back yesterday of all days. Where were ye?"

Tannin couldn't have given an answer even if she had one. She could only try and swallow the lump in her throat.

Eve gave a disgusted sigh. "Get out, Tannin. I've covered for ye. I've gave ye second chances, made allowances for ye, but this is the last straw. I need a dependable worker, and that's not you so get out and don't come back."

"Eve..."

"Dinnae 'Eve' me. I needed ye and ye bailed. Yer lucky it's me here and not the Fletchers 'cause they're ready to skin ye alive." Tannin's heart felt like it was breaking as Eve's voice cracked. "I needed you! Yesterday was hell, and now I have to find a new assistant. Maybe even two now that..."

She trailed off, but Tannin immediately clocked the way her hand instinctively moved to her belly, which now Tannin noticed sported a gentle bump that hadn't been there before.

"Wait, are you...?"

"Another reason ye need to go," Eve snapped. "I dinnae ken what kind of shady business ye've got yerself into. Don't think I havnae noticed, but I need that shit as far away from me and this baby as possible. I worry about ye, I do, but ye've crossed a line. I'm done bailing ye out."

"I'm so sorry –"

"Just get out."

Tannin moped in her rooms for days, alternating between napping and rereading snippets from either the journal or passages from the Remnant Accounts. She thought about having to tell Flint about losing her job when he finally got back from Tayfort and groaned. He was definitely going to have some choice words for her too.

She confirmed her suspicions that none of the stories involving the Triquetra had a happy ending. There had been a couple more attempts to infiltrate the group but whoever they were, they always seemed one step ahead of these poor saps. If any of it was even real and not some made up fairytale. But the names... the journals...

She couldn't wrap her head around it all. Remnants? Magic? It was all too weird. But what had happened to her had been real.

Urghhhhhh! It makes no sense!

Tannin had no idea when Princess Avalyn would next be at the crypt. She wished she'd jammed the trapdoor open so she could go back and get the second book. She needed answers. Thankfully, she didn't have to wait long until a solution presented itself, rapping intently on her door.

"Hello?" called the thin voice of Mrs O'Baird. "There's a letter for ye here."

Tannin cracked the door open just enough to snatch the letter and mutter a thanks, snapping it shut before Mrs O'Baird could see her mess of her room and have a heart attack. Dirty cups and a few plates covered most of the surfaces while various items of clothing were strewn across the floor where she'd let them fall. She'd clean up later, she told herself.

The envelope was nothing special, just plain with her name and address and sealed with a non-descript wax seal. She slit it open and shook out the contents.

Dear Thief,

Bring it back. Tomorrow 9pm. You know the place.

A

Tannin smiled.

Aha, so she has noticed.

Chapter Eighteen

An Uneasy Alliance

Tannin arrived early and perched on a mushroom-covered stone slab looking out over the view. The citadel was a city within a city surrounded by crumbling walls which had stood for hundreds of years when the castle was little more than a fort and the citizens had all lived comfortably within the surrounding battlements.

From her perch on the raised hill of the necropolis, Tannin could see it all – from the silhouette of the castle illuminated by the tail end of the sunset, the sloping streets of the walled city and further to the sprawl outside and the distant tree line. She could probably work out which one of those little roofs was the bakery if she bothered. She took a deep breath and took in the earthy scent of the foliage and the headiness of the evening air. It was going to rain again.

The creak of the trapdoor brought her back to why she was there. She slipped off the slab to make her way behind the broken pillars to where she knew the hidden entrance was.

"Evenin'," she called as she peered into the opening.

Torches glowed in their sconces, but no reply came from the depths. With only the briefest of second thoughts, she ducked through into the gloomy cavern. She needed answers.

She saw the princess immediately, leaning over the sarcophagus seemingly intent on some document or other. All the royal adornments had been left behind and she was simply dressed in black, her thick dark hair pulled back from her face. This was Ava, not Princess Avalyn.

"Give me back my book," she said without looking up.

"Straight to the point, I see. Tell you what, I'll trade you for the second one."

CLANG.

Tannin swore colourfully as the princess's bodyguard emerged from the shadows behind her after slamming the trapdoor shut.

"What do you want it for? I thought you weren't interested?" Ava still wasn't looking at her.

"They're an interesting read," Tannin replied eyeing the bodyguard cautiously. As long as he kept his distance, she wouldn't make trouble.

"You have two options here. Give me my book back and be on your way or we can work together, and you can have all the information you want."

"What's in it for me? Information doesn't pay my bills."

Ava finally looked at her. She seemed a lot more assured of herself than the last time they met "I'm sure we can agree on a compensation of some sort for your trouble."

Tannin laughed. "Honestly, when we met before you should have led with that. It would've gone a lot better, and I wouldn't have jumped out the bloody window."

"So, are we agreed?"

"Well, you already got me fired so..." She shrugged. "Make it worth my time."

"There's something else too. You've read something that has your interest piqued, haven't you?"

"So, no apology? All right then. Clearly, I did read something interestin', or I wouldn't be asking for the second book. There was a symbol I recognised. And a name," Tannin said. "When do I get paid? And how much?"

"What name?" Ava smiled, ignoring Tannin's questions.

"Who's he? You trust him?" Tannin indicated the bodyguard who was still lurking in the shadows.

The light of the torches illuminated a scar intersecting his lip, which set his mouth in a permanent grimace under his thick beard. The simple roughspun shirt and brown wool kilt he wore could have belonged to any common man but the rigid, militaristic way he was standing suggested he was anything but.

"With my life," Ava answered simply. "This is Captain Attilo."

The man didn't offer a greeting just a curt nod. It wasn't lost on Tannin that his hand rested casually on the hilt of his sword that hung from his hip.

"Not the friendly type, huh? Fine by me." Tannin leaned against one of the supporting pillars.

"Hey, I have a question, princess." The thought suddenly came to her. "If you think I am what you think I am, how come you aren't scared of me? You think I killed those men on Pine Street. Tore them apart. Yet you wanna work with me."

Ava finally stood up straight and gave Tannin her full attention, those blue eyes staring straight through her. "Not work with you. You're going to work for me. Clear?"

"Whatever."

"We looked into those men. My theory is it was self- defence – am I right?"

Tannin didn't respond.

"You've lived here for, what, five years?"

"Six-ish. What does that matter? And how did you know that?"

"I did my research. Six years and only one incident? I'd say you're just coming into whatever abilities you have. I doubt you could do it again even if you wanted to, just yet. But this is all just theory. So why don't you tell me? Should I fear you?"

"Maybe." Tannin tried to sound confident, but she really wished Ava would blink. That intense stare was unnerving.

"Usually, Remnants display abilities when they hit puberty. Like a growth spurt. And that's usually when they're most visible because they don't know how to handle it yet." She looked Tannin up and down. "I'm guessing you're a late bloomer."

Tannin couldn't help the flush that rose up from her collar.

"Also, Remnants tend to stick together. Close-knit families and packs. But you're on your own, aren't you? You have no idea what's going on and that's why you're here." Ava finished assertively with her hands on her hips. "It's probably why you made a mess like that in the first place too. You are clueless."

"You know what? Screw you." Tannin turned to leave.

Attilo blocked her way.

"Ah, ah." Ava tutted. "I thought you wanted paid?"

"You know where you can shove your money? Get out of my way." She tried to push past the bodyguard, but he was like a rock and blocked her again. "Move!"

"You've got a temper, haven't you? We'll need to work on that," Ava chided.

Tannin was seething. "What is your problem?"

"We've still got more to talk about," Ava said primly. "Let's talk family. Remnance is genetic after all. Where are yours? More drunken accidents?"

Tannin rounded on her. "Ohh, I see what you're tryin' to do. It's not gonna work. You think you're so smart, but two can play at that game. You wanna talk family? Let's talk family. You're down here in a damn crypt plottin' against yours. What's the matter? Mummy and daddy don't love you enough? Didn't buy you enough sparkly things? They love your perfect brother more than you, is that it?"

Ava's carefully put-together expression twitched. Tannin nodded in satisfaction.

"Thought so. Are you done?"

"For now." Ava smiled, slyly. "A lot of Remnant attributes present themselves under stress, can't blame me for being curious."

Tannin shook her head in disbelief. "You were gonna goad me until I Changed is that it? Are you stupid? You just said you think I don't have control."

"What do you mean Change?"

Ah, fuck.

"Nothin'."

"Ah, ah. You said Change. A transformation is extremely rare." Ava was alight with excitement and rummaging through the books until she found what she was looking for and flipped it open. "Come here, look."

Tannin approached cautiously and looked at the carefully drawn watercolour figures on the pages before her. Humanesque figures with great taloned wings erupting from their shoulders, others with spiked tails and claws and one that was covered in scales that sparkled like gems.

Ava was looking at her expectantly.

"What? Am I a giant half bird thing?" Tannin raised her eyebrow. "I thought you said you knew what I was? Are there more types than were in that book I read?"

"I mean, yes and no. And yes, there are." Ava frowned at her and then sighed. "You don't even know what you are do you?"

Tannin shuffled her feet and didn't answer.

"Would you like some tea?" Ava said suddenly.

"What?" Tannin thought she'd misheard.

"Tea. We are getting to know one another after all." She sat down on the floor where a fur rug covered the bare stone and gestured next to her. Tannin sat down a little further away, eyeing the princess distrustfully.

"So, what about the rest of you?" "The rest?"

"Yeah, don't you have a group or somethin'?" "It's just us."

"Oh." Tannin frowned. "What about those men from before?"

"They were just hired muscle. You sound disappointed."

"Kind of. The folk in here," she said and held up the Accounts, "they always had clans or like a whole underground thing going on."

"That was centuries ago. And it's what we're trying to build up again. With your help, of course."

Attilo produced a flask and cups from somewhere while Ava pulled over a stack of books and placed them in front of Tannin, shuffling closer.

"These are probably the most important to start with," Ava said, blowing steam from her cup.

Tannin waited until Ava took a sip before trying her own tea. It was hot and herby. *Not bad.*

"So, what's with the lens thing?" Tannin asked, ignoring the books.

Ava took the cracked lens from her pocket. It was now bordered by a gold band attached to a thin chain which disappeared into her tunic like an old man's monocle. "This?"

"Right, yeah. I think it's time you told me what that thing actually does." Tannin set her cup aside.

"Take a look." She offered the lens to Tannin.

Tannin had to lean in close to put the lens up to her eye, close enough to smell the floral soap Ava must have bathed with. The slight blueish white colour of the glass tinted the room. "What am I supposed to see?"

Ava wordlessly handed her a small handheld mirror. Tannin stared at her own reflection and breathed a sigh of relief. She'd expected to see a horrific monstrous face looking back at her, but it was the same old face she'd been looking at for seventeen years. The only difference was a coppery hue and a bright golden flash from behind her eyes as the light caught them.

"All right, so what does that mean?" She looked up at Ava. "Well, if you hadn't broken it, you would be able to see much more."

"I didn't break it – it got broken." Tannin clarified pointedly.

"Mhm." Ava took back the lens. "Anyway, that was just a final clarification. I didn't need to look at your eyes to know that you're a Remnant. And an Inherent Remnant at that."

"What d'you mean?"

"You gave yourself away the first time we met. There's no way human hearing could have heard the ticking from the device this lens was in. And the way you reacted to the whistle proved it further."

"Whistle? That was you in the alley? That bloody hurt!"

Ava took a thin reed-like instrument from a bag beside her. Tannin immediately clamped her hands over her ears, sending her half-drunk tea flying.

"Oh, calm down I wasn't going to blow it."

"Put it away then," Tannin said angrily, wiping splashed tea off her overalls.

Seemingly oblivious to Tannin's annoyance, Ava continued. "So, all in all, that proves that you are a Remnant. Heightened hearing – I'm guessing sight too, but we can test that later. There's a number of things you could be. I need to do some tests. How are your reflexes?"

"My what?"

Ava flung a nearby book at Tannin's head. She ducked quickly but not quickly enough to avoid a glancing blow on the forearm she'd thrown up to shield herself.

"OW! What the hell was that for?!" Tannin rubbed her arm.

"Hm, reflexes seem normal. For now, at least. Your abilities will develop over time... Attilo, could you get my notebook?"

"The only one not normal here is you, you crazy woman!"

"I'm just narrowing down options, calm down."

"You calm down!" Tannin snapped back. It was childish, but her arm was throbbing.

Ava pursed her lips in thought. "Maybe a different approach."

"You think?" Tannin said sarcastically.

"Here." Ava took the cracked monocle from around her slender neck and tossed it to Tannin.

"What am I meant to do with this?" Tannin asked putting it up to her eye again. "I already... Oh shit." She took the lens away and Ava's appearance turned back to normal. Peeking back through the lens, the bluish hue to her skin and reflective green glint returned. "So. This makes more sense."

Ava smiled. "Trust me a bit more now?"

"Trust is maybe a little strong."

"We don't have to be friends. Just allies."

"Allies I can do."

"Excellent." Ava took a tiny, razor-sharp blade like the one a healer would use from her pocket. "How are your healing abilities?"

"You stay the fuck away from me with that."

Chapter Nineteen

You Learn Something New Everyday

"So, what are you then?" Tannin asked as Ava, prompted by Attilo, reluctantly put the blade away.

"A Wielder. My blood is the blood of the druids to be precise." Ava took the lens back and gave Tannin a wink. "Another reason I wasn't scared of you. I can Sense things; and I didn't Sense any threat to me."

"So, the royal family are Remnants? Why was I in danger at the castle then?" Tannin's mind was swimming. "What else can you do? What's a Wielder?"

"I'll answer a question every time you do. Fair?" "Sounds fair. So?"

"No, the royal family are not Remnants. Where are you from?"

"I don't know. So, if they're not Remnants and you are that means you have a different bloodline?"

"Answer for answer. You didn't give me a real one."

"I genuinely don't know. East in Woodren somewhere but I'm not sure. I got some bad blood poisonin' when I was wee, and I don't remember much before that."

"Blood poisoning..." Ava mused. "Wait a minute." She dived into a stack of books to pull out another old volume. "There was something about blood poisoning in here."

"So, you're a bastard then?" Tannin asked again.

"Apparently," Ava said, not looking up from the book but flinching slightly at the word.

"Isn't that a big deal?"

"I've made my peace with it."

"And that's why you're doin' all this weird stuff?" Tannin gestured to the crypt with all its training materials. "They won't let you anywhere near the political stuff 'cause you can never take the crown is that it?"

"No."

"Then what –"

"Excuse me, you owe me about three answers by now. Slow down."

"Fine, ask away."

"I'm still on blood poisoning, give me a minute."

Tannin huffed and drank her refilled tea quietly until Ava found the right passage.

"Here we go… 'A transformation brought on by extreme circumstance before the subject is of the natural age can result in the poisoning of the blood and the decay of the body. Survival is unlikely.'."

"Huh." Tannin shrugged. "He always did say he saved my life."

"Who? Your grandfather?"

Tannin nodded. "So that means I Changed before?" Her eyes widened. "It's not a dream. It's a memory!"

"What is?"

Tannin blushed. She hadn't meant to say that out loud. "I have, uh… nightmares. About running from somethin' and then my body gets all distorted and torn up and…" She trailed off, embarrassed at Ava's rapt attention.

"Interesting. And this would be around the time of the blood poisoning?"

"Probably. My turn?" Tannin continued without waiting for a response. "What's a Wielder? And what can you do?"

"That's two." Ava considered the question for a moment. "There are two kinds of Remnants just like there were two distinct kinds of Fair Folk. Those who can use magic and those who have magic within them. There's a subtle distinction but –"

"Witches and monsters?" Tannin interrupted.

"Well, if you want to be crude about it," Ava said, annoyed. "The actual terms are Wielders and Inherents."

"Oh, get off your high horse, you already called me a monster," Tannin said half-seriously. "So, witch, tell me about your magic."

Ava sighed loudly and Tannin got the impression she was trying to stop herself snapping at her. Tannin tried to hide her smile. It was far too much fun to wind her up.

"I'm not a witch. I have druid blood – there's quite a distinction. And the answer is not much without a teacher. I can make some salves, and I have my Senses."

Tannin pondered this for a moment. "Okay, onto my main question though, what are you actually doing here?"

To her surprise, it wasn't Ava but Attilo's gruff voice that answered.

"There's Remnants in hidin' all o'er the city and in other cities too. They're being hunted by a group who call themselves the Triquetra – which you'll have read about in there. We think they believe a Remnant with any power'll end up causin' another Dark Age."

With a little prodding, Attilo – helped every so often by inputs from Ava – explained further.

The legends got most of it right – thousands of years ago, the Fair Folk and humankind lived as separate species and over time the bloodlines merged and mixed and diluted the Fair Folk's magic. What the legends left out, however, were the years and years of blood-soaked conflict that had led to the current state of things.

Animosity between the Folk and humans had been around since the dawn of time, but it wasn't until they first coupled and produced living offspring that the fallout on both sides became catastrophic.

Clans of Folk separated themselves from society and took to the deep forests to conserve their power in their own tribes. Groups of humans also formed clans, declaring the power of the Fair Folk unholy and demonic. Wars and battles raged for centuries, but eventually the power of the Folk proved too much for their human counterparts. Many of the human-only tribes were wiped out in a series of bloody massacres.

The Folk clans combined into one, which they called the Empire that ruled over almost all of what was now the five kingdoms with a vicious Emperor at their head. His thirst for power consumed and corrupted him until his own people overthrew him with the help of the remaining human clans and the first true alliances were formed.

But for some of the humans who survived, their ideology remained. The demonic nature of the Fair Folk's power had been proven through the Emperor's crimes. They gathered in secret and vowed to never again let one with such power rule over any kingdom and so the Triquetra was formed and under the guise of friendship infiltrated the society of Folk and human. The history of what exactly happened was lost to time but over the early years of the new alliance, hundreds of the Folk succumbed to a mysterious plague which ravaged every town and settlement until humans outnumbered them significantly. With dwindling numbers, magic became increasingly diluted until even the notion faded into myth and legend.

"Now, the Triquetra hunt everyone with the bits o' that magic in their veins, Remnants, to stop a Dark Age ever happenin' again. They target any Remnants who have even a wee bit political power, but none o' them are really safe."

Tannin paused for a minute, digesting all the facts. She had magic power in her blood. And a mysterious centuries old secret society would want her dead for it if they found her.

Wonderful.

"I'm not human?" Tannin frowned. "I'm a...a...?"

"Hybrid, I presume, is the word you're looking for." "And you're like me too? What about Chuckles here?"

Tannin asked, jerking her head in Attilo's direction who still looked stony faced.

"Attilo is fully human," Ava replied and then paused. "You and I are similar but slightly different. The history is a little jumbled on the details."

"But we're both Remnants? Technically, I mean."

"It would appear so."

"Okay," she said slowly, "the point I'm stuck on is still what you want to do about it. You want to warn me about this Triquetra? Consider me warned."

"We want tae fight them! They're murderin' people!" Attilo's voice was full of unexpected passion.

"Why not go to the guards about it?"

Ava scoffed. "For one thing, they would think we were mad and for another the Triquetra seems to be a part of every level of law enforcement, government... even local councils."

"Sounds like a hopeless fight to me. Everyone in that book died 'cause of it." Tannin tapped the book she'd borrowed.

"It's not hopeless," Attilo stated firmly.

In response to Tannin's raised eyebrows he continued almost reluctantly.

"Before I got to be Princess Avalyn's personal guard, I had tae dae the trainin' again. There was this lad that shot up through the ranks.

He had this talent to know when someone was lyin', and there was no one quicker on their feet. You couldnae get the drop on him if you tried. Now, I'd been in the army. I knew Remnants were the real deal, I've seen some things." He paused and shook his head as if shooing away memories to keep on track with his story. "Anyway, I kinda thought this lad had that kinda feel tae him. First couple of times he's out, he's bringing in criminals left, right and centre, and then one night he's just gone. News came back after a few days that he'd fallen in one of them big grain containers. Suffocated under it all. Crushed."

Attilo's face screwed up in a frown. "Now, I never saw that lad even stumble. No way he'd fall in one of them things. And there was no reason for him tae even be up there and no explanation ever came. No one even looked intae it. I asked around a wee bit, and the more I asked the more I felt someone following me. So, I left it."

"Grains..." Something stirred in Tannin's memory. "Was his name Morellis?"

Attilo stared. "Aye."

"I've got to go. I'll be back though" Tannin leapt to her feet. "Thanks for the tea. Tomorrow?"

She didn't wait for an answer as she rushed out into the cool evening.

Tannin's mind was racing as she ran home.

She arrived breathless and ignored Mrs O'Baird's usual small talk as she rushed to her room and bolted the door. Her grandfather's old books had partially fallen apart from water damage and also just indelicate handling. Loose pages scattered across the bed, and she scoured them looking for the name Morellis. Eventually, she found it and sat down on the floor to read it properly.

"I think I've found another. The problem is he's in the Guard and talking to him alone is going to be difficult. I got his name from Carter – Morellis."

"I've been watching the Guard, and I think Carter is right. I saw him chase down a man outside the glassblower's, and it was like he was running on air. I've got to get to him before they do."

"He replied to my message. I've arranged ameeting with Morellis for tomorrow night."

"Morellis is dead. I saw it this time. I don't know who they were, but they threw that poor lad's body in the grain silo. I now know for certain that my poor Laurel's death was no accident. It was Them."

Chapter Twenty

Breaking Bread

Tannin pulled the hood of her cloak up against the relentless misty rain. She could already feel the damp seeping in through her clothes. She hated this type of weather.

Just rain properly and be done with it.

This was a dishonest type of rain. Enough to soak you through – and from all directions – but without the decency to make any nice pitter patter sounds on the roof or to wash the muck from the streets. She hoped the journal in her satchel stayed dry at least.

She'd only made it a few streets from her house when she paused. She should really bring something. It was tradition – not to mention polite – to bring a gift to someone's house and she couldn't just show up empty-handed.

She gave herself a mental shake. What was she thinking? This was a secret gathering in an underground crypt not a damn tea party. But then again, if this was all true and she was entering an alliance, she should take something anyway. If they accepted an offering from her, and she from them, then the rules were that they couldn't do each other harm. The ancient rules of hospitality.

Decision made, she picked up her pace a little but couldn't help rooting around in her pocket to see what money she had on her. Her fingers traced the thin discs. Coppers. She had almost nothing to her name right now. She bit her lip. Technically, Fletcher's still owed her a week's pay...

The grumbling of her stomach decided for her, and she changed direction. Her agreement with Mrs O'Baird included an evening meal, but with no money Tannin hadn't eaten anything else all day. The familiar sight of Fletcher's bakery came into view as she rounded the corner.

"Old habits die hard," Tannin muttered as she slipped around the back.

It had been a cold winter five years previously when she'd last slunk into Fletcher's to steal their bread. Her grandfather had been away somewhere on what he called "business", but he hadn't come back when he said he would. Tannin, hungry and coinless, had found the bakery door open and with the warm sweet air pouring out she'd been helpless to resist. Eve had found her hunched over the table stuffing still warm bread into her mouth by the handful and instead of calling the guards or even just throwing her out, she'd made Tannin some hot tea with honey and let her eat her way through almost a whole loaf in exchange for sweeping up the floors and cleaning some dishes. By the time her grandfather finally did turn up a good week later, Tannin had been officially employed as Eve's assistant.

Sorry, Eve.

Rain fogged the kitchen windows. Tannin couldn't make out any movement within. The light was on, so Eve or one of the owners was around somewhere. She had to be quick. She eased open the door and peeked in. A rush of warmth and the scent of hot, buttery bread blew in her face. Her mouth involuntarily watered. A row of dark loaves sat cooling on racks on the big table a couple of steps away.

They would, of course, know that one was missing but they'd never know for sure it was her. Tannin's forehead wrinkled up as she frowned. Eve would know it was her in a second.

But it didn't matter. She was sure she'd burnt her last bridge with her anyway, Tannin thought as she stole quickly into the kitchen, dripping water everywhere to grab the still warm loaf. She tucked it in beside her grandfather's journal, checking carefully that the pages weren't wet, and left as quickly and silently as she'd come.

The rest of the walk to the necropolis was miserable. The wind dragged Tannin's hood down every time she pulled it up. Eventually she gave up and left it down, the drizzle settling in her hair like dew and occasionally dripping down her neck, making her shiver. Cracks in the leather of her worn-out shoes let the rainwater in and her feet were numb and cold by the time she climbed up the slick grassy side of the necropolis. When she reached the hidden trapdoor, it wouldn't budge so she stomped on it three times like a knock. The wind whistled through the gravestones. She stomped again.

"Open. Up. Arseholes!" She grunted. "I'm freezin' out here!"

A scraping sound rose over the howl of the wind and the trapdoor jutted open. She lifted it up and slid into the gloomy cavern, squelching loudly.

"Finally!"

"The whole point o' a secret meetin' place is that it's a bloody secret," Attilo growled as soon as Tannin reached the bottom of the stairs. "Which means, no yellin' yer head off at the door."

Tannin shook water off her cloak as she shrugged out of it.

"Well, let me in quicker then."

"Were ye followed?"

Tannin hesitated. "I don't think so."

"Were you?"

"I dunno, I didn't check."

Attilo gave Ava a meaningful look. "This is what I was talkin' about."

"I'm new to this, remember." Tannin reminded him.

He grumbled something she couldn't make out as she rubbed her hands together and blew on them to warm them up.

"Tea?" Ava nodded to the canister on the table.

"Oh please, aye," Tannin said gratefully, helping herself to a steaming cup. She held it in both hands and let the heat and sweetness warm her.

"Uh." She reached for her bag. "This is for you."

She offered the loaf. The rain had gotten to it and the top edge was a little soggy.

She awkwardly held it out, a little unsure of the proper etiquette. "It's not much, but I couldn't come with nothin' if we're going to work together so, uh, here."

She trailed off as Ava accepted the loaf. "Thank you," she replied graciously if a little amusedly, a smile hiding behind her serious face.

"Wait." Attilo stormed over, snatched the bread out of her hand and started squishing in the sides, cracking the crust and sending crumbs crumbling all over the table.

"Hey!" Tannin protested. "What are you doin'?"

Ava sighed. "He's checking it for weapons. You can never be too careful."

"He's ruinin' it is what he's doin'! The crust is the best part!"

Attilo, seemingly satisfied with his squishings, tore off a corner and sniffed it. He licked it suspiciously. He then held the rest of the bread out to Tannin obviously meaning her to eat some to check for poisons. She rolled her eyes as she tore herself off a chunk and stuffed it in her mouth. It was still a little warm and it practically melted in her mouth. Slightly sweet from the dark molasses and dense with a crunchy crust. It was no wonder Fletcher's was so damn popular.

She spread her hands wide. "Satisfied?"

He grunted in affirmation and took a small bite. She watched his face for a reaction and saw an eyebrow twitch.

"It's good, right?"

Another grunt and another bite.

He nodded grudgingly, placing the loaf down in the middle of the table.

"Well," Ava said a while later, brushing crumbs from her lap, "now that we've broken bread together, we can get started properly."

"Okay, where do we start?"

"Here." Ava dropped a tome onto the sarcophagus-table causing dust to puff up from either side.

"Yay, more books," Tannin said sarcastically.

"Knowledge is the most important thing for what we're doing."

"I get that, but can't we do somethin' a bit more... I dunno. Just a bit less... dusty?"

"Books are where we start," Ava said with a tone of finality.

Tannin rolled her eyes behind her back and turned her attention to the cabinet that she'd noticed previously standing in a shadowy alcove behind the sarcophagus. Its shelves were filled with odd contraptions, bottles and jars along with countless old books. Tannin recognised the broken and bent brass form that once held Ava's sightlens.

"Ooh. What's this?" Tannin asked, picking up a soft velvety pouch with silver stitching. It rattled when she shook it. She tipped the contents out into her hand and inspected the strange symbols carved into smooth black stones. "What are these for?"

"Put that down."

"Aye okay, I'm just lookin'," Tannin said, dumping it back on the shelf. "Hey, when do I get a sword?" she asked crouching to examine the rack of dulled weaponry.

"Never. Those are for training."

"What's the point of trainin' to then not have a sword?" She picked one up out of its stand and hefted it in both hands. She'd never held an actual sword before. She would have usually had her small knife on her for protection, but Ava's goon had stolen it. This, however, was a beast of a blade.

"Put that down."

"In a minute." Tannin grinned and swung the sword around loosely. "ZZzzzschooom! Zzzzschoom. KKrrshh. Krrrrrshhh!"

"Attilo, I think we need to get some of the materials from my brother's nursery so Tannin can start learning at an appropriate level for her maturity," Ava snapped irritably. "I said put it down!"

"Oh, good idea," Tannin replied mockingly, returning the sword to its place. "Hey, Attilo, do you think we could get some more candles down here too so the princess can lighten the fuck up?"

Attilo's snort turned into a cough as he choked on a mouthful of bread. Ava glared at him. He shrugged an apology, eyes watering. Once he'd verified it wasn't poisoned or hiding secret blades in the crust, he'd half devoured the thing.

"Or maybe we can just put all the shiny things up on the higher shelves out of reach," Ava said, glancing at Tannin.

"Oh, ha ha. Very funny, princess." Tannin rolled her eyes. "Way to take the moral high ground."

Ava took a deep breath and closed her eyes. "Will you please just pay attention for a few minutes?"

"Well, since you said please."

Tannin returned to the table and rested her elbows on the hard surface, looking at Ava expectantly.

"Thank you. So, if you don't want to start with some actual work – you ran out of here last night because of the name Morellis. Why?"

"Oh aye." Tannin grabbed her bag and drew out the damp journal with its loose pages stuffed roughly back in the cover. "I read it in this. It was my grandad's. He knew Morellis or knew of him I think."

She flipped it open to the right page and slid it across the table for Ava and Attilo to look at. Ava wrinkled her nose at the soggy, dog-eared parchment. They read in silence for a few moments before Attilo nodded solemnly.

"Aye, that's him. Poor bastard."

"Your grandfather was investigating Remnants?" Ava asked sharply, shuffling through the pages.

"I know as much as you. I've only got that to go on." Tannin nodded to the notebook. "I didn't even know about this Laurel woman and apparently they had a whole thing goin' on."

"Very observant," Ava muttered with raised eyebrows.

"Right, listen –"

"Enough," Attilo said. "There's people here that we've come across in our research and some we've not. It's good information."

"Except every person mentioned here is dead," Ava muttered.

"If you're insinuatin' somethin' just come out and say it. By all logic, my grandad would have been a Remnant himself if I am, right?"

"Not necessarily and no one is insinuatin' anythin'." Attilo sounded tired with the pair of them already. "Is there anythin' else useful here?"

"I don't know. There's a few more notebooks worth."

"Next time bring them all here and we can compare."

"Okay." Tannin agreed. "What about this thing? This symbol. Is that for the Triquetra you think?"

Tannin pointed to the chaotic swirls inked over the pages and filling the margins. Upon closer inspection, it looked like each one was a solid line without an end in a vaguely triangular shape.

"Could be." Attilo tilted the page to look at it closer.

"Let me see." Ava nudged Tannin aside to grab a page. "Yes, three points, see. Triquetra means three. I've been thinking it could refer to Wielders, Inherents and humans but there's no way to be sure."

They mused some more on possible theories before Ava dived back into her books again.

Chapter Twenty One

Practice Makes Perfect

"Alright. Show me what you've got."

Tannin gripped her wooden practice sword, her face set in a grim line. Every time they'd tried sparring up until now, Ava had knocked her on her arse, but she was determined to get her this time. She adopted the wide-footed stance she'd been shown and adjusted the plated vest slightly. The added bulk was uncomfortable and restricted her movements a little, but even a wooden sword swung with force could do damage so they both wore thick leather vests with wooden plating and helmets.

Tannin watched Ava carefully as they circled each other around the training ring. Ava was the taller of the two and certainly the more practiced at this kind of thing, but Tannin was willing to bet she was faster. Maybe she'd challenge her to a race next time and finally win something.

Attilo had begrudgingly accepted training Tannin in self- defence after she'd pestered him. He seemed to be more tutor than bodyguard down here in the crypt and clearly had considerable skill.

When he was out of earshot one day, Ava had told her, almost boastingly, that although he may have been older, he was no less capable than anyone else she'd seen when she watched the guards training in the castle courtyard. Even in his fifties, Attilo put most of the younger men to shame. He always said experience and practice outweighed strength and youth every time. The slight limp that emerged on colder days was one of the many injuries he sported that whispered of his experience in the field, including that scar that split his lip and curved round his chin.

He watched from the side lines as they faced off, offering Tannin pointers on how to hold the sword and on where to put her feet.

"Her left side is weaker, aim yer strikes careful like," he called.

"Stop playing favourites, Attilo." Ava grunted, jabbing at Tannin with her wooden sword.

"Jealous cause he likes me more now?" Tannin's dodge was clumsy, but she still grinned as she taunted the other girl.

"Well, if you keep feeding him of course you're going to be the favourite!" The swords whacked together as Ava effectively blocked Tannin's attempt at a retaliation.

"Pay attention!" Attilo barked, spraying crumbs from the pale, nutty-tasting loaf Tannin had stolen that day. She wondered what he'd say if he knew she wasn't paying for his snacks.

Tannin's mind snapped back to the fight at hand just as Ava made a sneaky low swipe at her knees. She yelped and twisted away, avoiding the blow but barely, her feet sliding on the smooth stone floor. Cheap shot.

"Nicely done, Ava!" Attilo called.

Ava's smug grin irked her. She clearly revelled in Attilo's praise. Tannin seized the opportunity. Knocking Ava's weapon to the side with her own, she leapt forward ramming her shoulder into Ava's chest like a true Skirter brawler and she went down hard. It wasn't skilful or classy, but it worked. Ava landed on the floor with a grunt as Tannin kicked her sword away and straddled her. She tapped the tip of her sword against Ava's armoured vest.

"And you're dead. I am the champion!" She raised her other hand in mock celebration. "Now yield!"

"Never." Ava grinned back.

"No?" Tannin said, eyebrows raised, resting her sword under Ava's chin.

"I will never yield."

Tannin scowled. She was supposed to yield. Those were the rules of the challenge. If either one of them lost their weapon irretrievably or was knocked down, they had to yield the competition to the other. Tannin had already swallowed her pride and yielded multiple times and had to deal with Ava's gloating smugness every time. There was no way she'd let her get away with not giving in when she had her dead to rights.

"Attilo," Tannin whined. "She's not yield- ooft!"

As soon as Tannin had taken her eyes off her, Ava had pushed her sword away with one hand and given her a hard shove to the side with the other. In a split second, she was on top of her and had Tannin pinned to the ground flat on her stomach.

"Hey! That's not fair!" she complained, trying to reach for her fallen sword that was just within arm's reach.

"Life's not fair," Ava replied smugly, casually grabbing Tannin's wrist and pulling her hand away from the weapon to pin it uncomfortably behind her back. "Yield."

"Absolutely not. Fuck you!" Tannin wriggled under Ava's weight but couldn't shift her or break her grip. "Get off me!"

"You lost your focus. Just because you have the upper hand doesn't mean you can get complacent," Ava said matter-of- factly.

"If that was a real sword, you would have cut yourself to pieces on it. Cheater!"

"That's also where you went wrong. We're not aiming to kill or hurt anyone. Just defend and disarm. We've got to be better than they are." Ava spoke chidingly and Tannin fought a little harder.

"You're hurtin' me right now, arsehole." She grunted.

"Ladies. Enough. Let's take a break."

Tannin could only glare at the floor furiously until Ava finally relented and let her up with a wink. "I win," she mouthed when Attilo turned away.

Tannin called her some more impolite names under her breath as she unstrapped her helmet and brushed dust off her vest. She was still taking that as a victory no matter what Ava said. She glared at her as she turned and walked away.

Goddamn cheat.

Her eyes drifted. Gods, Ava's breeches were *tight.* She tore her gaze away hastily and took a swig of water.

Oh no. Bad thoughts.

"How're you gettin' on with practicin' yer Changing?" Attilo asked as Tannin stomped over to the rug to sit down.

"No joy."

"Keep trying. There's some things here on meditation…" Ava launched into yet another explanation of the body's connection to the mind and the soul, but Tannin was feeling sulky and zoned out.

She'd been trying without success to connect with whatever remnants of power might lurk in her blood but, so far, she had nothing to show for it. If it weren't for the recurring nightmares and the stolen coat that was still shoved under her bed, she would have said she'd imagined the whole thing.

And she had other, more pressing problems. Stealing the occasional loaf of bread wasn't her only money issue. Without her job, her meagre savings weren't going to pay rent this month. She'd sated Mrs O'Baird for now by doing more odd jobs around the house, but her good humour wouldn't last forever and Clach's next payment was looming in the not-so-distant future.

"Hey, princess?"

Ava looked at her in surprise, mouth still open forming the words of a sentence Tannin hadn't heard. "You're not listening to me at all are you?"

"Not in the slightest," Tannin replied. "Also, I can't help but notice you still haven't paid me."

Ava exchanged a glance with Attilo. "About that..." "I knew it. Unbelievable. No wonder you cheat."

"I do not cheat," Ava insisted. "And I am going to pay you. Just not in coin."

"Excuse me?"

"Here." Ava threw something in her direction. Tannin had to stretch to catch it, but it still fell short.

"Nice throw," she muttered drily. "What's this then?"

She picked up the shiny thing from the floor and looked at it. It appeared to be some sort of pendant, and it was heavy with gold.

"Is this a charm or somethin'?" she asked, holding it up so that the light from the lantern made the edges of it sparkle.

"It's your pay. I hardly have any need for physical money so getting a hold of some isn't as easy as you may think. Trinkets like that, however, I have plenty. I'm sure you'll find somewhere to sell it."

Tannin groaned. More legwork. At least this looked like it was indeed worth some money. Which was good, she thought, because she definitely needed it.

Chapter Twenty Two

The Gold that Glitters

"Hey, stranger." Flint grinned widely from underneath a wide brimmed hat. "What's the craic?"

"Long time no see." Tannin bounded up to him to wrap her arms around his neck, and he responded with an even tighter embrace that lifted her feet off the ground as he spun her around. "Two weeks, huh? Liar. How was Tayfort?"

"Tayfort was... profitable." He grinned. "Did you bring me a present?"

"Of course not."

"Mean," Tanning said with mock offense and punching him lightly on the arm. "Nice hat, scarecrow."

"Magnificent, isn't it?" he said eyeing it fondly. "What've you been up to these days? Heard you got kicked from Fletcher's."

"You know. Keepin' busy. And I didn't get kicked... it was mutual."

"Whatever you have to tell yourself, Tan," he said airily. "And your mystery friend? I'm glad you're not dead by the way."

"Why, thank you. And yeah, surprisingly mystery friend is actually a friend." Tannin shrugged. "Could also be a profitable venture."

They strolled together through the markets just inside the city walls, eating the hot, smoky flavoured roastnuts and chatting idly. Tannin couldn't help shooting glances at every stranger they passed, wondering if they could be Remnants. Was that muscly man a balor-blood or was he just buff? Was that apothecary something more than just medicine? Was there a druid-blood at work there?

"So, what is it you asked me here for?" Flint said, flicking a roastnut shell into the gutter.

"Who says I didn't want to just see you after all your time away?"

"Your face says so, so spill it."

Tannin crunched a nut between her teeth to open its shell before answering.

"I need to sell some gold. I want to talk to your contact."

"What, Barrel?" Flint shook his head. "Nah, Tan. Just go to a pawn shop or something. Barrel is bad news."

"I need someone who won't ask questions."

"Stolen?" His tone was light, but a crease appeared in between his eyebrows.

"Not stolen, no," Tannin said carefully. "But questionable."

"Let me see it."

They both cast furtive glances around the street, but in the hustle and bustle they may as well have been invisible. Tannin slipped the pendant that Ava gave her from an inner pocket and then held it out for Flint to inspect.

He whistled. "That's a pretty piece," he said and then frowned. "You sure about this? You know why he's called Billy Barrel right? Some eejit sold him fakes for a ton of coin and when Barrel found out, he had him nailed into a barrel with a rabid dog and thrown in the river."

Tannin flashed him a skeptical look. "That seems extreme. And also untrue."

"I'm telling you if you meet this bloke, you'll believe it."

"How come you do business with him then if you're so feart?"

"Because he doesn't ask questions."

"Exactly."

It only took a little more wheedling until an hour or so later they arrived in a back street that Tannin had never been to before. The shop fronts looked empty and lifeless. Flint led her to one of them where the once red paint was peeling off and worn lettering above the window spelled out "Cosy Collectables".

Tannin raised an eyebrow. "Cosy Collectables?"

"Yep. Come on." A bell's tinkling echoed through the shop as Flint pushed the door open.

The shop itself was cluttered and dingy with broken furniture piled against the walls where the wallpaper was peeling as much as the paint on the outside of the shop. Glass fronted cabinets displayed dusty baubles and trinkets and half a dozen lopsided chandeliers hung from the yellowish smoke-stained ceiling. At an antique desk in the back, a newspaper rustled and pipe smoke billowed.

"Help ye?" A gravelly voice came from behind the paper.

"Afternoon, Billy," Flint chirped.

"Aw it's you." The voice sounded disappointed. "What shite am I buyin' today?"

The newspaper crinkled loudly as it was folded and set aside, revealing a grey-faced man with a scraggly yellow-grey mane falling from beneath a rounded hat. Puffs of thick, greasy smoke slid from his slack mouth and the end of his long black pipe. His watery eyes narrowed as he saw Tannin.

"What's this, lad? I dinnae like new faces."

"She's a mate," Flint said with confidence, leaning on one of the precarious furniture piles. "And she's got something to sell that I think might be of interest to you.

Tannin felt like those watery old eyes could see through to her very bones as they scanned her up and down.

"What ye got for me then?" He growled.

Flint gave her an encouraging nod to which she set the gold pendant on the desk.

Billy grabbed it with the quickness of a much younger man and scrutinized it with a magnifying glass. He hmm'd over it for a few minutes before setting it down with an air of finality.

"Two hundred," he said.

Tannin knew enough about these kinds of things to know that it was probably worth a lot more than that. She'd expected that he would give a low offer first and see how much of a fool she was. She opened her mouth to start haggling when Flint interrupted her.

"Excellent! We'll take it."

As Barrel turned to creak open a rusty and ancient-looking money box, Tannin rounded on Flint.

"What the hell? That's too low," she hissed. "I was gonna haggle."

"You don't haggle with Barrel," Flint whispered, his mouth barely moving.

"That's right." They both jumped. Apparently, he had excellent hearing. "And you, lass, are lucky I'm takin' this at all. Royal stamp on there and all."

Barrel had managed to come around to the front of the desk without them hearing. His bulky frame towered over Tannin. Even Flint, who was tall and gangly, seemed to shrink down with his proximity.

"There's more where that came from. If you give me a better price for it." Tannin stared solidly up at him with crossed arms.

A few tense seconds passed before Barrel released a deep belly laugh. "Tell you what, lass, I'll give ye another ten for having the balls. But don't dare be askin' again."

"Done." They shook on it.

Flint and Tannin left the shop in silence. Tannin's pockets were heavy with coin and she was thinking fondly of a hot lunch when Flint suddenly rounded on her, stopping her in her tracks.

"Royal stamp? What was he talking about, Tan? What've you got yourself into?" he asked urgently.

"Nothin' I can't handle." Tannin tried to brush him off, but he wasn't letting it go so easily.

"Tannin." He grabbed her arm to stop her walking away from him. "These people are dangerous. Barrel is dangerous. You're not taking this seriously. And dealing in royal stamped goods? That's just asking for trouble. Do you know the penalty for that?"

His tone was a long way from his usual joviality.

Tannin pulled her arm back, annoyed. "I said I'm handlin' it."

"Oh really? It doesn't look like you're handling it to me. It looks like you're drowning." The crease between his eyebrows had reappeared and his voice softened. "You had a good thing at Fletcher's. What the hell are you doing in shitty places like this?"

"Fletcher's just didn't work out. I told you. And I'm doing fine," she insisted.

"I know you haven't been paying your rent, Tan."

Tannin blinked. So now he was checking up on her behind her back?

"Oh really?" she said, anger seeping into her voice. "And how would you know that?"

"Tan, I'm worried about you!"

"Well, don't be! I don't need you babying me. I've got this." "I'm just trying to help."

"I didn't ask for your help."

"Fine."

"Fine."

They walked back to the bustling market without another word.

"See you around, Tan," Flint said stiffly when they reached the next crossroads and took off without a second glance.

She almost called him back to apologise but stopped. She didn't need bloody parenting. And who was he to lecture her on what she chose to do with her time when more than half the things he owned were stolen and the other half was bought with dirty money?

Tannin left the market and all thoughts of Flint along with it, the heavy coins burning a hole in her pocket. It had been a long time since she had money to actually buy things for herself, and she wasn't sure where to start. Her shoes were worn through the soles and she would need a warm cloak for the coming winter.

Tannin chewed the inside of her cheek. In the bakery, it hadn't mattered that her breeches had holes in the knees or were frayed at the bottom but now she couldn't help but compare herself to Ava, who was always perfectly put together even if it was in her simple training outfits. Apart from the grey dress from Fletcher's for the disastrous commission at the castle, Tannin hadn't had new clothes in years.

It was a simple decision in the end really. She needed new everything.

As she was heading home for the evening, the sweet smell of roasting meat stopped her in her tracks. It was a bit extravagant but with the coins jangling in her pocket, Tannin let herself be a little reckless. It would be a nice change from their usual cheap scraps.

The hog leg was hot through its wrapping, and the sweet honey dripping from it was already soaking through the paper. Her hands were sticky with it by the time she got home.

"What's this?" Mrs O'Baird asked suspiciously as Tannin entered the kitchen with her fragrant offering.

"A present for you," Tannin said, laying it down on the table. "To say thanks for bein' lenient with rent this month. And for bein' the best landlady ever." She fluttered her eyelashes.

"Hmph. Flattery is it? And I've not been that lenient. I've been tryin' tae chase ye down for days, ye wee besom! I dinnae run a charity here, ye ken!"

"I have it here." She scattered a handful of gold coins on to the table. "For last month and this month," she added a little smugly.

"Mhm." Mrs O'Baird snatched up the coins and secreted them away in the folds of her apron. She sniffed suspiciously at the meat and couldn't help but smile as she opened it. Tannin had remembered her fondness for pork.

"You're welcome," Tannin called on her way out in a sing song voice.

"Oi! Dinnae think this means ye can be late all the time!" she called after her.

That night, generous slices of honeyed hog as well as roasted vegetables and rich gravy made their dinner into a feast. The food lightened the moods of even the dourest of the tenants as they all sat together for the first time in the dining room. Mrs O'Baird had cheerfully roused them all for dinner with the clanging of a bell. Tannin suspected she had already been at the wine as she was unusually animated when she bid them all take a place at the table.

Tannin had seen the other tenants, of course, but she had had no great desire to speak to any of them. She heard enough of them through the thin walls to last a lifetime.

Mr MacTavish was separated from his wife and cried through the night, Mr Lynch was a travelling salesman and would corner anyone he could find to talk about walking sticks, and Tannin was pretty sure that Mrs Hewat had a different man home with her every night of the week. She wondered how she bribed Mrs O'Baird to allow such things in her respectable house.

After they had eaten, Mrs O'Baird cracked open a bottle of whisky and splashed out a generous measure for each of them.

Mr MacTavish, it turned out, was a keen lute player although he never practiced in the house. He said he'd had neighbours complain before but when he started to play, they all agreed that there was nothing to complain about. It was only when he started to sing along with his strumming that they began to understand the source of the complaints as he screeched in a thin reedy voice that seemed to only hit the right note by accident. Luckily though, he was more than happy to just strum a tune as they settled into conversation by the fireside. Tannin didn't even mind Mr Lynch's usual spiel about walking sticks so much now that her belly was full and her mouth was pleasantly tingling from the whisky.

They retired sometime in the early hours when Mrs O'Baird had started snoring in her armchair and they unanimously decided to call it a night. As Tannin fell into bed, she felt warm and heavy with a kind of contentment she hadn't felt in a long time.

Chapter Twenty Three

Making Friends

"Well, don't you look sharp," Ava said as Tannin descended into the crypt in her new outfit. She wore her crisp new shirt, that she'd actually pressed for once, under a soft brown jerkin. Her breeches had no holes, and her new boots hugged her calves in black leather. She'd even spent extra time pinning up her hair in a much neater knot than usual.

"See?" Tannin replied while giving a playful twirl, her thick black cloak flapping around her. "It works wonders when you actually pay people. Speakin' of, that royal stamp on that thing cost me at least half its value."

"You got paid, why you complainin'?" Attilo grunted, cracking his knuckles with an audible crunching sound.

Crack.

"Can you not?" Tannin said with a disapproving wince. "And I'm not complainin', just makin' a point. Nothing else to do around here anyway."

Ava and Attilo shared a look and then quickly dropped it.

"Oi, oi," Tannin said accusingly. "What was that look?"

"There was no look."

"There was definitely a look. What are you two up to? Why so secretive?"

"There's another Remnant we've been tryin' to recruit."

Crack.

"And you didn't want to tell me because...?"

"He's ignoring us so we're going to pay him a little visit. And it is a tactful operation," Ava said pointedly.

"Okay. So?"

"Yer not tactful," Attilo said bluntly. Crack.

"Rude. I can be tactful. Did you send him those creepy 'we know what you are' letters? 'Cause, if so, I can definitely see why he isn't respondin'."

"You did."

Tannin shrugged. "It was touch and go. And honestly if you'd mentioned money first, it would've gone a lot better."

"Ye were alone, desperate and already in trouble. An easy mark," Attilo stated simply. Tannin opened her mouth to object, but he continued talking. "He's a bloody Laird. A minor one but still."

"Woah, back up," Tannin said, frowning. "What d'you mean 'mark'?"

"Nothing," Ava said, shooting Attilo a look.

"A mark is someone you con. What –" Tannin narrowed her eyes as it dawned on her. "There was never a Seer, was there?"

"Oh." Attilo's brow furrowed with discomfort over his mistake. "Shite."

"Ava?" Tannin demanded.

She sighed and closed her eyes for a second before answering, sharply. "No, of course there wasn't. A Seer would have Seen me if there was one at the castle and you know already that my Remnant status is a secret."

Tannin gaped.

"Then why the hell did you say there was?" She couldn't stop herself from raising her voice. "I lost my job 'cause of that!"

Ava crossed her arms and stared resolutely back. "You wouldn't have believed us if we had just told you what was going on. You needed to see. Of course, I could have just offered you money but then you'd be in it for the coin and not because you're invested in it."

"I... you..." Tannin spluttered over the start of several sentences before spitting out, "Eve hates me now!"

"I didn't intend that."

Tannin ran her hands through her hair, messing up her neat knot in the process, and paced. "You deliberately cut me off so that I would have no choice but to come here!"

"No," Ava said firmly. "I didn't intend for you to lose your job."

"I told you I would!"

"I thought you were exaggerating." "You are unbelievable!"

"Well, what's done is done." Ava waved a hand dismissively.

"It is not!"

Ava raised an eyebrow at her. "Then what do you propose? If you want to leave, go ahead. If you want to stay, continue to get paid more than you did at the bakery and actually do something worthwhile then calm yourself and lower your voice."

"You... I..." She couldn't leave. She needed them now and Ava knew it. "URGHH!"

"We're settled then? Good, because I'd like to continue with the plan for tonight without further distractions."

"I hate you so much."

Ava merely rolled her eyes.

"Our Remnant, Laird Campbell, I think is a selkie-blood. The plan is to get into his estate where he's hosting a soiree and talk to him directly," Ava said, rolling out a map of the city. "The Triquetra target any Remnants with political power, so a Laird will be high on their list regardless of if he actually brings attention to himself or not."

"What the hell's a soiree?" Tannin asked sulkily.

"A party."

"Then say party. Honestly, what is wrong with you people?"

CRACK.

"Attilo!" Ava and Tannin barked at once.

"That was the last knuckle," he said defensively.

Ava didn't take long to explain the plan. It wasn't uncommon for wealthy families to send representatives to social events when they were too busy or simply had no interest in attending themselves. It was a good way to maintain contacts and appear social without having to do any of the hard work.

Attilo was going to pose as the nephew of one of the invited barons as his representative. They'd managed to intercept the baron's invitation before it had even left the city. Ava seemed especially proud, and she spoke quickly and fervently about what essentially boiled down to plain old bribery and an underpaid postman. Tannin was solidly unimpressed, feigning mocking amazement when Ava produced the invitation with a flourish.

Ava herself would sneak into the house via the tunnels and disguise herself to blend in with the staff. Attilo explained that most of the old families had at least one smuggler's tunnel running under their properties from hundreds of years ago. Few people knew they still existed.

"And you think no one will recognise you or notice that there's a new girl just swannin' about?"

"They're bringing in extra staff to cater since it's such a large event. No one will notice one extra new face," Ava said primly.

"Okay, so that's how you get in. What about when you're there? Are you just gonna go up to the honourable Laird Campbell and say 'Hello, we broke into your house. Wanna be pals?'"

"That's none of your concern because you're not coming."

"Uh, why not?"

"We've got it covered."

Tannin grumbled and griped the rest of the day while they were training. She was still fuming over Ava's deception and couldn't focus on the stances Attilo was trying to teach. It culminated in Tannin chucking a shield at Ava's head after a takedown that she thought was far more violent than was necessary. Attilo confiscated it with a few sharp words on sportsmanship and declared training over for the day.

"I still want to come tonight."

No one answered her, and they continued to tidy up the training area, steadfastly ignoring her. They must've made an agreement to try and keep her out of the plan. *Sneaky weasels.*

"You know I'll follow you anyway." She crossed her arms.

Ava groaned. "Fine, Tannin. Fine. But you stay outside and far away from the house."

The night of the party came and Tannin sat grumbling in a tree in the grounds of the Laird's estate with her spyglass focused into the windows of the manor. Heavy rain the night before had left her vantage point wetter than she cared for. Dampness was seeping into the seat of her breeches, but she couldn't abandon her spot.

She'd been there for what felt like hours already, and she was thoroughly bored. Soon the guests would be arriving in their fancy carriages.

Until then, her only entertainment was the servants bustling about through all four floors of the house.

Working your arse off for a party you don't even get to enjoy sounds shite. At least they have warm, dry arses though.

Ava should already be underneath the house in that seemingly never-ending maze of smugglers' tunnels. Probably how rich folk kept themselves rich, Tannin thought.

Crooks the lot of them.

The arrival of the first carriages distracted Tannin from her worries for the later parts of the plan, which she still hadn't managed to squeeze out of either of them. These were no ordinary carriages. Large enough for six people to ride comfortably and pulled by two pairs of magnificent steeds, the first carriage was a shining black lacquer with golden inlay and golden wheel spokes. Tannin focused her spyglass on the doors as it pulled up and stopped at the entrance. Three figures gracefully alighted. Two men and a woman by the looks of it, dressed in fine silks and velvets.

More carriages arrived shortly after and the party began in earnest. Even from her perch, Tannin could faintly hear the music booming from the band in the main hall, and the vibrations were setting the leaves in her tree fluttering.

It seemed this Laird really had spared no expense. It was far more luxurious an affair than the party that had been going on during the sightlens job. Tannin wondered idly if there would ever be an occasion where she was actually invited to one of these things.

Probably not.

She scanned the windows for Ava or Attilo. They should be out and about by now. She shifted uncomfortably. Her stomach was growling, and seeing the platters of delicacies piled high wasn't helping.

Aha, there you are. She spotted Attilo at one of the upstairs windows and clicked the spyglass a notch further to focus in. He wore the same dark blue doublet he'd worn before. She reasoned that Ava probably wasn't far away and sure enough found her a few windows over carrying a tray laden with goblets of wine. Tannin couldn't help a little smirk at Ava's catering uniform. She watched as they circled various rooms in tandem, seemingly invisible to the partygoers.

Abruptly, Ava's smooth circuit of the room stopped and she spun around. Through the lens, Tannin saw the purposefully relaxed way she exited the room that contrasted with the tension in her shoulders. As soon as she was within eyesight of Attilo, she paused and tugged sharply on her earlobe. A signal? Something was wrong.

Tannin bit her lip.

Should I stay here or go help?

She only had to mull it over for a few seconds. Stay in this damp tree bored out of her mind or get in on the action. Not a hard decision.

She slid down the branches and brushed bark and muck from her hands. She took one last look through the spyglass. Attilo was still visible at the upstairs window, but Ava had disappeared.

Tannin made her way into the tunnel that had brought her into the grounds of the Laird's estate, and a few twists and turns later she pushed up a drain cover slowly and winced as it grated along the stone floor of the cellar.

"Who's there?" a sharp voice came from above.

"Me, eejit. Who else?"

"Tannin, what are you doing here? You're supposed to be outside!"

"Uh huh. Sittin' and watchin' with no way of even lettin' you know if I see anythin'. Very valuable use of my time. What happened anyway? I saw you give a signal. Fucked up, didn't you?"

"No, I did not... mess up. It was one of the guests. He's the son of one of the other Barons and he has... expressed an interest in me before. He'd recognise me in an instant."

"If only someone had mentioned the probability of you gettin' recognised before," Tannin said sarcastically, stroking an imaginary beard as if in deep contemplation.

"Quiet." Ava sighed and leaned heavily on a shelf full of boxes, pinching the bridge of her nose. "Tonight's not going to work. We'll come up with a new plan."

"The plan's not a bust yet, that's why I'm here. I am the cavalry." Tannin spread her arms wide with theatrical flair.

Ava simply blinked at her. Tannin dropped her arms with a sigh.

"Give me your uniform, and I'll go up and be you," Tannin said slowly, spelling it out for her. "Did you even get any sleep last night?" Where before the poor light had hidden them, Tannin now clearly saw the dark circles under Ava's eyes. Not even the fancy powder she wore could conceal them fully.

"You have no idea what to even do up there. There are rules and etiquette and..." Ava shook her head. "Best go home."

"You're givin' up?"

"No, I'm re-strategising. You can't just charge in and hope for the best."

"I can if you give me your uniform."

Ava gave her a withering look. "No." "Fine. Plan's a bust then." Tannin huffed.

She was about to climb back down the ladder when a thought occurred to her that cheered her up immensely – an opportunity to wind up Ava. "Wait, this is a wine cellar, right?"

Ava nodded towards a door. "In there is the wine cellar, this is just storage why?"

Tannin grinned and waggled her eyebrows mischievously.

"No, Tannin, wait –"

But Tannin was already through the door and inspecting the rows and rows of bottles and casks.

"Damn, this place is huge!"

"You cannot steal from the man we are trying to recruit!"

"Oh, like he'll notice." Tannin said gesturing at the huge cellar which held enough wine to drown a small village. "There must be a thousand bottles here. He'll survive the hardship of nine hundred and ninety-nine."

"Tannin..." Ava groaned, following her in.

"Gimme a recommendation," Tannin said, moving along the rows and peering at labels that meant nothing to her. She'd been joking about taking one but the more she saw, the more tempted she actually was. This was good stuff. Even the cheapest bottle here would have probably been way out of her price range.

"I'm not participating in this." Ava crossed her arms.

Oh Ava, you make this almost too easy.

"Bore."

"I do not condone this," Ava hissed and turned on her heel in an attempt to storm off. "Do not break anything."

As she turned the handle of the cellar door, however, an abrupt crunching sound stopped her in her tracks.

"Don't break anythin' huh?" Tannin smirked.

"Be quiet. It's not broken." Ava pulled the handle, and it flew free sending her staggering backwards a few steps, the handle still clutched in her hand.

Tannin cackled as Ava tried frantically jamming the handle back into the hole in the door.

"It's not funny!"

"It is."

"The door won't open!"

"Awk aye it will," Tannin said, coming to help. "You've just got to get the edge and - oh."

The door was completely flush with the wall with no edge to use to pull it open. The hole that the handle came out of was no larger than a screw, and although the handle slid back in, there was no grip on it from inside and it flopped down sadly.

"Well," Tannin said, putting her hands on her hips, "fuck."

Chapter Twenty Four

The Best Laird Plans

"You sure you don't want some? It's pretty good."

"No, thank you," Ava said, her voice clipped. She had finally stopped her anxious pacing and slumped down onto the cold stone floor opposite Tannin.

"Suit yourself."

They sat there for a while, Ava brooding and Tannin drinking sweet red wine from a bottle she'd grabbed at random. Nothing else to do, she'd reasoned, and it was true that the Laird really wouldn't miss it. They'd have to wait until someone let them out anyway. Hopefully, it would be Attilo. She didn't want to have to explain to some servant what they were doing lurking about in the cellar.

"This is your fault, you know!" Ava hissed suddenly.

"Uh, no. It isn't. You're the one who broke the door."

"We wouldn't even be in here if you hadn't felt the pressing need to mess around."

"You're just mad your plan didn't work. That all your manipulative schemin' didn't pay off."

"No, I'm mad because I'm stuck in a cellar because of you!"

"Because you broke the door," Tannin said pointedly.

"Ughh just... Someone will come sooner or later." Ava pinched the bridge of her nose again.

"Fine by me."

Silence fell between them, with only the sound of wine sloshing in the bottle as Tannin occasionally took a sip.

"You know, this is why you weren't even supposed to come," Ava blurted. "You're too irresponsible. These things have to be carefully planned and instructions followed."

"And look how your perfect plan turned out without me doing anythin'." Tannin shot back.

"Well, you certainly didn't help."

"You weren't even going to give me that chance!"

"Can you blame me? Look at us now."

"Shh!" Tannin held up a hand and looked towards the door. She was sure she'd heard footsteps. The sound grew louder, and they both scrambled to their feet.

"What do we say?" Tannin whispered. "Leave it to me."

There was a scraping sound as the handle to the wine cellar turned from the outside. Tannin was conflicted about whether to try and talk their way out of this or just charge at the door when it opened. She still hadn't reached a decision when Ava grabbed her and pulled her close just as the door swung inwards.

Tannin barely had a split second to steady herself before Ava's mouth crashed into hers. Shock sparked through her whole body. Every thought rushed out of her brain and there were only warm lips on hers and Ava's hand cupping her cheek.

Ava broke away as quickly as she'd initiated and babbled something to the stunned servant in the doorway. Tannin couldn't quite process the words. Her lips were tingling. Ava giggled girlishly like a lass at her first Beltane festival and took Tannin's hand and pulled her out of the door past the gaping, flush-cheeked man who looked as dazed as Tannin felt. *Giggled.* She would never in a million years have thought Ava would giggle like that. It sounded so strange.

Ava dropped her hand as soon as they ducked back into the storage room when the man was out of sight.

"Right, let's go." Ava was back to being all business.

"Uh, excuse me?" Tannin shook the fuzz from her mind. "What the hell was that?"

"A distraction." Ava shrugged. "That worked, I might add."

"I'm sure there was another option."

"You're complaining?" Ava challenged with that smug smile creeping up the corners of her mouth.

"No! I mean yes!" Tannin floundered. "Oh, shut up."

Ava laughed as they climbed down into the tunnel and along the passage. "You should feel lucky. Not many people can say they've kissed a princess."

"You think you're out of my league, don't you?" Tannin said, clutching her heart dramatically. "I'm so offended."

"Oh, I am definitely out of your league, peasant. Where are you going?"

Tannin paused on the first rung of the ladder that led up to the streets above. "We've been underground all night. I need some fresh air."

Ava hesitated but followed Tannin up and out of the tunnel which surfaced beyond the outer wall of the Laird's estate. She seemed to be about to ask something but was interrupted when the silence of the cool night air was shattered by a blood-curdling scream.

Someone was dead, that much was clear. They crept through the gardens to see a finely dressed crowd bunched together around the front entrance to the manor. The nobles whispered anxiously to one another, their expressions drawn, as some of the ladies strategically jostled each other to aim their faintings in the direction of the most eligible bachelors.

"We need to get closer," Ava hissed. "If we get seen –"

"We won't."

Tannin didn't argue further. They skulked through the shadows to an archway decked in wilted honeysuckle where they could crouch unseen. The nobles were thinning out now. Someone had taken charge and was directing people back inside the house and away from the body. Crimson blotches were already blooming on the white sheet.

They waited, huddled together in the shrubbery, until only one man stood guard over the corpse.

"Distract him."

"What? How?" Tannin asked, taken aback.

Ava paused for a second. "Go over there, behind that bush. Count to ten and then shout for help."

"And then run away?"

"Exactly. Go, now."

Tannin dashed around to where Ava had indicated and, feeling immensely stupid, called out a shrill, "Help! Someone help!", in as affected an accent as she could, hoping to emulate a noble lady.

The man guarding the body reacted far quicker than she'd expected and dashed off to attend to the apparent damsel in distress. Tannin cursed quietly as she raced out of sight, back around the garden and to the front door and the body in front of it.

She rounded the last corner at speed and then leapt back, skittering on the gravel, to avoid her new boots being splattered with vomit.

Ava heaved once more, and Tannin swore.

"You alright?"

She shook her head weakly and spat. Tannin glanced over to where the blood-soaked sheet covered the body and took a step towards it.

"Don't." Ava panted but it was too late. Tannin stooped to jerk the sheet away from the face. From what had once been a face. Tannin recoiled.

The skull had been crushed so brutally that it was difficult to immediately tell what she was seeing. A thick line was squashed into the pulverized flesh so deep that Tannin could see the bloody gravel underneath. A wide, gaping mouth with the jaw angled alarmingly away from the rest of the head. A lone eyeball hung from a shattered eye socket.

Tannin felt bile rise up in her own throat. She quickly re- covered the corpse and joined Ava. She was leaning heavily on the wall, pale-faced.

"We have to get out of here."

Ava nodded numbly. A sheen of sweat glistened on her forehead and her queasy expression suggested another round of vomiting wasn't far off. She let Tannin ease her away from the house and back into the privacy of the shadowy gardens.

"It was him," Ava said quietly. She was shaking. "Who?"

"The... the body." Ava gestured back to the house. "It's Laird Campbell."

Chapter Twenty Five

Apolog-tea

It had been the wheel of one of the massive carriages that had crushed his skull. The spooked horses had been found, still snorting and stamping, in the grounds of the manor along with the blood-splattered carriage. The general consensus pointed to an unfortunate freak accident. Tannin, Ava and Attilo knew better. The murder had the Triquetra's stink all over it.

Infuriatingly, the guards had been quick to write it down as an accident too and there was no investigation to speak of. Any chance for the trio to investigate the death themselves was also a dead end since it had all been cleaned away disconcertingly quickly. Their only hope was to try and uncover details about the Triquetra and piece together the scraps.

Ava had purchased a whole wagon full of old texts, which they trawled through, painstakingly, for information on Remnants. By now, the crypt resembled a library much more than mausoleum, complete with a sturdy pinewood desk alongside the sarcophagus they used as a table.

"Tannin, fetch me the Atlas."

"Say please, arsehole," Tannin said automatically without giving her companion so much as a glance. Ava quite often forgot she wasn't a servant or someone she could boss around, and Tannin quite enjoyed reminding her, especially since she hadn't forgiven her for all that fake Seer business. Attilo was absent today, and when it was just the two of them, she could quite happily call the princess names without getting a telling off.

Ava sighed dramatically. "Please, Tannin, would you do me the great honour of fetching me the Atlas?"

"Much better. You know, for a princess you have terrible manners."

She was tempted to still tell Ava to get it herself, but she wanted to stretch her legs and take a break anyway so she sauntered over to one of the overstuffed bookcases and scanned the spines for the Atlas. She scowled when she spotted it on the second highest shelf and had to drag a stool over and stand on her tiptoes to get the heavy book down off the shelf.

"Not a word." She warned as she saw Ava watching her and smirking over the top of her book as Tannin hopped down off the stool.

"I wasn't going to say a thing," Ava replied lightly, still smirking.

"Mhm." Tannin dropped the book onto the desk in front of Ava and leaned over to peer at the text Ava had been scrutinising for the last hour. "So, what's so interestin' in there then?"

She flipped a couple of thin pages. Ava stuttered in protest.

"OHHHH." Tannin squealed gleefully spying the intricate drawing of entwined bodies on the previous page. "This is dirty!"

"Don't be childish," Ava hissed, colouring slightly. "This is research."

"Call it what you want, princess. I can see why you've been so absorbed over here."

"Oh, be quiet." She hastily lifted the Altas over to cover the drawing and flipped through the pages until a map of the five kingdoms was displayed before them.

"I liked the other picture better."

"Shush." Ava trailed her fingertip over the inked lines until she found what she was looking for and compared a cluster of lines showing river tributaries to a sketch she'd made on scrap parchment.

Tannin followed along over Ava's shoulder in semi-interest. The texts were, on the whole, mind-numbingly dull and whatever concentration she had was chased out of her head by a tantalisingly sweet scent. Ava's hair, she realised with a slight twinge of embarrassment. The candle on the table illuminated the coppery chestnut tones in the dark waves.

Gods, it smells good. Like fresh spring flowers... I bet it's really soft.

Ava turned her parchment scrap this way and that, trying to match it up with the map. When it didn't, she gave a muted grunt of frustration and screwed the sketch up into a ball angrily and tossed it to the floor.

"Now who's childish?"

Ava gave her one of her withering looks.

Tannin was about to say they were getting nowhere so she may as well go home when she stopped in her tracks. The crypt always smelled dusty and vaguely deathlike but there was something new. Something florally but not like Ava's soap. She sniffed.

"Why do I smell roses?"

Ava's eyebrows shot up. "I'm impressed."

"That I know what roses smell like?"

"That you can smell it at all from over there. That must be another one of your intrinsic Remnant abilities. I should write that down..." Ava rose to take a box from the shelf behind her and held it out to Tannin.

"What is it?" She turned the box over in her hands.

"It's for you."

Tannin opened it. The little wooden box was filled with dark slivers and shrivelled pink petals. The scent blossomed from them. Rose tea. Her favourite.

Ava sighed. "As way of an apology. You were right, and I never should have lied to you about the Seer. I should have just been honest. The other night..." She trailed off. "It's reminded me that this is serious. And that I'm glad to have you."

"How did you know...?"

"That it's your favourite? You blabber on a lot, Tannin, but I do pay attention." Ava laughed lightly. "You mentioned it a few weeks ago."

"And you remembered."

Tannin immediately busied herself pouring hot water from the flask into two cups so that Ava wouldn't see how touched she was. It was stupid. It was clearly an attempt to buy her forgiveness, but still.

She got me rose tea.

The first sip was heavenly. Tannin closed her eyes as the delicately scented steam rose up from her cup. She groaned happily.

Ava joined her on the rug, picked up another book and sipped her own tea quietly until Tannin shivered. A draught had managed to find its way through the thick stone walls.

"Cold? Me too."

Without waiting for an answer, Ava fetched a thick patchwork blanket from a chest behind the weapons rack, draping it over Tannin's shoulders and scooting in beside her.

"You're being suspiciously nice to me today."

"That's not true."

Tannin raised an eyebrow at her.

"All right." Ava stared down at her hands, which fidgeted in her lap.

"I am a little worried that you'll give this all up. We're not getting anywhere and people are dying. When we started this, I told you I'd help you understand what you are, and I promise I am following up on leads, but I haven't given you many reasons to stay. I'm worried you'll leave."

For a second, she looked not like the devious scheming princess that Tannin had come to know but a lonely seventeen-year-old who was far out of her depth. It tugged at Tannin's heartstrings and she cursed her own softness. She nudged Ava's knee gently with her own.

"What else would I do?" she said with a small smile. "Break my back pumpin' bellows for coppers again? I'm too used to the easy life now." She stretched luxuriously and leaned back against the sarcophagus, tugging the blanket tighter around her shoulders.

"You mentioned leads for me?" Tannin yawned. She hadn't slept much the night before.

Ava seemed grateful to change the subject and regained her poise. "I know someone who might be able to help. It's a long shot, but I'm trying to set up a meeting. I'll let you know as soon as I have anything."

"How did you end up doin' this?" Tannin asked. It was something she'd been curious about for a while. How did a princess come to spend all her time in a crypt deciphering old texts and plotting against secret societies?

"My brother. Florian." Ava slid down so that she lay on her back on the rug and Tannin stretched out next to her.

They shuffled closer until their shoulders touched and they could both still be covered the blanket. "He knew about me, about what I am, and he wanted to protect me. He'd known the truth about Remnants since before I was born. I don't know how but he knew so much. It was always secret, but he told me what he could when we were alone and passed on some of his contacts. The crypt was his idea."

"I'm sorry," Tannin said quietly. "For your loss."

"Thank you." Ava sighed. "I keep wondering if his death was truly an accident. A rogue arrow when he was out hunting. It would've been all too easy for the Triquetra to... but he wasn't a Remnant, it doesn't fit... and to kill a prince..." She bit her lip. "It doesn't fit, but I can't shake it."

"You must miss him."

"I do."

As Ava spoke more about her brother, about how he taught her to swim and how they would pick apples together, Tannin closed her eyes and listened to the sound of her voice. As much as she hated Ava's condescending way of talking, when she spoke all slow and quiet like she was doing now, she had a low comforting quality to her voice that was almost soothing.

Tannin jerked awake at the sound of Ava sucking in a sudden breath through her teeth.

"Whassit?" she mumbled blearily, blinking grogginess out of her eyes.

They were still lying on the rug under the blanket, but Tannin's head rested on Ava's shoulder and her arm lay across her stomach. "Oh, sorry," she mumbled. "I didn't..."

"It's fine, Tannin, but could you, uh…" She blushed suddenly deep crimson and swallowed hard, staring resolutely up at the ceiling. "…could you move your leg please?"

"What? Oh. *Oh.*"

In cuddling up to Ava in her sleep, Tannin had unconsciously thrown a leg over her and her thigh was now pressing into Ava in a very intimate way. Tannin felt her own cheeks heat. She blabbered another apology as she fought to extricate herself.

Sitting up, she rubbed her eyes hard and gave her head a shake with a groan.

"Wouldn't have guessed you were such a cuddly sleeper," Ava teased.

Tannin scowled at her.

"You're not sleeping well these days, are you?"

"Neither are you," Tannin replied pointedly. The dark circles under Ava's eyes had become more pronounced in the days since the Laird's murder.

"I don't sleep because I have things to do. Is it the nightmares? You were mumbling in your sleep as well as trying to get between my legs."

"I was not trying to –! I didn't –!" Tannin protested, her cheeks burning.

Ava laughed at her obvious discomfort, and Tannin shoved her. "Shut up!"

The princess chuckled a little more before asking, "The nightmare. It's your first Change isn't it?"

"Aye."

Tannin told her about her recurring dream. About being chased, the fear, her body tearing itself apart. Bone splintering and teeth cracking.

"That's…"

"Grim? Mhm."

Ava considered it for a moment. "It could have been Redcaps chasing you. Especially if you came to Armodan from the northeast."

"Redcaps?"

"Not all Fair Folk mixed with humans, you know. There's a few of the originals out there – mainly ones whose physiology would be incompatible with a human mate. Although, Redcaps also didn't mate because they tend to kill anyone who ends up on their territory. It's why so few people know about them too; they don't like to leave survivors."

"Charming," Tannin said, furrowing her brow. "What are they? What other Fair Folk are out there?"

"Goblins. They're why people say the Bluewoods are haunted." Ava gave her a strange look. "You're lucky to be alive. You must be really something to scare off a pack of Redcaps all by yourself."

"What can I say?" Tannin grinned and spread her hands wide. "I'm pretty fearsome."

"The most fearsome." Ava agreed with a serious expression. "As for the other Fair Folk out there, it's difficult to know, but some of the wraith types and others who live in secluded places I imagine are still around. In cities, people know even less – or pretend to anyway. In rural places, people still leave offerings for the Folk, perform rituals and observe special days for them."

"How do y'know that?"

"I hear things." Ava shrugged. "I read things."

"You wouldn't be able to go to any of those places, would you?" Tannin asked, struck by sudden sympathy. As much as she was Ava down here, she was still Princess Avalyn to the world.

"No," she said, wistfully. "Not unless I could get away for a while. Without my entourage. Without my guards." She shook her head. "I don't see it happening. You'll have to go for me and report back some day."

"Alone?"

"You can take who you like as long as you get me the information I want." Her offhand demeanour didn't quite hide the bitterness.

"You know what?" Tannin said, struck by a sudden idea. "We should go out. You and me. We've been at these bloody books for ages, and I don't know about you, but I need a break and you should experience some damn life other than dusty old graves."

Ava arched an eyebrow. "Are you asking me on a date?"

"Don't get ahead of yourself, princess," Tannin said quickly. "Just to get out of this place for a bit. I feel like I'm half dead spendin' all my time in a crypt."

For all the princess's teasing, there were probably laws against royals being involved with non-royals anyway, Tannin thought, and she was about as unroyal as a person could get. There was the whole obsession with babies and lineage to think about as well.

The blossoming spark she felt between them could just be her imagination anyway. It probably was. Even so, she could often feel Ava watching her over the top of a book and couldn't help wondering if Ava looked at her the way she looked at Ava sometimes.

"I can't."

Tannin's heart drooped.

"I mean, I would want to, but I can't." Ava remedied quickly. "It's too big a risk. Especially with the Rill delegates here and the engagement." She bit her lip. "Did you hear about that?"

"I heard there were suitors."

"Yes well, my father accepted one."

"Oh."

"Mhm."

"Who?"

"The second son of Rill," Ava said bitterly. "Prince Erlan."

"And?" Tannin prompted, swallowing down the hollow feeling inside her. She could at least try and be supportive. Her little crush was nothing in the face of royal engagements. "Is he... nice?"

Ava scoffed. "No one cares what I think."

"Well, I'm asking."

Ava took a moment to ponder the question. "He's a prince. Reasonably handsome. A bit full of himself. All that matters is strengthening the alliance and gaining access to their navy now that there's unrest in Gormbrae and the Cascairn borders." She sighed. "He's a social climber. He wants power – that much is obvious. He's been nothing but courteous to me and so far none of my servants have had anything untoward to report about him or his people."

"Why am I not surprised that you have spies in your own house?"

Ava gave Tannin a serious look. "The Royal Court is a dangerous place – possibly more dangerous than your streets, I'd wager. The stakes are high and the amount of cloak and dagger operations going on would surprise you. I fully expect him to have people looking into me as well." She smiled. "Not that they'll find anything. I hide my secrets well."

"Cockiness won't help you after the wedding." Tannin laughed and then made a face. "Oh gods, you have to actually get married. You'll have... marital duties. You're gonna have to –"

Ava interrupted her. "I'm well aware of what a marriage is, thank you. I'll do what I have to for the Brochlands. It is what a princess is for, after all."

Tannin nodded slowly.

I wouldn't bloody do it for the whole five kingdoms.

"Will you have to go to somewhere in Rill after?"

"Tayfort. After the wedding." She bit her lip, "I'd have to leave all this here. Attilo would obviously come with me but we've just gotten started with this whole thing, and I have no idea what I'd do there and..." She blinked hard. "I think I'd miss you."

Tannin gave her a gentle elbow in the ribs, trying to hide her smile at the thought of Ava missing her. "Of course, I'd visit. Do you know how bored I'd be without you? I can hardly go back to regular life now."

She hadn't actually realised it until she heard the words come out of her own mouth. She really couldn't go back to a normal life now. Not with all that she knew.

"Besides, you pay me too much."

Ava rolled her eyes. "I think you like me enough without my money."

"The money definitely helps." Tannin grinned.

"I'd be bored without you too." Ava sighed. "My life is boring."

"Oh, what a tragic life you lead, princess."

"It is actually," Ava said archly. "I'm not allowed to do anything. I've spent most of my teens learning how to sew silly patterns on handkerchiefs and learning which spoon to use at banquets."

"Well, aren't you glad you've got me to be such a bad influence." Tannin nudged her playfully and grinned. "I'm sure your sewin' was very pretty."

"Oh, shush."

Tannin grinned and then said, "I should get goin'. I need a proper sleep."

"Sweet dreams."

Tannin paused at the trapdoor after shrugging on her cloak and turned grinning widely. "Hey, Ava? Thanks for the apolog-tea."

"Get out."

Chapter Twenty Six

Old Allies, New Problems

Tannin wandered around the inner citadel on one of the days where Ava and Attilo were off doing royal things and found herself thoroughly underwhelmed.

There were none of the curious little shops that filled the streets near the citadel walls, overflowing with weird and wonderful contraptions and potions and plants and pottery. It was all just fancy clothing or jewellery. Of course, drunken men still smoked and brayed outside bars and heavily powdered ladies called lewdly from balconies as soon as the sun disappeared behind the roofs and the oil- filled streetlamp cast long shadows. You'd have to go a long way from Armodan to avoid those sights.

She was headed back in the direction of one of the bridges out into the Skirts when she caught a glimpse of motion in one of the streets to her left. She wasn't sure what had caught her attention. Maybe the furtive way the man was creeping around that suggested he really didn't want to be seen or the fact that she recognised his pointed mousey face.

Ben? Berk? Beck! That was it. The creepy man from the lens job. What is he doing sneaking around?

She paused at the mouth of the alley, keeping out of sight. She expected to see Beck consorting with other shady types, but she didn't expect those shady types to be accompanied by a guard. He stood out against the dark colours the others were wearing. They all had hoods pulled up or caps pulled low to shade their faces.

Her curiosity was well and truly piqued now. Gangs bribing the city guards was hardly a secret. Afterall, they would be pretty useless if this many gangs were still operating and they were actually trying to stop them. But this didn't look like a simple pay-off. As she watched, the guard seemed to be doing the talking with the men hanging onto his every word. She cocked her head to catch some of their conversation.

Warehouse... payout... tonight...

Even with her heightened hearing, she could only catch a few words and then even less as they took off at a leisurely stroll down the alley, looking determinedly nonchalant. Tannin ducked back behind the wall before any of them spotted her.

Oh, something is about to go down.

It took her a second to work out where they'd gone, but after a moment's pause, she heard voices and quickly ducked behind the wall again. They spoke in hushed tones, making it impossible for Tannin to make out exactly what they were saying as they headed to the back of a shop that had boarded up windows. It seemed that even up here in the fancy parts of town things weren't as pristine as they pretended to be.

One of the men pried the padlock off the door and they entered with surreptitious glances over their shoulders. The door closed behind them. Things became still and quiet until a tall bald man in a black cloak swept straight up to the door. Unlike the others, he walked with long, purposeful strides and his head held high. He disappeared inside.

After several long minutes of nothing happening, Tannin sighed as she studied her nails and leant on the alley wall. Somehow the inner citadel managed to make everything boring – even crime watching. A chill was seeping in now that the day was drawing to a close. Tannin had decided to leave and was half turned when the creak of hinges reached her. The door opened and the bald man, the Guard and Beck came out. Beck was now wearing a flat cap that one of the men had been wearing.

He stole his hat?

Tannin frowned, puzzled. That seemed weird.

Without a second glance at each other, the three of them parted ways. Tannin pressed herself flat against the wall as Beck passed her by. He had his collar pulled up around his chin and the stolen hat low over his eyebrows as if he were trying to hide within his clothes. He walked quickly. As quickly as someone could without breaking into a run.

That is suspicious.

Approaching the warehouse, intending to peek in through one of the windows and maybe have a nosey around, she smelled it before she saw it. That sour, metallic tang in the air as she crossed the street. Blood.

It only took one glance through the gap in the boards to show her the source. The floor was slick with it, and it ran in thin streams from the far wall where it had splattered in abundance. A stricken face stared unseeingly in her direction. Several feet away, the corresponding corpse lay in a misshapen heap. Another lay still at the end of a red streak across the floorboards as if he had tried to haul his mangled body to safety.

Tannin stared open-mouthed at the butchery.

I should get help... I should...

But there was nothing to be done. The four men who had entered the building were very, very dead.

"Okay, so there's a pile of dead bodies in the back of a shop in the inner citadel, and I think I just saw the Triquetra kill them," Tannin blurted as soon as she dropped into the crypt.

"Sorry, what?" Attilo looked up sharply from the table.

He hastily tried to put away the scraps of parchment in front of him. "Uh...Yeah, lemme just –"

"What are you doin'?" Tannin raised an eyebrow in suspicion.

"Nothin', I – give that back!"

He snatched for the parchment that Tannin had grabbed, but she danced out of reach. The parchment was covered with lines and lines of shaky letters in blotched and smeared ink. Attilo turned a deep shade of red.

"I'm still learnin'," he said quietly. "I didnae want you and Ava to know I can't – I mean, I can read, sort of, but I've never done the letters myself before." He shuffled uncomfortably.

"I'm sorry for bargin' in," Tannin said. She felt so bad. He was obviously embarrassed. "It's good," she said handing the paper back.

"It disnae matter. I was just practicin'," he mumbled.

Tannin cleared her throat. "So. Murder? Dead bodies?"

He cleared his throat as well, shuffling the papers together and stuffing them into a drawer. "Right, aye bodies. What bodies?"

Tannin told him what she'd seen.

"We've been thinkin' that it'd make sense for the gangs to have Remnant members. Kelpie-bloods for smugglin' and the like. Balor-bloods as the muscle." He scratched his beard. "It could be ye've just seen the Triquetra at work. Unusual they're not makin' it look like an accident."

"Gonna pass it off as a gang fight maybe. But that was four at once, and it's gruesome. That's a serious clean up. Oh! Maybe the killers were Remnants! That's why it was so messy!"

Attilo sighed. "There's nothin' we can really do until the mornin'."

"They might've gotten rid of all the evidence by then!"

"Aye, but what can we do, the two of us if we go there and there's a whole bunch of 'em? I'll get some pals of mine to check it out, all right?"

Tannin reluctantly agreed as she stifled a yawn. The adrenaline had worn off.

"Go home and get some sleep. I'll take care of this, all right?" he said. "And Tannin, don't you be goin' back there alone, you hear me? Straight home."

Tannin promised him she'd go straight home but chuckled inwardly. If it were any other day and she wasn't this bone tired, she probably would have gone to check it out again. He was starting to know her too well.

When she arrived back at the crypt the next day after a surprisingly good night's sleep, all things considered, she was met by Attilo's grim news that, while they'd found the shop she'd spoken of, there was nothing left but scrubbed bloodstains on the floor. The bodies were nowhere to be found and there wasn't a scrap of evidence pointing to what had happened or who had done it.

Tannin frustratedly filled Ava in on the details and was promptly scolded for following Beck in the first place.

"If I hadn't, we wouldn't know about any of this." Tannin pointed out.

Ava glowered but didn't argue. "Tell me more about what the bald man looked like."

"I don't know." Tannin shrugged. "Generic bald middle- aged man. Kinda pale. Kinda tall but not hugely. Black cloak."

"He was a Black Cloak?" Attilo asked sharply.

"No," Tannin said exasperated. "He had a black cloak. He wasn't one of the Black Cloaks."

The black-garbed heralds of death could be found all through the Brochlands, spouting messages of various hells and paradises that awaited people after the end. A Black Cloak at the door meant someone was dying and begging for assurance that they had lived a good life and that the darkness wouldn't claim them. Of course it wouldn't, they'd say. In exchange for a small offering. Tannin wasn't sure if they were employed by the city to guilt people into obeying the laws while they were alive or if they had made up their own guild to fleece the poor saps at death's door.

"It could be the Master of Confidence," Ava said quietly. "He's bald and pale and influential enough to make this go away."

"Could he be Triquetra?" Tannin asked. "Also, who the hell is the Master of Confidence?"

"I thought that was one of those secret but not really secret at all things," Ava replied. "You really don't know?"

Tannin shook her head.

"He's the head of Armodan's scouts to keep an eye on everything, except he watches the city too. They say that no letters leave the city without one of his employees reading it and none of the underground activities happen without him having some stake in the outcome."

Tannin stared at her for a moment. "So, he's a spy. And you don't think this is exactly what the Triquetra would need to find all the Remnants and make them disappear? Why didn't we talk about this before?"

Attilo and Ava looked at each other shiftily.

"I have honestly had it with you two keepin' things from me. Out with it."

"He's my uncle," Ava said in low tones.

"Wonderful." Tannin threw her arms up exasperatedly. "You know that doesn't make him automatically not evil, right?"

"I know that," Ava snapped. "I just mean he's really close to the inner workings of things. It's difficult to look into him."

"Oh. Sorry."

"We'd never get anywhere close," Attilo said. "We've been thinkin' he might be at the heart of the Triquetra for a while."

"You should tell me these things." Tannin insisted. "Like, I know it's always been you two and I'm new and everythin', but you've got to let me in if this is gonna work. It can't be you two and then me on the outside."

"You're right." Ava heaved a tired sounding sigh. "From now on, we'll tell you everything. But until we know more, no more risks, okay?"

"Awww. You worried for me?" Tannin asked cheekily, and Ava rolled her eyes.

"I just don't want to lose the only recruit we've gained in all this time."

"Mhm sure. Purely business."

It turned out there wasn't much more that Tannin didn't know as Ava and Attilo showed her stacks and stacks of notes on the Triquetra. It was all just details and nothing majorly interesting. It was all in Ava's handwriting too, and Tannin noticed Attilo giving her sidelong looks as they spoke. She wondered if Ava knew he couldn't write. She must do if she wrote everything down. Although maybe not. Ava did tend to get absorbed in the details, Tannin thought as she turned her attention back to her. She hadn't paid attention to what Ava had been saying for the last five minutes and she had not noticed in the slightest. She hadn't even looked up from her notes, speaking quickly and more excitedly by the minute. She got such a glint in her eye when she was talking through her schemes and plans and research it bordered on manic. Those blue eyes really were intense.

Like little shards of sky.

"What?"

Ava had noticed Tannin staring.

"Nothing, nothing," she replied quickly. "Just listenin'."

"I asked you a question."

"I was... listenin' so hard I didn't hear it?"

"You are ridiculous," Ava said slamming her notes down on the table. "You ask to be included and then you don't pay attention?"

"I -"

"You want information? It's all here," she said crossly. "Read it yourself. I'm done for the day."

"Ava, wait!" Tannin tried to apologise but Ava was having none of it and just said a curt goodbye as she disappeared up the tunnel that led up to the castle. Attilo exhaled heavily and gave a shrug before following.

Tannin rubbed her eyes.

Ugh, I'm an eejit.

She was tired, but the lure of a night of mindless frivolity was never far away. It wasn't late enough to truly call it a night and there was a ceilidh at the Swords tonight...

Chapter Twenty Seven

Answers

"As requested," Tannin said with a flourish as she dumped her load of packages onto the sarcophagus table. "And by the way, callin' these shopping trips you send me on "acquisition missions" does not make them any more fun."

"Did you get everything?"

"Aye." Tannin rolled her eyes.

"Don't get comfortable," Ava said as Tannin started to take off her coat. "We've got to get going."

"Goin' where?"

"Remember I told you I was trying to organize a meeting with someone who can hopefully get you some answers? That's today."

"Right now?"

"Yes. Unless your memory has miraculously reappeared."

"It has not. Lead the way, then."

To her surprise, they went not up to the surface but through the tunnels that Tannin thought only led to the castle. Attilo pulled back some half-broken boards to reveal another offshoot.

"These tunnels never end, do they?" Tannin muttered as she ducked inside.

It was not a short walk and she was soon impatient.

"Where are we goin'?" she whined.

She had ended up staying at Flint's after a they'd had a late night of cheap whisky and ceilidh dancing until their feet hurt. She'd made amends with him after their previous argument which more or less consisted of buying him a drink and all was forgiven. He snored like a hog though and she'd hardly slept. Flint had sheepishly bought her a hot sweetroll for breakfast as thanks for not kicking him during the night, but it had only perked her up for as long as it took her to eat it. She was hopelessly grouchy, her feet were still sore and, if she had to be truly honest, she was a little hungover. She knew her complaints made her sound like a petulant child but this walk was far longer than anticipated.

"To get some answers," Ava replied. "I told you."

"That doesn't tell me anythin'."

"Then I suppose you'll have to stop dragging your feet and hurry up."

The passage they walked through had a trough of brown, muddy water running through the middle of it that stank of decay. They walked in single file. Attilo's torch in front did little to lighten the mood.

"I really hate your tunnels," Tannin grumbled. "Why can't we just walk there like normal people on streets made for walkin' on? In the sunlight. Do you remember sunlight?"

"Stop yer complainin'." Attilo called from the front. "We're doing this for you."

"Quiet. We're here." As Ava stopped in her tracks, a distracted Tannin walked straight into her with a grunt.

"Finally," she muttered.

"Hey." Ava stopped as she was about to climb the ladder and turned back to Tannin. "Best behaviour. This is a good contact but flighty."

"Best behaviour." Tannin snorted. "I'm not a child! Hey, I'm older than you!" she called up at Ava's disappearing form.

"Only marginally. And yes, you are a child," came the curt reply.

The ladder surfaced from a drain cover in a weedy courtyard behind some residential buildings. The once white walls long turned grey, now streaked with rainwater stains and rust from dripping gutters. Thick, black beams crisscrossed the walls, and sections of the once-white paint were chipped away revealing the red brick underneath. Ropy climbing plants clung to the cracks in the walls and pulled at rotten shutters.

"Lovely," Tannin muttered under her breath.

"This way."

She followed the other two to the backdoor of one of the houses where Ava gave a curt rap on the door with her gloved knuckles followed by a pause then another two knocks.

Almost immediately they could hear movement on the other side. There was a click, and a tiny window in the centre of the door opened. A rheumy eye regarded them with suspicion. It blinked, and the little window snapped shut. Chains and locks clinked hurriedly before the door creaked open.

"Ava, my darling!"

The door was thrown wide and enveloped them in a heady cloud of incense. The man it revealed was dressed in a long dark blue robe with wide flapping sleeves that whipped around with every flamboyant and exaggerated movement as he ushered them inside. His watery eyes were rimmed in black, and his grey moustache was waxed into curled points.

"Are you serious?" Tannin whispered at Ava as she gagged on the humid perfume.

Ava waggled a hand to shush her.

"Tiberius, darling, it has been too long." Ava swept forward to plant a kiss in the air somewhere about a foot to the left of Tiberius' cheek as he did the same.

Tannin realised for the first time that Ava was not dressed in her usual black. Under her cloak she was all ruffles and... pearls?

Tannin raised an eyebrow at Attilo for an explanation, but he merely shrugged as he leant casually on the wall.

"And what have we here?" Tiberius grasped Tannin's shoulder with bony fingers. She resisted the urge to slap him away.

"A new acquaintance. I was rather hoping you would read her fortune for her. Somewhat of a curiosity, you see." Ava had taken on a gratingly slow and deliberate accent that made Tannin want to hit her.

"And my fee?" he asked, critically eyeing Tannin up and down. She crossed her arms and stared solidly back.

"On my tab, darling."

"Well then, marvellous! Follow me, my dear."

He led them through a curtain to a room decked from top to bottom in cushions and fabrics. The floor was layered in an assortment of carpets and rugs, and floaty ribbons of material hung in loops from the ceiling. Tannin followed Ava's lead and sat on one of the fluffy cushions, choosing to sit cross-legged instead of fully reclining across three of four them as Ava did. Attilo stayed standing at the curtained entrance.

Tiberius took his place on the other side of the table and paused briefly to balance an absurdly large, bejeweled turban on his head and flip the trailing fabric scarf around his shoulders. From where she sat, Tannin could see the beads of glue squished out from behind the gaudy gems.

She shot Ava a look of disbelief, but the princess simply winked.

"And now!" Tiberius said with an intensely serious voice. "We begin!"

The lights dimmed from somewhere outside of their fabric cocoon. Tannin had to stifle a laugh and turn it into a small cough. This was absurd.

"Ahhhh yes. Speak to me spirits!" He closed his eyes and reached up as if to draw in the "spirits" towards himself.

"Speak to m— what?" His tone changed sharply, and his eyes snapped open to look directly at Tannin. The curtains rustled.

"Go." Ava commanded to Attilo and he leapt into action. They seemed to have been waiting for this. Tannin watched open-mouthed as Attilo pounced through the fabric, ripping it from where it was nailed into the wood panelled walls, to seize a fleeing figure in its folds.

The figure shrieked and fought, but between the net of curtains and Attilo's strong arms wrapped tightly around them, they had no hope. He simply lifted the struggling mass clear off the ground and strolled back with it.

"What in the name of –"

"Save it." Ava's fake accent was gone, and she was all business as she pointed at the cowering magician. "Stay."

She strolled over to where Attilo was still holding the squirming mass of fabric. Slippered feet peeking out of the bottom hammered his shins but he stoically held on. She tilted her head and observed the bundle carefully before parting the fabric in the top.

A litany of profanity poured out of the hole in the thick material. Ava pushed it back to reveal a furiously cursing teenage girl.

"Let me go!" She howled in a curiously accented voice, still kicking.

"And here she is, the real star of the show."

"Uh, what's goin' on?" Tannin asked, still cross-legged on her cushion.

The girl in Attilo's arms fixed her with a penetrating stare that made her neck prickle. One eye was a deep brown, almost black, but the other was such a piercingly pale blue it was almost silver. Even from where Tannin sat halfway across the room, its fierce brightness unnerved her.

Ava stepped in front of her, breaking that chilling glare.

"We have a couple of questions, if you'd be so kind."

The girl merely howled again in response and struggled harder.

"Very well, tire yourself out and then we'll talk. Tiberius?"

"...yes?" All the extravagance was gone from the man, and he curled in on himself as if trying to hide inside his robe.

"Talk to me," Ava commanded.

"Uh, yes. Well, uh..."

"What's her name for starters?"

"Rozhin."

"Shut up, Tiberius!" the girl roared.

"Well, Rozhin, it's clear that you are a Seer. Can't really hide that, can you?" Ava said lightly, indicating the girl's odd eyes. "So, what we want to know is everything you can tell us about our friend here."

"Ask her yourself, you horse's ass." Rozhin spat.

"Ohoho, I like her." Tannin laughed.

"Go and die, abomination!"

"I like her less."

"Rozhin," Ava said, attempting to rally the conversation. "I need to know what you see."

"Why should I tell you?" Rozhin had finally stopped fighting and hung limply in her curtain cocoon, breathing hard.

"I'll make it worth your while."

Rozhin thought about it for a minute and shared a glance with Tiberius. "Show me the money."

Ava inclined her head and lay a drawstring bag on the table, tipping it over to reveal the glint of gold. Rozhin craned her neck and examined the gold as best she could.

She nodded. "Acceptable. Now put me down!"

Attilo waited for a nod from Ava before setting the girl's slippered feet back on the ground and releasing her from his bear hug. She shucked off the curtain indignantly.

"I do not appreciate this method of business," she snapped.

Ava laughed lightly. "If we'd approached and asked to talk, you would have been off like a shot."

Rozhin nodded knowingly. Now that she was out of the curtain, Tannin could see the long black braid that swung low down her back. "You have known this whole time you've been coming here."

"I suspected."

"I suspected you suspected, but you always pay full price." Rozhin shrugged. "Shall we sit then? You can go."

This last remark was directed at Tiberius, who gratefully scurried out, his turban abandoned.

"Why does he do this and not you if you're the Seer?" Tannin asked, poking at the turban. She immediately regretted asking when she was met by a cold stare.

"I keep myself safe, and people pay for what they expect. Which is him in his stupid hat."

"Good business model." Tannin conceded.

"No one asked you," Rozhin snapped, sitting down on the cushion Tiberius had vacated and settling her wide skirts around her.

"What's with the hostility? I haven't done anythin' to you."

"You are an abomination."

"Aye, we've established that," Tannin said irritably. "But why?"

Ava cut in. "She doesn't know what she is."

Rozhin scoffed. "Sure."

"It's true!"

"Hm." Rozhin fixed Tannin with an unblinking stare for a few moments as she fidgeted with a cushion tassel. She then leapt up from her cushion and crossed to a cabinet that would have been hidden behind where Attilo tore down the curtain. There were clinkings of glass bottles as she rummaged in the cupboards and then with a noise of satisfaction she returned with a dark green bottle and two small glasses.

"Here." She thrust a glass at Tannin and poured out a healthy measure.

"What is it?" Tannin eyed it suspiciously as Rozhin poured a second glass for herself and downed it in one gulp.

"Drink."

Ava nodded encouragingly and so Tannin brought the little glass to her lips and took a sip. The smokey taste filled her mouth, and the liquid burned her throat. She choked.

"This is whisky," she said in surprise. "*Good* whisky."

"You will need it. Drink."

"Sláinte." Tannin toasted to no one in particular as she gulped the rest of fiery spirit with a grimace.

"Okay." Rozhin cleared her throat. "I will say one word and you will say the first thing that comes into your mind."

"Come on." Tannin rolled her eyes. This was a children's game.

"Tannin," Ava said and shot her a knowing look. "You wanted answers."

"Fine, fine." Tannin sighed. "Go for it."

Their gazes locked and Rozhin began. "Red."

"Blue."

"Mother."

"Father."

"Bird."

"Fly."

An uncomfortable warmth was rising up from under Tannin's clothes. The spicy drink plus the closeness of the room were getting to her.

"Fire."

"Heat."

"Ice."

"Cold."

It seemed Rozhin's mismatched eyes were boring into her soul. The rest of the room seemed to disappear, fading into the black edges of her vision until there were only those eyes.

"Night."

"Day."

"Light."

"Dark."

"Life."

"Death."

"Red."

"...Blood."

Tannin's vision filled with red.

She blinked hard and rubbed stinging blood out of her eyes. It ran down the side of her face from a cut over her eyebrow.

"And that is why you never let your guard down!" A booming male voice filled her ears. She blinked again. The man stood over her and offered a hand. She took it.

A girl stood opposite her with a mop of black hair. She held a short sword in each hand, one which was tipped in blood. Her blood.

"Dana is today's winner. The rest of you, clean up!"

"Home." Rozhin's voice broke into the memory, sending it swimming back out of sight.

"Safe." Tannin gasped reactively, tracing where a scar should have been above her eyebrow.

"Win."

"Lose."

"Fear."

"..."

"Wake up! It's time!" Someone shook her awake. "It's today!"

"I'm awake!" Excitement thrummed through her entire body. Initiation day.

Dressed in their new white tunics, the novices waited for their names to be called in the grand hall. It was empty apart from the white line of excited youths. They fidgeted and giggled as much as they tried to stay quiet. Today was the day they learned whether or not they would make it to the ranks of the Golden. The tension and excitement were palpable in the air.

One by one they were called, and one by one they disappeared through a side door to their fate.

"Tannin."

She almost skipped to the door in her excitement. She couldn't have kept the cheek-aching smile off her face if she'd tried.

"This way."

Tannin followed the faceless figure down several flights of stone stairs which dipped in the middle from centuries of use. Down to the laboratory.

The faceless figure led her inside and bade her to sit up on a wide stone table. The lab was filled with bubbling glass receptacles, steaming and sending puffs of coloured smoke into the air. Pickled things in jars lined the shelves. The floors were the same wide flat stone as the walls. Tannin felt the smile fade from her face as she saw the grooves in the tiled floor were crusted with what looked like blood. A drain next to where she sat was also lined with red.

"What's going on?"

The faceless figure turned around and lifted a goblet filled with dark liquid to her lips and urged her to swallow. "Lie back. This won't be pleasant."

Her vision faded to black as screams filled the air.

"Tannin!"

The screaming stopped. Tannin realised with horror that they'd come from her own throat and now it felt raw. She sat up wild-eyed.

"What did you do to me?!" she demanded, panting.

"Nothing. I just helped with some memories. Is that not what you wanted?" Rozhin asked tauntingly.

"What do you remember?" Ava asked urgently.

"She was right." Tannin gasped in dismay, nodding to Rozhin. Her heart was thudding impossibly fast. "It's not natural. I was made into this."

"Made you into what? I don't understand."

"Warg," Rozhin hissed grimly.

"What's a warg?" Ava demanded.

"A darkness. A beast. A monster. A thing that should have died out long ago." Rozhin snarled. "An abomination."

"An old type of Fair Folk. I must've been a warg-blood Remnant before or it would have killed me and then they did something..." Tannin stared at her hands. "The blood knows. That's what they would say."

"Who?" Ava said. "Who would say?"

Tannin scrambled to her feet. Her legs felt like jelly. She desperately wanted to breathe fresh air that wasn't clogged with incense. "I have to get out of here."

She burst out of the door into the courtyard, squinting against the sudden change in light. She breathed heavily, doubled over with her hands on her knees. She still felt like she couldn't take in any air. Her limbs shook violently.

"Tannin?" Ava had followed her out and gently touched her shoulder.

"No!" She jerked away.

She didn't want to be touched. She didn't want to talk. She didn't want to be seen. Tannin looked around desperately for a way out of the courtyard that wasn't back down into the stinking tunnels. She felt like a wild animal, cornered and frantically looking to escape. There was a gate.

She ran.

Chapter Twenty Eight

Painful Memories

Tannin had no idea where she was. After she'd shouldered her way out of the gate, she'd run until she couldn't run anymore. Her legs and lungs were burning. She was pretty sure she'd never been to this part of town before. Or maybe she had and her treacherous mind was just hiding more memories from her. She sunk down into a doorway and held her head in her hands. A fierce ache was building up behind her eyes and unwelcome flashes of memory kept stabbing into her brain.

A school. Lessons. Training. Mountains. Thick forest. Blue flowers. A dark lab. Jars. Bitter black liquid.

Tannin squeezed her eyed shut and raked her nails through her hair.

It can't be true. It can't be real.

But the more she thought, the more she remembered. The next swallow of chemicals had turned her veins to ice and then fire in turn as the faceless figure noted figures on a chart while she screamed. That had been the first dose.

Others came later. Months or weeks later, she didn't know. Of the thirty novices in her class, twelve had survived. Dana, her usual training partner and friend, had made it but she'd lost other friends. A lot of friends.

Her throat felt tight as the memories flooded in.Blood-stained white sheets covering a pile of small bodies. The unworthy. They had all been of noble blood, she remembered with a start. She was a noble. That felt weird to think. She'd had a home. A nice home. Parents who died when she was young, in childbirth and in some accident.

Her grandparents had raised her. Grandparents, plural. She had a grandmother. The blue flowers. Her grandmother planted blue flowers in the window boxes all around the house.

Tannin held her head in between her knees in an effort to stop the world from spinning. Assaulted by memories from all sides, she reeled. At some point, she ended up laying on her side, half in the doorway, curled into a tight foetal ball with her arms wrapped around her aching head.

Her grandmother had died. Illness. Fresh pangs of old loss gripped Tannin's heart and she moaned into the dirt. Her grandfather had found out about the Programme soon after. It had been a secret. A big secret. A pain of death secret.

But someone had told. There had been a revolt. A coup. The city streets had blazed in a terrible fire. It had been that night that they'd run. Under the cover of smoke and chaos, they'd run into the night and not looked back.

It was too much. Too much information. Too many feelings. Numbness took over as she lay there shivering, drenched in cold sweat. She wasn't unconscious – she could hear rumblings and footsteps and the gentle patter of the rain starting, but she couldn't bring herself to move or even open her eyes.

The dream started as it always did with running and drums and sharp tree branches reaching for her, but this time she wasn't dreaming. The same panic and fear that had plagued her for years filled her chest and closed off her throat.

Her grandfather held her hand and pulled her onwards and away from the danger. He dragged her behind a huge tree, where they huddled down in the hollow of its roots.

"I'm so sorry." He panted.

"Are we going to die?" Tannin cried.

"I wish there was another way." He reached into the ragged bag he'd managed to hang on to and drew out a long case. She knew that case.

"No." She gasped. "No, you can't!" She tried to squirm away, but he pulled her back.

"If there were any other way, I would! This is our last chance!" He grabbed her arm tightly and held the little vial to her lips. The final dose.

She tried to shake her head no, but the bitter poison seemed to force its way into her mouth of its own volition. She retched at the taste as the serum forced itself into her bloodstream. She knew she had maybe seconds before she felt it.

An arrow whistled overhead and thudded solidly into a tree just a head of them.

"We have to go!" Her grandfather grasped Tannin's small hand in his large one and again pulled her through the trees which reached to snag their clothes and trip them up.

The all too familiar burning wasn't far behind. Muscles screamed and bones crunched. Teeth spilled, broken, from her twisted mouth and tumbled onto the wet leaves.

Tannin woke with a gasp and then a groan as the pounding in her head started up again.

"Hey, wake up." The guard gave her leg another booted kick. "Time to go home."

She groaned and sat up. Her neck was stiff, and her back was killing her from sleeping curled up in the doorway.

Sunlight trickled through the clouds.

"What time's it?" Her mouth felt cottony, and her tongue was heavy as she formed words.

"Time to get going," came the helpful reply.

Tannin heaved herself to her feet. Even a night of extra heavy drinking with Flint hadn't made her feel this bad before. She rubbed her forehead. Along the street, traders had just set out tables and had begun piling them with reels of fabric or crates of fruit.

She grumbled incoherently, brushing off most of the dirt from her clothes and turning her collar up against the morning chill, setting off at a brisk pace to try and warm up. She stopped.

Where the hell am I?

She looked at the stalls filling up along the sides of the street. Mornings in the citadel meant markets lined almost every street. Was she even still in the citadel? She looked around for a reference point and saw the edge of the wall curving off in the distance. Still in the citadel. And the sun was to her left, which meant that way was... West? No, east. She cursed herself for never being able to remember and decided to just keep trudging along until she found somewhere she recognised. She couldn't be far from something she knew.

"FRESH FISH!"

Tannin clutched at her head and whimpered as the fishmonger's yell echoed around her skull like the toll of a bell. People skirted out of her way.

I must look as shite as I feel.

The streets were bustling and colourful, the city awake and full of life by the time Tannin finally got home. She mumbled a greeting in the vague direction of the kitchen where Mrs O'Baird usually spent the majority of her time and headed up to gratefully collapse in the comfort of her bed. A night out on the street had chilled her to her bones.

Tannin spent most of the day in bed, nursing a seemingly unshiftable headache. Sitting on her bed with her quilt wrapped around her shoulders, she chewed thoughtfully on a hunk of bread and butter that she'd swiped from downstairs. She still couldn't quite process it all. The memories weren't assaulting her brain quite like they had been, but the flashes still kept coming.

She'd grown up in the mountains to the north, technically in the kingdom of Cascairn, not in Woodren like her grandfather had told her, past where anyone here in Armodan would think there would ever be a city. Nestled deep in the forest and half built into the mountain face itself was Stonestead. Tiny compared to Armodan – maybe the size of the inner citadel – but still thriving with life. It had been an isolated community. Home of the warg-bloods.

That far in the wilderness, there was no outside trade or visitors of any kind, and they kept it like that. Outsiders were not welcome.

They kept to the lifestyle of the Ancients, the ones who came before, when magic flowed freely through the veins of most living creatures and conflict was rife between the races.

They fought for food and land and resources. Why be a farmer when you could be a warrior? They used to share those forests with other Remnants in the old days until those of the warg-blood had all but slaughtered them and claimed the far north as their own.

When Tannin was a child, the greatest thing you could hope to be was one of the Golden. The elite. The old warg- blood was potent within them. They were the fiercest warriors known to Stonestead. They staged great battles between themselves for the crowds, fought wild beasts in arenas and dragged in huge kills from the animals of the forests. Tannin had hoped to be one of them.

There were, of course, farmers and shopkeepers and street sweepers but there was no honour in that, and as a noble she was expected to do something great. A warrior, an academic, an Elder. Like all her family before her. Not like any of them had been involved in warfare in centuries, but it was the principle of the thing. No one south of the mountains even knew they existed, but the people of Stonestead were too proud to ever admit that. The power of the old blood was almost like a religion to them. Those with warg-blood were faster, stronger than the rest. Heightened senses. The spirit of the mountain, they said, that was what made them warriors.

Tannin frowned. None of that meant physically becoming a warg. She'd never heard of anyone Changing, even a little bit. She shuddered. That was what they were doing. What they did to her. Her appetite left her.

She set her meagre meal aside and pulled her blanket closer. Why had her grandfather never told her?

Because it's fucking traumatic, that's why.

She pulled the blanket up over her head and slumped back into her pillows.

It took a few days for Tannin to sort out all the memories that had suddenly crammed themselves into her brain.

She'd tried to jot some of it down, but it all got jumbled as they spilled from her mind onto the pages in a flurry of ink. She had to talk to someone about it. She had to go back to the crypt.

The day had begun with the promise of clear skies, but as Tannin neared the necropolis the heavens opened and dumped a week's worth of rain down on her. The long walk to their hidden headquarters was getting really tiring.

She wasn't generally superstitious, but as the rain condensed into a thick fog around the graves she suppressed a shudder. It was Samhain soon when the fabric between this world and the after was thinnest and it was said that spirit could cross through on that night. She gave herself a shake.

Ghosts aren't real.

"It's me," she called, shucking her sodden cloak and squelching into the crypt.

"Oh, she returns then." Attilo's arms were crossed.

"Yeah, yeah," Tannin muttered, rubbing her hands together to warm them.

"Ye cannae just go runnin' off like that," he replied. "What the hell happened?"

"Where's Ava?"

"She had a thing."

Tannin raised her eyebrows. "A thing?"

"She's dinin' with Prince Erlan."

"Oh yeah, I keep forgettin' about him."

"Aye, so does Ava. It's bad form." Attilo shook his head reprovingly. "He's gettin' insistent about havin' the weddin' early."

"Why?"

Attilo shrugged in an offhand way. "Politics. Probably wants his power good an' solid as soon as. Doesn't help that Ava's been neglectin' the whole business. Prince's probably rushin' so she won't call it off."

Wish she would call it off.

"Anyway, don't change the subject," he said sternly. "What happened with that Seer? What got you chargin' off like that?"

Tannin let out a long breath. "I remembered," she said simply.

She recounted as much of her memories as she could. About where and how she'd grown up, about the Golden and about what they'd done to the novices. She told him about her dream too. That it was her grandfather that had given her the final dose to escape from the Redcaps.

She told him about killing the men in the alley, which he had already known about, and the horse which he had not.

"I'm a monster." She stared at her hands.

"Yer not a monster," Attilo said surprisingly softly. He reached over and gave her hand a reassuring squeeze. "We've all got demons. It's how ye live with 'em now that matters."

"Since when are you all wise?" "Since always."

Tannin got the feeling he was going to say more, but at that moment Ava stormed into the crypt, wordlessly going straight to her table and slamming open a book. Her expression was thunderous. Tannin and Attilo exchange a glance.

"Well, hello there," Tannin said. "You good?"

"Oh." Ava straightened up and swept her hair back. She must had forgotten she was wearing kohl around her eyes because she left a black streak down her cheek as she rubbed at one. "You're back. Good."

"I am." Tannin cocked an eyebrow. "Trouble in paradise?"

Ava gave her one of her speciality withering looks. "You could say that, yes."

"Wanna talk about it?"

"I do not." Ava said firmly but when Tannin raised her eyebrows pointedly, her defiance wilted somewhat. "It's Erlan. Prince Erlan. He's getting very serious about this whole marriage business. He keeps wanting to spend time with me."

"Your fiancé wants to spend time with you? Oh no, how terrible."

"I had to spend three hours in the sanctuary with him today to maintain my cover because he wouldn't leave me alone." Ava snapped. "And it's not just that. He keeps already calling me his wife and ordering my servants around like they're his."

"He sounds like a charmer." Tannin leant casually on the sarcophagus. "Here's a thought – don't marry him."

"It's not that simple. It's all arranged." Ava rubbed at her eyes again, further streaking the black smudges and Tannin had to clench her hands to stop herself reaching out to wipe them away. "The actual marriage is just a formality at this point. Prince Erlan has well and truly ingrained himself in Court here. Everyone loves him, of course, and all of his ideas. Rill's navy is a marvel, I'll admit. They have weaponry that can blow pirates out of the water these days." Ava sighed. "I thought I could stall for longer."

Tannin wished she could think of something to say. Something comforting or motivating or, hell, just something nice but before she could come up with anything, Ava was speaking again.

"Oh, and Rozhin is gone."

"What do you mean gone?" Tannin blinked.

"I mean gone, Tannin. As in, packed up and left the city."

"Guess we're still just a merry band of three then," Tannin said.

"Guess so," Ava said with no small amount of resentment.

"Not good enough for you anymore, huh?" Tannin quipped.

"That's not what I meant, and you know it. I thought I could convince Rozhin to join us. She would have been a powerful ally. She was my plan B after the sightlens broke for finding and recruiting other Remnants or at least stopping them from revealing themselves and being picked off by the Triquetra. Now we're back at square one."

"Not quite square one," Attilo said gently. "We've got Tannin now, and she actually has some good news for ye." He gave Tannin a meaningful look and gestured to Ava who Tannin thought would actually be better off with a nap.

"Are you sure now's the time? You look like you're gonna keel over any second. When did you last get some sleep?"

"Just tell me," Ava said, annoyed.

"I remembered. Everything. I know what I am."

"Ah," she said, brightening. "Finally."

Chapter Twenty Nine

The Past Comes to Light

Tannin told them about life in Stonestead to their mounting horror.

"They experimented on children?!" Ava paled at the notion.

Tannin shrugged and coiled a loose thread around her fingertip. "It wasn't really experimentin'. I think they knew what would happen."

"But how could they do that?"

"Because warg-blood is everythin' to them, so the opportunity to enhance it probably outweighed the sacrifices somehow."

"But how did they explain all those dead children?"

"We lived in the trainin' academy all year round except for a couple weeks. It was like one of those schools or whatever you have here that monks go to except it was for warg- bloods who were trainin' to be Golden and it was all hush hush. When they died, the Elders said it was a sickness."

"And people bought that? Surely, they can't have accepted that year after year?"

Tannin shook her head. "Stonestead is so isolated, they didn't really have a choice not to accept whatever they were told. The word of an Elder was law and we'd suffered sicknesses before. It didn't take a lot though to convince people of the truth once my grandad found out what was really going on. And don't ask me how he found out, he just did. We were sworn to secrecy."

"What happened when they learned the truth?"

"All hell broke loose. The families of the dead novices practically tore down the academy walls. That was the night we left – me and my grandad, I mean. The buildings were all on fire. Hell, the whole city was on fire, and my grandad just showed up in the madness and told me to run. I have no idea what happened after we left."

"But how did you lose your memory?"

"I think it was the serum or potion of whatever it was. My grandad gave me the last dose because we were getting chased by the Redcaps in the woods, like in my dream remember? I don't think he was expectin' a fully formed warg. I bloody wasn't. But something must've been wrong with the timin' – you said I Changed too early or something like that? The blood-poisoning? – anyway, after I Changed back, I damn near lost my mind. I was sick for a long time, and then we came to Armodan. Before that, we travelled around a bit going from inn to inn. Spend quite a bit of time out in the marshes in a wee cabin on a lake."

Ava scribbled so frantically that her quill was in danger of tearing the parchment.

"Why did you come to Armodan?" she asked, not looking up from her parchment.

Tannin shrugged. "That was all my grandad's plan. I guess it's easy to hide in such a big place. Also, he was lookin' for other Remnants, remember? Maybe he was looking to join in with some other group."

"And you had no idea you were a warg?"

"How would I if I didn't remember and he never told me? I didn't even know that word until the other day." "What was in this enhancing potion?"

"No idea."

"I thought you remembered everything?"

"I don't remember what I never knew, Ava." Tannin pressed her fingertips into her temples. This was giving her another headache.

"What is a warg?"

Tannin smiled wryly. "Wargs are monsters. Rozhin told you as much."

"Interesting," Ava said, absentmindedly sucking on the feathered end of her quill. "Do you know anything specific about your Changed state?"

"I really don't know. Just that it frightened off Redcaps. And I can apparently take out three arsehole muggers at once."

"I wonder if other Remnants can change their shape still." Ava had that slightly crazed look of intensity in her eyes when she was working on a theory.

"They'd need the same kind of potion, right? Otherwise, the magic stuff in Remnant blood is too diluted for a Change."

"Maybe others managed to make one."

"Could be." Tannin yawned. "Aren't you tired yet? I'm tired."

Ava ignored her and kept scribbling. "We could write a whole new volume of Remnants in the Age of the Sun with this." She muttered mostly to herself.

"Oh yeah, I wanted to ask." Tannin suddenly remembered. "What on earth is the Age of the Sun?"

"It's just the name for the time after the fall o' the Fair Folk's Emperor. You know, the evil one?" Attilo explained.

"Sounds a bit overly dramatic," Tannin said. "What came before the Sun?"

"There's not much on that, but it was somethin' like the Age of Darkness."

"Age of Darkness. Who even speaks like that?"

"It was a long time ago," Ava said almost defensively, finally looking up from her notebook. "And I think it sounds poetic."

"You would, princess."

Ava made a face at her.

"Are we done here?" Tannin griped. "My head is killin' me with all this."

"Yes, yes. You can go home," Ava said, re-reading what she'd written. "Oh, tomorrow we won't be here. Duty calls." Her expression turned sour.

"Looks like you're thrilled about that." Tannin remarked.

"It's... wedding stuff."

"Oh," Tannin grimaced. "Can you really not get out of it?"

"This was all arranged when I wasn't even in the room. What makes you think they care what I want?"

"That is a fair point," Tannin said. "Good luck I guess?"

"G'night," Attilo said, graciously opening up the trapdoor for her, letting the night air swirl in.

"Hey, make sure Ava goes to bed too, all right? She looked dead on her feet," Tannin said, poking her head back into the gloom one last time.

"Easier said than done once she gets her teeth into somethin'." Attilo grinned. "Get home safe."

"Oh please." Tannin rolled her eyes. "Weren't you paying attention? Even durin' Samhain, I'm the scariest thing out there."

Chapter Thirty

If You Go Down to the Woods Today

Tannin tramped through the overgrown grass in between the towering trees. She swung her satchel down on an upturned stump, sat down next to it and unlaced her boots. She liked these boots and wasn't going to risk them getting all torn up. She remembered what she was going to transform into, and they definitely wouldn't fit. The bag had a spare set of clothes, a waterskin and an apple grabbed hastily from Mrs O'Baird's pantry for a late morning snack.

She sighed. She'd been at this for weeks. Trying to find whatever it was inside that made the beast – the warg – come out, but it was like striking a dud match. As much as she tried to strike it, she just couldn't catch that spark. The woods were the obvious choice for a place to practice – far enough away from any onlookers or potential casualties depending on how badly it went, but close enough that she could get there on foot.

Ava had initially suggested taking a horse but quickly rescinded the offer when Tannin reminded her that she'd eaten one the last time. On foot was best. And alone. Both Ava and Attilo had wanted to come with her, but she had no idea if she could control herself in that state. She certainly hadn't made any choices herself that night with her would-be-muggers.

Or had she? She wondered. If she had made the decision, would she have chosen any different? Probably not. If she'd had her knife on her that night, she would have used it without hesitation, she knew that. She'd lain awake at night a few times since then trying to work out if she felt guilty or not about killing them. Taking a life was a big deal but, curiously enough, she didn't feel any different for having done it. It had been them or her. The horse was a different story though. Remembering the joy she'd felt ripping into it made her feel sick to her stomach. That definitely hadn't been her. That was whatever beast lurked under her skin. The thought of it gave her uncomfortable goosebumps.

Memories of that night weren't the only ones that plagued her. Ever since the meeting with Rozhin, she'd been having intense flashbacks. Sparked by the most mundane of items or words or scents, they would come crashing in until she felt like her head was too full to cope anymore.

Being out in the forest helped. The clean air and most importantly the silence. It was calming and let her shuffle through all the disjointed memories like she was trying to organise a deck of cards until they fell near enough into place.

Even so, as she noticed a spray of brambles peeking out from a tangle of thorns, another memory flashed behind her eyelids.

"Are you sure you can eat them?"

Dana nodded fervently, shoving more berries in her mouth and giving her a purple grin with juice dripping down her chin. "I eat them all the time."

Tannin plucked one from the bush and inspected it before popping it in her mouth and making a face at the sourness of it.

"I'm taking some home," Dana announced, holding the bottom of her tunic up to make a makeshift basket. "I'm gonna pick so many, and my mum is gonna make a bramble cake."

Tannin perked up at the word "cake". "Do you think my grandma knows how to make it?"

"All grannies know how to make cakes," Dana said confidently and so Tannin filled her own tunic, staining the white fabric with streaks of purple.

She chuckled a little at the memory. She'd gotten in trouble for ruining her tunic, but her grandmother still thanked her for bringing her them and said it had been a thoughtful gift but next time to use a basket. Little Tannin had just wanted bramble cake but had accepted the thanks glowingly anyway. Almost every autumn after, she had filled a basket to take home until she was sent away for training. There had been no bramble bushes in the novice compound.

Tannin closed her eyes as she sat down on an upturned tree and let her heartbeat settle after her hike. Deep breaths left puffs of white in the air. She felt the tree under her, the gentle breeze, a slight tickle on her hand. Her eyes snapped open, and she slapped at the tiny spider marching up her finger.

Ava's books had all talked about control when it came to transformations or energy transfers, but weeks of meditation and soul searching had dug up nothing but impatience and a quickly growing hatred of bugs.

Maybe I'm just not that deep.

She took out her apple and bit into it. The two times that she'd managed to transform were times she'd been in danger. There had been a need for it. She'd tried to bring this up with Ava, but she was set on her theory of "know thine own self" as the book put it. But Ava wasn't here now. Tannin finished the apple and threw the core into the undergrowth. What kind of danger could she find out here, she wondered? Would the warg come out if she went over a precipice or did she need a physical opponent?

The snap of a twig somewhere in the trees sent her instinctively into a crouch. She watched, barely breathing, for any sign of movement. If she hadn't already been watching, she would have missed it. The slow, deliberate step of the doe sniffing for berries in the mess of wild thorns. No, an opponent wasn't what she needed, Tannin thought with growing excitement.

Prey.

This time the match struck smoothly. An undeniable flicker of heat sparked in her chest. The heat again rose to become almost unbearable, but she was expecting it and gritted her teeth while keeping her eyes glued to that soft pelt. White and creamy brown. Hot blood pulsing through long, elegant limbs and up through that long, elegant throat. She bit back a cry as her muscles swelled and gripped her shifting bones. She tasted blood as her clenched teeth grew and sharpened, cutting into her skin that wasn't quick enough to drag itself out of the way of her lengthening fangs. She could see the pulse in that silky throat so clearly. It was calling to her with every beat.

The doe was on alert now. It couldn't see her yet, hidden as she was crouched amongst the grass. Maybe it heard. Maybe it caught her scent or some other keen sixth sense was sending signals of danger screaming into its brain. She took a careful step forward, glowing yellow eyes never wavering from the creature. The motion broke whatever spell had frozen the deer in place. It shot from the undergrowth, its hooves pounding the earth in a flurry of desperate movement.

Tannin lunged after it. Except she wasn't Tannin anymore. She was more. She was something wild and fierce and free. A beast. Her own feet, now four colossal taloned paws tore through branches and propelled her, snarling, through the forest. The air she breathed carried the tang of deer but also of dirt, grass and wildhog. The doe was fast, she was faster. She was gaining. Yearning to sink her fangs into that soft flesh and feel the blood drench her fur. Feel the life drain away to be soaked up by earthy roots in the quiet of the forest. As it should be. Prey and predator. Life and death.

The doe darted sideways through a narrow gap between two wide trunks, and the beast skidded, raking deep grooves in the dirt with needle-like claws to pounce after it. She clawed at the trees, propelling herself forward with powerful front legs when she couldn't run freely as the trees became thicker and closer together and springing cat-like from branch to branch. The deer struggled too as the roots became bigger and wilder, tripping its spindly legs and causing it to stumble. A thrill shot through the beast's spine as the deer fell and she leapt for the kill.

The deer's golden eyes were wide with terror. Golden eyes. Black eyes. Glassy black dead eyes. The beast faltered at the last second and careened into trunk with a thud and a confetti of falling leaves.

Tannin coughed as she swept her loose hair out of her face and lifted her head to see the doe scrambling over a fallen tree and racing into the foliage. She blinked and a grin stretched itself over her face. She'd done it. It was unbelievable, but at the same time it felt like the most real thing she'd ever experienced. She couldn't suppress a bark of laugher. And then a whoop. And finally, she let out a wolf-like howl that bounced off the trees and echoed through the forest. She was dangerous. She was powerful. She was – she looked down at herself – naked.

Fuck.

Chapter Thirty One

Accidents Happen

She'd chased the deer further than she thought, and it took an age to follow the trail of broken branches back to where she'd left her spare clothes and thankfully unharmed boots. She shivered violently as she redressed. Her numb fingers fumbled on the fastenings. She rubbed her hands and blew into them. Her nose was numb too. She was almost certainly going to get sick from this, she lamented, and her arms were covered in scratches from where she'd had to push through twigs and thorns. At least on a day like today, there was no risk of anyone else being up here in the woods. She grimaced at the thought of being caught up here bare for the world to see, in the freezing cold. That would be fun to explain.

Between her hike up there in the first place and finding her clothes again, time had gotten away from her, and the day was already drawing long by the time she saw the first roofs of the town, smoke piping merrily from their chimneys from roaring fires inside. Tannin quickened her pace, eager to be back in the warmth.

She'd sent Flint a note asking to go for a drink that night as way of an apology for blowing him off for ages while she dealt with her new-found realisations but was now deeply regretting it. She did miss him these days, and she probably owed him a bit of an explanation, but right now she was so so tired.

And cold. Now that she was close to home, the chill felt even more biting, and her teeth were chattering when she finally arrived back home.

"Ms Hill? Ah, there ye are. I'm havin' some work done in the kitchen, dear. So, there's nae hot supper I'm afraid. There's sandwiches on the table. Everyone else is away oot at the tavern," Mrs O'Baird called from the hall.

Tannin heard her sniff as if offended that her sandwiches weren't good enough for her lodgers.

"Thank you, Mrs O'Baird," Tannin called behind her as she climbed the stairs. Gods, she was tired. Tired to her very bones. She didn't want to cancel on Flint again, but maybe she could sneak in a nap before it was time to meet him. She was about to collapse onto her bed when there was a loud thud and then a crash from below.

"Mrs O'Baird?" Tannin yelled. She did say she was getting work done, so maybe it was builders messing about in the kitchen. The lack of reply set the hairs on the back of her neck prickling uncomfortably.

Did the old woman just have a fall?

Despite her exhaustion, she heaved herself back up and went down to the kitchen.

"Mrs O'Baird?" she called again as she approached. "She went out," a thickly accented voice answered from behind her.

Tannin jumped. A broad, bearded man in overalls blocked the doorway to the lounge. One of the builders. The hairs on Tannin's neck again prickled.

Something's wrong.

"Did she say where?" Tannin kept a careful distance from the man and edged towards the kitchen door.

"No. Don't go in there, Miss." He warned as she reached for the kitchen door.

"Why?"

The pause was enough. She darted the last few steps to the kitchen and wrenched open the door. The sight that greeted her made her recoil. Mrs O'Baird was sprawled over the tiles, eyes wide open and blood still pooling from where the skin had torn around her cracked skull.

Tannin shrieked and immediately tried to go to her but out of the corner of her eye she saw the man in overalls lunge for her. She slammed the kitchen door on him and braced her back against it.

Mrs O'Baird...

Blood was filling up the gaps in the tiles and creeping across the floor like lines on a map threatening to engulf one of Mrs O'Baird's discarded house shoes.

Tannin shoved her shoulder against the door as the builder pounded on it. He was three times her size. The door began to force its way open. She changed tactic and leapt back, letting go of the door and letting him fly through, tripping over Mrs O'Baird's prone body as he went. He crashed into the old stove with a flurry of curses.

Tannin didn't waste any time seeing if he would get up again and dashed towards the now unobstructed kitchen door. She only just managed to skid to a stop as another figure blocked her way. One she recognised.

"Hamish? What -?"

Hamish was wearing the same overalls as the bearded man. He held a length of rusted pipe in one hand that was dripping an altogether non-rust-like red onto the tiles.

"Aw hell. It's you." Hamish rubbed the back of his neck and rolled his shoulders.

"What – what's goin' on? Did you kill Mrs O'Baird?" Tannin's voice was shrill and panicky. She looked between the two men frantically. "Why? She never hurt anyone... she –"

"She wasnae supposed tae be here." The bearded man dropped his fake accent. He'd gathered himself up from his fall and was approaching her.

"Then..." Realisation dawned.

They're here for me.

Hamish swung the pipe.

Tannin ducked, and it smashed a cabinet behind her to splinters. She straightened up just in time for Hamish's fist to meet her face. Warmth spurted from her nose, and she fell to her knees with a cry. She desperately tried to reach for that inner spark to call her powers, to Change, to do something, but just as before the match refused to catch.

She was spent. Exhausted. Her eyes were streaming and when she put her hand to her face, it came away wet with blood.

Tannin stared at the blood covering her fingers and angrily held her sleeve to her nose to stem the flow.

"What the hell, Sommer?" she asked thickly. They had been supposed to be practicing blocks and parry manoeuvres with mock spears, but her training partner for the day, her cousin, had zoomed straight in and punched her. At four years older, Sommer was not only taller, stronger and more practiced, she was fiercely competitive. It was completely unfair for them to be paired together.

"Strike first, strike hard," Sommer replied primly, swinging her spear through the air expertly and tucking a strand of red hair behind her ear. "Or have you forgotten that lesson already?"

"Please stick to the lesson plan, Sommer, no sparring today." The tutor's voice sailed overhead. "A solid attack though. Tannin, work on your defence."

"Thank you, Master Theo," Sommer said, glowing with the praise. "Maybe one day you'll be half as good as me Tannin but not today."

Tannin called her a flurry of names in angry indignation as she launched herself at her smug older cousin, tackling her to the ground and covering them both in dust and blood.

She got a good few hits in before the tutors pulled them apart.

"Come on." The bearded man grabbed a fistful of Tannin's hair and dragged her upright. "Got tae make this look accidental. Get the door," he barked at Hamish.

Tannin yelled and tried to grab at the man's arm to release some of the agonising pressure on her scalp, but he caught her wrist and twisted her arm up behind her back until she cried out. Her shoulder screamed in protest as she was half- steered half-dragged out of the kitchen and towards the stairs. Attempts at bracing her feet against the steps failed, as did trying to grab at the handrail with her free hand. She tried screaming for help until a savage jab to the ribs from Hamish's pipe knocked the air out of her.

The bearded man managed to wrestle her all the way to the top of the stairs before she was able to drag a breath of air into her aching chest.

"Please. Don't," she gasped, spraying flecks of blood where it had run down from her nose to cover her lips and chin. She stared Hamish straight in the eye, hoping to find some kind of mercy there, and upon finding none she managed a weak, "Why?"

"Just business." He almost looked a little uncomfortable.

"Accidents happen."

And with that he gave the other man a nod. The grip on her hair and on her wrist released suddenly, but her relief was short-lived as the rusted pipe smashed into the side of her head and she careened down the steep stairs.

Chapter Thirty Two

Left For Dead

It was the smell of smoke that roused her. Drawing in a breath made her cough, which sent spasms of pain ricocheting through her body. Through hazy, half-shut eyes, Tannin could see the smoke swirling around the ceiling in clouds and lazy whorls. She coughed again and winced at the ache in her head as she rolled over. Something in the back of her mind told her she should have been dead already.

Bastards.

She had to get out of here. She dragged herself along the carpeted hall on her stomach to keep below the thick

smoke bellowing out from the kitchen.

Mrs O'Baird...

She was beyond help.

Tannin scooted along slowly, her bruised limbs protesting and begging to rest, until she could see the front door. And the hallway cabinet tipped over in front of it.

Fucking bastards.

They hadn't taken any chances. The other way out was through the kitchen, where she could already feel the heat of the flames emerging. Glancing backwards, the angry orange flames that were licking at the doorway told her she was out of time.

With a grunt and redoubled efforts, she crawled her way into the dining room where she had to pause, panting and seeking support against the wall. She couldn't let herself lay down completely. If she did, she'd never get back up again. The flames were getting closer, inching across the black, curling wallpaper. The smoke stung her eyes and clogged her throat as she crawled her way past the table with its platter of untouched sandwiches. Tannin groaned in effort as she dragged herself to the window using the ledge to haul herself partway up to fumble at the latch.

Fuck.

Her hands were slick with sweat and blood, and the latch wouldn't budge. She slammed her hand into the glass.

Fuck, fuck, fuck.

She slid back to the floor and rested her head on the wall, coughing weakly. She couldn't see anything she could break the glass with. She could barely see anything at all.

Breathing was getting difficult. The glow of the fire was flickering in the doorway. She gave a wry, hacking laugh.

What a way to go.

She had just about given up when there was a thud from the window above her. Another loud thud. The pane gave way with a final thud, and a crack showered her with tiny shards of glass.

"Tannin! Tannin, is that you?!"

She could have cried at the voice.

"Flint!" She tried to shout but it came out as a croak. It didn't matter, he was already fighting his way in through the window. Surprisingly strong arms lifted her out through the shattered window and lay her down on hard ground. She sucked in lungful after lungful of clean, cold air and coughed out the thick black smoke.

Concerned eyes swam into sight as she struggled to blink moisture into her dry, stinging eyes, and Tannin felt her hand grasped tightly. "Can you hear me? You all right?"

She tried to answer but only managed another wracking cough.

"Been better." She croaked.

The weakened wood of the house behind them cracked loudly and spat sparks into the air as the flames engulfed the upper floors. Smoke poured from every orifice of the building.

"Is there anyone else inside?"

Tannin shook her head, coughing.

The coughing sent pain stabbing through her ribs and back. She grimaced, holding her arms tight around herself. She couldn't suppress a groan as Flint helped her up. Her legs barely held her weight and the sudden elevation made her feel faint. Pain shot through her head as she staggered into him and then sank back to her knees.

"Shit. When you didn't show up, I thought you'd forgot or..." Flint breathed. His shirt and hands were already covered in her blood. "You need a healer, Tan. Your head–"

She shook her head and regretted it instantly. "I need to go to the necropolis."

"What? The hill of the dead?" Flint took her face in his hands and stared into her eyes, wiggling his fingers in front of her. "How many fingers?"

"Three, and I'm serious. I need to get there." She stubbornly tried to take a step on her own only to fall back on him as her shaky legs weakened again. "Trust me, please."

"Tan..."

"Please, Flint. I'll explain later I promise. Just get me there," she implored.

He bit his lip and then nodded. "Okay, okay. You can't walk that far. Uh, wait here. I'll get a horse."

"Round back." Tannin gasped as Flint lowered her to sit on the ground.

Flint dashed off round the side of the blazing building, ducking as a wave of heat sent broken glass shooting from an upstairs window.

Tannin sat alone on the pavement and gingerly traced her fingertips along her ribs. She didn't know how to tell if they were broken. They hurt a lot. Her leg too where she'd crashed into the stairs. Her head... He'd definitely hit her hard enough to break bones. Another cough wracked her body, and she collapsed fully onto the ground.

Frantic whinnying came quickly from the back of the house and almost immediately Flint came charging around the corner with the skittish brown and white horse.

Hooves slid and clattered on the stone while the horse fought against Flint's hold on the reins as it tried to flee from the flames.

"Tannin, get up!"

She tried, but her body had given all it could and all she could do was lay as a motionless heap in the muddy cobblestones. Flint had to tie the protesting horse to the fence to come and haul her up onto the saddle, which she did with much swearing and wincing. He climbed up behind her and reached around to take the reins.

The jolting of the horse's gallop was torture, but Tannin gritted her teeth and reminded herself it was the quickest way. As soon as they dismounted, the terrified mare jerked free and sprinted and honestly, Tannin couldn't blame her.

"What the hell are we doing here? You need to go to a healery, Tan," Flint asked anxiously as he looped her arm around his neck and half carried her through the graves.

"I'm fine," she lied through clenched teeth. "Up here."

"If I get eaten by a Sluagh, I'll never forgive you," he muttered, his eyes scanning the decrepit tombstones warily.

Tannin dug the bulky key that Attilo had given her out of her pocket and indicated for him to open the latch.

"Help me down."

"Into a tomb? Are you insane?"

"Please. Trust me."

Flint let her use him as a crutch once more. They climbed down the crumbling stairs, awkwardly ducking under the low ceiling. The crypt was unsurprisingly empty as they reached the cavern. Flint lit a lantern as Tannin lay on the rug.

"What is this place?" he asked half wary, half in awe.

"It's... a secret place. Promise you won't tell anyone about it."

"Tannin." He knelt at her side, his brow furrowed in concern. "What is going on? What is all this? Who did this to you?"

Tannin was about to answer when the door to the tunnel crunched open and Attilo marched in. He drew his sword at the sight of Flint.

"Who are you?!" he barked.

"Attilo." Tannin croaked weakly. "He's a friend, it's okay."

Attilo gave Flint a stern look just as Ava burst out of the passage and rushed to Tannin.

"Oh gods, what happened to you?!"

"Triquetra... I think."

"Are you okay?"

Tannin was going to say that she was fine, but the lie caught in her throat.

"Move away," Attilo commanded, and Ava reluctantly

shifted a little. "Anything broken?"

"...don't know."

Attilo grunted and then took his time inspecting her limbs and moving her joints. He spent a lot of time peering in her eyes and examining her head wound.

"May I?" He indicated to the hem of her shirt.

Tannin gave a shrug. He lifted it slightly then grimaced at the already mottling purple and black bruising.

"It doesnae look like anythin's broken, but ye've taken a hell of a beatin'. Ye'll need some stitches too." He eased her shirt back down. "What happened?"

Tannin swallowed hard. "They were waitin' for me when I got home. They killed Mrs O'Baird and attacked me. Threw me down the stairs. Set the place on fire. Flint got me out." She looked at him. "I would've died."

Flint, who had been hovering awkwardly this whole time, was pale-faced and had gasped at the news of Mrs O'Baird's demise. Attilo and Ava both looked at him now.

"Thank you, Mr Flint," Ava said.

"It's just Flint," he muttered, eyes still wide and fearful. "Who are you? Can you help her?"

"Friends of Tannin," Attilo said curtly. "Thank you for yer help, we can take it from here."

"But -"

"It's all right, Flint. They are friends of mine," Tannin rasped, eyes already closing. "You saved my life... thank you."

The rest of the conversation between Ava, Attilo and Flint seemed to swim through the air and only reached her ears distorted and heavy. She couldn't even tell who was speaking as consciousness drifted away.

Chapter Thirty Three

Bedside Manners

The first thing Tannin saw when she opened her eyes was smoke swirling in clouds and lazy whorls around the ceiling.

She gave a strangled cry and leapt to her feet. Or tried to. The blanket that had been covering her tangled around her legs, and she ended up rolling off the couch in a heap. She cried out as her bruised body thudded onto the tiles. Tiles? What?

"Hey! Shh! It's okay." Ava knelt beside her and cupped her face in her hands.

"Ava? There's a fire..." Tannin babbled, still wild-eyed and panicked.

"Shh, it's okay. You're safe. You're in the castle. You're with me."

Tannin blinked and slowly took in the room. She was in a large, fully tiled room with elaborate pipes and sinks lining one wall and a huge sunken pool in the middle of the room filled with water and some kind of petals. Ava's bathing room. The swirling smoke she'd seen was steam rising from the water and coiling around the domed ceiling.

She sighed in relief and sagged against Ava.

"Come on. Up you get. Easy. You can tell me more about what happened after we get you cleaned up a little. You're bleeding again."

She helped Tannin to sit back up on the couch and gently sponged her face with a soft white cloth dipped in warm water.

"There are oils in the water that will help. I already stitched up your head, but honestly it was closing itself as fast as I could stitch. You'll have to thank those ancestors of yours," Ava said as she cleaned away the fresh blood that leaked from Tannin's nose. "You heal so quickly now."

She paused, looking at Tannin with those serious eyes of hers. "What happened?"

Tannin shrugged and then winced. "I think they must've been hired by the Triquetra. I knew one of them. It was the man Attilo knew from when we tried to steal that lens, remember? They were waitin' for me... They killed my landlady... Attacked me with a pipe, threw me down the stairs and set the place on fire," she said between Ava's dabs with the cloth.

Ava shook her head almost in disbelief. "We should have known. We should have taken better care of you." Her fingertips lingered on Tannin's cheek. "I should have taken better care of you."

"I'm fine."

"Your face tells a different story."

Tannin laughed and then winced again sharply and clutched her ribs.

"Argh, don't make me laugh. It hurts."

"Sorry." Ava reached up and brushed a tangled strand of hair from Tannin's face.

"You're fighting a losing battle there." Tannin looked down at herself. Between the blood, smoke and dirt, she was pretty sure her clothes were ruined. "I'm a mess."

"Mhm." Ava agreed. "That's why I ran you a bath. It will help the pain and any swelling as well as clean you up. I was going to let you sleep a little longer, but I guess you're awake now."

Tannin groaned happily. "A bath sounds lovely. Thank you."

Ava knelt in front of Tannin and deftly unlaced her boots for her, waving off Tannin's embarrassed protests. "You've had a long day."

Tannin chuckled weakly. "Beaten to a pulp and left to die in a fire is not my ideal evenin'."

She let Ava help her out of her jerkin but quickly assured her she could get the rest on her own.

"You really could have died tonight."

"I know." She grinned. "But you're not gettin' rid of me that easily."

Ava only managed a weak smile at her joke. "You can't go back into the town for a while, you know that. It's not safe. You can stay here until you're healed. After that, Attilo will find you somewhere to stay."

Tannin nodded. "Where's Flint?"

"We sent him home well paid I assure you. He says he won't say anything," Ava said. "I'm so relieved he got there in time."

"Me too," Tannin said in earnest. She would've suffocated in the smoke or been burnt to a crisp without him. She shuddered. "Gods, I owe him a hell of an explanation. And many, many drinks."

"All in good time. I'll be right outside if you need anything." Her hand lingered on Tannin's arm for a moment.

Getting the rest of her clothes off was slow going but she managed it and let them fall next to the couch. She definitely needed new ones. Tannin paused. If the fire had gotten to the upper floors, she'd need new everything.

Everything would be gone. She groaned at the thought. She could worry about that later. The air in the bathing room brought goosebumps to her bare skin while the sweetly- scented steam lured her aching body down the tiles steps and into the water.

A mirror on the wall showed her battered face, and she grimaced. She gently shook out the remainder of her hair that hadn't already come down out of its knot and let it settle messily about her shoulders. Ava had cleaned some of her face but down her neck was still grey with ash. A neat line of stitches ran from her forehead into her hair line.

"What do you know, her sewin' is pretty," Tannin muttered, inspecting the stitches.

Tannin gave a contented sigh as she steeped in the perfumed water.

Standing in the deepest part, the water reached to her elbows, and as she lowered herself in fully, she breathed in the flowery scent of the petals. It smelled like Ava. She sat on one of the stairs and leaned her head back on the ledge, eyes closed, the warm water up to her chin.

Oh, this is nice.

She sat there a while letting the heat seep into her stiff joints and bruised muscles. Dipping her head under the water, she let the warmth cover her entirely and soak the dried blood from where it clung to her hair.

Coming back up from under the water, she pushed her hair back and wiped the beads of water from her eyes to see Ava's face smirking down at her.

"Enjoying yourself?"

Tannin jumped and accidentally swallowed a mouthful of water.

"Ava! What are you doin'?" she spluttered.

"Checking that you haven't drowned. You've been in here a while."

"Ava, I'm naked!" Tannin squealed, folding her arms over her chest.

"I can see that," Ava said with a smirk and a raised eyebrow.

Tannin scowled at her.

"How're you feeling?" she asked a little softer.

Tannin wiggled from side to side. The stabbing pain was no longer as biting. "Bit better actually."

Ava nodded knowingly. "Does wonders, doesn't it? It's the oil from these petals." She paused and then said in a more serious tone, "You scared the life out of me coming in all banged up like that. You could have really died."

Tannin smiled. "You were worried about me?"

"I always worry about you."

"Oh, is that so?"

"You can't even fight me, how are you supposed to take on Triquetra assassins?" Ava replied smugly.

"You're such a prick. I've kicked your arse more than a few times and you know it!" Tannin said slapping a hand in the water, launching a spray up to drench Ava. She squealed.

"That's what you get for sneakin' in on me bathing," "Tannin, I'm soaked!"

"May as well join me then." It just slipped out. Tannin froze.

Ava's eyes widened and then her mouth twitched up in a mischievous smile. "All right then."

"What, seriously?"

"Turn around."

Tannin turned her back and waited, listening to the rustling sounds of Ava shedding her clothing and then the gentle splash as she entered the water. She risked a glance and got a face full of water as Ava splashed her.

"I didn't say you could look." Ava's tone was playful.

"Hey! I am injured. You're supposed to be nice to me."

Tannin wiped the water from her eyes again, and when she opened them, Ava was fully immersed across the pool from her. She leaned back against the side, arms outstretched, and eyes closed. She gave a quiet moan as she sunk a little deeper into the water. Tannin's eyes followed the smooth lines of her outstretched arms to her shoulders, her neck and down to where the water reached the gentle curve of her...

She looked away. The water suddenly felt far too hot. She cleared her throat.

Ava opened her eyes. "Yes?" That mischievous smile played on her lips. Lips that were full and soft-looking.

"Nothin'," Tannin said, still averting her gaze.

"You're not shy, are you?" Waves rippled over the surface of the pool as Ava glided closer.

"No."

"Good."

Tannin couldn't help but meet Ava's eyes.

A strand of dark hair had fallen from its fixing and lay on her flushed skin. Tannin instinctively reached up to tuck it back behind Ava's ear as Ava had done for her before but couldn't bring herself to take her hand away. It rested there against her cheek. Her breath caught in her throat as she felt Ava's own hands come to rest on either side of her, pressing into the wall behind her. Those blue eyes were like pools themselves. Those lips...

"Princess Avalyn?" Attilo's shout came from the other room and the spell was shattered. They froze and then jumped apart.

Ava muttered something and splashed out of the pool. "Just a minute!" she called back, grabbing a thick white robe the second she was out of the water and throwing it around her still wet shoulders. She was still muttering as she stalked out of the room.

Tannin stayed in the warmth a little longer, slightly dazed, until her heart had stopped racing. Ava had left her a stack of impossibly soft white towels which Tannin quickly dried off with and then wrapped around herself. Now that she was out of the pool and its medicinal oils, the ache in her body was creeping back in.

It didn't take long until Ava returned. "He's gone."

Tannin nodded and made to stand up from the couch where she'd sat down to wait. Ava must've noticed her pained expression.

"Come. I have some balm for the bruising."

Tannin perched uneasily on the cushioned bench at the end of Ava's magnificent four poster bed as she fetched a tub of strange smelling balm.

"Here. Rub this on wherever hurts and it'll help."

"Wait," Tannin said as Ava turned to leave.

Dare I?

She took a deep breath. "Help me with it?" She held out the tub.

Ava smiled almost shyly and took the balm back.

"Show me," she said softly.

Tannin swallowed hard but let her towel fall to bare her back. She heard Ava hiss through her teeth as she saw the patterns of livid bruising from where she'd hit the stairs.

The balm that she smoothed onto the angry purple blotches was cool and tingled.

"What is this stuff?"

"Ground leaves and roots and all sorts of things that if I try and explain you'll stop paying attention like you always do." Ava chided. "I make it myself to use after trainings. The perks of being a druid-blood. You can't exactly have a black and blue princess, can you?" She smiled. "Speaking of which, you have a really black eye. Look at me."

Tannin turned to face her and stayed still as Ava applied a generous layer of the balm to the bridge of her nose and around her eye. She added more daubs along her forehead above her eyebrow where the pipe had cracked into her skull.

"Where else?"

"Here." Tannin shifted her towel to bare her thigh where another deep bruise had already formed.

Ava reached across her lap and placed her hand where Tannin indicated.

"Here." She echoed rubbing the soothing gel in small circles.

Tannin was still clutching her towel against her chest as Ava trailed her fingertips along her leg and up to her ribs. "Here?"

Tannin nodded. She couldn't speak. Her heart was thundering as she let the towel fall away completely.

Ava was silent as she massaged the balm into Tannin's skin and then trailed her fingers further up to Tannin's bare chest and paused there. Her feather-light touch was questioning.

Ava's eyes flicked to her eyes and then her lips.

Fuck it.

Tannin leaned in and closed the space between them. The instant their lips met, it was like nothing else existed. Ava kissed her back with thrilling ferocity, pulling her in and entwining her hand in Tannin's still damp hair.

Sparks danced at the point of contact as they rose together and stumbled towards the bed. Tannin looped one finger into the tie keeping Ava's robe closed and gave it a suggestive tug. Ava loosened it to slip the soft covering from her shoulders and tossed it aside.

They toppled together onto the sheets. Touching, exploring, kissing hungrily.

Ava ended up on top and her mouth left Tannin's to trail along her jaw. Her teeth scraped gently, tantalizingly until her lips met that sensitive spot under Tannin's ear and then down the side of her neck. She shuddered and a tiny groan escaped her as goosebumps leapt up under Ava's touch.

"Careful," Ava murmured playfully against her neck. "These walls aren't as thick as they look. You'll have to be quiet."

Tannin chuckled and then flipped them over so that Ava was underneath her, making her squeal in surprise.

She captured Ava's chin in one hand and gave her a devilish smile. "Oh princess, it's not me that's gonna have a problem with keepin' quiet."

Chapter Thirty Four

G'morning

The stained-glass window bathed the room in muted colours. It took Tannin a second to remember where she was but when she did, she smiled and nuzzled into the soft sheets with a contented sigh.

Rolling over, she saw Ava lying next to her in the bed. She lay on her stomach facing away from her with her hair splayed messily over the pillow and the sheets bunched around her hips. Tannin watched the rise and fall of her slow, deep breathing. She propped herself up on an elbow and stroked a finger gently down the sleeping girl's back, across the little bumps of her spine and traced the few moles that marked her skin. How could a person's skin be so soft? Tannin had marvelled at it the night before, and she marvelled at it again. The softness. Under her fingers, her lips, her tongue.

Ava's breathing changed, and she turned her head groggily. Upon seeing Tannin smiling at her, she smiled back.

"G'morning." Her voice was husky with sleep. "Mornin', you."

"Mmm. Keep doing that." Ava closed her eyes again and snuggled into the pillow as Tannin resumed lazily grazing her nails up and down.

Ava was clearly not a morning person, Tannin mused as she ran her fingers up and through her dark waves, curling one around her finger and watching how it sprang back.

"Ava?" Tannin said, struck by a sudden thought.

"Mhm."

"I don't have any clothes."

At that Ava opened one eye and smiled mischievously. "Who says you need any?"

"Ah, so that's your plan, is it?" Tannin shuffled back down on the bed and leaned in to leave a trail of tiny smiling kisses along the back of Ava's shoulder.

"No plan." She yawned and stretched in a way that made Tannin's breath catch a little. "No plans, no rush, no need to get up. And besides you should be resting anyway."

"I feel fine." The truth of it actually surprised her. A dull ache lingered along her back and in her head, but she could move without the stabbing pain of the day before.

"Maybe wargs are just hard to kill," Ava mumbled sleepily before shoving her face back into the pillows.

Tannin crept out of the bed, briefly fighting Ava for a sheet to wrap around herself and wandered around the room.

Not many people had the opportunity to snoop in a princess's room and Tannin was especially curious. Where did Ava meet Princess Avalyn?

Apart from the rumpled bed, the rest of Ava's rooms were impossibly, oppressively neat. As she padded around, Tannin saw little trace of the Ava she knew. The flowers in their vase were pretty, and plump cushions and fur rugs were rich and luxurious but to Tannin it all just felt a bit... not empty – there were plenty of decoration and shiny trinkets – but just... impersonal? Did everyone in the castle think she was this bland? Then again, she was supposed to be some sheltered, pious princess. It was a clever cover.

Tannin approached a little table and chair set at the window where a book was laying open next to a half-melted candle. It looked like Ava had been up reading before she came down to the crypt the night before.

"How did you know to come to the crypt last night? Is there an alarm or somethin'?"

Ava moaned and rolled over onto her back, one arm over her face to block out the light. "Sensed you."

"From that distance?" Tannin said. "That's actually impressive."

"Only for some people."

"What?"

"I can only do it for some people," came the grumpy reply.

Oh, Ava really isn't a morning person.

"Is it 'cause you like me?" Tannin jibed.

A prolonged groan came from the bed, and Tannin nodded satisfied. "It's 'cause you like me."

She turned her attention to the book. It was set open at a page with a stylised painting and a page of compact, tiny text. She dismissed the text immediately. She may have been awake but not awake enough to tackle that, and she looked instead at the drawing.

Thin lines in red ink showed glowing eyes and fangs in a contorted tangle of furred limbs. Below the picture "The Transformation" was inked. The image thudded into her mind like a physical blow.

She grabbed the book and bounded back to the bed. "Ava!"

"Shhhhhhhhh."

"No, wake up!"

"What?" she demanded groggily.

"This!" Tannin tipped the picture towards her. "I managed the Change yesterday. I'd completely forgotten with the fire and attempted murder and everything, but I did it and I chased a deer!"

Ava blinked at her and slowly sat up rubbing her eyes. "A deer?"

"Yes!" Tannin sat back and revelled in the memory, letting the forgotten feeling of freedom and power wash over her. "I really am a warg."

It felt right. She scanned the text excitedly, the remains of sleepiness shaken from her mind.

"Strong of bone, tough of muscle, it is difficult to cause injury to a warg in a transformed state. They are weakest in their human skin. However, the human form is also durable and resilient against attack. If one wishes to destroy a warg, they must do so carefully, quickly and without hesitation."

"Fearsome as warriors and as beasts, their mentality is always toward physical strength. A warg attack can always be expected to be a full-frontal assault."

"They will almost always travel as a pack, yet the lone warg is vulnerable. To kill a warg you must first isolate it."

Tannin frowned, her brow furrowing, as she flipped the pages looking for more. This was all about how to kill a warg.

"Guess we were never popular," she murmured to herself as she again studied the vicious drawing. She nudged Ava with her foot.

"Oi, princess?"

"Mmm?"

"This book is entirely about how to kill me. Should I be worried?"

"Maybe," came the grumbled reply. "If you keep waking me up."

"It makes us sound like big dumb beasts that will just kill anythin'." Tannin closed the book with a disgusted snap. "Where did you even find this?

Ava turned around with half opened eyes and reached over to pat Tannin on the head. "There, there. You are very smart."

"Arsehole." Tannin pushed her hand away but couldn't help the grin that stretched across her face.

Eventually, Tannin's restlessness roused a still grumbling Ava from the nest of blankets as she dragged Tannin away from the book and into her dressing room.

"I'm not wearin' anythin' with ruffles," Tannin said seriously as she looked at the racks of frilly dresses with dismay.

"I think you'd look lovely with ruffles."

Tannin snorted.

"Here." Ava rolled her eyes and tossed her a loose grey shirt with crisscross laces at the front. "This was my brother's. It's his clothes I wear down in the crypt. All my clothes have ruffles."

Ava dug out a pair of breeches to go with the shirt that fitted Tannin's small frame well enough if she tightened a belt around them. Ava helped her get dressed despite Tannin's protests that she wasn't hurting as much anymore.

"You just want to touch me a little more, don't you?"

Ava slapped her arm lightly and shushed her.

"Oh, so you mean you don't want to? Shall I do the touchin' instead?" Tannin murmured suggestively.

Ava reached over and pulled her close by the front of her shirt. "Those are dangerous words."

"Mm? What are you gonna do about –"

Ava silenced her with a kiss.

Tannin chuckled, using their closeness to run her hands over Ava's goosebumped skin and deliberately grind her hips into Ava's, making her gasp.

"So much for the pure and innocent princess," Tannin said, kissing the side of her neck and feeling her pulse race under her tongue.

"Aren't I just full of surprises?"

Tannin grinned up at her. "Surprise me, then."

Ava twirled a lock of Tannin's pale hair in between her fingers as they lay entwined on the furs covering the dressing room floor, their clothing strewn across the room.

"I've never done someone else's hair before."

"Neither have I, to be honest. Unless you count seeing how many toothpicks I could stick in Eve's hair before she noticed." Tannin rolled over to prop herself up on her elbows and noticed with amusement how wistfully Ava was looking at her. "Knock yourself out if you want to."

What Ava lacked in skill, she more than made up for in enthusiasm as she attacked Tannin's tangles with a comb. When it was finally brushed through and soft, Ava let it fall through her fingers as she rattled through a list of styles she could try – none of which Tannin knew, so she didn't offer any opinions. Besides, she was enjoying Ava just running her fingers through her hair.

She sat with her eyes closed as Ava tried out a few things and decided they were too difficult.

It took a few attempts but Ava, having ultimately decided on something simple, finally and with a flourish, pinned back the twin braids she'd made with the locks of hair at the front with a white floral clasp.

"It looks nice," Tannin said, tilting to see the sides in the mirror. "Looks like I've got my own wee tiara."

Ava nodded. "That's the idea. I have this in summer usually and then get flowers woven in."

"You don't stay here in summer, do you?" Tannin said, remembering a snippet of conversation from the bakery.

They swapped places and Tannin took up the comb. She stared at Ava's mass of dark hair. In the daylight, it had tints of chestnut and copper. She really had no idea what to do with it.

"No, we summer in Highholde. It's a really beautiful place."

Highholde was a smaller city in the Brochlands, nestled in the lush glens to the southwest.

"Better than Armodan?"

"Prettier definitely. And fewer people, so I can go out more there." She sighed. "My brother used to take me out on the loch in a rowing boat."

"Florian?"

"Of course." Ava snorted. "My brother Justus and I don't get on very much. Florian didn't like him much either even though they were closer in age."

Tannin tried not to pull the comb too harshly. "You must miss Florian a lot."

"I do. He would've been a really good king. He was always looking out for me and trying to make things better for everyone." She sighed. "I always assumed Flo would take care of things."

The comb was now fully entangled in Ava's thick waves and Tannin tried as carefully as possible to extract it.

"Uh huh. What's Justus' stance on Remnants by the way? He'll be king here one day, right? Should we be worried about that?"

The more she tried to tease the comb out, the more it seemed to tangle itself in.

"I'm not sure. He really doesn't talk to me." "Does he know you're..."

"No." Ava shook her head and Tannin lost her grip on the comb. It hung suspended in its nest of hair. "It's kind of a bigger secret than I let on. Only a few people know. Even I don't know who my real father is."

"I kinda guessed it was a touchy subject. Do you wanna talk about somethin' else?"

"No, it's fine. It's actually nice to have someone to talk to."

"Any time," Tannin muttered, distractedly. She had entirely lost sight of the comb now. "And what would your, uh, fiancé think of me being here right now?"

"It's none of his business," Ava said firmly.

"What goes on in your bedroom isn't your husband-to-be's business? Mhm okay."

"I never wanted to marry him anyway, and I never gave him any indication that I did. He can't blame me if my interests lie elsewhere.

"Is that so?" Tannin purred, leaning in close so that her lips grazed the outer shell of Ava's ear. "Bad princess."

She laughed as Ava's playful slap cracked against her thigh before fruitlessly tugging at the comb. "How is this so impossible?!" she asked, exasperatedly.

"Are you all right back there?"

"No!" she said in frustration. "Your hair has a life of its own, and it's eaten your bloody comb!"

Ava ended up insisting on calling in her attendants to finish off Tannin's failed attempt at hairstyling while Tannin hid in the bathing room, sulking. She was sure she would be able to fish the comb out of there eventually.

Her stomach squirmed as she listened to the muted sounds of polite conversation from the other room. Ava had assured her that no one would enter the bathing room and she'd be safe there, but she still felt trapped as she tried to pace as silently as possible. She wondered what the punishment would be if they found her here? Was this technically trespassing or something more serious? It felt like forever before Ava finally came in to tell her she could come out now.

Except it wasn't Ava. This was definitely Princess Avalyn. Along with doing some sort of dark magic to make her hair glossy and sleek, her attendants had also plied her with makeup to give her red lips and lined her striking eyes in black kohl.

She seemed to hold herself differently too – stand a little straighter with her head a little higher. Tannin couldn't help feeling of being looked down on more than just due to their height difference. She scowled and crossed her arms.

"I thought I had the day to myself today, but duty calls," Avalyn said hurriedly, chiding Tannin towards the tapestry that covered the hidden doorway. "Go down to the crypt and entertain yourself and I'll be down in a few hours."

"But –"

"Just a few hours. And it's not safe for you to go out either, okay? So, stay there."

"Fine, fine." Tannin let herself be ushered out. Once she'd ducked through into the dark tunnel, she turned to say goodbye only to be met with the curt click of the closing door.

She tried not to feel to dismissed but found herself grumbling regardless as she picked her way down the tunnels. She marveled at how well she could see in the dark now compared to the first time she'd stumbled her way down these passages to the crypt. She could see offshoots here and there along the passage that were boarded up or blocked off and she wondered where they went. Maybe she'd explore them sometime. Of course, she had no idea where they led and the idea of having to explain what she was doing if she was caught was not an appealing one.

Especially since she was wearing Ava's brother's clothes. She didn't know what would be worse. The implication that she'd spent the night with the prince, the king to be, or the truth that she'd spent it with the princess.

Either way, I'd be royally screwed if anyone sees me.

Tannin chuckled to herself in the dark.

Royally screwed. Gotta remember that one. Ava will hate it.

Whatever Ava said, Tannin knew that Prince Erlan would be furious and embarrassed if he knew how she'd spent the previous night. It could even lead to a political incident between Rill and the Brochlands. Tannin bit her lip. Was it worth all that?

Yes, a small voice in the back of her mind whispered. And she really had to agree. She replayed the memories of the previous night and found herself involuntarily grinning.

Tannin wandered around the crypt, playing with the various artifacts and trinkets in the shelves, but even that couldn't stop her from getting bored very quickly. She wondered what Ava was doing. Princess duties. What did they entail apart from marrying princes and waving from the window of golden carriages at the common folk? Whatever it was, it was taking ages.

Finally, after she was finished with whatever royal business she had, Ava poked her head out of the tunnel and invited a thoroughly impatient Tannin back upstairs for a late lunch. Tannin had been steadily getting hungrier as she kicked about in the crypt and was thrilled to see the spread laid out on the low table when they re-entered Ava's rooms.

"Help yourself. You must be starving. I'm so sorry I forgot about breakfast."

"What on earth is that?"

"Haven't you ever seen a waterfowl before?"

"From a distance, and it was still flappin'."

At Ava's guidance, Tannin tried a little bit of everything, including a strong-tasting bitter drink that Ava swore was good but made Tannin splutter.

"So, what do you peasants usually eat at home?" Ava asked playfully, biting into a slice of something Tannin had already forgotten the name of.

"I'm no peasant, remember?" Tannin sat up straighter and fluttered her eyelashes. "I'm a noble lady of Stonestead."

"You are a peasant at heart."

Tannin made a face at her and then thought for a moment.

"I don't know. Depends on the season. Bread of course. Oats. Eggs. Riverfish on fish market days. Mrs O'Baird makes really good soup with roots and turnips... Made."

Tannin trailed off with a sudden rush of guilt. She'd almost entirely forgotten that Mrs O'Baird was dead. Murdered.

She'd been so caught up with Ava...

Ava seemed to guess what she was thinking and laid a hand on her arm. "I'm really sorry. I don't know if you were close?"

"I wouldn't say close, but she seemed so constant, you know? Reliable, old Mrs O'Baird. 'Dinnae be tracking muck on my floors, ye wee besom!'" Tannin rasped and

shook her finger in an imitation of the old woman and then sighed. "I don't know what I would've done without her. You know she let me be three weeks late on rent when you hadn't paid me?" She dug her elbow into Ava's side.

"Ow. I paid you a good wage."

"Mhm eventually." Tannin rubbed at her eyes and exhaled slowly. "What am I gonna do now?"

"Long term, I honestly don't know. But we'll figure it out. Together." She gave Tannin a surprisingly tender kiss on the cheek. She then speared a cube of something yellow that Tannin suspected was some kind of fruit and held the fork up to Tannin's lips. "Short term, you're going to let me educate you on the finer things in life."

Chapter Thirty Five

Restless

It wasn't long before Tannin was itching to get back to the peace of the forest. She wanted to Change again. No, needed to. As her injuries healed rapidly and her bruises had dulled to a sickly yellow, she found herself unbearably restless.

She had all the luxury she could ever ask for, but she found it impossible to relax. Every tiny sound made her think some servant or other was going to come bursting into the room to find her there or even worse – find her and Ava together in a compromising position.

Attilo was tracking down leads on Hamish and the fire, so they had a lot of time to themselves. When they weren't tumbling all over each other, they read over the passages about wargs in the old book again at Ava's insistence, and Tannin told her more about her Change. She felt stupid trying to tell her about her little "warg-fire" as she'd taken to calling it. The sensation of her transformed state was difficult to describe beyond that it just felt so intensely real. She was craving the feeling again.

Ava had told her a bit more about her Sensing too. It was subtle. She wouldn't have known to pay attention to these "gut-feelings" if it hadn't been for her nursemaid as a child. She said she strongly suspected that nursemaid knew who her father was and what he was. She had been the one to first tell Ava the stories of Remnants and Fair Folk in hushed tones and only when they were alone or sometimes with Florian. She knew the woman only as Mo. She taught her to pay attention to the signs and feelings that she saw and felt. Ava didn't know what had happened to Mo. She had simply been told one day that she had no need for a nursemaid any longer and she had been replaced by a symphony of tutors and instructors in everything from history and politics to languages and art who had no time for her Senses.

She'd never forgotten Mo's lessons though, and when she'd found *An Account of Remnants in the Age of the Sun* in a hidden latched panel in the castle library, she knew she had to keep it secret. She read the old tomes cover to cover as a child, and her understanding grew as the legends began to overlap with her history tutor's lessons. Questions about Fair Folk, however, had earned her harsh rebuke and ridicule. Children's bedtime stories had no place in the royal courts. Only Florian spoke about it with her and always in secret.

As an only child, Tannin was fascinated by Ava's tales of her brothers. By all accounts, Justus was a complete arse, and Ava crinkled up her face in distaste every time his name was mentioned. As for her younger brother, Prince Sontar or Sonny as she affectionately called him, Ava didn't see much of him. He was still a baby and other than crying and drooling on himself, he didn't do much. Although, apparently, he was particularly cute when dressed up in his little royal kilt.

Tannin loved the quiet time of just talking in the comfort of Ava's rooms, but nagging in the back of her mind was the knowledge that she knew couldn't stay there forever. She was hopelessly fidgety and stifled, so despite Ava's protests she ducked out of the crypt in the early hours of the next morning. She went long before anyone should be around and stole silently through the morning dew into the trees.

Going into the woods from the necropolis instead of starting from home meant she was far away from the paths that she knew, and she kept having to doublecheck her bearings.

The foliage here was wilder and whatever pathways there were in between the towering trees were overgrown and rough.

"Arghh." Tannin cursed. She'd stepped over a tree root straight into a deep mud-filled puddle. The hem of her breeches was soaked through where it trailed longer than it should. She was sick of tripping over them.

She took a dagger from its little sheath on her belt and slit through the fabric to shorten them. "There."

She was pretty sure this dagger was Attilo's sgian dubh and was supposed to be strapped to the ankle instead of on the belt, but she was used to carrying one there. Although it looked more ceremonial than practical, it was one of the only weapons she'd found in the crypt that wasn't dulled down to practice with and there was no way she was getting caught unarmed again. She turned it over in her hands, admiring how the light glinted off the gold inlay in the handle.

She hoped Ava wouldn't mind too much that she'd cut up her breeches.

Ava.

Tannin smiled.

When she thought she was far enough away from the town, Tannin stopped. She'd reached a patch of long grass where the trees had thinned out a little. This was as good a spot as any.

Now to just find a deer.

It wasn't nearly that easy. After hours of trailing around in the grass, getting steadily hungrier, colder and more impatient, Tannin was ready to give up. The woods didn't seem to have any deer today. Or even one measly rabbit for her to chase. Without a target, she'd been trying to coax out her little warg-flame without a shred of success. She remained stubbornly in her tiny, useless human body.

She was in a foul enough mood walking back when she realised the path she'd taken led back into the town and not to the necropolis. She hadn't been paying attention and had been about to waltz straight into town where anyone could see her.

Stupid.

She was about to turn and head back the way she saw the stone wall surrounding the ruins of the old watchtower. A little further and she'd be at the graveyard. They say talking to the dead helps.

Tannin didn't have any flowers. She wondered if Mrs O'Baird had even had a funeral yet. Was she already in the ground? Had there been enough left after the fire to bury? It had been her fault she had been murdered, Tannin thought not for the first time. The memory of Mrs O'Baird's broken body splayed out on the kitchen floor felt like a punch to the gut. The least she could do was say sorry.

Tannin hopped the low wall instead of walking around to the gate. The shortcut seemed vaguely disrespectful, and she immediately felt judged by the corbies that perched on the higher gravestones. She made a rude hand gesture at them. Who were birds to judge her when they would just as soon peck the eyes from the corpses themselves?

Looking around, it was clear there were no freshly dug graves. No new gravestones and no snatches of bright flowers showed between the dull brown earth and grey stone. Her guilty conscience would have to wait for another day.

She paused. There was another grave she could visit. She hadn't visited his grave since the funeral, and a dried up, half mushed bundle of what was once a bouquet suggested no one else had either. And why would they, she thought bitterly. Arsehole. There was so much he'd kept from her. Important things! Half of this shit was his fault.

If he'd just told me...

She kicked at the headstone savagely.

A tutting sound behind her shocked her back to her current surroundings and she spun around.

"That wasn't very nice was it?" came the drawling voice of the last person on earth she wanted to see.

"Clach?" She gasped bewildered. "What are you doin' here?"

"I could ask you the same question. A lot of people have a lot of questions for you."

She didn't answer as he came around from the tree he'd been leaning on, leering at her.

"Like how is it that a lodging house suddenly catches fire right after the landlady is murdered? Coincidence?" He paused. "Maybe a disagreement between a respectable landlady and a disreputable tenant turns into a murder most foul. Maybe it's lucky that the house is empty of other tenants, maybe it was planned, who knows.

Maybe the murderer sets the fire to cover the crime and walks away without a scratch, nowhere to be found." He spoke slowly and deliberately, his soulless eyes raking over her.

"That's not what happened." She took a step back as hecame closer.

"It's what the guards will believe."

"And who's gonna tell them that pack of lies?"

"Perhaps a group of concerned citizens who all grieve so for poor Mrs O'Baird. A gentle soul. I suppose... accidents do happen but what are the chances?"

"It wasn't me."

"Oh, you and I both know the truth, but the question is what will be believed?" He grinned unpleasantly. "Maybe if you turn yourself in and confess, then this doesn't have to get messy. There don't have to be any more... tragic accidents."

"If you know the truth... why would I confess? I didn't do anythin'."

His smile was replaced with a slight frown as if waiting for her to understand a joke.

"You will confess," he said slowly, "or things will get complicated."

The penny dropped.

Accidents. The fire. Mrs O'Baird. The sightlens. Hamish. My grandad.

Tannin's mouth fell open as the pieces of the puzzle clicked into place.

He's one of them. Triquetra.

"I see that we're on the same page," he said. "There's a reward for you as well, which is always handy. Come along."

He reached for her elbow, clearly intending to frog-march her back into town and to the nearest guard. Tannin flinched as his thick fingers closed around her arm.

She didn't mean to do it.

One second his stupid arrogant face had been gloating as always and the next his eyes and mouth were wide open in disbelief.

They both looked down in shock at the hilt of the dagger jammed into his chest and Tannin's hand clenched around it.

"You...!" He wheezed.

She wrenched the blade free. Blood spouted from his chest. Warm flecks of it hit her face as he fell.

A sickening crack of skull meeting stone filled the graveyard, and then silence. Nothing moved. Tannin was sure her own heart didn't even beat. She didn't breathe.

The only motion was the slow drip of ruby red blood falling from the blade clutched in her hand.

She dropped it. The resulting clatter broke some kind of enchantment, and the corbies seemed to rise as one flapping, screaming mass into the dull sky. She staggered backwards.

"Oh no, no, nonono."

Clach's head lay at an impossible angle against the stone with blood leaking across the grave.

Tannin was frozen, staring at the body when a flash of movement caught her eye. It was the flapping tails of a thick black coat. A thick black coat on the muscular back of a burly man sprinting away from the graveyard and towards the town.

Graeme. Eve's secret lover.

"Oh fuck." She raced after him, vaulting the low wall and charging down the path.

She was never going to catch up. He would go to the guards. Panic surged through her.

"Graeme!" She yelled. "Graeme! It's not what it looks like!"

His long legs propelled him far ahead, and she was losing him already. Adrenaline let her run the full length of the path back into the town, but her throat was soon burning with the cold air. She looked around desperately trying to see which way Graeme had gone. If she could only explain. Explain what though? Her blood ran cold. She had stabbed him. She had killed him. Of course, she had technically killed before but that was an accident. This was no accident. Or was it? She hadn't meant to kill him. She had just... stabbed him in the chest.

Oh gods. Oh gods. Oh gods.

Tannin ran desperately. He had to be somewhere. She rounded the corner into a small square and the blood drained from her face.

Graeme was talking animatedly with two red-clad guards who listened with rapt attention. She hadn't even thought to keep close to the buildings. Graeme saw her immediately and started gesturing wildly with the limp, bedraggled bouquet he still held in his hand. The two guards started towards her with their hands on their weapons.

"Stop!" one of them yelled.

Shite.

Tannin turned on her heels and ran.

She skidded around the corner. She could lose them in one winding street or another and get back to the safety of the crypt if she just kept going, but with the next step she took she knew something was wrong. Her leg jarred awkwardly as she put her weight on it and she stumbled. Her other leg didn't seem to work either and she crumpled to her hands and knees.

What...?

Her arms couldn't hold her up either, and she tipped face first onto the cold ground. She fought her closing eyelids for as long as she could. Long enough to see a long barb tipped with feathers jutting out of her thigh and two sets of heavy boots thudding towards her.

Chapter Thirty Six

The Gaol

Tannin lay on the floor of her cell. The rest of her body was taking longer to shake off whatever she'd been shot with, so all she could do was lie there with her cheek pressed to the floor and stare at the row of thick iron bars that crisscrossed each other in a solid grid.

Feeling crept back into her arms and hands, which she was pleasantly surprised to find were free of shackles. She, like everyone in Armodan, had heard the stories coming out of the Gaol of prisoners chained up and left for hordes of rats to gnaw on while they were still alive, unable to fend them off. Her legs too were free. Not that it made a difference at the moment – they were still numb. Tannin dragged her useless legs over to the wall so that she could at least sit up and lean on something.

The flickering torchlight outside the bars revealed how small her prison cell was. If she lay across the cell, parallel to the bars, she could have probably touched both sides. It was longer than it was wide, dug deeper and cave-like into solid rock. A tall man would have struggled to stand straight without his head banging the rough ceiling.

It gave the distinct feeling of being buried alive, and Tannin had to fight off the claustrophobia that was threatening to overwhelm her. She focused instead on rubbing feeling back into her legs. Her pockets were, of course, emptied but also her boots and coat were gone, leaving her barefoot and only with her thin, borrowed shirt to stave off the cold. It wasn't doing a good job at all, she thought wrapping her arms around herself. As her hair fell forward about her face, she realised as well that they'd taken the pin holding the braids back that Ava had done for her and they were half unravelled.

Tannin ground her knuckles against her eyes to stop them prickling. Eve had always joked with her if she hadn't taken her on she would have ended up in the Gaol sooner or later.

Looks like she was right.

When she had full control of all her limbs again, Tannin pushed herself to her feet and peered out through the bars. They were thick enough that holding onto them her hands barely made it all the way around. The door set in the middle was locked with a bolt and a solid iron padlock. She tugged it without enthusiasm. It barely even rattled. Even in her Changed state, she wouldn't be able to get out of this cell until someone let her out. Claws wouldn't do much against cold hard steel. The corridor outside continued in the same stone walls, floor and ceiling except with flickering torches every few feet. Further down was another set of bars on the other side of the corridor, but they were too far for her to see inside.

"Hello?" she called. "Anyone there?"

The slight echo of her own voice was the only reply.

"Hey!" she yelled, rattling the door as much as it would budge.

A series of thuds from somewhere down the corridor told her she'd been successful in rousing someone. The sound of heavy footsteps approached followed by a heavy man. He was dressed in the usual red of a city guard minus the armour or helmet. His droopy moustache made him look like one of those old horses. A fat old horse. He rapped on the bars with a baton causing Tannin to jump.

"Didnae expect ye up for hours yet. Those darts pack a punch. They're no supposed tae use them on people, but if they insist on runnin'..." The warden chuckled, seemingly at nothing. "What's aw this noise aboot then?"

"I have to talk to Captain Attilo." She could hardly mention Ava but Attilo was just as good a bet.

"Uh-huh." He picked up a wad of parchment that had been pinned beside her cell and leafed through a couple of pages. His expression soured.

"He knows me."

"Sure, he does." The warden took a stick of charcoal from his pocket. "Name?"

"Captain Attilo. I don't know his last name. Or maybe that is his last name." She was surprised to find she really didn't know.

"Your name, prisoner." The warden rolled his eyes.

"Oh." She bristled at being called "prisoner". "Tannin Hill."

He scratched away at the paper.

"Address."

She gave it to him and waited impatiently until he finished writing.

"Can you please get Captain Attilo?"

He scoffed but didn't look up from the paper.

"Hey! This is important!"

He rapped again on the bars, narrowly missing her fingers. "If ye dinnae want tae starve in there, yer gonnae speak tae me with the proper respect." All trace of humour had left his voice.

"You can't do that."

He scoffed again. "It says here multiple murders. Yer no long for this world anyway."

"I'm innocent," Tannin blurted.

"Sweetheart, it says witness and evidence here. Ye've even got blood on you. If yer innocent, I'll eat my hat." He laughed at his own hilarity in a deep booming bark.

Tannin looked down and saw he was right. Red flecks stained the front of her shirt along with dust and dirt. Goddammit. Clach was still screwing her over from the underworld.

"Make yer peace with whatever gods ye have now cause yer gonna swing with the rest of them, sweetheart."

"Wait!"

He hung the clipboard back on the nail on the wall and left, ignoring her continued shouting.

Tannin groaned in frustration and thudded her forehead gently against the cold metal. She had to get a hold of Attilo. She looked up. But first she wanted a look at that parchment. She squeezed as close to the bars as possible and stretched out her arm.

"Yer wasting yer time."

The voice came from one of the cells diagonally across from her. She squinted and saw a pair of hands resting on the bars.

"Thanks for the tip," she said grudgingly. She pulled her arm back in and flopped to the floor with a huff.

"I dinnae mean just with that chart. Yer man – Attilo was it? He ain't comin'."

"He will if he knows I'm here," Tannin insisted. She craned her neck to try and see any more of her fellow prisoner. That voice sounded familiar.

"These soldier boys are all the same. They promise ye the world."

"He's not my "man" man. He's a friend."

Harsh laughter erupted from the other cell. "Oh aye? And just how friendly has he gotten?"

"Ew. It's not like that."

"Whatever, newbie."

A switch clicked in Tannin's memory. That woman from the heist. What was her name?

"...Nyesha?"

There was a pause. "Dae I know you?"

"Kind of. I helped on a job with you and Hamish and-"

"Dinnae say that name!" The venom in Nyesha's voice surprised her.

"Why?" she asked. "And you should know he also tried to kill me, so I think he's a piece of shit."

"He's the reason I'm in here. Fergus is here somewhere too. He sold us out." She spat.

"Lovely."

"How'd ye end up here? We thought ye were a one-time thing." Her gruff voice carried a note of sympathy.

Tannin exhaled slowly. "It's a long story." Nyesha laughed harshly. "I got time, lass." Can't really argue with that.

She explained about her grandfather and the debt and how Clach had been taunting her at the graveyard about framing her for Mrs O'Baird's murder.

She trailed off, but Nyesha seemed to be able to connect the dots about what had happened next.

"That is some rough luck."

"What about you? What did they get you for?" "Murder. Fraud. Robbery. You name it."

Tannin was about to ask for the story when the sound of heavy footsteps returned, this time accompanied by a creaking and clinking sound.

"Supper," the warden announced. He was pulling an old wooden cart behind him with wheels that squeaked with every step he took.

Tannin didn't even know how long it had been since she'd eaten, but the tense knots in her belly hadn't relented. She didn't know if she could stomach anything at all. As it turned out, the wooden bowl of slimy looking gruel dropped unceremoniously outside her cell door did nothing to entice her appetite, but she gladly glugged from the small pitcher of water. She could have easily drained it but stopped herself.

"Pace yerself, lass. There's no more comin' for a while."

Tannin poked at the gruel but couldn't bring herself to put it in her mouth.

"How long have you been here?" she asked Nyesha.

"A week, I reckon. Give or take," came the reply. "Cannae really judge time in here."

Even though she'd apparently slept for hours after being darted, Tannin still felt exhausted. It had hardly been a restful sleep. She lay back on the hard ground and tried to get comfortable. Her cell didn't have a bench let alone a bed to sleep on. All she had was her bowl, pitcher and a sad-looking bucket in the corner that she dreaded having to use. Despair was creeping in, but exhaustion was stronger and sleep pulled at her eyelids.

Chapter Thirty Seven

Passing Time

"What is this - a wee baby guardling?" Nyesha's amused voice woke Tannin from a fitful sleep and she shuffled to the bars.

The new guard couldn't have been any more than sixteen with fluffy ginger hair and a nose flecked with freckles. His lankiness was only made more apparent by the loose uniform that made him look like a half empty sack. His breeches in turn were several inches too short. He straightened up to his full height.

"I am a member of the Armodan city guard, prisoner." His attempt to sound authoritative was thwarted as his voice cracked.

Nyesha cackled. "Sure, you are, baby boy. What did ye dae tae earn this shitty assignment?"

"MacDubh! Get moving." The order was barked from somewhere further down the corridor.

"Aye sir."

The boy sloshed water from a bucket onto the floor and scrubbed at the stone with a tattered broom, sweeping the water into the long drains that ran alongside the cells.

As he diligently scrubbed his way towards Tannin's cell, an idea came to her.

"Hey, MacDubh?"

He ignored her, but she could tell by the sudden stiffness in his shoulders that he'd heard her.

"MacDubh! Don't worry, I'm not gonna ask anythin' crazy. Can you just get a message to Captain Attilo for me?"

"Hey! What did I tell ye!" The booming voice came from along the corridor.

"Aw hell."

The warden had been still within earshot and now stormed over, smashing his baton into the bars and making them ring once again.

"I told ye no requests for murderers."

"Alleged murderer," Tannin corrected, irritably.

He gave her a glare and then noticed her untouched bowl still on his side of the bars. He nudged it over with his foot splattering the mush out onto the floor. He gave a triumphant smirk and left, again barking at MacDubh to scrub harder.

The boy looked in dismay at the sludge seeping across the floor then glanced over his shoulder. He continued sweeping but distractedly, coming closer.

"Say I did ken yer Captain. What's in it for me?" he murmured out of the corner of his mouth.

"Coin," Tannin said simply. Everyone had a price.

"Aye, I got that," the boy grumbled. "How much? It's got tae be worth my time."

He splashed more soapy water from his bucket onto the floor and scrubbed the remains of what was supposed to be Tannin's dinner down the drain.

"Twenty? There's coin in my pouch. It'll be with the rest of my stuff."

"Mate, any coin ye had on ye when ye came in is long gone. As for yer stuff, it gets sold unless any of us fancies it."

"Seriously?"

He shrugged. "Ye ain't goin' tae be using it."

"We'll see about that. Tell Attilo where I am. He'll get you your money."

The boy shook his head. "Money first."

"How am I meant to do that from in here?!" Tannin hissed.

"Hey, baby boy." Nyesha's husky voice sailed across the corridor. "I'll get yer money. Go to the porter at the Thistle and tell him Ny sent you. He'll give ye fifty, no questions."

MacDubh sauntered over to Nyesha's side to hash out the details before returning.

"What's the message?"

"That's it. Just tell him I'm here and to get me out."

MacDubh looked like he was going to say something else, but he quickly shut his mouth as he saw something along the corridor. The warden probably.

Suddenly, the boy flipped up his broom and smacked it against her bars, flicking filthy water in her face.

"Urgh!" Tannin gasped, spitting and wiping her face with her sleeve.

"No requests, prisoner!" he shouted, giving her a sly wink.

"Good lad," came the response from out of sight. "These criminals will say anythin' tae avoid the noose."

Tannin spat onto the ground through the bars to get rid of the taste of floor water that had splashed into her mouth and cursed.

"First days are the hardest," Nyesha said softly.

"Why are you helpin' me?"

Tannin imagined the older woman shrugging. "What else am I gonnae dae? Maybe I'll get a wee bit good karma at the end. Gods, I never thought I'd be back here."

"Done this a lot have you?"

"It's my first time doon here in the dungeons, but I'm no stranger to this place. Been in an' out a couple of times over the years."

"What for?"

"Thievin' mostly."

"I thought people lost a hand for that."

The law in Armodan was notoriously harsh. Why keep people locked up and taking up space when you could chop off thief's hand or have them flogged to remind people to behave?

"Not if ye can pay to keep it." Nyesha laughed mirthlessly. "Money will get ye anywhere you want to go 'til some bastard with more wants ye in a place like this."

"Hamish?" Tannin asked hesitantly.

Nyesha took an age to respond, and Tannin was worried she'd killed the conversation by mentioning his name. "Aye," she said quietly.

"What happened? You may as well tell me – there's nothin' else to do."

And so Nyesha recounted her tale of woe.

She'd grown up in Armodan– a Skirter her whole life. It hadn't been a kind life, and she'd gotten mixed in with the wrong sorts of people at an early age.

"Not unlike you," she chuckled.

She'd been taken in by one of the smaller gangs that roamed the Skirts and spent years shaking down local businesses and hijacking merchant wagons to turn a coin. She explained that at the time it seemed her only options were that or work in one of the seedy brothels that operated out of the backs of inns and taverns. She said she'd seen the crime world as a more dignified way to earn her living instead of on her back.

She'd proven herself to be smart and cunning and was quickly taken under the wing of the gang leader. It was widely acknowledged that she was his apprentice of sorts, being groomed to take over when he retired. And that was when Hamish appeared. He'd swept in and stolen her place at his right hand from under her nose with barely an effort. He was charming and capable and dazzled the crew with his daring schemes and network of contacts while Nyesha was pushed out of the inner circle.

The original gang leader had been killed in a scuffle with a rival, and Hamish was seen as the natural successor. He wasted no time expanding the crew. Nyesha had soon

found herself in a place of prestige at his right hand. She'd enjoyed the new pace of life. They'd graduated from picking off wealthy merchants to taking on commissioned work from people like Clach. Bigger jobs. Heists. And she couldn't deny she loved the thrill of it. Hamish, however, was a more bloodthirsty leader than the others and thought nothing of dispatching witnesses. Nyesha didn't so much mind it when it was necessary, but the more time progressed, the less necessary the killings became. They even took on hit contracts. It had sat wrong with her, but the money was too good to be ignored, and she had done what she had to do. Even though most jobs could be passed off to underlings so that she didn't have to get her hands dirty, she still had some regrets. The night they had met to steal the sightlens was one of the first jobs she'd done herself in months, but Hamish had insisted inner circle only. He also refused to tell even her what the strange bundle truly was.

"That's somethin' ye don't do wi' a crew on jobs like that. If ye cannae trust yer lads, then the job's already fucked," Nyesha explained. "Hamish was so angry when we lost that prize."

"Really? He didn't seem that bothered to me."

"Nah, when he gets all quiet-like there's some serious rage brewin'. Back at our place later, he beat the shit out of some lad for lookin' at him wrong. I'd never seen him so mad."

Nyesha went on to say it only got worse from there. He'd become withdrawn and moody and would barely talk to any of them. He had secret meetings and disappeared for days on end to the point where the day to day of the gang leading fell to her and she semi took over in his absence. She vetted the commissions and recruits, and the gang became stable for a while. And then Hamish had come back in a blazing rage of paranoia and anger and accused her of mutiny. He'd pulled a blade, she'd pulled hers. Blood was spilled, but ultimately it had been a stalemate. He'd left and taken half of her men with him and threatened to destroy her. He'd been in a wild state. She'd heard through the grapevine that he'd become even more of a mercenary, taking any job no matter how bloody.

"That explains what he was doin' at my house." Tannin told her about his attempt to murder her.

"You had a hit on ye? Oh lass, who did ye piss off so bad?"

"A few people," Tannin said grimly. "He messed it up though."

"That's not like him. Usually, if Hamish wants someone dead, they may as well start diggin' already. Maybe he let you live."

The memory of a rusty pipe swinging in her periphery flashed though Tannin's mind. "No, he definitely meant to kill me. I'm just not as easy to kill as I look."

"A lot of good it did ye in the end." The sympathy in Nyesha's voice had returned. "Yer too young for an end like this."

"It won't come to that," Tannin said firmly.

"Aye. Yer soldier boy," Nyesha said sadly. "Whatever helps ye keep on hopin'."

"How did you end up here?"

A loud sigh echoed from Nyesha's cell. "He said he'd destroy me. I thought he'd at least have the decency to kill me himself. Then I could've gone out with some dignity instead of danglin'. But no, he sent me a parlay. O' course, I went. I've got my honour. Turned up to a warehouse full of corpses and a whole company of guards."

"That's a bad day."

"Mhm," Nyesha said bitterly. "And now I'll never get the chance to smash in his slimy face."

Tannin didn't know what to say. She wanted to say that there was still time, but she knew as well as Nyesha what the penalty was for murder. And for multiple murders... there was no hope of a reprieve.

Tannin had never been to an execution. It was more a spectacle for the richer citizens of the citadel, but she'd seen the looming gallows that stood permanently in the square outside of the Gaol. The sight of them was enough to make anyone shudder.

She settled back against the wall, picking at the loose threads at the bottom of her breeches where she'd sheared off the excess material. She got one loose and twirled it in her fingers. How long would she have to wait until Ava got her out of this? Maybe she could convince her to recruit Nyesha too.

Chapter Thirty Eight

Rock Bottom

Long days passed with no news. Whenever MacDubh was on duty, Tannin tried to talk to him but with no success.

Nyesha's cruel taunting didn't make him any warmer to either of them either, and Tannin was tempted to tell her to knock it off, but she was the only thing keeping her from going mad in the quiet gloom of the dungeon. As time went on, conversation eventually dried up. Nyesha seemed in no mood for talking, merely giving one-word answers to any of Tannin's questions, if she answered at all. Tannin couldn't blame her. Between monotony and stabs of anxious worry, she could feel herself giving up too.

The dungeons of the Gaol were cold and draughty, and Tannin's nail beds had become a blueish purple. She paced and jumped on the spot to try and warm up a little, rubbing her arms and blowing into her hands. She'd relented after the first day and eaten the tasteless grey mush she was given, but it hardly gave any relief to the gnawing hunger in her belly. She didn't know how much more of this she could take.

"Tannin?"

The quiet voice cut through the dreary silence. Tannin practically leapt up from her slumped position huddled against the wall.

"Ava? Oh, thank the gods you're here." She could have cried in relief as she rushed to the bars. Ava stood there in the freshly swept corridor, hood pulled up over her dark hair and a thick scarf around her neck. It was jarring seeing her all perfectly put together in such a depressing place.

"I had to come. To see for myself..." Ava looked at Tannin, trying and failing to hide the horrified expression as she took in the cell and Tannin's unkempt appearance.

"Well, here I am. Let's go." Tannin jiggled the cell door pointedly.

"Did you kill him?" Ava still hadn't approached the bars, neither did she meet Tannin's eye. Instead, she studied an invisible speck of dust on her sleeve.

"Can we talk later?" Tannin frowned. This was not the place for long conversations.

"Tell me the truth." There was a hard edge to Ava's voice that made Tannin nervous. When she finally did meet her eye, her gaze was stony.

"Ava, what is this? Get me out of here." She rattled the door again to emphasise her point.

"You killed a man."

"So what?" Tannin hissed quietly, glancing down the corridor to make sure they were alone.

"So what?" Ava said, exasperatedly. "That's murder, Tannin!"

"It was actually more like a public service, in my opinion. I'll explain everythin' as soon as you get me out of here."

"I can't."

"What do you mean you can't? You're...you... You can just say the word and get me released."

"It doesn't work like that." Ava shook her head. "There would be questions."

"So find answers." Tannin could hear the panic rising in her own voice.

This can't be happening. Don't you dare.

"Tannin..." Ava actually had the good grace to look apologetic for a second.

"All of what we're doing is illegal! So, what, gangs and bloody treason are fine, but killing an arsehole who absolutely deserves it is too far? Where's the line?!"

"Murder. Murder is clearly the line." Ava's face was flushed and her eyes shining as she snapped back. She lowered her voice to barely above a whisper. "You weren't even in your other form. There's no excuse!"

"You can't actually be this naïve. What would you do with a member of the Triquetra, huh?"

"I'm trying to make things better not worse. Without bloodshed."

"Oh really. Ask Attilo. Ask him what would he do if he was face to face with one of them."

"That man wasn't one of them," Ava whispered. "You don't think we checked him out?" She shook her head. "You have to face the consequences."

"He wasn't...?" Tannin felt the blood drain from her face. "Consequences... You're not serious? Ava, they won't even give someone like me a trial!"

"They caught you with blood on your hands. What do you expect me to do?"

"I expect you to care about me!" Tannin bit back what she was about to say next. That she thought they'd had something. Something special. It sounded pathetic even to her.

"I do care." Ava's voice softened. She finally approached to lay her hand on top of Tannin's where it was clenched tightly around one of the bars. "But you killed a man. I can't change that."

"You can't be serious," she repeated, barely louder than a whisper. "Don't..."

"You're just not the person I thought you were." Ava let go of Tannin's hand. "I'm sorry, but this is goodbye." Her eyes glistened as she turned away.

"NO! Ava. Ava, don't you dare walk away! AVA!" Tannin pounded on the bars until her hands ached. "AVA, DON'T LEAVE ME!"

How could she?

She tried to call out again, but the words stuck in her throat and she choked on them. Ava was long gone.

Tears clouded her eyes. She'd managed to keep the tears in since she'd first woken up in this cell, and now that the dam had broken, they poured out. Hot and salty, they rolled down her cheeks as she sobbed, hanging onto the bars for support and eventually sliding down to crumple on the ground. She clutched her chest, gasping and choking, the air suddenly feeling very thin. Her lungs refused to fill.

She'd never thought for a moment that Ava would leave her here. That she'd walk away.

Was any of it real?

The stark realisation of being well and truly fucked hit her like brick wall. Without Ava, she had no hope.

Oh gods, I'm going to hang.

Chapter Thirty Nine

It's Time

Tannin stayed curled up at the back of her cell, swamped in misery for what felt like an eternity until the growling of her stomach and Nyesha's chidings forced her to crawl to the bars to accept her usual bowl of tasteless slop. Without even a spoon, she tipped the gruel down her throat, fighting the urge to gag at the texture.

"We ain't dead yet, lass," Nyesha had coaxed. She'd tried to talk to her several times since Ava's visit, but Tannin had ignored her.

She must have heard everything. She must think I'm pathetic.

Tannin didn't even have the energy to pace anymore. She wasn't sure if it was from lack of food or simply lack of motivation. Her last hope had given up on her and walked away. Her days passed in a daze of dozing and shivering.

She'd initially tried scratching a tally into the chalky stone, but now she just listlessly scratched at the wall with long, dirt encrusted nails to watch the dust float down. She imagined the little specks racing each other to the floor and picked one each time to cheer on in her head. It must've been over a month already. She hadn't bled, but then again she was being half starved so who could tell.

The only benefit she'd found was that she didn't have nightmares anymore. Although the monsters in the trees were nowhere to be seen, she woke every time back into a real-life nightmare.

Stories about the Gaol rats hadn't entirely been untrue either. Sometimes in the quiet, she could hear scrabbing and gnawing from the drains that echoed and distorted through the prison. She'd only actually seen one once. It had squeezed its slick, hairy body from the barred drain and scuttled along the corridor. MacDubh had screamed shrilly, and Tannin had let her cracked, dry lips curve up in the semblance of a smile.

There was something different in the air the moment the guards came into the corridor. The sense of foreboding practically dripped off them. They were accompanied by a pair of men in black robes. Black Cloaks. They were never a good sign even if you saw them on a cheery summer's day, let alone here in the depths of the city dungeons.

"On your feet," the warden barked, standing straighter than usual. "It's time."

"Time for what?" she asked but she already knew the answer. Her stomach clenched.

She got shakily to her feet as the door was unlocked and opened with a pitiful whine. It was the first time since her incarceration that the door was actually open. She could Change. She could transform and escape and... who was she fooling?

She had barely enough energy to stand up, let alone transform. And besides, what was the point? It didn't matter anyway. Her heart thudded in her hollow chest. Ava had abandoned her. She had no family. Nonetheless, she felt around for that little spark. It was like a feeble glowing ember in a pile of spent ash. *Useless.*

Tannin didn't fight it as the warden firmly bound her hands behind her back. What was the point? As Tannin was led past the other cells, she saw Nyesha spit in the face of one of the black robed men.

"Burn in hell!" she hollered as she was dragged out of her cell.

"You'll experience that soon enough yourself," the Black Cloak replied almost gloatingly. It was only now that Tannin remembered their other job alongside comforting the dying. To escort the condemned.

They were marched through a muddle of corridors and up a mass of stairs that strained Tannin's unused leg muscles. Eventually they were prodded to join a line of male prisoners already lined up. Tannin recognised the solid mass that was Fergus in the queue and saw him give a stoic nod to Nyesha as they drew closer. Guards lined the corridor, hands at the ready on various weapons in case of trouble, but from the hollow eyes and stooped postures of the ragged prisoners they looked like they had already resigned themselves to their fate.

The door at the front of the queue opened. Tannin winced and ducked a little to shield her eyes as they were stabbed by a pale sunlight she hadn't seen in weeks.

"No! NO. You can't do this to me!" One of the prisoners screamed as the doors opened. "Do you know who I am?"

The man was dressed distinctly finer than the rest of them, but judging by the rips and stains, he had been there just as long. His hair hung like rat tails around his face and flailed as he fought with the guards struggling to restrain him.

Two of the Black Cloaks left the back of the queue to assist. One carried a long brutal-looking hammer, and with a quick gesture the man was thrown to the floor. From where she stood, Tannin couldn't see him anymore, but she saw the prisoners who could see recoil. She heard the thuds and the cracks and the man's pitiful screams. When they hauled him back up, his face was ashen. Somehow, he was still gibberishly protesting and crying but much more quietly.

Two guards held him up by his arms as his shattered legs dragged uselessly on the ground and carried him out into the sunlight. A further four men, including Fergus, followed to the sound of a jeering crowd. The door closed again, muting the noise.

"You have the choice to face your punishment with dignity," one of the Black Cloaks addressed them piously, "or be dragged with bones as broken as your pitiful souls."

Whatever feelings of rebellion and escape that still flittered in the prisoners' minds were as shattered as that man's shin bones. The Black Cloaks were not messing around.

The jeering of the crowd sailed through the door along with the intelligible murmur of a speech being given. The bloodthirsty masses loved a good execution, and it seemed they were getting their money's worth. The Gaol seemed to be emptying its cells all in one go by the number of prisoners gathered. Behind Tannin and Nyesha, more had joined them.

The rumble of the crowd stilled for a heartbeat and then exploded louder than before. Behind her, Nyesha began to hum. Tannin recognised the tune. Nyesha started to sing words in a language she didn't know. Her voice was surprisingly high and lilted sorrowfully throughout the corridor they stood in. The raw emotion of it pricked at Tannin's eyes, and she squeezed them shut. She would not go to her death weeping. As Nyesha's last note petered out, the doors opened again and they were marched forward into the unrelenting sunlight.

The sight that greeted them was worse than Tannin could have ever imagined. The faces in the gathered crowd, pink- cheeked against the cold wind, were twisted in hatred and feverish with bloodlust. She looked away. There were going to be people she knew in that crowd. Usually, these sorts of things were for the more affluent citizens to enjoy but from the scale of it there could be anyone out there. Neighbours. Customers from the bakery. Vendors from the vegetable market. All screaming for her death. Did they know it was her already? If not, would they recognise her? Maybe not. She hoped they wouldn't recognise her in her filthy, bound and ragged state. Her cheeks burned.

At least she knew Eve wouldn't be here. She'd always said she couldn't stand the sight of death and would never cheer the loss of a life. That was a good thing. If Eve saw her here like this, she'd most likely die of shame before the hangman had the pleasure.

The view away from the crowd wasn't any better. Five bodies lay in a heap, half covered by dirty sheets. One was very large. A set of legs protruded from under one of the sheets, stuck out at odd angles and leaking blood. Healer's apprentices were already edging closer like wary vultures. A full set of dentures was worth a pretty penny even if they were ripped from the mouths of the condemned.

Despite the chill of the day, Tannin's shirt was damp with sweat as she climbed the wooden stairs on shaky legs. Someone was crying loudly. Another black-clad man was making a speech to the crowd from a raised podium.

"...in defence of this great city, we must first cleanse it of the evil within! And thus, we are fortified to resist the evil which this very day approaches! ..."

Tannin's mouth was dry, and try as she might to keep her composure, her knees still trembled at the sight of the gently swinging noose that came closer with every step.

"... to protect you! The honourable citizens of Armodan! Today evil is swept to hell! ..."

She closed her eyes as the man neared the end of his speech and she reached her place above the trapdoor. She kept them closed as the rough rope was looped over her head and pulled snug against her throat. Sounds faded against the ringing and pulsing in her ears and her own ragged breathing.

Her warg-fire was nothing but dry ash in her chest. She was no longer aware of Nyesha or the nameless man on her other side.

There was only the wooden platform beneath her bare feet and the breeze that sent strands of hair tickling across her face. She breathed in a deep breath that smelled of horseshit and sweat.

And then the world fell away.

Chapter Forty

Fluffy

Nine Years Earlier

Tannin knelt on the sun-warmed pantry floor and glanced around furtively before lifting the latch of the cage. The rabbit cowered from her a little, but its nose twitched at the leaves she held out for it. She'd been working on gaining its trust for days and made soft cooing noises until it happily chomped at the greens and she could stroke its soft little head.

"Good Fluffy," she murmured, giggling when the rabbit sniffed at her fingers and tickled her with its whiskers. They both froze at the angry sound of the hallway door slamming.

The rabbit fled to its corner while Tannin quickly tucked herself in the small space under the shelves and next to the cage. She was good at hiding.

"Just because they can't give me answers doesn't mean it's wrong to ask!"

Tannin groaned internally as squished herself further into her nook. The voice, unmistakably, belonged to her cousin. If she found her here, she'd never hear the end of it.

"It is not the way to question the Elders!" The voice of one of their tutors increased in volume as they strode into the kitchen.

"It is if they're being stupid!" Sommer retorted. "If someone just had an answer to why we are hiding instead of fighting – "

"Sommer. Enough."

"But if warg-blood is so great then – "

"You already have kitchen duty. Do you want latrines as well?"

Tannin chewed her lip. If Sommer had kitchen duty, then she was the one who had trapped Fluffy. She would kill him and roast him for tonight's supper.

"No," Sommer responded sulkily.

"Then stop making trouble and peel some vegetables. We've got to – TANNIN!"

The tutor had spotted her as tried to sneak the rabbit out of the cage. She squealed, grabbed it, shoved it under her arm and raced for the kitchen door.

"Oh no you don't." He ducked almost lazily to catch her before she made it.

"Noooooo!" Tannin wailed, twisting in his arms. "What do you have there?" he demanded.

"You can't kill him! Please!" she yelled, wriggling for all she was worth. "I'll look after him, I promise!"

"You're such a baby," Sommer sneered as Tannin started to cry.

"I'll look after him." She sniffed, cradling the rabbit close. "Please!"

"Give me the rabbit, pipsqueak." Sommer tried to grab it, but Tannin bit her hand hard. "OW!"

"No!"

"Let go! It was in my trap. I caught it!"

"Enough! It's food, Tannin, not a pet," the tutor said sternly, grasping the rabbit by the ears and tugging it out of her grasp and passing it to Sommer.

Tannin howled and fought but it was too late. There was a crunch. Sommer smirked as she dropped Fluffy's limp, broken body onto the kitchen counter.

Chapter Forty One

A Swing and a Miss

The world jerked violently back into existence as the noose snapped taut.

Tannin's eyes involuntarily snapped open, bulging from their sockets. Her whole weight dangled from the rope around her throat. The pressure was excruciating. Blood pulsed nauseatingly in her head and the skin of her face grew tighter and hotter. Her legs jerked with frantic spasms.

The braying crowd was hidden from view behind the wide wooden panelling of the gallows platform. They would only be able to see the wiggling of the rope at the top as the condemned fought for air like fish on a hook.

Tannin choked as she twisted and wrenched, trying to free her hands so she could tear off the noose, but the grip of the rope around her wrists was unrelenting. With each pulse, the edges of her vision became darker. The heat was overwhelming.

Heat?

Heat!

Her adrenaline was like fuel to the flame, and Tannin frantically, desperately threw it all into that cavern in her chest where she first found that little spark.

The roaring in her ears was deafening and her vision was clouding, the black edges getting denser and denser.

Just when her legs kicked their last frenzied kick, the spark caught onto that fuel and blasted her dying ember into a roaring, furious, glorious flame.

As claws erupted from her fingertips, she sliced through her bindings. Her body grew and morphed, bones shifting and straining under her skin. She grasped desperately at the rope crushing her throat and digging deep into her skin as her slender neck expanded with the rest of her and became corded with muscle. With a last burst of energy, she reached up to slice the rope from above her head.

She fell the last few feet and landed with a thud, sprawling on the sawdust covered ground. Choking and spluttering, she clawed the shrinking noose from around her neck and sucked in a ragged breath.

Above her, four sets of barely twitching legs dangled. She leapt before she even decided to, the fire in her veins making the decision for her. The wooden panelling splintered beneath her gigantic paws as she propelled herself back up to the platform of the gallows. An outstretched claw to the neighbouring ropes sent the limp bodies crashing to the ground.

By the time Tannin had scrambled her way back up onto the gallows, her muscles had grown and her fangs sharpened. The hooded hangman stood frozen in fear as she shook her terrible form to shift the last of her bones and joints into place with audible crunching.

The look of fear stayed carved onto his face as his head parted company with his shoulders and showered the frozen crowd in a crimson rain. The following screams of the crowd were drowned out by the guttural and savage roar that ripped itself from Tannin's throat. If rage had a sound, it would have been that roar. It was a scream that would forever haunt those who heard it and lived to tell the tale.

The massacre was quick and brutal. Those at the front of the crowd met death in an eruption of claws they didn't even have time to see coming. Any black-robed figures were swiftly mauled, their remains left strewn in the square. The spectators trampled anyone who stumbled and ground them into a pulpy mess on the paved street.

It was over in seconds.

Daylight forced its way through the mass of thick clouds overheard as Tannin stalked wild-eyed through the streets, not bothering to hide in the shadows. Anyone who caught a glimpse of her darted out of her way, probably thinking her insane. She did look insane. Or dead. A walking, staggering corpse.

A ragged, brown cloak covered her skinny body from shoulder to knee. She wasn't sure where she'd gotten it from. She didn't even remember shrinking back into her frail human shape. Her shaking hands gripped the cloak around her, shedding drops of blood onto the pavement with each tremble.

A glimpse of her reflection in a cracked shop window made her laugh. A hoarse, gasping death rattle that made her throat ache. Gore streaked her gaunt, pale face, and a livid purplish band encircled her throat. Around the blackish brown centre of one of her eyes, the white was blood red with ruptured vessels. It matched the wetness spattered across her face and dripping from her bared teeth as she rasped manic giggles.

A monster through and through.

A drunk who hadn't yet seen her stumbled into her path. His laughing face went slack at the sight of her. She shouldered past with a snarl, wrenching a half empty bottle from his limp hand. The sweet wine was heaven in her dry mouth, but swallowing was hard and painful, and half the mouthful she swigged ended up spluttered out down her front. She cast the bottle aside with a grunt, relishing in the sharp sound of shattering glass, and staggered onwards.

A walking corpse. The unforgiven dead. *Sluagh.*

She hadn't known where she was heading until her bare feet, sliced up and bleeding from a hundred small stones, met soft mossy grass. The necropolis.

Ava.

A fresh growl grumbled in her chest. She pressed on using the gravestones as supports. If there had been a fence, she'd climbed it without noticing, her blood-shot eyes fixed intensely on the pile of pillars she knew concealed the hidden entrance.

"Ava!" She gasped in a thin voice that she didn't recognise as she finally saw the trapdoor nestled in the wreckage of stone. A new padlock hugged the lock. Tannin banged on the trapdoor with all the feeble strength she could muster.

"Ava, you piece of shit, get out here!" Her voice cracked and ended up more of a whisper than a yell as her swollen throat closed around the words. She grabbed a rock and hefted it at the trapdoor. It struck the lock with a clang and disappeared, bouncing into the long grass.

Her legs gave in at that point, and she slumped down in the weeds, her shoulders wracked with silent sobs. "Ava! You did this... you did this!"

A rustle in the grass made her yelp and try and rise but her legs refused to listen and buckled under her weight. She snarled.

"Tannin?" The scarred, bearded face peeked over the mound of stone. The relief in Attilo's eyes gave way to horror at the sight of her.

"Go to hell!" Tannin scream-croaked, chucking another rock in his direction. It fell pitifully short even as he moved closer.

"Lemme help ye." He reached for her. Black hardened nails sprouted from her nailbeds for an instant and she swiped at him. He jerked back in alarm.

"I'll kill you!"

"We were comin' to get ye, I swear it." He held his hands up almost like a surrender. His voice caught slightly as he sank to his knees in front of her. "I swear it."

"Liar!" She struck at the long grass, looking for something else she could throw at him.

"We were! We had a plan, we were comin' to get ye, but the execution dates got changed."

"You left me." She mouthed the words, a slight breeze carrying away the feeble sound of her voice.

"I know. I dinnae have the words to say how sorry I am."

"She left me." Tannin slumped back as tears rolled down her cheeks. She didn't have the energy to fight anymore. The burning heat had long since died, and she was numb with cold.

Attilo warily shifted closer and when Tannin didn't swipe at him again, he laid a hand on her knee. "I know. Ava told me what she'd said. You should've seen her though. When we heard about the execution, she rode like a hellion down from the castle tae try and save ye. It was really somethin'."

"She was... too late." Tannin choked. Her throat burned and closed up around her words as she forced them out.

Attilo let out a regretful sigh. "I know. And that's why I'm here and she's not. I figured you wouldnae want tae see her."

"I'll kill her, I swear." She expected some sort of response, but Attilo didn't give any. Instead, he waited quietly until her tears stopped and she sniffed.

"How did you find me?" she asked haltingly.

"Ye left a hell of a trail. And I willnae be the only one followin' it, so we don't have much time 'til the whole city guard comes down on us. Will you come with me?"

Tannin stared at her shaking, blue-nailed fingers for a moment but eventually nodded and let him help her up. She didn't know where else she could go. Her thoughts were too scrambled and muddled. Her head hurt. Attilo half supported, half lifted her down the other side of the hill. By the time they reached the bottom, he had scooped her up and her eyes had closed as the soft patter of rain mixed with her tears.

Chapter Forty Two

Pastries

"Ava was asking after you again."

"Tell her I still hate her guts," Tannin replied, taking a sip from her mug. "Actually, tell her that if I see her, I'll rip them out and strangle her with them."

It had been a few weeks since Tannin's execution, and the rough hoarseness had finally left her voice and she was able to eat solid food again, albeit only soft ones. She sat with Attilo at the tiny wooden table in his rooms, sharing a pot of stew.

More often than not, a small fire burned in the grate to warm them both. The cold still lingered outside with delicate icicles hanging from the gutters outside Attilo's window, even though the snow this year had long turned to muddy slush piled at the side of the roads.

"You have to forgive her eventually."

"I absolutely do not."

Attilo sighed. He'd done the best he could with Tannin's physical recovery, and she was grateful, but inside was still a seething mess that he could do nothing about. Especially since he'd let slip that they could have gotten her out on day one, but Ava had wanted to let her suffer a little so that she could learn her lesson.

She had been locked up even longer than she thought. She'd missed the Yule celebrations for the winter solstice entirely, and to her surprise it made her heart ache for them. She'd never seen it as anything particularly special – it was just a week in the deepest part of the winter where bonfires burned in every public square of the city. On the first day, a procession lined the streets from one bonfire to another to light them all as people stood around to sing and drink hot spiced wine in the glow of the flames. Tannin had been to the celebrations every year that she'd lived in Armodan, and now that she thought about it, she did always look forward to those cold nights all bundled up in her thickest scarf and woolly hat against the chill, crunching through snow, and the sweet smoky smell of burning wood. Attilo had warmed up some spiced wine for her when she mentioned it, but it was a poor substitution.

"Lang may yer lum reek." Tannin had toasted sulkily when they had to spend Hogmanay alone in his apartment. *Long may your chimney smoke*. It was a traditional saying for the new year's celebrations that they could hear raging in the nearby taverns. Another one she was missing.

"Well, you have to find a way to work with her regardless."

"I don't think you're really getting my whole 'gut-strangling' stance on the issue."

"What we're doin' is too important to let slip. Especially now that Remnants are under the microscope thanks to your... whatever you want to call it."

"Resurrection? And don't try to appeal to my better nature or sense of morality. I haven't got one. See outstanding murder charge for details." She popped her last scrap of bread into her mouth. "I really don't care."

"Tannin." He gave an exasperated sigh.

"Attilo," she parroted back at him, failing to hide the twitch of a smile.

Apart from a rather lacklustre selection of reading material – mostly old war stories –Tannin's only entertainment these days was raising Attilo's blood pressure. And dangling the occasional string for the cat.

Tannin set her mug down on the table, wiping beer foam from her upper lip as she did so and ran a finger around the edge of her bowl. She held it out for the purring mass winding itself intently around her ankles. Attilo's cat was one of the many surprises she'd found in his rooms.

Room, actually, would be more accurate. A low bed stood in one corner and a table and two chairs in the other.

Originally, it had just been one chair, but Attilo had salvaged a second beat-up wicker chair to set at the table once Tannin was finally up and about. A cot had been set up at the foot of the bed, which Tannin had tried to insist on taking. She felt bad for kicking the man out of his own bed, but since he was hardly around to use it, the bed became Tannin's while he crashed on the cot whenever he was back from babysitting the princess.

She thought he would have slept in the barracks with the other soldier types or maybe that he had his own accommodation in the castle somewhere. She'd asked him about it early on and he'd confessed that, while he did have sleeping quarters at the castle, this was his late mother's place and he liked having a place to escape to.

"I never saw you as a cat person." Tannin mused as the cat's rough tongue lapped up the gravy.

He shrugged. "Cannae let the wee thing starve."

At first, he had been insistent that the bedraggled little ginger cat was just a stray that came in sometimes, but Tannin quickly clocked the blanket-filled basket in the corner and the little water bowl set out for him. For all the feigned indifference to the furry creature, Tannin had heard Attilo talking to it when he thought she was asleep. There had been a lot of "good boys".

And he was a good boy, she had to admit. Her old nightmares had returned, this time with the lovely inclusion of twisted vines in the shape of a noose that looped around her neck, choking the life out of her no matter how fast she ran and how hard she fought. She would jolt awake, gasping and sweating with panic. The little cat, who had taken to sleeping at the foot of her bed, always gave her an indignant meow at being shaken from its slumber. Soothing the creature by stroking his soft fur soothed her too and helped her heart rate return to its usual, slow thud. His deep rumbling purrs were calming even in the depths of the night when she had only her night terrors for company.

Tannin moved her bowl from the table to the floor and stroked along the cat's back as he stuck his eager face straight into it, lapping noisily. Attilo smiled, but Tannin could see the lines in his forehead were tensed.

"What's up?" she asked propping her elbows on the table.

"Nothing."

"Liar."

"I don't know if you're up for hearin' this." "Tell me anyway."

Attilo was always reluctant to tell her bad news as if it would send her into some sort of spiral. She alternated between finding it sweet and annoying. He always seemed to know when to give her space and when she needed to bury her face in that big barrel chest of his, breathing in the earthy scent of his lacewood beard oil and have a good cry. But she did still have to figure something out someday and Attilo's babying wouldn't help her get back on her feet. She needed to be able to take care of herself.

He begrudgingly filled her in on the latest news from the castle. Armodan scouts had arrived earlier that week, weary and frightened from investigating the unrest in Cascairn to the north. With them, they'd brought more rumours of a roving army mercilessly attacking towns and villages around the capital, Tark, burning homesteads to the ground and salting the fields. There were never many survivors.

By the time the party of scouts had been sent into Cascairn to see the truth of the rumours, they had been met with scenes of absolute desolation. Bands of refugees were arriving daily now into Armodan from all over the northern regions, forced into travelling by the threat of a slow and terrible death from starvation.

"Okaaay," Tannin said. "I get that that's bad, and I know this is going to sound terrible, but why should I care about this?"

"The attackers are wargs, Tannin."

"Oh," Tannin blinked. "What? The wargs left Stonestead? Why?"

Attilo paused. "These aren't just random attacks. This is coordinated. The displaced people from the towns all went to Tark before comin' here. They're full to burstin' up there and don't have the resources. Tark is gonna fall, and the wargs won't burn it – they'll occupy it. And from there, it's a straight road down here and we're already fillin' up with the refugees that Tark couldn't take. The Golden, you called them, right? It looks like they're wagin' some kind of war up there. The stories from some of the refugees coming in are... Well, they're not pretty. These wargs are vicious."

"Maybe people tried to hang them," Tannin said, evenly.

"No one even knew they even existed a year ago," Attilo replied, ignoring the bitterness in Tannin's comment.

She nodded distractedly. "It makes no sense. Why would they leave Stonestead?"

"It seems they decided now is the time." The little shrug he gave didn't convince Tannin that was all to the story.

"What aren't you saying?"

"It's just... the timin'. I think they know you're here. Rumours spread like wildfire in this city, and the monster of Armodan has been no exception. Especially after... you know."

"After I tore apart half a crowd? Aye, I know." Tannin raked a hand through her hair. She wore it loose these days. "So, what now?"

"Wait and see what happens. The king's sent an army up to Tark. We have to just wait and see what happens now. Although this definitely isn't good for you. They've doubled patrols around the city after... y'know. The only good thing is you're not the only one unaccounted for."

"Oh?"

"Yeah, other prisoners who got cut down in the scuffle."

"Nyesha," Tannin said softly. "She has a lovely singing voice."

Attilo gave her a reproachful look. They hadn't discussed his views on capital punishment for obvious reasons, but Tannin was pretty sure what they were.

"Don't you look at me like that – I didn't exactly have time to conduct interviews as I was swinging about up there. Well, I would have saved Nyesha regardless but still."

The aftermath of the failed execution had been messy. The identification of the bodies had taken days, and even then they couldn't be certain which limb belonged to which body.

The guards had tracked her to the necropolis but according to Attilo, the hidden entrance to the crypt remained

undisturbed. It didn't really matter if it was, Ava had moved all their things from there as soon as Tannin had been arrested. Tannin had balked at that information. She was no snitch. Even after Ava had left her alone in that dungeon, it had never even occurred to her to sell her out. Did Ava think she was that weak?

With the blood trail ending in the necropolis, rumours flitted around that the beast had come from the graves themselves. Attilo had told Tannin all about it after she'd recovered a little. Everyone was talking about Remnants.

It seemed everyone had always known, or at least suspected, but now that it was all out in the open, fear and mistrust spread through the streets like a plague. Tannin did feel partly responsible for it being that it was her rampage that sparked it off, but her guilt hung onto her in a detached sort of way. What else was she meant to have done?

"You worried I might go join them? The wargs up in Tark I mean," Tannin asked, bringing the conversation back. "Get all murdery again?"

"It crossed my mind."

Tannin sat back and crossed her arms. "I don't know," she said truthfully. "There's nothing keeping me here, and I really should get out of the city when I can. I'm no soldier though. I'd happily never kill anyone again, you know that. I don't know what I'd do there."

"What is it ye want?"

"I don't know what I want." She stretched. "Peace of mind probably."

"And pastries?" Attilo said with a twinkle in his eye.

Tannin brightened considerably as he took a grease-spotted paper bag from the pocket of his coat.

"And pastries." She agreed firmly, accepting the bag eagerly. They were a new discovery to her, and she was never going back to life without them. Fletcher's had made sweet breads and buns filled with dried fruit but nothing like these flaky, buttery pieces of heaven. Her favourites were the ones topped with sourberry jam. She brightened further when those were the ones Attilo had brought.

"You spoil me." She sank her teeth into the sweet crust.

"Don't get used to it," he grumbled. "They ain't cheap."

Tannin held up her hands. "Hey, I would contribute but y'know the whole wanted for murder thing is putting a little bit of a damper on my job search."

He shook his head exasperatedly, but she saw the hint of a smile. "I'm needed back at the castle tonight." "Again?"

"I'm still Ava's bodyguard, and things are getting' messy up there. There's the Cascairn stuff an' Prince Erlan's makin' all sorts of trouble. Wants more influence. Won't commit his navy. Wants to move the weddin'. Wants on the council." He groaned. "I hate politics."

Attilo washed his face and changed into his uniform with a soldier's efficiency before smoothing a healthy amount of lacewood oil into his beard. Tannin wrinkled her nose.

"Of all the scents you could pick."

"It's manly."

"It's ugh."

"The ladies like it."

"I'm a lady and I don't."

He snorted. "You're no lady." He tugged on his coat and pulled a cap down over his ears against the chill of the evening. "Not sure when I'll be back. Sleep tight."

As Attilo left with a wave, Tannin glanced guiltily at the deep claw marks scratched into the wall beside the bed.

In her first few days here, she had spent almost all of her time curled in a ball under a quilt. Attilo had tried to coax her into eating with hardly any response until he'd tried making her porridge. The sight of the lumpy grey mixture in the bowl had looked too similar to Gaol gruel and it had sent her into a half-formed terrified fit.

Her claws had ripped through the bedding and scraped chunks out of the walls. The porridge itself had ended up thrown across the room and Attilo himself was lucky to keep his hand. He'd stayed, quietly standing by, until her hoarse roars had become sobs and she'd retreated into the pile of shredded fabric like a frightened animal. He'd never made porridge again.

She'd also managed to successfully beg Attilo to deliver a note to Flint for her to ease some of her worries. The last time she saw him, he'd saved her life and been given nothing but a few coins and some cryptic nonsense until he'd probably heard through the grapevine that she'd been arrested. And he would have heard about the hanging. He must've been confused out of his mind and she owed him so much more than a scribbled note, but it was the best she could do.

Flint,

I'm not dead, and I was framed. Mostly.

I can't give you answers, but I want you to know I'm safe.

Don't come looking for me.

Love, T

Chapter Forty Three

Warg

Tannin hadn't properly considered the city's reaction to her in the aftermath of what had happened at the gallows, but now fear gnawed at her daily.

The mobs that circled the city in the dark of night would tear her limb from limb if they got a hold of her. Not even all the muscle of a warg would help her if folk put their minds to it. The only time she'd leave this room was if she got the codeword from Attilo for her to run.

If that happened, the plan was to hide out in the crypt and the underground tunnels until it became safe again. He'd already packed her an emergency bag to grab on her way out the door and planted a cache of food and water down there.

"What would I do without you?" Tannin had asked him that a million times. He was so quick to think of all the things that were vital but that she would have never thought of, and although she shuddered at the thought of being stuck down underground for that long, she was eternally glad that he had a contingency plan.

She would deal with her fear of being underground again if it came to it. Just being stuck in the house was making her impossibly irritable.

She filled her days with trying to write an account of everything she knew and remembered about wargs, Stonestead and her own experiences with Changing. How it felt. She wrote so much her hands cramped and her already child-like handwriting became illegible. Not that she expected anyone to read it. The only person who would be interested was Ava, and she'd already told Attilo she'd tear his head off if he even thought of giving it to her. Ava didn't deserve her wisdom unless she was going to choke on it.

Tannin also experimented with her warg-fire. Secretly, when Attilo was away and the cat was safely tucked in his basket, she played with trying to control her power and direct it within her body. Since her last Change, the desire for it had been burning steadily and begging to be released.

So, she released it.

It was a disaster. Attilo's small room had barely been large enough to contain her. She broke almost all of his dishes as she crashed into the cabinets simply trying to turn around and she buzzed furiously with the need to run, to leap, to hunt. It took all her willpower and several hours to calm herself enough to Change back. She had stood stock-still with her eyes closed until the flames ebbed and she shrunk back into her human form.

Exhausted and unnerved, she had crawled back into bed. Attilo had returned home to utter carnage. He didn't yell at her, but Tannin could tell he very much wanted to.

But her need for it didn't fade for long. Her wargish side scraped against her control. It jarred.

She wanted to be out. Forests. Fields. Running. Hunting. *Free.*

Tannin swallowed it all down. She had to get control of it first.

Every day she tried again. Fighting to work towards a controlled Change left her shaking and dripping with sweat. The process drained her every time and left her with a ravenous appetite. But she managed it.

Then curiosity prodded her to take it further. Did she have to completely transform every time? It sapped her energy so completely, and if she wasn't prepared enough to be already be undressed, the Change would shred any clothing on her body as it grew. What if she stayed small but had those blade-like claws? She'd never be unarmed again. That night in the necropolis, hadn't she grown out just her claws? And the porridge fiasco?

She tried again.

The first time she attempted to limit it, the fire inside took hold way too fast for her to control and her body warped itself into its beastly form even as she fought against it.

She tried again.

She focused. She could feel the power flow through her and concentrate in her hand. The air around it shimmered with the heat of it, and her veins bulged under her skin. Growing and writhing like horrible blue worms. Slowly, she allowed the power to grow in the tiniest increments. The first time her wrist clicked, she recoiled, panicked that she was just going to break it. The second time, the intense throbbing of her veins, straining so hard she feared that they would rip through, made her shudder with revulsion and she drew her power back.

After many attempts at controlling the flow in her bloodstream, she managed to channel just the right amount – a trickle of energy – into her right hand.

Tannin watched with breathless focus as her hand contorted. Thick black fur sprouted along the back of her hand and down her fingers. The bones in her knuckles ground together as she concentrated her power to expand them. Her obsidian claws were as sharp as newly smithed blades as they tore jerkily through her fingertips, splitting and tearing the skin down the sides of her fingers.

She couldn't keep them very long and collapsed on the bed panting as her hand shrunk back to a shaky normal size. Her time in the Gaol had left her weak, but she swore that she would get stronger. Day by day she would recover. As her skin knitted itself back together, Tannin let out whooping laugh. She grinned widely as she looked down at her hand and wiggled her rapidly healing fingers. She'd never be unarmed again.

Come at me now, you Triquetra bastards.

The Triquetra had shown no trace of themselves but Tannin and Attilo knew they were lurking in the shadows, waiting for the scent of opportunity to arise. If she somehow miraculously wasn't on their radar before, she definitely was now. The words "Remnant" and "Fair Folk" were on almost every breath of spring air that rustled through the new green leaves. Tannin's dramatic re-emergence had rejuvenated people's belief and the legends of old were suddenly on everyone's lips. Apparently, out in the Skirts where she was seen as some sort of folk hero, people were proclaiming themselves Remnants publicly and proudly in the streets and inciting more violence in the aftermath of the unrest than was already expected. The guards were spread thin. Attilo filled Tannin in on various snippets of information in hushed tones whenever he made it back to the house. It was only a matter of time before the Skirts descended into all- out civil war.

Chapter Forty Four

Tactful Negotiations

Tannin drummed her fingers on her chin in thought.

"Taking the west road would only end up taking me north into Cascairn... which is apparently overrun by monsters such as myself. East is to the marshes. Maybe I could go to the sea. I've never been to the sea." She ran her hands through her hair.

She'd had this conversation with herself a million time with little success. The truth was that she didn't want to leave at all. But Tark had wargs. Tark could have answers. She bit her lIp. At what cost though? She'd gotten snippets from Attilo about warg sightings, and she got the impression he was downplaying the violence in the stories from the refugees. Reading between the lines suggested it was probably a full-blown battleground. She appreciated him trying to keep that away from her. She was dealing with a lot in her head and she caught him more than once watching her with a concerned regard.

"I need tae tell ye something'."

Tannin leant back in her chair, arms crossed. "What?"

She had been trying to decide where to go for days – she couldn't stay here that was for sure, but sneaking out was going to be damn near impossible. Half the city was out for her blood. Whenever she thought she'd settled on a destination, something nudged her towards elsewhere.

Maybe she could be a nomad for a while.

"Now isnae the best time tae be leavin' the city, Tan."

When did Attilo start calling me Tan?

Tan had always been Flint's nickname for her. It seemed like a lifetime ago that they'd walked through the market eating roastnuts together. On bad days, her longing for his company was like a painful knot in her stomach. He would definitely have seen the Wanted posters. Eve too. Maybe they hated her now. Maybe they thought she was dead already.

Would they light a candle for me?

"There's trouble beyon' the Sheybridge. There's an encampment doon there. They came up from Ravensmore doon in Gormbrae and they've been pickin' up more support along the way."

"What? Why?" Tannin asked in alarm.

Attilo ran a hand over his grizzly face. "Old agreement for trade wi' the Gormbraeans. Harvest was rough again, so they didnae deliver. King Florian, o' course, demanded more in retributions. Same old, same old, 'cept the southerners are fed up. So here we are."

"Why didn't you tell me?"

Attilo sighed. "If I'd told ye they were comin' ye might've left quicker, an' I don't think yer ready yet."

Tannin scoffed. "What d'you mean not ready?"

He gave her another hard look. "Ye know what I mean. Plus, this place is burstin' with soldiers now. Ye'd never make it oot."

"It's not up to you to make that decision for me, Attilo," Tannin argued. "You must've known about this for ages! So, what, I just stay here in this room through a whole damn siege?"

"I dinnae ken!" Attilo yelled suddenly, tearing at his hair and making Tannin jump. "I dinnae ken," he said more gently. "Between you and Ava an' aw this politics, I dinnae ken a damn thing anymore."

He stayed quiet for a few moments.

"I'm not a smart man – no, really I'm not – aw this plottin' is not for me. I'm a soldier. I know a battlefield like I know the back o' my hand, but aw this... I dunno what to dae." He exhaled. "I know one thing, though, a siege is a bloody terrible thing."

It seemed like he needed something off his chest, so she waited and surely enough he continued.

"It was years ago. Before you were even born probably. It was the start of aw the trouble. The Gormbraens had been encroachin' on Brochlands land a wee bit more every year and King Florian decided to make an example o' them."

Attilo didn't look at her as he spoke and instead addressed the scratched wood of the table – something else she'd done accidentally while trying out her powers. "We went south. Wasnae much more than a bunch of villages clumped together just past the border that kept takin' more o' the land – and they were gonnae take a stand." He laughed without humour.

"A bunch of peasants used tae raidin' each other for sheep were gonnae take a stand against the Brochlands army. They took one look and ran for their fort. Well, we surrounded the fort. Killed aff stragglers. And they still wouldnae give up. So, we starved 'em oot." He shook his head. "It wasnae pretty. Took a while, but the king was adamant. They ate their horses an' their dogs and then started on their own dead. By the end, they were half-mad. Threw their Laird over the walls when he wouldnae give in and opened the gates themselves begging us to either feed 'em or kill 'em."

He had a faraway look in his eye as if he saw them still. "No wonder there's war brewin'."

The biggest excitement of Tannin's time with Attilo came early one morning. Attilo swept into the room at first light to rouse a very groggy Tannin from her sleep.

Notices had been pinned all over the city, featuring not only the royal stamp but the king's signature itself. Attilo had slipped one into his tunic as they were distributed and now unfolded the crumpled parchment over the table. It was thick and expensive with a gilded border and painstakingly neat lettering.

"What's this?" Tannin asked as he lay it out on the table.

"A possible way oot of this mess," Attilo replied. "The Crown wants tae make the Beast of Armodan an offer."

Beast of Armodan. Ooh, I like it.

"In the interest of peace and prosperity for all, the Crown offers the Beast of Armodan the position of Defender of the Realm in order to pay the blood debt accrued by the Gallows Massacre. Upon acceptance of the terms, the Beast shall be pardoned and the debt forgiven in lieu of service.

His Majesty allows for three days before an answer is expected. Should the Beast decline, a royal mandate will decree a search of every home in the city to apprehend the Beast whereupon it will be put to death."

Attilo paraphrased the best he could as he read slowly, but Tannin saw straight through his placations as she scrutinized the text.

"So basically, be a slave or be executed?" Her eyebrow arched with scepticism. "Those are the options they're givin' me?"

"It's not a bad –"

"Don't you dare say it's not a bad idea." She pointed a warning finger at him. "I'm not doin' it. I'm gettin' out of here as soon as I can, and they can all go to hell."

"The damn whole city is on high alert. It's too dangerous tae run now. Maybe we can negotiate. Will ye think about it?"

Tannin reread the notice.

"Why do they keep callin' it a massacre?" she asked with a pout. "It was, like, five people."

She poured two mugs of tea and passed one to Attilo, who accepted it with a grunt. He clearly hadn't slept.

"The final count was fifteen includin' the Black Cloaks and those who died later."

"I wasn't includin' Black Cloaks. They're soulless," Tannin said flippantly, but Attilo persisted with his expectant look.

"And what's to stop them just killin' me on the spot?" Tannin asked pointedly. "If I show up and they really want me dead, it's all over."

"Nah, yer of much more use to them alive. 'specially wi' Gormbrae at the bloody gates. They want tae use ye."

"Oh, I can see that."

"I could go in yer place to the negotiations. In disguise, o' course."

Tannin narrowed her eyes. "Mhmm. Aye, that's not gonna happen."

"Why not?"

"You'll want to choose what you think's best for me."

"And that's bad 'cause...?"

"'Cause I get to decide that. My life. My choice."

"Tannin..."

"Fuck it. Let's do a meeting."

The meeting conditions were simple. Neutral ground. No guards. No weapons. No transformations. Attilo had suggested an old sanctuary as the meeting place because the network of tunnels had an exit just a block away. Tannin had no desire to come face-to-face with one of the warg- hating mobs that roamed the streets.

The morning air was clear and crisp as they made their way to the old sanctuary. Inside the evacuated zone, nothing stirred except for the odd rat darting through the gutters, but even that unnerved her. Attilo looked stern and calm.

Tannin hoped she could absorb some of his tranquility just by keeping close to him and had to clench her fists in her pockets to stop herself from actually hanging onto his sleeve.

The old sanctuary wasn't used as a place of gods anymore –it was just a big empty hall where people could hold meetings. Even so, carvings of huge figures lined the walls with empty slabs at their feet where people once laid offerings and lit candles.

In the middle of the main hall, a long table and several chairs had been brought in – probably from the castle itself, Tannin imagined given the carved and polished finish that it must have cost more than what she used to earn in a year at the bakery. The chairs were made of the same wood but with cushioned seats stitched with the royal coat of arms and floral touches.

They had arrived early and the emptiness of the streets outside and the echoey silence inside the hall gave Tannin the intense feeling of being somewhere she shouldn't be. Somewhere forbidden. The building itself might have been beautiful once, but now it just felt desolate. The roof was high, and a draught whistled in from somewhere up near the beamed rafters and something winged fluttered out of sight.

Their footsteps echoed on the worn floor as Tannin trailed after Attilo while he made his inspections. He held a mask loosely in his hands which he would wear during the meeting. Tannin had half-heartedly tried to suggest he shouldn't come at all even though she was desperately thankful she wasn't alone. It was a risk, though. Helping her amounted to nothing short of treason and wouldn't just lose him his job and status but his head as well.

Attilo had made pained noises at the state of Tannin's appearance before they had left. They had an audience with the king. He really should have gotten her something appropriate to wear, he had said ruefully.

Tannin really hadn't cared at the time, saying as long as she looked vaguely human they wouldn't mind, but now that the meeting was looming, she rolled up her too-long sleeves and tried to smooth her hair.

"If it comes tae it, dinnae try an' go through the stained-glass ones. There's wires through it tae strengthen it – see here?" He pointed out the diagonal edges to the coloured panes.

"I'd rather this didn't result in me jumpin' through a window."

"That's why I said if. They should be here any minute. Sit yerself doon," he suggested.

Tannin was too jittery to sit still and after just a few moments on the luxurious chair, she jumped to her feet and began to pace along the length of the table.

"What if they just come through the door, shoot me and drag me back to the Gaol?" she said, twisting her hands together.

"They willnae."

"How do you know?"

"It's an honour thing," he said. "The whole city knows aboot this meetin', and it'll probably reach the other kingdoms too before long. If it got oot that King Florian doesnae keep his word..." He shrugged. "Ye can always go all murder-beastie again if it comes tae it."

"Oh, ha fucking ha."

The king might keep his word, but that didn't stop him from being late. The minutes ticked by maddeningly slowly. Tannin drummed on the back of one of the chairs. She was half convinced no one was going to show up so when the door finally opened, she jumped.

She'd expected a little pomp and flair as the king swept into the room to confront the legendary beast terrorising his city and not the lone figure that slipped into the chapel.

"You." A growl rumbled in Tannin's throat before she could stop it. Attilo quickly put himself between her and Ava. She ducked around him, rage boiling in her blood.

"Wait, before ye do anythin' –"

SMACK.

Ava staggered at the force of Tannin's palm cracking against her cheek but managed to stay on her feet, gasping and blinking tears.

"You bitch," Tannin hissed, lunging for another hit or maybe to try and throttle her, she wasn't quite sure.

Attilo caught her around the middle, and she had to fight against her instincts to elbow him in the gut.

"Hey, hey. Wait a minute." He glanced at Ava. "I asked her tae come."

"You did what?!" Tannin wrenched herself out of his arms. Her knuckles turned white as she clenched her fists. Anger did not even begin to describe the raging fire within.

"The meetin' isnae for another half an hour, but you two needed tae talk. We'll go tae the back room. She's here to help, Tan."

Attilo propelled her into the storage room at the back of the sanctuary and Ava followed closely behind.

"Get off me! I don't want her help, and I don't need it." She sneered and gave Ava the filthiest look she could. "You used me and then you left me to die."

"I was going to come back for you, I promise!" Ava cried. She looked tired. She was wearing her usual black, but somehow it didn't look as sleek as it once had and across her left cheek was a furious red welt.

"Oh aye, how could I forget? You only wanted me to think you were leavin' me to die. Of course, what's a little psychological torture between friends?" Ava looked like she'd been slapped all over again as she winced at the venom in Tannin's voice.

"I –"

"Save it. I don't care. And I don't want you here so fuck off." She turned away and jabbed a finger at Attilo. "Lie to me again, Attilo, and I swear you'll regret it."

"I didnae lie, I –"

"Is there even a meetin' at all? Did you make it all up as a ruse?!"

“There is a meetin’.” He assured her, laying a hand on Ava’s shoulder and giving it a squeeze. “And Ava can help. She knows the ins and oots of the royal courts. She’s a valuable ally here.”

“Oh, there’s plenty of things I’d call her, and ‘ally’ isn’t one.”

“Tannin –”

“Fuck you! Keep my name out of your lyin’ mouth,” Tannin hissed, rounding on Ava. “There is nothin’ you can say that will make me forgive you. Nothin’.”

“This is a mistake,” Ava said urgently. “This whole negotiation.”

“Oh really,” Tannin said, making no effort to conceal her sarcasm. “Because clearly you always have my best interests at heart.”

“They’ll never let you go. You’ll be in their debt the rest of your life even if you agree to only ten years’ service or something.”

“I’d never agree to ten years, are you mad?”

“Tannin.” Ava groaned. “What exactly are you hoping for here? They see you as a mass murderer, and they will wear you down until you are their little pet or they will kill you.”

“I’m not a mass murderer!” Tannin insisted. “I just... lost control a wee bit. I’m not givin’ up half my life because of it.”

“You’re not going to get a solution you want here.”

“I want to just leave. Get out of Armodan and never come back.”

“They won’t let you go.”

“And what do you want, Ava?” Tannin asked irritably. “Why are you even here? Atoning?”

“Yes,” she hissed back. “I tried to come back for you. I tried. I was too late, and I can never take that back.”

“You left me to rot,” Tannin hissed savagely.

She rubbed her forehead for a moment where a migraine was threatening to bloom. She was suddenly so overwhelmingly tired. “I can’t do this,” she said quietly. “I can’t.”

Tannin shouldered past the princess and stalked out of the storage room and into the main hall. She got about halfway across before the doors were thrust widely open from the other side and she came face to face with the King of the Brochlands.

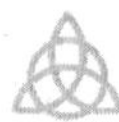

Tannin had only ever seen the king from a distance, and if she’d seen him on the street, she wouldn’t have thought anything special about him. The only thing regal about him was the purposeful stride at which he entered the sanctuary. He had gone without his crown and gemstones for their meeting and was dressed simply in a blue leather jerkin and thick wool cloak. A dark bushy beard streaked with grey and white covered half his broad chest and matched his thick eyebrows, which knitted together in a frown.

"His Majesty, King Florian of Armodan, King of the Brochlands," announced one of the men accompanying him.

Tannin skittered to a stop as the king took in her appearance with no small measure of surprise. His gaze leapt to the door behind her as Attilo, now masked, strode out to stand behind her like a bodyguard. Ava had most likely scurried out the back door.

The king bowed stiffly and then gestured to the table. As they took their seats. Tannin had to pinch herself to make sure she wasn't imagining the bizarre scene.

I'm sat across from the King of Armodan. The King of the Brochlands. The king wants to make a deal with me.

She shook her head slightly. She couldn't afford to get distracted by the weirdness of it all. She sat with Attilo on one side of the table while the king and his two accompanying advisors sat opposite.

"This is my advisor MacLeod and Sir Everard our Royal Chief of Confidence," the king said. "And I am King Florian of Armodan and the Brochlands Kingdom."

Obviously.

Tannin recognised Sir Everard immediately with his bald head and sunken eyes. He was definitely the man who'd been with Beck that night. The back of her neck prickled.

The king looked expectantly at Tannin and she cleared her throat. Their intense focus made her feel two inches tall.

"Uh, I'm Tannin. This is... " She glanced at Attilo. "Bob," she finished lamely, noticing how the King twitched at her poor lie.

"Are we to believe you are the Beast of Armodan? A warg?" MacLeod, the advisor, said, his wide froglike eyes filled with distaste. "I'd like to see some proof."

"Now, now, MacLeod. Be courteous. Things aren't always as they appear." King Florian turned to Tannin. "Please excuse my advisor's rudeness. Although I admit you are... younger than I had expected."

Tannin didn't know how to respond. The king's tone had taken on a silky-smooth quality, and she had the horrible impression he was trying to charm her.

When Tannin still hadn't responded and King Florian, taking her silence for impatience, he continued. "I see we'll have to cut the small talk short. Simply put, what we're aiming for here today is a solution that benefits everyone."

He smiled a wide smile. "Things have been... messy up until now."

Nope not charming. Patronising, Tannin realised.

He thinks I'm a damn child.

As she kept her thoughts to herself, the king nodded to his advisor, who brought forth a bundle of parchment scrolls and writing implements. He handed the king one of the sheets.

"Let's make sure we're clear on the current situation." He squinted at the paper. "Miss Tannin Hill accused of the murder of Mrs Ermina O'Baird and Mr Morey Clach. Found guilty. Sentenced to death. Further accused of the deaths of fifteen persons including members of the Royal Household at the event of the so-called Gallows Massacre. Sentenced to death."

He rolled up the parchment and raised his eyebrows expectantly.

"Well, technically, I already got hanged, so strike off that first part," Tannin pointed out. "Also, I didn't kill Mrs O'Baird."

"But you admit to being responsible for fifteen deaths at the Gallows massacre?" Sir Everard asked sharply.

"I admit nothin'," Tannin snapped back. She wondered if she should say what she knew about him or not.

I'll bet there's more blood on your hands than mine.

But was the king Triquetra too? How much danger was she really in here? There were so many questions and so many unknowns, Tannin wanted nothing more than to disappear into the floor and escape from this. This was a mistake. She felt waves of heat ripple through her as she fought to keep herself still and not bolt for the door.

"Get to the point. What d'you want from me?" she spat.

"We are reluctant to have you executed as that seems like a waste of your... unique abilities shall we say? It doesn't help that the city is already so strongly... interested in your case. The Remnant issue is becoming increasingly pressing. Making you into a martyr may only exacerbate matters, do you see?" Sir Everard said, seeming to savour the sound of his own voice.

"What... do... you... want?" Tannin said slowly and deliberately, taking immense joy in the fact she could be as rude as she liked to people who were wholly unused to it.

The advisor, MacLeod, looked like he was about to explode. He gaped and puffed indignantly while the king's eyes only slightly narrowed.

"As outlined in our first communication, we would like you to aid against the threat of the Gormbraean army which encroaches on our lands and act to protect the interest of the city and the Crown if there are attacks or if the need for counter attacks presents itself."

"And if I did this, I'd be able to do whatever I liked when we're not under attack?"

"Not... exactly."

"Uhuh," Tannin said. "Give me all of the details or I'm leavin' right now."

"You would perform all and any duties required – whatever they may be – and when not directly in combat or under other instruction you would be confined to appropriate lodgings. A fixed period of time, of course, after which you would have earned your pardon," he said. "Twenty years is a generous –"

"Oh fuck off," Tannin interrupted.

"Tannin!" Attilo yelped. "I apologise, Your Majesty. She meant no disrespect."

"Aye, she did," Tannin replied hotly. "Twenty years...? Are you taking the piss? None of this is my fault."

"It's not aboot fault, it's aboot fact," Attilo replied in a hushed voice before addressing the royal party again. "Would ye accept five years indentured?"

"I wouldn't accept five years!" Tannin said sharply. "Stop speaking for me!"

"I do not understand why we are even entertaining the idea of compromise with this... creature. It should be begging Your Majesty to spare its life and be honoured at the offer to serve the Crown." MacLeod gave her a filthy look.

Tannin stared at him in appalled amazement.

It? IT?!

She pushed back her chair with a loud scraping and paced a few steps as her blood pulsed in her ears. She stopped and gripped the back of her chair and glared at the advisor.

"I'll do one year if I get to punch him in the face right now."

"Are you insane?!" he yelped.

"Oh, quite possibly. It's been a stressful couple of months."

"That is not on the table," the king said sternly. "Let's keep this professional."

"This would go a lot smoother if it was on the table," she reasoned.

Attilo gaped at her.

"What? He has a very punchable face." Tannin shrugged.

"Claws," he hissed.

"What? Oh." Tannin looked down to see her nails had become long and black and were curving slowly and digging into the soft dark wood. She let go of the chair.

"That violates the agreement!" Sir Everard said triumphantly.

"Kiss my arse."

"That is two-hundred-year-old mahogany," MacLeod said weakly, staring at the dents left by her claws.

"Oh really?" Tannin raked her claws along the wood, leaving vicious scratches in her wake. "The craftsmanship is *wonderful*."

"A pause? Gentlemen?" Attilo hurriedly grabbed Tannin's arm and dragged her back from the table and the ruined chair. "What are ye doin'?!" he whispered desperately.

"Take this seriously! These are dangerous people. Take a damn deal!"

"They don't scare me."

"Dinnae be so flippant! This is exactly why I didnae want ye goin' aff on yer own. Yer not ready. Yer reckless! Yer..."

"I'm what? Go on."

"Yer out of control," he said. "Look at ye." He gestured to her clawed hands.

"Oh, this is entirely under control," Tannin said, flexing her hands.

She held them up and shrank some of her claws back down while keeping some up to make a rude hand gesture, which she directed at MacLeod. His face purpled in indignation. Tannin dropped her hands as she caught the king's eye with a smirk. He held her gaze in an angry stare.

She had made her decision.

"No deal, gentlemen," she proclaimed as she swept past the table and to the exit, making sure to drag her now fully elongated claws along the back of every chair she passed.

Chapter Forty Five

Start Talking

The rooftop was flat with one side flush with the old city wall and paved with yellowish stone slabs that had brown and wrinkled weeds springing up along the edges. Someone had obviously tried to make a garden up here, and their failed attempts rotted in various pots that had been strewn about by the wind. There was a bench that looked like it had been stolen from one of the city parks with several slats missing and surrounded by empty bottles that clinked against each other when the wind pushed at them.

Tannin pulled her collar up around her chin against the chill. She'd tried to put on one of Attilo's woolly scarves before she left the apartment and it had been a terrible idea. As soon as the fabric touched her throat, she was back on those gallows fighting for her life against the noose. She'd ripped it off and sat huddled on the floor until her knees had stopped shaking and she could make it out of the door.

Attilo hadn't been talking to her much since the disastrous meeting with the king - which was fine by her because she wasn't talking to him either after that stunt he pulled with Ava. She knew he was furious at her for her attitude and disrespect but she knew he was also worried about Ava.

With yet more political upheaval with the Gormbraens, the atmosphere in the castle was apparently very tense. He was at the castle almost every day and night now.

For Tannin, being alone in the apartment had become suffocating and the slightest ruckus outside had driven her up on the roof to see what was going on. It was a stupid risk, but she couldn't bear another day inside with only her own thoughts for company. Still, her heart hammered against her ribs.

When she was feeling brave, she tiptoed to the edge of the roof to look down at the cobbled street but there was nothing to see. Attilo's building backed into the old citadel wall and it called to her from her periphery. She hesitated and chewed her nail a little. She'd never been a nail biter before, but in the quiet of Attilo's home, they were never not bitten down to the quick.

It can't hurt to take a look.

Jutting bricks in the old wall let her clamber up without much problem even with wind buffeting her and whipping her hair into her eyes.

Even though no one was up here on the ramparts, she kept her head ducked. There was no telling who would look up from below. The wall was wide enough for two people to walk abreast comfortably, and a thinner chest-height wall circled the outer edge with slots cutting down through it presumably to shoot from.

The remains of a tower built into the wall stood, partially roofless and open, where the wall curved around. She ducked inside to shelter from the bitter wind. The walls of the tower blocked it almost completely. She only realised how loud its howling had been as she stepped in and the noise was cut off.

An uneasy feeling settled in the pit of Tannin's stomach as she leaned forward enough to peer down into what used to be an empty ravine under the old walls. It was now filled to the brim with mud coloured water while sharpened stakes lined the edges. The moat hadn't been filled in years. She instinctively ducked back at the sight of a heavily armed patrol below even though they couldn't have seen her through her small window.

The streets beyond the newly filled moat were not nearly as quiet as they were under Attilo's window. It was a frantic sea of activity as the inhabitants scrambled to add more boards to their already boarded up windows and barricade their doors. A thin line of red tunics at the main gate halted a crowd of people clamouring to get inside the citadel for refuge.

Tannin knew immediately what was going on. Riots.

Two shopkeepers were brawling in the road. The last time there had been a full-scale riot was when the taxes were raised. It had been a blood-soaked, three-day affair, which only ended when the military was deployed and a harsh curfew set. Tannin had hidden in the bakery with Eve for days, afraid to venture out into the streets.

Even when it was over, the tensions were high for months and tempers were spring loaded and volatile. With the encroaching army, the crown must have put up another levy to raise funds. No wonder people were up in arms about it.

The crowd pushing to gain entry through the main gate weren't rioters now though. They were terrified common folk trying to reach safety before they were caught up in the madness. Something happened to the Skirts folk when there was violence in the streets. It was like an infectious disease that ravaged people's minds and sensibilities as if one broken window shattered the bonds they used to keep themselves in check. It would be a free-for-all, and gods help anyone who got caught in the crossfire.

She clutched at the rough stone as she watched uselessly, almost pressing her face to the gap. The small figures were too far away for her to make out any faces as the guards bore down on them, batons raised.

I can't watch this.

Tannin staggered backwards out of the tower nook and leaned against the edge of the parapet wall. There was nothing she could do. She should go back to the room. She should –

CRUNCH.

The old stone parapet was less stable than Tannin had realised, and as she used it to brace herself, the mortar at last gave in to age and her weight against it. She scrabbled at the stone on either side, but it was too late.

"FUCK!" Tannin shrieked as the stone slid out completely and she toppled off the wall after it.

She plummeted into the filthy water with a screech, flailing limbs and a big splash. The fall was long, and the impact jarred her bones as she smacked into the moat. It was freezing, and the shock of the cold made her gasp, taking in a mouthful of gritty water. It would have burned in her throat and lungs if she wasn't burning all over anyway. The adrenaline of near death seemed to be an inescapable a trigger for her Change. The water around her thrashed and broiled as her other form took hold, wrenching her body apart.

A moment's stillness ensued as the ripples settled. One of the soldiers guarding the bridge peered into the ravine, taking a short break from his baton brandishing to see what idiot had just hurled themselves off the wall.

He leapt away from the explosion of wet fur and fangs as Tannin erupted from the ravine, frantically scrabbling at the edges to haul herself out.

Cries for weapons and back up filled the air as the rest of the soldiers spotted the soaking wet, growling beast. Most of them had the good sense to run into the citadel instead of attacking, and Tannin huffed a sigh of relief. Now it was just a case of getting herself out of here before –

A trumpet blared, and the drawbridge shuddered as the company of mounted soldiers thundered through the gate.

Shite.

They were armed to the teeth with bows and axes and swords. Tannin quailed as a volley of arrows thudded into the ground right before her paws.

RUN.

Streets and alleyways blurred together as she sprinted, paws pounding and claws skittering over the cobbles. She threw herself over a low wall, out of sight of any pursuers.

Change.

It seemed as soon as she made the decision, her body obeyed and shrank, cracking and popping as her joints realigned themselves and her claws shrivelled back into her skin. She shuddered at the unpleasant sensation. Satisfied that she was fully human shaped again, Tannin slipped into a covered alleyway, snagging a tunic that was hanging out to dry as she went. Hoofbeats sounded worryingly close by.

She didn't even dare peek out to see which way they were going but pressed herself against the rough stone.

I have to get out of here.

But there was nowhere for her to go. She couldn't go back to Attilo's – the gates into the citadel were probably locked up tight now and would be heavily guarded now that she'd shown herself. Even waiting for nightfall was risky and she could hardly keep wandering the streets. The guards would be looking for her. Bloodthirsty mobs too. Even in her human form, if anyone recognised her from her Wanted posters then she was in trouble. Skirters would sell out their own grandmother for a few crowns, so she had no doubt she'd end up facing a murderous mob with the fortune being offered for her head.

Tannin chewed her lip for a second. There was one place she could try.

Fletcher's. Her old home away from home. The big front window was smashed behind the broken boards that were supposed to protect it, but the bakery stood as it always had – proudly and solidly. Tannin approached the backdoor with caution but there was no movement from inside.

She eased the door open slowly, thankful that it didn't creak, and stepped into the dark interior with a sigh of relief. She was still pulling the door gently closed when a voice startled her.

"I thought ye'd come here eventually."

"Eve." Tannin gasped.

She sat with her arms folded at the old wooden table. She looked more tired than Tannin had ever seen her but still the same. Eve.

Eve, who had taken her in, who had given her more than she ever deserved, who had always looked out for her. Whom she'd disappointed and hurt more than anyone else.

She instinctively stepped forward to embrace her old friend but stopped at Eve's sombre expression.

"Eve, I... I..." Tannin fumbled over words before blurting out, "Please don't turn me in."

She couldn't handle it if Eve tried to turn her over to the guards. That would truly break her.

"I willnae turn ye in but –" Eve held up a hand to stop the torrent of thanks that was about to spill out of Tannin's mouth. "Ye have to explain yerself. Fully."

"Then we decide if we turn ye in or not," Graeme's voice rumbled from the corner where he'd been waiting, causing Tannin to jump. He held a crossbow loosely in one hand.

They must have seen her approach and agreed Graeme should be armed and close by in case she was a fully-fledged maniac.

That's reasonable, I guess.

Tannin opened her mouth to speak when a soft gurgling reached her ears and her head snapped to a bundle of blankets on the counter behind Graeme. She gasped and looked from Eve to Graeme.

"You...when? ... baby?" She stuttered. She'd entirely forgotten.

"Sit. Talk." Graeme gestured with the crossbow and moved to block the bundle from her view.

She sat around the table across from Eve awkwardly. She could feel the crossbow's sights on her back and forced herself to breathe evenly.

He's not going to shoot me. It's just a precaution. I hope.

Tannin took a deep breath and spoke looking at the table so that she didn't have to see Eve's disapproval. "It started when my grandad died...."

It was as if more and more weight lifted from her shoulders with every piece of the story she revealed. She told them about the debt and about working for Clach, about the first time she Changed and then the threatening letters and then about teaming up with Ava and Attilo. She neglected to mention that Ava was in fact Princess Avalyn, but that was the only omission she made.

When she told them about regaining her memories, her voice cracked and she had to take a gulp of lukewarm tea Eve had brewed while she spoke. Tea had always been Eve's first instinct during times of stress or worry and it was something Tannin had picked up from her.

"Let's just say there were some not so fun memories, but I remembered where I grew up and what happened to me and how I became... this."

"And Mrs O'Baird? The fire? Mr Clach?" Eve prompted.

Tannin nodded wearily and took another sip of tea before continuing. It was exhausting going through it all, but she told them of the Triquetra, the conspiracy and how they were waiting for her when she got home that day. She left out the details of her time with Ava and just said a friend helped her get better.

"And then I was at my grandfather's grave and Clach showed up." She risked meeting Graeme's eyes at that point. They were unfathomable, and she hadn't a clue whether he was believing her or not but continued regardless.

"He basically admitted being in the Triquetra, or I thought he did anyway. He said I should confess or things would get messy and I didn't plan to... I mean, I didn't mean to... I stabbed him..."

This time when she looked up, Graeme wasn't looking at her at all but was staring off into the distance biting his thumb. When it got to the part in the story about the execution, Tannin couldn't bring herself to say the words. She'd avoided thinking about it, let alone talking about it, and it was threatening to overwhelm her. She wrapped her arms around herself tightly and swallowed hard. "I... escaped. I didn't mean what happened. I just lost control." She forced the words out, skimming over the noose and how close she'd come to the end of it all, dangling on the end of a rope, and rapidly continued as if she could run away from it all over again.

"I've been staying with a friend and then when there was maybe gonna be riots, I was up on the wall. It was so stupid, I know that, but I couldn't just stay inside anymore. I wasn't thinking. I just..." She took a deep breath. "I fell off and now I can't get back into the citadel and there are patrols everywhere." She looked up at Eve then. She'd been avoiding looking at her face this whole time and now saw the tears that streaked her cheeks.

She wiped tears of her own from where they'd snuck out as she'd been talking. She threw her hands in the air, laughing a little manically. "There you have it. My whole sad, shitty story."

Her laughter spawned more tears, and she fought a sob. "I – oh!"

Eve was out of her chair and launched herself at Tannin before she could say anything else and enveloped her in a spine-crushing hug. Tannin held her back just as tightly and buried her face in Eve's shoulder as they cried together.

Tannin eventually broke the embrace and sniffed as Eve hiccoughed and dabbed at her tears with her sleeve. She waited, twisting her fingers awkwardly until Eve composed herself enough to speak.

"Tannin, I am so sorry. I had nae idea ye were –" Eve waved a hand at Tannin's general self. "Ye could've told me, ye could've... and with Mr Clach, I dinnae know what happened. I told Graeme he should've let ye explain –" She dissolved into more hiccoughs. "And the Remnant thing – I knew there was truth in it, but I didnae think..."

Tannin shrugged awkwardly. She had never seen Eve cry before, and it was breaking her heart. "It's okay."

"It's not bloody okay!" Eve exploded. "Ye could have died! I promised I'd take care of ye!"

"I'm fine," Tannin forced a smile through tears that refused to stop. "I promise, I'm fine. I'm in a hell of a mess but I'm all right."

It took a further ten minutes to get Eve to a point of steady breathing and rational thought.

"We're not turnin' ye in. Yer staying here for now, and then ye need to get somewhere safe," she said with a decisive nod. The old Eve was back as she barked out a list of supplies she could spare for her and told Tannin to check the stock.

"What about the Fletchers?"

Eve frowned. She explained that they had fled to the citadel at the first hint of rioting. They were staying with friends until the situation blew over.

Graeme still hadn't said anything or moved but he had lowered his weapon.

"Um, Graeme?" Tannin asked tentatively as Eve bustled around the kitchen. "Are we... good?"

He snorted as he shook himself out of a daze. "Yer a murderer," he said quietly so that Eve couldn't hear. "But if Evie is willin' tae give ye a second chance..."

More like hundredth chance.

He shrugged.

Tannin breathed a sigh of relief. Not exactly forgiveness but she'd take it.

"So how does it work?" he asked frowning. "Yer whole monster thing?"

"I'm a warg, not just a monster," Tannin corrected gently. "And I don't really know. I'm still learnin' about it." She rubbed her eyes tiredly. "It does take it out of me though. I'm starvin'. Is there still bread from today?"

Eve had more questions too as Tannin scoffed down slices of bread thick with butter.

What had happened at the castle that day? Were there more like her? Could she do magic?

All residual awkwardness slipped away, and it was as if no time had passed at all since they used to spend their mornings together chatting and joking the time away.

"And... the baby?" Tannin asked gently. She'd been avoiding the topic while the news of her beastliness was still fresh, but it couldn't be avoided.

Eve beamed and moved to take the bundle from Graeme, who had scooped it up and had been rocking it while Tannin ate.

"Born a week ago. We named him Jaimie after my da."

She adjusted the fluffy blanket the baby was wrapped in so that his tiny face peeked out. He looked like a walnut, Tannin thought, his little brown face screwed up tight and scowling at the world.

"He's adorable," Tannin lied.

All of a sudden, she desperately did not want to be near the baby. He was so small, so fragile, so... so... She couldn't find the words for it, but she suddenly felt unbelievably wrong for her to be here with Eve and her new baby and husband. Cooing over this brand-new, tiny creature. She felt like she was looking in through the window, a ghost of her former self. Who she was now was some kind of creature of chaos, and this bubble of domesticity was all at once startlingly human. Like a punch to the gut, she realised that this was a world she just wasn't a part of anymore. She wasn't human at all.

Tannin swallowed hard as Eve told her she and Graeme had been married in a quick ceremony just before the birth. Eve assured her she would have been invited in other circumstances in that joking voice that usually cheered her up. Tannin faked a smile.

"What else did I miss? Did you get a new assistant?" she asked, changing the subject. Eve suddenly looked sheepish. "What?"

"Ye were... y'know, and I think it really scared him. I dinnae think he took breakin' the law that seriously until... y'know, and he came around lookin' like a wee lost pup. He was truly a sorry sight tae see," Eve gushed quickly as if saying it faster would soften some kind of blow.

"Eve. I don't mind that you replaced me. Honestly."

Tannin laughed. "You fired me for good enough reasons, but are you tellin' me that Flint took my job?"

"He -"

Eve was interrupted by a gentle knocking at the door. Tannin dove under the table, heart leaping up into her throat. If she was caught here with Eve and Graeme, they would be in trouble along with her. Just as her mind was about to start spiralling into panic, Eve said just about the only words that could have calmed her down.

"Speak of the devil!"

"Eve, are you all right? You weren't home. The baby?"

Tannin's heart swelled at the familiar voice. She popped her head out from under the table.

"We're fine, we're fine." Eve shushed him and stroked his messy hair out of his face. "As a matter of fact, there's some good news."

Eve smiled over at Tannin who emerged grinning ear to ear.

"Hi Flint."

Chapter Forty Six

Last Minute Plans

Tannin had never seen so many emotions in one face in such a short space of time. Surprise, confusion, relief, joy, fear... anger?

"A note?" he said finally, his voice shaking. "You sent me a note?"

Tannin's smile faltered. "Well, I -"

"A note?!"

"I could hardly stop by the pub," she replied with a weak attempt at humour.

"You..." Flint clenched his fist in his hair. "A NOTE!"

Tannin had to fight to keep control of herself as he suddenly grabbed her by the front of her stolen tunic and shook her hard.

"I watched you die, and you send me a note?!"

"You did what!?"

"I saw it, Tannin. I saw it all," he hissed, his eyes wild. "I saw you on those gallows."

"No." She moaned. She couldn't bear it if he'd seen that. "No, gods, Flint. Tell me you didn't."

"I watched my best friend die." His eyes filled with revulsion. "And I saw what happened after."

He saw me kill them...

"I didn't -" She stopped talking as he shook her again hard enough to rattle her teeth.

"A fucking note," he whispered pushing her away roughly.

"I did what I could under the circumstances!" Tannin retorted.

"Let's all just take a wee minute," Eve said, positioning herself between the two of them. "Flint, Tannin has explained everythin', and I think ye need tae hear her out. Tannin... well, Tannin, I think ye owe him that."

It took a whole hour and lots of talking for Flint to finally stop glaring at her, but when he did, it was worse. He looked like he was in pain.

Flint shook his head in disbelief. "All this time and you never told me what was going on?!"

"And how exactly would I have worded that?"

"'Hey, Flint. You're looking especially handsome today. Also, I'm a huge murderous monster.' would have done it!"

"Watch it!" Tannin snapped. "I still don't fully know what all this means. I didn't want to drag you into my mess. I had assassins and all sorts after me and this is just the tiniest wee bit confusin' for me!"

"At least Ava had the decency to send proper letters!"

"She did what?" Tannin's eyes widened.

"She wrote to me. After I went to that goddamn hill looking for help when you got arrested." Flint glared at her. "And then after. After I saw everything. She wrote to me telling me you were safe and recovering. Said you would have wanted me to know." He scoffed at that. "Her letters arrived way before your note, by the way."

"Stay away from her," Tannin said bitterly. "She's a snake."

"Better a snake than whatever you are."

Tannin flinched and then narrowed her eyes. "You got somethin' to say to me, Flint?"

"Maybe. If I say something you don't like, are you going to tear me apart like you did all those people?!" "I didn't mean to do that!"

"That's worse!"

"Flint." Eve tried to interject.

"No! Have you seen what she is? What she can do? 'Cause I have." He looked at her in undisguised fear and disgust. "I saw the bodies. Whatever you are, whoever you are –"

"I'm still me!"

A heavy silence hung in the air before Flint whispered, "I can't believe you even survived that hanging."

"I can't believe you watched my bloody execution. Thanks for the valiant rescue attempt. Oh wait..."

"Well, I can't believe –! "

"Enough!" Eve hissed as little Jaime started to fuss in her arms.

"I'm sorry, all right, Flint?" Tannin murmured. "You were right that day at Barrel's. I didn't know what I was doin' and I still don't. It all just felt so bizarre and unreal. I'm sorry I didn't tell you."

He looked at her with tired, hollow eyes.

"Flint, I'm still me. Would you just talk to me?!" She tried taking a step towards him but he recoiled.

"You might've survived that hanging," he said in low tones, "but the Tannin I knew died that day with all the other victims of that massacre."

"I didn't –"

He stalked away from her as far as he could without leaving and folded himself against wall. He was trembling.

He's scared of me.

Tannin thought her heart couldn't possibly break any more than it had when Ava had walked away from her, but this was a whole new kind of destruction. It tore through all the little strings she'd used to try and hold herself together over the past few months. In all her time being disgusted and afraid of herself, she'd never imagined how crushing it would be to see those same feelings on the face of a friend.

Eve started to say something calming but Tannin shushed her as sounds outside pricked her sensitive hearing.

Someone was coming. Tannin flung herself in front of Eve and the baby as the door slammed open with such a bang Tannin almost thought it had been ripped off its hinges.

Sporting a full set of claws, she faced off against the intruder and prepared to strike.

"What the hell were you thinkin'?!"

"Oh, Attilo it's you." Tannin let her claws slide back into her fingertips and pretended she didn't see Flint and Graeme's horrified faces out of the corner of her eye.

"I didn't plan it, I promise," she began but Attilo interrupted.

"Yer supposed tae be layin' low! Instead, yer oot here and half the damn city is huntin' ye now! They want yer head on a bloody spike. If they dinnae decide to burn ye at the stake. Or both."

Attilo rubbed his scraggly chin.

"I found ye here nae problem. Anyone with half a brain who knew ye before will think tae look here. We've got tae go. Right now."

Tannin felt herself pale as knives of guilt twisted in her belly.

"What about them?" She turned to face her old friend. "He's right. Oh, gods, I'm so stupid. You have to get out of here. If anyone works out that it's me then they'll burn you just to get to me. Oh gods..."

"I understand," Eve said stoically, looking over at her husband. "Graeme's parents have a farm ootside of the city. We'll be safe there. Flint?"

He looked at her, bewildered.

"Yer comin' with us. Grab some things and be ready tae leave in one hour. One hour, ye hear me? We leave today."

Eve's tone allowed for no arguments. "And Tannin?"

"Eve, I'm so sorry. I didn't even think – "

Eve shushed her and cupped her cheek. "Take care, okay? Go now and go quickly. And you, you make sure she's okay."

This last remark was barked in Attilo's direction. He gave an automatic salute in response to the command as he hustled Tannin out of the bakery.

"Eve, I...."

I don't want to go alone.

She knew the words were true, but she couldn't bring herself to say them. She couldn't bear to put Eve in danger. Flint hated her. Attilo couldn't leave. He had Ava to worry about. She would have to go it alone eventually no matter how much she wanted to stay. She just wasn't ready yet.

"Take care," Eve said again simply and closed the door.

Tannin gritted her teeth as she drew her hood over her head and she hurried after Attilo. She couldn't afford to spare her fears or regrets and thoughts right now. She needed to concentrate on staying alive.

Even taking the route Attilo had carefully planned, she could still hear the distant trampling of feet and yells that announced one of the warg-hunting mobs coming closer – no doubt with pitchforks sharpened and torches held high even in the middle of the day.

Her unexpected reappearance had been like blood in the water, and every Skirter whose greed outweighed their common sense was chasing down the scent.

Their path had plenty of places to hide and took them to one of the hidden entrances to the tunnels without incident. Tannin would follow it alone out to the suburbs, close to where she had broken into that house with Hamish and his crew, and then start walking to the first village. Once there, she would send word for Attilo to organise transport for her as far away from Armodan as possible.

The entrance to the tunnels that was to be her escape route was near a park fountain. It had long ago been drained of water, like the one in the merchant's quarter where she'd met with Ava all that time ago. This one was undamaged, however, and stood as a decorative statue in the open, grassy square. One of the gutter grates doubled as a secret opening mechanism for a hole just large enough for a person to squeeze through. Tannin's fingers shook as she fumbled with the latch, casting wary glances left and right for any hint of an angry mob approaching.

"Maybe we could just live out our days in the tunnels like rats and then in a hundred years when they find our skeletons, we'll end up as scary stories people tell each other about the Tunnel People."

Attilo blinked at her. "Ye awright?"

"No, I'm really not." She hugged her arms around herself, peering down into the dark hole in the ground.

"I'm tired, Attilo. And I'm scared. I don't want to go down there. I don't want to be alone. I don't know what I'm doin'. My home is gone. My friends –"

Her voice caught. It was easier to focus on things like claws and angry mobs than the fact Flint wanted nothing to do with her anymore.

"Hey now. Yer strong. Ye can dae this." He laid both hands on her shoulders and gave her a reassuring squeeze. "This isnae how I pictured my life either. Creepin' aboot the city wi' some tiny, half-feral warg girl who told the king tae fuck off tae his face."

Tannin couldn't help but smile as she rubbed at her eyes. "Who're you callin' tiny?"

"There ye go," he said with a grin, tapping his knuckles against her jaw. "There's that fightin' spirit."

"Ye've got to run," he said gently. "It's been the only option for quite some time now, and I think ye know that as much as I do. The timin' is never gonnae be good so ye'll just have tae settle for luck."

"I don't have any luck." Tannin grimaced. "What about you? You're in this as much as I am now."

He chuckled. "Not quite. And I swore an oath tae protect the princess. I have tae go where she goes. And I think I've kept my cover."

Tannin nodded and scuffed her feet. "I get it. I wish you could come with me though. I need a grownup."

At that he really did laugh and then stopped abruptly, catching sight of something over the top of Tannin's head. "Go, go now!" he hissed urgently.

She didn't need telling twice as she half-threw herself through the grate into the hidden tunnel below. She cringed at the loud, wet squelching sound she made as she landed. She didn't want to even think about what she was standing in.

"Captain!" The shout echoed through the tunnel and made the voice sound alarmingly close. Tannin froze, her pulse racing, but Attilo must have moved away from the grate to meet whoever it was because their conversation became muffled. She breathed as much of a sigh of relief as she dared.

Should I go already or…?

Her question answered itself as Attilo's familiar footsteps sounded from the surface and the grate above her head creaked open. Moss and algae coated the walls in slimy green where rainwater still trickled into the tunnel. Tannin recoiled as she accidentally brushed a hand against it as Attilo dropped down.

"What is it?" she whispered, scooting out of the way. The hair on the back on her neck was standing on end.

One look at his face told her something was very, very wrong, and Tannin immediately felt queasy.

"Ava –" He cleared his throat. "The Rill troops... they've staged a coup. Prince Erlan has her as a hostage."

He looked utterly horrified. "I should've been there."

Tannin started to say that it wasn't his fault, that he couldn't have done anything, but he wasn't paying attention.

"We'll take the tunnels," he said commandingly. "They willnae be expectin' that."

"Wait, we?"

He frowned at her bewildered for a second. "Aye, we. She's in danger, Tannin. They could kill her."

"But..."

She was supposed to be fine. She was supposed to go be a princess like she was always meant to be. I was supposed to leave my stupid broken heart behind with the rest of the wreckage of my life. I was supposed to leave. To forget her.

Tannin raced through her thoughts, but she couldn't escape the truth of it. Even after everything she couldn't bear it if Ava got hurt. Or worse.

Attilo added quietly, "The guilt ate her alive. She asked aboot ye every single day. Aboot how ye were doin'. She was so worried. She didnae eat or sleep. And I know things between the two of ye are... complicated, but she cares for ye. Whatever ye believe, I can say that's true. She needs yer help. Tan, I need yer help."

He was looking at her so earnestly. He'd done so much for her and asked so little in return. Tannin felt her doubts melt away. Her anger at the princess was somewhat stale now and with all that she had ahead, she didn't have room in her heart or the energy for it. And for a tough, old warrior, Attilo had such puppy dog eyes.

Damn it all to hell.

"I'm doin' this for you, though," she lied, pointing a finger at him as she stalked past him up the tunnel. "Not for her."

Chapter Forty Seven

Spilled Secrets

"Where are we even goin'?" Tannin panted. "Even if they haven't left the castle, that place is huge!"

"I've got a hunch."

They carried on in silence. Attilo's stress made the air buzz with anxious energy until they arrived at a passageway that was like none she'd ever seen.

"This is not what I expected," Tannin breathed.

The corridor was brushed clean of dust and cobwebs and the uneven stone floor was laid with a lush, red carpet runner. The narrowness of the corridor and the bare walls, however, suggested they were very much still inside the thick castle walls.

"Here," Attilo muttered as he pointed out a small wooden shutter built into the wall and jammed his eye to a matching one on the opposite side. Beyond the tiny window was a fine mesh over a hole straight through the wall into the room beyond.

Tannin squinted through the shutter into a huge arched hall with a towering, golden throne flanked by Armodian banners. The back of the throne rose high into the air and branched off into imposing spikes and swirls like a golden mass of twisting vines and thorns.

Cushions in vibrant royal purple lined the seat. But the ostentatious display of luxury and power wasn't what made Tannin hiss through her teeth.

A man whom she reckoned must be Prince Erlan stood on the throne platform pacing, his blade drawn and swinging. He was dark haired and broad shouldered and held himself proudly. He had the long, lithe body and tanned skin typical of the coastal regions and he would have looked very regal if not for the fact he was red faced and raving. Rill guards in their blue-green tunics secured every entrance to the throne room, weapons drawn and doors barred. Towards the edge of the platform, flanked by a further two guards was Ava.

She had clearly been surprised by them and her dark chestnut hair was loose about her shoulders, covering the delicate satin straps of her pearl-white nightdress. Her cheeks were tinged pink, not from fear but from fury as she argued with her captor.

"This is insane, Erlan!" The princess's voice echoed in the empty throne room and bounced into the secret passageway.

"Shite," Tannin breathed.

"Is it Ava?" Attilo bumped her out of the way of the spyhole.

Tannin heard his breathing catch in his throat as he took in the scene. She fidgeted nervously as he watched. Not being able to see was frustrating, even if their voices flooded into the small space and were as loud as if they stood on the throne platform themselves.

"Unhand me this instant!" Ava's voice rose shrilly.

"You are a traitor!" Tannin assumed this was the voice of the Prince. It was deeper than she'd expected from the look of him and rumbled into the passageway.

"I have no allegiance to Rill. I can't betray what was never there." Ava spat.

"Oh no?" Prince Erlan sneered. "Were you not promised to me? To Rill? For our continued alliance with the Brochlands?"

"I made it clear I had no interest in it. Can you really be surprised?"

"I was not surprised at your indifference – a spoiled brat like you could never be satisfied." His tone was scathing. "But your impurity and faithlessness were unexpected."

There was no reply from Ava. Tannin, too, was struggling to decipher his words. What exactly did he know? The crypt, the Remnants?

"Explain yourself," Ava demanded, although her tone had softened.

"I know." He laughed. "I know everything."

Tannin tugged at Attilo's sleeve to see again but he brushed her off. She could see a vein pulsing in his neck.

"Firstly," the prince's voice reverberated off the stone. "The mere fact you were offered to me is a sham. Did you not think I would have my people do some digging? Do you not think I don't know you're nothing but a bastard?!" His voice rose until he screeched the final words.

"Uh oh," Tannin muttered.

"I am offered tainted, paltry goods in exchange for my kingdom's resources. The disrespect." He spat on the floor. "Do you hear that, Your Majesty?!"

Tannin's forehead crinkled up in confusion. She rushed to the other wall where the spyhole looked into what looked like a meeting room. Sure enough, the king sat at the round table with his head slumped in his hands. He must have been barricaded in.

"And furthermore," Prince Erlan continued, "not only is my wife illegitimate and quite frankly an insult to me and my kingdom, she is as impure in faith as she is in blood."

Tannin scoured the tunnel, running her hands over every part of the walls to find some way through. There had to be a way in. The pitiful light in the corridor didn't do anything but cast long shadows and merge everything into a murky grey.

Only by running her hands along the stone did she find the crease in the wall. Definitely a door, but she couldn't find an opening mechanism anywhere. It could have been broken off years ago, she thought in despair.

There must be a way through!

"That's right. Did you think your depraved activities went unnoticed? Did you think I wouldn't know that my wife was entertaining a lover right under my nose?"

Tannin froze.

Oh no.

"And a commoner too." His voice dripped with disgust. "I must say, my dear, you have terrible taste. Your little plaything was nothing more than a criminal in the end. They always are. These peasants can't help themselves." Tannin could hear the mockery in his voice. "What a pity you couldn't save her in time. Quite a show you put on trying though. I did enjoy that."

"You bastard!" Ava screamed.

Whatever else she said was lost on Tannin as blood pounded in her ears.

It was him. He tried to have me killed. As a pawn in his game. To get back at Ava.

Her breathing turned to panting as the heat emanated from her chest. She couldn't have stopped it if she'd wanted to. She grabbed the back of Attilo's jerkin and tossed him aside with ease to press her eye to the spyhole.

Ava struggled against the grip of the guards as she slung one expletive after another at the prince. Tannin had never heard her utter a single curse before, let alone the torrent of profanity that she came out with now directed at her former fiancé. She even spat at him as he approached. He recoiled in revulsion before cracking the back of his hand across her face.

"Ava!" Tannin saw red.

Her claws slid out of her fingertips without prompting, and she threw herself to the crease in the wall and jammed them into the gap. The pain was excruciating as they bent under the pressure.

Her sleeves burst open at the seams as she channelled powerful heat into her arm muscles to drag the wall apart in a cascade of dust and stone, roaring with effort.

The wall opened up enough for her to squeeze past, pulling herself though the gap with a scrabbling of half-extended claws and Attilo close behind. She fought against the urge to transform fully – she'd never get through the gap if she did. Her glowing eyes were so fixed on the prince that she misjudged the drop on the other side. She stumbled and fell hard. Attilo, however, landed in a practiced cat-like crouch and drew his blade in one fluid motion.

"Release her!" he bellowed as he charged.

"No! Attilo they have –!"

Ava never managed to finish her warning as a little package thrown by the nearest Rill guard landed by Attilo's feet. A split second of confused silence was followed by a thunderous explosion of flame and clouds of suffocating smoke.

Attilo's body shielded Tannin from much of the blast, but she was still thrown back against the wall with bone- crunching force. All she could hear was a high-pitched whine as smoke and dust stung her eyes. She shakily pushed herself up from the floor. The flagstones of the throne room were cracked and curved in a crater from where the bomb had landed. She should have known. Rill's navy were known for the unforgiving explosives they used on enemy ships. Great barrels of the stuff. She didn't know they had fashioned it as hand weapons too.

It was for blowing great holes in ship hulls. To use it on people was barbaric.

"Attilo," Tannin croaked hoarsely.

He lay in a heap of shattered stone a few metres away from her.

"No!" She gasped, crawling towards him. Bloodied, scorched flesh showed through the smoking tatters of his jerkin. Reaching him, she felt his chest for that tell-tale rise and fall of a breath.

At first there was nothing, and Tannin felt her despair rising, but then with a gravelly rattle his chest finally rose.

"Hey, hey," she tried desperately. "Stay with me. You're gonna be okay."

"A...va," he wheezed.

"It's okay. You just... lie still." Tannin stared in dismay at his ravaged body. His limbs bent in awkward angles that could only mean broken bones. Tannin didn't dare touch him in case she made it worse. Blood seeped seemingly from everywhere. Too much blood. His eyes stared upwards blindly.

"Help...her." He choked, blood bubbling from his mouth.

"Don't try to speak." Her voice quivered as she shushed him. Her hands hovered over him, unsure but desperate to do something. "I'll do it. I'll help her. And then I'll get you help, okay? Just hang on."

He managed a weak smile before his mouth went slack.

"Attilo?! Att- argh!"

She'd been so focused on Attilo, she hadn't noticed how close the Rill guards had gotten. One of them grabbed her by the hair and dragged her backwards. She struggled but found herself thrown to the floor. The impact knocked the air out of her before she was seized by the arms and dragged to the front of the throne room. The guards forced her down onto her knees and kept her there with a hand on each shoulder.

She looked up into the smirking face of Prince Erlan and felt her claws grow.

I'm going to tear his fucking face off.

"Ah, ah." He tutted, pointing over his shoulder to where Ava was still standing with the two guards. Tears streaked her face as she trembled but she stood perfectly still, a dagger resting at the hollow of her throat.

"You piece of shit," Tannin spat.

The prince ignored her. "You know, I had my suspicions that my dear Avalyn's overnight guest and the Beast of Armodan were one and the same after that terrible incident at the gallows."

He paced a few steps languidly. "Really, Avalyn. A beast? Have you no shame? I imagine you'll both face trial after this. I know you had some sort of negotiation going on but after all this." He gestured to the general destruction. "I think that's all over now."

"In Rill, the whole murder and monster thing aside, I would have you both executed immediately for adultery. Maybe if you, my dear, were actually of royal blood, we could have come to some sort of arrangement but as it stands..." He shrugged exaggeratedly. "And I'm sure His Majesty," he yelled in the direction of the barricaded door, "would simply love to know how you ended up with the most wanted criminal in the city in your bed. Would that amount to treason, I wonder?" He tapped his chin in thought.

"If you think you're gonna come out of this well then you're insane." Tannin chuckled humourlessly. "You've betrayed the king. I doubt he's happy with you right now either."

The prince crouched in front of her and took a hold of her chin, tilting her head from side to side.

"Don't fuckin' touch me," she grunted but the dagger at Ava's throat kept her from pushing him away.

"It's amazing. You could almost pass for human and not the pitiful, soulless creature you are." He smirked, drawing his own dagger from his belt and placed it under her chin where his hand had been, forcing her to look up at him. "Maybe I should just cut your throat right now? I'd be a hero."

"You can do whatever you want. You'll still be a worm," she snarled.

He chuckled cruelly as he pushed the tip of the dagger against her throat until a warm trickle of blood seeped down her neck. She gritted her teeth.

This piece of shit.

He'd had her hanged. He'd taken Ava hostage. He'd *blown up* Attilo. And now she was supposed to just kneel here as he slit her throat? No fucking way.

A low growl rumbled deep in her chest.

"No, don't!" Ava gasped, grabbing at the arm of the guard holding the dagger to her throat.

"Silence! You will not tell me what to do!" Erlan roared.

"I think she's talkin' to me, arsehole." Tannin growled savagely. She grabbed his wrist with one hand, pulling the blade away from her skin and plunged the claws of the other into his forearm.

Skin, muscle and bone gave way under her claws as she dug them in as deep as she could and twisted. Blood coated her up to her elbow like a red silken glove as she raked her talons down the length of his arm and pulled them out again with a last twist and cracking of bone. It took a moment for him to register what she'd done before he started screaming.

Tannin didn't have time to think, but some little piece of her mind remembered Attilo's lessons on armour. And its weak spots.

She thrust her claws out to both sides, slashing across the backs of the guards' knees. The scraping of her claws on metal jarred up her arms and set her teeth on edge, but at least some of her claws found their mark. She wrenched herself out of their grip as the guards shrieked and toppled.

She sprang up from the floor and shoulder-slammed into Erlan, who was cradling his ruined arm and gibbering, as she launched herself at the guards still restraining Ava.

In grabbing the guard's arm, Ava had given Tannin a couple of inches worth of time until the blade plunged into her throat, and that was all she needed. She barrelled into them, grabbing the dagger out of the stunned guard's hand and flinging it away. She followed it up with a vicious swipe that tore open the man's face like wet parchment and sent him staggering backwards. The other guard still had a grip on Ava's arm as Tannin turned to face him.

"Kill them!" the prince screamed deliriously as he cradled the remaining tatters of his arm. "Kill them both!"

The last guard stood firm for only a moment before the look in Tannin's glowing eyes made him back away with raised hands.

"No!" Prince Erlan shrieked, drawing his own blade clumsily with his left hand, wielding it with erratic swings. "Traitors!"

He slashed at Tannin. The swing was wild and he fought for balance, finding only the pool of his own blood beneath his boots. He stumbled and crashed face-first to the floor.

Tannin glanced at Ava and gave a tiny shrug before she aimed a vicious kick at Erlan's jaw. His head snapped back at the impact and he lay still.

"Av– ooft!" Tannin turned around just in time for Ava to crash into her and squeeze her tightly.

"Oh gods, Tannin, thank you!" she cried, stooping a little to bury her face in the crook of Tannin's neck. Abruptly, she let go and held her at arm's length. "Attilo!"

They turned to the back of the hall where Attilo's shattered body still lay. "Is he... ?"

"I don't know."

Ava ran to his side and pressed two fingers to his wrist and then to his neck. "He's alive!" she cried, tears springing to her eyes. "I need a healer!" She yelled in the direction of the doors. "Oh Attilo," she murmured, stroking his singed and blood-soaked hair.

A few Rill guards who had been manning the doors still milled around awkwardly, none of them wanting to engage Tannin but unsure of what they should be doing with their prince out cold and not issuing orders.

"Open the doors!" Tannin barked at them. "Now!"

There were a few exchanged glances and mutterings, but they did as she commanded and tore down the barricades to the main door.

Tannin poked her head out. "We need a healer in here!" It seemed most of the castle's staff had been nervously clustered around waiting to see the outcome of the prince's coup, and only few moments later a stretcher appeared and Attilo was loaded onto it.

"Take good care of him," Ava commanded. "And you," she yelled at the Rill guards trying to sneak out of the throne room. "Get the other door open and let my father out!"

They sheepishly removed the barricade from the meeting room door as Tannin watched over them, arms crossed and glaring.

"We could run right now and not deal with this," she said to Ava out of the corner of her mouth as the last of the barricade was removed.

"I have to..." Ava said puffing out her chest and smoothing her hair. "I have to face this."

The doors swung outwards, and the king strode out with an air of attempted dignity, along with MacLeod and what must have been an ambassadorial delegation that had gotten caught up in the drama. They were all dressed in clothes that were definitely not Armodian.

One in particular immediately captured Tannin's attention. She glittered with gold as she strode into the ruined throne room with poise and calm assuredness. She swept her fiery red hair over her shoulder to cascade elegantly down her back. Her gaze latched onto Tannin and she smiled.

Tannin's mouth dropped open. "Sommer?"

Chapter Forty Eight

The Trouble With Politics

For a moment, the world seemed to stop and the once regal throne room was a motionless tableau.

Tannin, bloody and open-mouthed in shock. Next to her, Ava, confused and tearstained. The king looked bewildered and angry. Prince Erlan lay motionless in an expanding pool of blood.

And the Stonestead delegates.

"Sommer?" Tannin asked again, blinking hard.

"Hello, cousin. I've been hoping it was you after all." Her voice had deepened over the years and had taken on a silky smooth tone.

"You look... different." Tannin gave her the once-over.

Sommer had always been tall but now she had grown into her lanky limbs and was all graceful curves. Her arms were strong and muscular under her pale blue, sleeveless tunic with swirling black tattoos inked into her skin. Her mane of red hair hung in loose waves around her shoulders, pinned back by a golden circlet around her forehead.

More gold glittered at her throat in the form of a torc, and gold bands encircled her biceps. Even her simple leather belt had gold detailing on the buckle that matched the engravings on the handle of the short blade she wore at her side. It looked mostly decorative, but Tannin was willing to bet it was still wickedly sharp.

"And you haven't changed a bit." Sommer laughed. A silvery, tinkling laugh. "Still getting into trouble, I see."

The king, who had been quietly purpling as Tannin and Sommer exchanged pleasantries, suddenly exploded. "What is going on here!" He turned to

Tannin, jabbing a thick finger in her direction. "And what are you doing in my castle?!"

"Oh, I come and go as I please." Tannin smirked as his face seemed to swell under the pressure of his rage. "It's not my fault your security is so lax."

The king gaped and fought for words in indignation.

"I see we've missed some details," Sommer said lightly, looking from Tannin to the king. "Why don't you fill us in, cousin?"

Before Tannin could open her mouth, a strangled cry erupted. Prince Erlan was struggling to rise from the bloodied floor and yelped incoherently at the sight of his ruined arm.

"Guards!" The king finally found his voice and called for his security. "Guards!"

"Did you do that?" Sommer asked, indicating to the prince.

"He attacked me first." Tannin shrugged. "Well, actually, he attacked Ava first. And Attilo."

A barrage of Armodian guards charged in and Sommer smoothly stepped forward and took over directing them. As she commanded them to aid the prince and the injured guards, she seemed to radiate an authority that even the king didn't challenge despite her ordering his men around.

"Your Majesty," she said gracefully, "let's try this again. Let me introduce you to my cousin, Tannin." She tilted her head at Tannin in curiosity. "I've got to say I'm surprised to find you here. After all, we'd heard about some misunderstandings and assumed the Beast of Armodan would have fled."

She gave the king a look filled to the brim with hidden meaning. "We assumed you'd be long gone from here, but I'd been hoping to pick up your trail."

"That was the plan. I got delayed," Tannin admitted, eyeing the line of guards. She still didn't trust them not to attack. "What are you doin' here?"

"Politics," Sommer said breezily.

"I'm so confused. What is going on? What kind of politics?" Tannin asked shaking her head.

"Well, as leader of Stonestead and, of course, the wargs, I have to make alliances and gain friends." She gave the king a twinkling smile.

"You're what now?"

"Ah, yes. You've been gone for some time." She frowned. "And how is your old grandfather? He's the one who took you away, isn't he?"

"Yeah, we left after it all went to shit. And he's dead, by the way."

"My condolences." Sommer touched a hand to her heart. "After you left and after the uprising, the council and the ruling classes all fell quite quickly. Naturally, my blood claim is the strongest, so I took my place at the head."

"Why are you here though?" Tannin persisted. "What about staying hidden and protectin' our heritage and all that preachy stuff?"

"Ah yes. Well, we've decided to finally stake our claim on the northern kingdom which, after all, is historically and rightfully ours. We want to forge alliances with the Brochlands, as good neighbours do." Another twinkling smile to the king. "It's time to come out of hiding and show the world who and what we are and take back what is ours."

She smiled. "And there's always a place for you near the top as well, cousin. Now what's your story? How on earth did someone of your blood end up in so much trouble and hiding like a little mouse?"

"That is a long story."

Sommer looked at her expectantly, so she recounted the events of the last year in the vaguest terms starting with her grandfather's death and her becoming aware that she was a warg, carefully leaving out much mention of Attilo and Ava, and ended with her negotiations with the king going a little badly.

"...and then I've just been listenin' for information since. Waitin' for the right time to get out of town."

"It seems you and my esteemed new friend King Florian got off on the wrong foot." Sommer's never-wavering smile seemed dangerous as she again aimed it at the king.

"Agreed," the king said graciously, finally getting his temper under control but determinedly avoided eye contact with Tannin. "Perhaps, in the interests of new alliances and friendships, it's time we revisited our ideas of peace."

"A toast then?" Sommer suggested, turning to the room at large. "To old friends and to new."

The king indicated to a servant, and within moments a platter appeared laden with cups and a flagon of wine.

"Please allow me."

Sommer took the flagon and filled the glasses, which were in turn passed to the Stonestead delegates in their pale blue finery, to Tannin and Ava, and the king and his advisor, MacLeod who had been stunned into silence. No one spoke as Sommer slowly and deliberately poured. Tannin stared at the Stonestead delegates wondering, momentarily, if she knew any of them from her childhood.

She knew instinctively they weren't wargs, but they could be Remnants maybe...

From the corner of her eye, she was suddenly aware of Ava frantically trying to catch her eye. One of the guards had brought her a silken robe and the sleeve flapped as she tried to wave without anyone else noticing.

Tannin mouthed a distracted "what?" at her just as Sommer finished handing out the cups.

"A toast! To peaceful times and friendship!"

The murmur went around the room as they all lifted their glasses to their lips.

"Don't!"

Tannin had barely tilted her glass when Ava lunged for her and slapped it out of her hand.

"What the hell are you doin'?" Tannin cried as the wine splashed over the floor from both her cup and the cup that Ava had dropped.

"Don't drink it," she cried to the room at large.

"What, why? What's goin' on?"

"Don't drink it," she repeated adamantly. "Something's not right. It doesn't feel right."

"Clever girl. But yours was perfectly safe." Sommer's smooth voice now dripped with a menace that had so far been absent. She tipped her own wine onto the floor in a steady stream of splattering red and then dropped the cup to clatter onto the stone.

"Sommer?" Tannin asked warily. "What's going on?"

"You have to understand, cousin, your claim to the throne is just as strong as my own. I would be amiss if I didn't try to protect it. After all, power taken for granted is power easily taken away." Her tone was still mild as if they were discussing the weather.

Tannin stared in horror at the red liquid seeping across the flagstones.

"You were gonna poison me?" she said in amazement. "I'm so *fucking* confused. I don't want your damn throne, Sommer!"

Sommer sighed sadly.

"Surely, you realise that you are a threat that needs to be eliminated. Not you personally, of course, but what you represent. Weakness." She turned to her own delegates and drew the short knife from its sheath on her belt. It was as cruelly sharp as Tannin had expected. "Even now can't you see?" She walked along the row of delegates with deliberate, calculated steps. Their necks stiffened as she came closer. "I see doubt in the minds of my people. And I can't have doubt. The warg, and Stonestead, need strength to succeed."

Sommer spun around to face them. Without even the slightest flicker of emotion on her face, she plunged the knife deep into the heart of one of the men. Blood gurgled from his mouth as his eyes bulged. The others barely flinched as they stood statue-still and silent, looking straight ahead.

Sommer shrugged and twisted the knife from the man's chest, watching him slump to the ground. "Unnecessary blood spillage, really, but I did need to make my point quite strongly. He had been voicing dissent for days now. A traitor. He would have had you on the throne instead of me in an instant. A clueless little puppet. All our hard work in Tark would have been for nothing." She eyed the rest of her group before she turned back to Tannin. "I hope you understand how much I really hate a weak link. And you...You could potentially weaken my whole chain of command."

She advanced on Tannin with the knife and then laughed in surprise as the king again called for his guards.

"You want her out of the way as much as I do." She took another step in Tannin's direction, her smile now looking much more like bared teeth.

Tannin backed away, hands raised. "Sommer, wait! We can work somethin' out! I honestly don't want your throne!"

"I'm sorry. This is how it has to be."

Tannin looked at the knife in Sommer's hands. She didn't have a blade herself but maybe she had something better. She channelled her energy through her chest and down into her fingertips and her claws ripped out through her skin.

Sommer's eyes narrowed.

"Wait!" The main doors were flung open by strong arms and two dark haired figures, each glittering with as much gold as Sommer. They raced into the hall.

"Dana?!" Tannin's heart rose at the sight of her childhood friend. The years had added almost a foot to her height, and she'd grown up a lot, but her sharp features and thick eyebrows were just as she remembered. She'd known Adair less so in their childhood as he was a few years older than her and Dana, but with his stark resemblance to his sister, Tannin would have recognised him anywhere.

"Ah, just in time. I'd really hate to get your blood on this dress," she said with a satisfied smile. "Adair, Dana, kill her."

"No," Dana said breathlessly, standing tall and puffing her chest.

"What do you mean, no?" Sommer snapped, one eyebrow arched. She twirled the knife in her long fingers.

"If this is a direct challenge then it has to be a one-on-one duel," Adair proclaimed, his rich voice echoing in the cavernous hall. He gave Tannin a meaningful look. "Honour demands it."

"Is that so?" Sommer replied sourly. Her catlike smile, however, returned as she turned back to Tannin. "Well then. Are you challenging me, pipsqueak?

Tannin flinched at the old nickname. She looked from Adair to Dana, who widened her eyes at her and gave her an encouraging nod.

"Yes?" she said hesitantly.

"Very well. Claws, was it?"

Her grin grew and became elongated as sharp fangs grew out past her red painted lips.

Tannin ran.

Sommer would have trouble with the regular sized doors in her Changed state, so Tannin bolted for the nearest and didn't stop to slam it behind her. She didn't even look to see if she was being followed. The howl filled with rage and thundering feet told her that much.

She just had to get out and into the maze of streets and she could lose her.

Or fight her. HA.

If anyone had asked, she would have freely admitted she was terrified. Her cousin was a trained fighter. A warrior. And Tannin had barely functioned as a baker.

In any case, she had to get her away from people. Away from any other collateral damage. The sight of Attilo lying broken on the floor was lodged in her brain. At least, he was safe in the healery for now. She couldn't let that happen to anyone else, so she sprinted as fast as she could down the corridor.

She burst out of the main doors to the wide marble staircase. Sommer would catch her in one bound if she slowed to take the stairs. Instead, she clambered up onto the sloped side and raced down, letting her momentum make up for her sliding feet and lack of balance. She leapt off the bottom, somehow managing to stay upright, and sprinted for the nearest alley. A roar shattered the peaceful morning air as the main doors were thrown open with a splintering of wood and Sommer's monstrous form careened out.

Tannin risked a glance back at the mouth of the alley and was stunned at the sheer size of the beast at the top of the stairs. She suddenly realised she had no idea what a warg looked like. Sure, she knew what it felt like – the fur, the teeth, the claws. She knew she had a tail. But seeing a full warg in all her glory brought her to a standstill.

Towering well above the height of a man and with the bulk of a colossal bear, Sommer's warg form had a distinctly lupine face with sharp fangs that poked out from under black lips that were pulled back in a snarl under bright orange eyes. Bright orange eyes that snapped directly to Tannin.

"Shit."

Tannin raced into the alley as the beast charged with a snarl that showed even more of those razor-sharp teeth. She took as many corners as possible hoping to slow Sommer down, but the crashings behind her seemed to be getting closer. She could almost feel hot breath on the back of her neck.

A window opened to her right and an old man popped his head out.

"What's all this –" His sentence ended there, half in fear of the creature galloping through the alley and half because Tannin had leapt through the window on top of him.

She gasped out an apology as she scrambled back to her feet. Outside, Sommer had skidded right passed the window and was now snarling and shoving her snout as far in the small window as she could.

Tannin threw a plate and grinned in satisfaction as it smashed off Sommer's nose and she retreated with a grunt.

Tannin rushed through another apology to the dazed man and dashed off through the rest of the house. Sommer would not take long to circle the building. If she was quick, she could head her off and lose her.

Tannin surged out of the other side of the house into a world of white as huge bedsheets fluttered in the breeze in every direction. She had only taken a few steps before she had to dive behind a low wall as the shadow of a monster loomed from behind the fabric, sniffing determinedly.

Tannin pressed her back against the brick and prayed Sommer couldn't hear the pounding of her heart.

At the sound of distant shouting, the warg froze and for a moment the world stood still. Tannin watched as the massive head turned back towards the castle, seemingly thinking. She must have reached a decision because as Tannin peered around the wall, she caught a flash of greyish fur between the sheets as Sommer charged off back the way she'd come.

Tannin let out the breath she had been holding and sagged against the wall. Her leg muscles were aching. She hadn't been this active in a long time.

Why had Sommer left? Tannin thought. She had been right there for the killing. Realisation dawned in the pit of her stomach. Sommer didn't have to chase after her in these cramped streets and waste her time. She could make Tannin come to her.

Ava.

Tannin could only manage a pathetic half run back in the direction of the castle, but the echoes of a crowd led her not to the marble stairs as she had expected but to the nearby main square where a small crowd had gathered – seemingly oblivious to the dangers – to catch a glimpse of royalty. She pushed passed a couple of people, who angrily pushed back and she found herself again at the back of the crowd. A line of guards had formed to keep people back.

Scrambling atop a vegetable cart, Tannin could see Ava standing with a group of nervous guards with lances facing off with a murderous Sommer. The fact that somehow her clothing had survived her Change registered dimly in the back of Tannin's mind as being interesting, but she was too concerned with that predatory look in her face as she looked at Ava. Dana and Adair stood off to the side, each holding a pair of short swords. Sommer shouted over the murmur of the crowd.

"It seems your girlfriend has run off," Sommer crowed. "How ever will I motivate her to come back and face me?"

"Leave her alone. She doesn't want your throne." Sommer laughed harshly. "It's not about want, Your Highness. It's about practicality. She needs to die. One life for the stability of a whole people – that's not unreasonable, is it? Now, are you going to call off your guards or do they have to die too?"

Ava must've given a signal because the guards backed up, if a little unwillingly. She walked towards Sommer so the two of them were alone in the middle of the square. The crowd started to mutter anxiously.

"Very good." Sommer drew a knife identical to the one she had thrust into the delegate's heart. "Let's have a wager, shall we? How many pieces of you do I have to cut off before your girlfriend comes running back, hm? I think I'd put money on less than five, wouldn't you?" She tipped Ava's chin up with the flat of her knife to look her in the eye and sighed. "That is if you actually do scream, and you look like you're going to try and be stubborn about this. Trust me, it's not personal."

Tannin watched in dismay as one of the guards charged at Sommer. Rescuing the princess of the realm would have made him a hero. Songs would have been sung about the noble, chivalrous warrior for decades to come. Sommer cut him down with a blade Tannin hadn't even seen her draw without ever taking her eyes off Ava's. She didn't even blink.

"Anyone else feel like being stupid?" she crowed, sliding the blood slick sword back into its sheath. "No? Shall we begin then?"

She raised the knife to Ava's cheek, smiling menacingly.

"Don't worry, we'll start small –"

The threat left Sommer's lips almost at exactly the same time as the turnip thudded pathetically onto the ground in front of them. She looked at it in amusement and then followed its line of trajectory to where Tannin had climbed up atop the cart to see over the crowd.

"Come and get me, you coward!" Tannin bellowed, launching another projectile.

And get away from her.

Sommer sidestepped the second turnip neatly before cracking the hilt of her knife into the side of Ava's head and sending her sprawling. Tannin snarled as Sommer turned to face her, grinning widely, her arms raised in challenge.

"Get out of here!" Tannin barked at the crowd as she slid down from the stall. They gave her a wide berth as she shooed them. "Now, go! Get!"

She had no plan at all, and her palms were slick with sweat. This was by far the stupidest thing she had ever done. Her knees were shaking as she reached Sommer in the middle of the square.

I am going to fucking die.

Behind Sommer, guards swarmed around the unconscious princess and carried her out of the square. Even from a distance, Tannin could see how much her head was bleeding. She tore her gaze away.

At Sommer's gesture, one of the Stonestead delegates threw a short sword at Tannin's feet. It matched the one Sommer had used to dispatch the unfortunate guard which she now drew again. Blood sparkled on the blade.

"Can't have anyone saying I didn't give you a fighting chance. I have my honour. Blades only and to the death. That means no claws, pipsqueak. Maybe then you won't run away like a coward." She smiled. "Agreed? Pick it up."

Tannin crouched to snatch up the sword, never taking her eyes off Sommer. As soon as her hand closed around the handle she felt the agreement like a physical weight. To the death. Blades only. She knew instinctively that she wouldn't be able to unleash her warg form on Sommer now even if she wanted to.

Oh, I'm absolutely about to fucking die.

"And so, we begin." Sommer bowed gracefully.

Tannin bobbed an awkward bow in return. She knew so little of how duels actually went, and her hands were slippery on the sword's hilt. Blades only...

Do we just go or... ?

CLANG

Tannin barely managed to get her sword up in time to deflect Sommer's first strike that struck her blade like a gong.

Scarcely a heartbeat passed before she lunged again. She was impossibly fast. Tannin didn't have time to block or even try to dodge. She gasped as the attack opened up a deep gash in her thigh and, as she saw Sommer's smile, she realized with appalling clarity that the first strike had been nothing more than a feint.

Tannin balanced on her uninjured leg and tried an attack of her own. It was batted away effortlessly. Blood soaked the leg of her breeches. Sommer slashed at her chest. She jerked backwards, off-balance. Another feint.

The tip of Sommer's blade whistled through the air, slashing Tannin's cheek and sending her staggering. She tripped and her knee buckled under her.

Tannin fought to get back on her feet but there was always another strike coming to cut into her. Sommer wasn't aiming for serious damage, Tannin thought desperately as the blade opened up another shallow cut on her bicep. She knew she had already won. She was the cat and Tannin was the helpless, bleeding mouse beneath her paws.

Almost like clockwork, Sommer spun and kicked at her with vicious precision. Her foot slammed into Tannin's chest and knocked her flat on her back on the hard ground. A savage stomp on her forearm made Tannin drop her weapon. Sommer scooped it up and tucked it into her belt with a triumphant smirk, not lifting her boot from Tannin's arm.

Tannin clenched her teeth against the pain. The bones in her arm grated against one another. She wouldn't scream, she told herself. No matter what Sommer did to her, she wouldn't give her the satisfaction.

"This is what your great Beast of Armodan really is. A weakling," Sommer called to the spectators, whose bloodlust kept their eyes glued to the violent spectacle that was playing out for them despite the evident danger.

If she wasn't concentrating on trying not to die, Tannin would have been humiliated to be beaten so easily. Sommer ground her heel into Tannin's arm again. Tannin groaned against her clenched teeth. "A weakling cannot be a ruler."

Sommer lifted her boot enough for Tannin to drag herself from under it as she levelled her blade at her throat.

"On your knees," she commanded.

"Fuck you," Tannin spat, wiping blood from her face and cradling her arm. She wished she had something more profound to say as her last words, but *fuck you* would have to do. She was losing so much blood from her leg with more trickling from a dozen cuts all over her body. It hurt too much to think.

If this is it, so be it. I tried.

And she had tried, but there was no way she could win this fight. Sommer was all warrior whereas Tannin hadn't even landed one blow. She hauled herself to her knees as best she could and closed her eyes to await the killing blow.

"Oh no," Sommer purred, "I may have won the duel, but I'm not done with you yet."

Tannin's eyes snapped open only to have the wind knocked out of her as Sommer delivered another kick that sent her crashing back to the ground.

Sommer laid the tip of her sword against Tannin's shoulder as she lay on the ground, right at the joint. "Where are the vials?" she whispered just loud enough for Tannin to hear.

"No... don't... vials?" Tannin gasped. She made a pathetic attempt to wiggle away, but Sommer bared her teeth as she leaned on the blade and blood blossomed on Tannin's shirt as it broke through the skin. Tannin's resolve broke and she screamed helplessly as Sommer pushed the blade in further.

"The vials your grandfather stole. From the lab. Where are they?" Sommer hissed, gripping her sword in both hands.

"I don't... I don't know... please don't..." Tannin's legs kicked feebly.

"I need to know. I'm not a fan of torture, but I will take you apart piece by piece until you tell me. Where are the vials?"

"I swear I don't..." Tannin's pleas turned to wordless screams as the sword plunged deeper without remorse. She was expecting the twist at any moment that would rip her arm from its socket and tear it off completely, but it never came.

"Stop." Through eyes hazy with pain, Tannin saw Adair with his own weapon levelled at Sommer's throat. Dana stood beside him, a short sword gripped tightly in each hand.

"I did wonder if it was one of my wargs pouring poison through the ranks." Sommer's voice was like ice.

"Step away from her," Dana commanded. "You won't risk taking us both on, so let her go."

A heartbeat passed in silence.

"As you wish." Sommer yanked the blade out of Tannin's flesh as she cried out weakly. Blood spurted and puddled on the ground.

"This will not be forgotten," Sommer said with a sneer. "Your days are numbered, traitors."

Chapter Forty Nine

The Healery

Tannin drifted in and out of consciousness for a while before she could focus her eyes and take in the room where she lay tucked under white sheets. Her bedding, the walls, everything about her surroundings seemed far too bright and white. Bandages mummified her injured shoulder and stretched across her chest under the crisp white nightshirt she now wore.

Bright red caught her eye. She cautiously turned her head to see two guards at the foot of her bed and another two in front of the door. As her eyes slid over them, one noticed her and nudged his partner. They straightened up and tightened their grip on their weapons that Tannin recognised as the dart-loaded crossbows that had taken her out before. She wiggled her uninjured arm and heard the tell-tale rattle of the shackle that was clamped around her wrist and sighed heavily.

Fuck. They got me.

Other than the guards, the room was almost empty. The beds across from her and to her right were unoccupied but the bed on her left, however, was taken up by a barely breathing, heavily bandaged man.

"Attilo," Tannin breathed and tried to sit up.

Her thigh where Sommer's sword had sliced her was also heavily bandaged, and Tannin felt the soft cotton as she failed to raise her battered body up further.

"Don't you be tryin' anythin'," one of the guards barked at her, alerting the others by the door that she was awake.

"Couldn't if I wanted to, arsehole." She grunted.

Attilo was a sorry state. He looked more bandage than man, with red patches seeping through the white.

"Is he gonna be okay?"

No one answered.

"I said, is he gonna be okay?" she shouted. The effort of raising her voice made her head spin and she slumped, groaning loudly.

A healer heard her shout and came hurrying through the guarded door.

"Wheesht now. Ye'll tear your stitches!" She showed none of the apprehension of the guards as she pressed the cool back of her hand to Tannin's forehead.

"Is he okay?"

"Let's just focus on you, hm? How's the pain?"

"I'll be fine. I heal quickly," Tannin half-growled, clenching her teeth and still trying to sit up. "He doesn't."

"No, he disnae," the healer said sympathetically. "He's comatose and we dinnae ken yet how bad the damage is."

Tears stung Tannin's eyes and a sob rose in her throat. "I could've stopped him. I could've –"

"Enough of that." The healer soothed her. "Just you focus on gettin' better."

Tannin glared at her. Her grey hair was pulled into a tight knot, but her face showed only a trace of wrinkles. She could have been thirty or fifty, Tannin couldn't tell.

"Why are you even healing me?" she asked. "I'm pretty sure I'm gonna get executed. It's doesn't make a damn bit of difference if I can stand or not when they take my head off."

The healer smiled that infuriatingly sympathetic smile. "I just heal the injured. And yer injured. It's that simple. I'm gonnae check yer shoulder, okay?"

Tannin begrudgingly allowed her to undo the mass of white wrappings. Underneath, it looked terrible – a bloody gash surrounded by dark bruising and held together with a crisscross of white thread. She swore as the last of the bandaging pulled at the tacky blood.

"Well, now," the healer said in a chipper voice that jarred against the sight of Tannin's mangled flesh. "That's lookin' good!"

"That looks good to you?" Tannin said in disgust.

"It's healin', and there's no sign of infection. That's good in my book. We'll know more about how the joint is fairing soon. However fast ye heal, that's no easy task. Ye might no regain yer full range of motion."

"It hurts." She moaned and then looked over at the sleeping form next to her.

"We don't know anythin' about his status, so dinnae ask again. We can only wait until he wakes up."

Tannin gazed at him forlornly. He looked so peaceful in his sleep with the blankets drawn all the way up to his neck. His serene appearance was marred only by the black-blue around his eyes under the bandages.

It wasn't long until the healer drew a curtain around his bed to stop Tannin staring at him, much to her annoyance, but the arrival of a steaming bowl of broth diverted her attention.

Propped up on her pillows, Tannin let the healer spoon the hot soup into her mouth. Although she hadn't eaten in gods knew how long, she only managed a few mouthfuls before she shook her head to indicate she was done. It irked her to be spoon-fed like a child but without the use of her arms, she had no choice.

"Can't you get them to take this off? You know I can't go anywhere." Tannin grumbled, rattling her shackle. "I can't even sit up properly by myself."

The chain locked onto her wrist led to a ring that was bolted securely into the floor. Its length was short enough that she couldn't lift her hand more than a few inches from where it lay on the bed.

"That's oot of my hands and also not my job," the healer said curtly.

"And dinnae make that face," she added with a stern expression when Tannin scowled.

Tannin was left mostly alone, bored and hurting until the healer unexpectedly announced she had a visitor.

She swivelled her head curiously and then groaned.

"Good afternoon, Miss Hill," King Florian said, sweeping into the room. The guards ducked their heads in respect as Tannin rolled her eyes.

"Here to gloat?" she asked, drily. "You got me, congratulations."

"I am not."

He settled himself into a chair next to her bed. He was wearing his crown today, nestled in his thick hair.

"Then why are you here?"

The king turned to the guards. "I require the room."

The guards exchanged uncertain glances. "But your Majesty–"

"That will be all," he said curtly.

They looked like they wanted to protest more but thought better of it.

"You're not worried I'll try to kill you and escape?"

"By the looks of you, I doubt you could." He smiled. "But no need for that. I bear you no ill will."

"Oh really? I'm not a prisoner here?" She tugged on the chain for emphasis. Its jangling echoed in the almost empty room.

"No. I will inform the guards that you will be leaving. In fact, I insist upon it."

"What?" Tannin was utterly bewildered.

The king sighed.

"After the events of this past week, it is clear that you are far more hazard than you're worth. Even if our original proposal were accepted, your presence here would only invite more trouble. It seems you have quite the target on your back."

"So why not just kill me?"

"Your warg friends are making their presence distinctly known. They want you back in one piece."

"My warg friends?" Tannin asked, wracking her brains for memories of what happened after Sommer stabbed her.

Dana?

"Plus, my Avalyn would never forgive me."

A weary expression settled on the king's regal face and he sighed. "You must think I don't know, but I do. I always have. She may not be my blood, but she is my child."

His weariness hardened into something decidedly sterner. "That is the other consideration for your banishment. I don't know the extent of your... relationship with my daughter but consider it at an end. You will never see her again. You will never contact her again. Am I clear?"

Oh gods.

Tannin felt her face redden. She'd forgotten he knew about her and Ava. She avoided his eyes and swallowed hard but nodded. It made sense. Ava had already been dragged so deep into this whole mess.

"Good. Three days from now you will be escorted from the city. Do not return." He made to turn away before adding, "Maybe I'll get lucky and that cousin of yours will tear you to shreds before long and save me the headache."

Her three days were up, and the lamps in the room were burning low. The curtain shielding Attilo was gone but his bed was empty, with fresh crisp sheets tucked across it. The healer told her they moved him somewhere more comfortable while she was asleep since he was going to be comatose for a while.

That's probably for the best.

Tannin didn't think she'd be able to say goodbye.

At the foot of her bed, someone had left a travelling pack as well as clothes for her which her healer had to help her into. She was sure that wasn't standard banishment procedure. Tannin suspected some other sympathetic soul was behind it rather than the king, maybe even the healer, and she was heartily glad of it. She needed all the friends she could get.

To anyone outside of this healery – to Flint, Eve and even Ava if no one told her – it would be as if she'd just disappeared off the face of the earth. At least until she got to another town and bartered for parchment and ink. If she even got that far. She railed against the anxiety knotting her stomach. She would do it. She would survive, if nothing else, out of spite and to see to look on the king's face if she ever saw it again.

"I really think ye need a few days more rest." The healer frowned sternly as she laced a wincing Tannin into her new leather jerkin.

She had freshly bandaged Tannin's wounds, and now that she was dressed, tied a thick strap around the back of her neck to act as a sturdier sling than the strip of cloth she'd been using. Tannin flinched at the contact with her neck, but as long as it didn't touch her throat, she felt she could stave off a panic attack.

"Thank you," Tannin said. "No, I really mean it. You didn't have to be this nice to me."

The healer cast a furtive look around the room to make sure it was empty before leaning in close to whisper in her ear.

"We look after our own." She winked.

"You're a –"

"Wheesht. Take these." She pressed a twist of parchment into Tannin's hand. "Bitterwart leaves. For the pain. Chew on one at a time, only one mind ye, 'til they get sweet and then spit it out. They might make ye a wee bit dizzy, but they'll help."

She disappeared behind a curtain for a moment before reappearing with a sturdy wooden walking staff.

"That, I definitely do need." Tannin hobbled over to accept the staff. She braced herself against it to take her weight off her bad leg. "Thank you again."

"You dinnae have tae thank me so much," she said with a smile.

"I never even asked your name," Tannin said suddenly realising.

The woman smiled. "It's Morag. Most call me Mo."

Chapter Fifty

Banished

Tannin gritted her teeth as she leant against a column to rest. The healery was part of the castle itself, as she suspected, and she was now being escorted through the grounds by group of guards. She could sense their annoyance about having to pause every few minutes.

"Can we get this moving a little faster?" one of them barked.

"If you want to carry me then sure. Otherwise, this is how it's gonna be," she sneered.

Gods, this really hurts.

She really should have been allowed longer to heal, she thought bitterly, this was cruel.

"Just get a move on."

It took them an age to reach the courtyard, where a carriage stood waiting to take her out of the city. She eyed it suspiciously but, upon seeing no locks or chains, awkwardly eased herself into the cushioned interior. Two stern-looking guards sat opposite her.

"I take it you lads are not up for chattin', huh?"

She was met with stony glares.

The carriage ride was long, and one of the guards would clear their throat menacingly whenever she tried to peek out of the window.

Finally, after maybe an hour, the carriage rumbled to a stop.

"Get out."

That was as much ceremony as she was going to get it seemed because as soon as she stepped out of the carriage, her pack was thrown out after her and the driver immediately cracked the reins.

She leaned on her staff and stared off after the trundling carriage and the looming outline of the city behind it.

I should get off the road.

There was still a bloody army close by. They'd no doubt have scouts all over the place. If she met anyone who wasn't friendly, she was as good as dead in her current state.

The setting sun tinged the billowing in pink and orange. High ground, she decided, high ground was always good.

As Tannin paused on the hill to rest, she looked back over the city that had been her home for so long. A curious column of smoke rose from somewhere near the centre.

The breeze carried the scent and when she sniffed, Tannin could smell the sweet, richness of burning wood in the air along with some kind of roasting meat smell. And something else that was hauntingly familiar. It had a muskiness to it and a hint of something floral. No not floral. Earthy.

Lacewood oil.

With a sudden awareness that was like being dropped into icy water, she realised the source of the smoke.

It can't be. It can't be. She said he was still sleeping.

As much Tannin told herself over and over as she retched, the smell was unmistakable. The tinge of burning flesh permeated the air along with the pungent scent of the beard oil. She couldn't breathe without breathing it in. She couldn't breathe at all. She heaved at the fresh wave of nausea and scrambled on her hands and knees to try and get away from the smoke. Her shoulder held up for all of two seconds before she collapsed face first in the dirt.

That was where Dana and Adair found her, sprawled halfway up the hillside path and shivering. She couldn't get any words out to answer their questions but let them steady her and make their way to where the pair had already set up a camp.

It was only there, sat around a small fire, that she finally answered.

"The smoke," she whispered.

"Yeah, we could smell it." Dana wrinkled her nose. She carried a longbow that rested on her back along with her long dark braid. Tannin noticed neither her nor her brother wore any gold anymore. "A funeral pyre."

"It was." Tannin stared in the cracking flames. "I knew him. I could... smell him."

"I'm sorry," Dana said softly, reaching to pat Tannin's knee.

"So, what's the plan then?" Adair said brusquely, brushing aside all sentimentality. "We're out of Armodan. What now?"

His sister threw a rock at him.

"Tactless idiot," she hissed. "Can't you see she needs a minute?"

He held up his hands in mock apology and muttered something under his breath as he went to check the tent posts again.

Dana sat with Tannin for a little while as she stared into the flames and chewed on one of her bitterwart leaves. The taste was awful, and she grimaced as she chewed.

"Why are you two helpin' me?" she asked. "I can't offer you anythin'. I literally have nothing, and Sommer has it out for me."

"That's exactly why we're helping you," Dana said. "Sommer is insane. Like more than you know insane. So far, you're the only one with a shot in the dark of taking her down."

"But I don't want that," Tannin confessed. "I don't want her stupid crown."

"It's not just about crowns though. It's about getting rid of her. She's a tyrant."

"Aye, I could see that." Tannin rested her head in her hands. "I can't do anythin' about that though."

"Not yet you can't," Dana said cheerfully, tapping Tannin on the nose. "Once you're all healed up, we can get you fighting fit and go kick her arse, how about that?"

Tannin smiled ruefully. "I think you overestimate my fightin' ability, Dana. It's less than zero. I'm no warrior. She'd tear me to shreds," she said, echoing the king's words.

"That just means a bit of extra training then."

Tannin spat the chewed-up mess of leaf into the fire and watched as it sparked madly and turned the flames vibrantly pink.

Dana was clearly not going to be discouraged, so Tannin merely smiled and yawned. She was immensely grateful that she wasn't alone and doubly grateful that the siblings actually had tents. Now, she wouldn't be sleeping in the open air no matter how mild the nights were becoming.

The bitterwart leaves did wonders. If she ever found her way back to Armodan again, Tannin thought, she needed to find that Healer and thank her again. Mo. Those leaves were a godsend, and she even managed a half decent night's sleep. Both the other wargs had waved off her offers of taking a watch and insisted that she rest. She was secretly relieved they didn't take her up on the offer.

She woke up stiff and aching and had a brief moment of calm before her memory came flooding back in. She was banished. Attilo was dead. Ava was... doing princessy things probably. Tannin pushed her out of her mind. She would leave her behind with the rest of Armodan. Dana and Adair packed up their camp with practiced ease as Tannin stood by awkwardly leaning on her staff.

"I don't know how far I can walk," she admitted. "My leg..."

"Pssh." Dana waved her off with a devilish grin. "Who said anything about walking?"

Tannin had to suppress the urge to whoop as they shot through the undergrowth of the forest. Adair's solid body beneath her surged to the beat of his massive leaps. She entwined her hands in his long brown fur like reins. Dana ran beside them and gave Tannin a dopey grin with her massive tongue lolling out the side of her fanged mouth. They really were odd looking creatures.

The sun was warm on the back of her neck and the wind whipped through her hair as Tannin barrelled through the forests and away from the city she once called home.

The End

Epilogue

Ava slapped a branch away from her face and then yelped as it came swinging right back.

This was such a stupid idea.

She was no adventurer. She was a planner. And where was her plan now? In the gutter, that was where.

She missed Attilo bitterly and sped up her stomping pace to clear her head. She was out of breath before long. Exercise was never really her thing except for the short sparring matches she's had with Attilo and Tannin.

Tannin.

How would she ever find her in this mess of trees?

Ava struggled through a particularly overgrown patch of forest lamenting that she had never been out into the wilderness much. She should have asked Attilo to train her for this too. She'd already had a difficult day's hike and a restless night's sleep, and her back was aching from sleeping on the hard ground. She had no idea how she was going to find food after she finished what was in her pack, and she was already running low on water. She should really find a stream, she thought to herself and then sighed.

Attilo would know what to do.

She'd insisted that a funeral pyre was built for him instead of a grave. He had told her once that he had seen such ceremonies as a soldier and said he'd rather that than being buried as worm food.

As the crackling fire sent thick smoke skywards to mingle with the clouds overhead, Ava had seen the appeal. Through the eye-stinging smoke, she'd stood with her head held high despite the tears streaming down her cheeks in a seemingly unending torrent. She didn't care what people thought even if she heard the whispers before the pyre was even lit. Attilo wasn't just a bodyguard to her. He was so much more. He was a dear friend. The sweet, smoky smell of wood and burning flesh had lingered for hours, and even now she caught another whiff of it as her hair fell across her face.

What was she thinking coming way out here, Ava lamented. She had no experience, few supplies and a crinkled map she'd ripped out of an old book. Who knew if it was even still accurate? She took it from her pocket and smoothed out the creases. Even the road she was on now, the main road out of Armodan, was little more than a dotted line on the parchment. The maze of interweaving forest paths wasn't pictured at all and most likely Tannin would have taken one of them. Her plan rested solely on finding her. She was supposedly injured and wouldn't get far.

Initially, that had given her some hope of finding her quickly but out here in the wilderness, she truly could be anywhere. Ava had found the tracks of the carriage that must have dropped her off before turning back, leaving an odd semi-circle in the dirt.

She'd found footprints small enough to be Tannin's embedded in some of the softer ground just off the path and followed them for a bit, but they became so jumbled and confusing that after a while Ava wondered if she was following any tracks at all.

"That," her travelling companion said matter-of-factly with his hands on his narrow hips, "is a pathetic excuse for a map."

"Do you have a better one?" Ava shot back. She was tired and beyond irritable.

Flint sauntered over and gave her a crooked smile. She frowned at him. He never seemed to just walk anywhere normally. It was always a swagger or a saunter or a lope. "Relax. We'll find her. And she's a big old beastie anyway. She'll probably find us before we find her."

"She could be injured and dying." Ava pointed out sternly.

"Or she could be avoiding you," Flint said. "Want to elaborate on that?"

"No." She sorely regretted her choice to go to Tannin's old friend for help, but going alone would have been nothing short of suicide. Besides, he'd been surprisingly eager to come along.

They had initially tried to keep to the smaller paths and routes through the trees so that there was less of a chance of meeting the unsavoury types who roamed these parts looking for unwary merchants to rob but the terrain had forced them back to the main road. Wherever Tannin was going, she had to head in this direction first regardless.

Maybe she could still find her, Ava hoped. And soon. She could hopefully fight off a highway man or two, but a broken ankle on these ridiculous forest paths would cripple her. She looked sideways at Flint and sighed. He would be useless in a fight. She'd bet money on that.

If she didn't find Tannin in the next few days, Ava thought, then she'd go home. She'd accept whatever convent or academy her father was going to send her away to. And he would send her away, she was sure of it. He'd threatened it before, and she really had gone too far this time. Ava sat down on a fallen tree beside the road and chewed her lower lip. She'd really messed things up. She just wanted to find Tannin and make sure she was okay. Out here alone and injured, she'd be easy pickings regardless of if a warg got to her or even just a common thief. And then even if she found her and Tannin forgave her, what then? Did she even want to be in the middle of a warg war? Should she just go home and face the mess she'd made?

She rubbed her temples. Even now as she tried to plan, all she could see in her mind was her. They hadn't let her see her in the healery.

A twig cracked behind her and Ava jumped and spun around. Flint swore and dropped his waterskin.

"Easy." A skinny, ragged-looking man ducked out of the treeline. "Didnae mean to startle ya."

Ava grabbed for the dagger in her belt and held it in shaky hands, stepping slightly in front of Flint. If he had any kind of weapon on him then she hadn't seen it. "Don't come any closer."

"Oh, dinnae be like that." The man smiled, showing rows of rotten and blackened teeth.

"Aye, we're just trying' tae be friendly." Another man followed him out of the woods. He hefted a formidable looking club in his hands.

"Stay away!"

"Ye all alone out here?" the ragged man asked with an evil grin.

Ava didn't answer and switched pointing between him and club man and back again. The man with the club started to circle so that she and Flint were between them. They stood back-to-back. Ava's hands were slick on the handle of her dagger.

"What's gonna happen now is – urrk!"

He'd spoken in a sickly-sweet voice until the arrow ripped through his throat. He slid to the ground, choking on his own blood. Ava whipped around in time to see the man with the club take an arrow straight into his chest. His eyes widened in surprise, but he too was dead before he hit the ground. Ava staggered, brandishing her blade wildly. Flint grabbed the fallen club and hefted it, his thin arms straining at the weight of it.

"Who's there?" She tried to sound commanding, but it came out shrill and fearful.

The forest stood still in shadowy silence. Ava kept her head ducked as she squinted in the direction the arrows had come from, but the dense trees hid their secrets well. She was just about to grab her pack and start running when a voice from behind her made her yelp in surprise.

"What the hell are you doin' here?"

Ava could have melted into the ground in relief.

"Tannin!"

Glossary and Pronounciation Guide

Aye Yes. Used by the Scots, the Irish and pirates

Balor A giant in Irish mythology sometimes depicted with one eye

Beltane Gaelic May festival

Besom A cheeky or immoral person, typically used for female persons. Pronounced bism

Bonnie Pretty

Broch Prehistoric circular stone tower in Scotland. Pronounced rhyming with loch – see further.

Ceilidh Traditional Scottish folk dancing. Extremely fun. Pronounced Kay-Lay

Clach Meaning stone this can also be a name. Pronounced with a rolled ch

Craic Social activity/ fun. Can also be used in the
context What's the craic? Meaning what's going on. Pronounced crack.

Corbie Crow

Dram A measure of whisky

Dinnae fash Don't worry

Druid Historically a high ranking figure in Celtic cultures. Also sometimes used synonymously with magic users

Eejit Idiot

Feart Afraid

Gaol Pronounced the same as jail

Graeme Scottish name pronounced Gray-am

Hogmanay Scottish New Year's Eve

Kelpie A shape shifting waterhorse from Scottish Mythology. Tends to be a bit murdery.

Ken Know

Lang may yer lum reek Long may your chimney smoke: traditional Hogmanay well-wishing

Loch Lake. It is not pronounced lock. If you say lock we can't be friends. Roll the ch at the back of your tongue.

Lugnasadh Gaelic harvest festival. Pronounced Loo-nah-sah

Mony a mickle maks a muckle Many smalls make a big. Quite an obvious statement but it's meant to be motivational as in "you'll get there someday!"

Peekit Pale. You can also say peely-wally

Redcap Murderous goblin who thrives on spilled blood which they dip their caps into

Samhain Gaelic festival marking the beginning of winter
on the 1st of November. Mostly associated with all hallows eve. Pronounced Sah-wen

Selkie Shape shifters from Scottish mythology also known as the Seal-Folk because they shape shift into seals and only seals.

Sgian dubh A dagger which is part of the traditional Scottish Highland attire worn in the sock.
Pronounced skeen doo

Sláinte Scottish cheers. It means health. You can also say Sláinte mhath which means good health. Pronounced Slan- jeh or Slan-jeh var

Sluagh The unforgiven dead from Scottish mythology. Less brain-eating and more thought to do good deads to try and earn forgiveness. Pronounced sloo-ah

Torc Solid metal necklace which shows a person's status common in a range of European cultures

Wheesht Shush. You can also say "Haud yer wheesht" which also means shut it but is a slightly nicer way of saying it

Wee Technically means small but in Scottish slang it just goes everywhere as a slight diminutive. You can have a wee behemoth if you like.

REMNANTS OF BLOOD

H.F. CUNNINGHAM

About the Author

I started writing properly in 2020 after being made redundant from an engineering consulting job due to corona. It actually ended up being a blessing in disguise because the sudden influx of free time was invaluable in the creation of my debut novel Remnants of Blood which you are holding in your hands right now. I plan for this to be a series of at least three books but we'll see.

I didn't study writing or English when I went to university because I wanted a "safe" and "sensible" career choice (spoilers: there's no such thing). I actually have a master's in electrical and mechanical engineering but creating fantasy worlds and letting my characters run riot in my brain is much more fun.

A lot of RoB is based on Scottish myths and aesthetics as well as having a lot of my characters speak with Scottish accents. This was fun to write. I am Scottish myself but I now live in Germany so I think some German influences will creep into the next books here and there.

My main aim for this book was to create a fantasy novel that doesn't take itself too seriously, has intriguing characters and to make it quite dark. And, of course, Make It Gay. I read a lot of fantasy and there is an overwhelming amount of boy meets girl and romance occurs and queer rep is a little lacking. So here are some useless lesbians written by a *reasonably* useful lesbian.

Of course, I didn't write this in a bubble and there are so many people who helped bring this to life. My friends and family have all been super supportive and the freelancers I worked with have all been amazing. Also my cat, Wilhelm. Who is jealous of my laptop and kicks it off my lap for cuddle time and steps on all the keys and generally makes it very difficult to write sometimes.

I hope that you really enjoyed this book (or that you will enjoy it if you've flipped to the back first. I certainly had a great time writing it. I would love to have your reviews and to hear any thoughts you have about this novel so, if you have a minute, I am on Goodreads and Storygraph and you can also review on Amazon, the Book Depository, Bookshop.org...basically wherever you got the book from.

You can also visit my website hfcunningham.com or find me on Instagram @hfcunningham.author and Twitter @hfcunningham.

Lots of love,

HF Cunningham

Printed by BoD™ in Norderstedt, Germany